Nemesis

Out of the Box, Book 17

Robert J. Crane

Nemesis
Out of the Box #17
Robert J. Crane
Copyright © 2017 Ostiagard Press
All Rights Reserved.

1st Edition

Prologue

Wolfe

**Norway
175 B.C.**

"To serve death is the greatest honor," Lethe said, surveying the fallen warrior that was being hauled from her quarters by two guards as Wolfe watched, impassive. He had seen such a tableau many times before, countless bodies hauled from her chambers, sometimes by the dozens, their final, screaming moments audible across the whole of the valley. Lethe's eyes flashed, beautiful blue and green, like sky meeting sea on a grim day, as she looked at Wolfe. "Do you not agree?"

"I serve Death," he said, reluctantly. Lethe was clad—barely—in animal skins, some mild concession to modesty that she made when others were in her presence. "But I prefer...strength."

The aged wood creaked beneath their feet as the guards dragged the body across the beams. They shot fleeting, fearful glances at Lethe, at Wolfe, and then crossed the threshold. The last one out shut the door, dropping a hand from the cold corpse as he did so, and Wolfe could hear their breaths of relief through the wood between them.

"I am strength," Lethe said, crossing the room to a small chest where a goblet waited. She lifted it, drinking contents in one gulp, then made her way to the small cask in the corner and picked it up, emptying the remainder into the goblet once more. She turned to look at Wolfe. "My father is strength. The strongest man in the world."

Wolfe stirred, arms folded across his bare chest. He hated to clothe himself, but he did—on his lowers—for her. And sometimes his upper body as well, when the cold of this accursed land was too wretched for even him to bear. Tanned hides for his feet too. Those he despised those even more, and put them on last of all. "Yes," Wolfe agreed. "Hades is strong. Stronger than Odin." He looked around; the walls could be watching, in this place, this meadhall of Odin and the Nords. "Yet we do not find ourselves in the halls of Hades."

Lethe's hand clutched the goblet. "Because my strength is great...but not as great as my father's, and I have no wish to take his place upon the throne in a dark cave, pursued by the gods of Olympus for all my days."

"You could strike a pact with them," Wolfe said. "They would gladly unseat him in your favor."

Lethe looked at him, eyes cool. "And become a kinkiller? Strength may be all you serve, Wolfe, but death—not him, but actual death—is not all I serve." She turned her back on him. "There are...other considerations in my life."

Wolfe made a snort, derisive. "Love?"

Lethe kept her back to him. "Yes. Love. For my family." She turned her head to look at him. "Is that so strange?"

Wolfe glanced away, taking in the feather bed in the corner, the rough cloth sheets turned out from her evening's activities—ones that had surely led to the corpse just dragged out of the room. Wolfe looked away again, finding a chamber pot—that was safer to look at. "Yes," he said. "That is strange." Or it was for him; he loathed his brothers, hated his father.

"Poor, sad Wolfe," Lethe said, and now he knew that the drink and the free feeling of wonder that followed her eating a soul had taken her. She wouldn't have goaded him like this if she weren't feeling her drink and the soul she'd just stolen. "I think you—"

"I don't need your pity," he said, and rounded on the door,

2

one of his toe claws gouging a long trail in the boards as he turned. "Find me again when you've slept off this drink and soul delirium."

"We can't all feed ourselves by blood lust alone," she said, still taunting, as he ripped the door open and stalked out. "Even you can't be sated by that only, Wolfe—"

He slammed the door so loudly the entire hall shook. His footfalls thumped until he regained control of himself, his feet carving little scratches in the wood as he walked. There were dozens, hundreds of them along this path already, measures of the time he'd spent in the quarters of daughter of Death.

Wolfe reached the main hall with its stone floors and burning pits of fire, smoking up toward the great holes in the ceiling. The whole place had an oaky aroma, the warriors of Odin gathered around the centers, smoke puffing toward the chimneys above. The remains of the evening's feast were beginning to curdle on the tables at the far end of the hall, beneath the banners and painted shields of Odin and his house. The idiot son with the hammer laughed loudly at one of the fires, a wench under each arm, and Wolfe avoided him, going toward the other fire, where he saw Freyja sitting, a cloth cowl over her head to ward off the chill of the night that crept in through the boards.

"You look like a man whose slumber will not be easy this eve," Freyja said as Wolfe slipped into the circle by the fire. He might have preferred to stalk off through the village, to leave the meadhall entirely, but it would have required cladding his feet, and Wolfe had no patience for that tonight, nor the biting chill outside these walls.

"My slumber is ever easy," Wolfe said, turning a feral grin toward Odin's queen. "It is the sleep of the untroubled mind."

Freyja was no fool; her eyes gleamed in the firelight. "Somehow I doubt that."

Wolfe turned his face away from her. "Wolfe doesn't care what you doubt." He looked up, catching sight of movement across the hall. That thin waif, Vivi, was staring at him again, dirty face and clear eyes finding him across the fires.

3

ROBERT J. CRANE

"Still you circle around little Vivi," Freyja said, eyeing him, far too fearlessly for his liking. "I would have thought you might have killed her by now." When Wolfe snapped his head toward her, Freyja merely smiled. "Did she tell you something?"

Wolfe stared down into the flames, away from Freyja, away from Vivi. "She avoids me—wisely."

"Hmm," Freyja said. "She has a prophecy, then. About you. Your…future."

Wolfe just bared his teeth. She needed to leave him be, though he could hardly make it overt. Perhaps he should find his foot covers, stalk into the snow for a time, leave all this behind him. "My future is my own business."

"Oh, I expect your future touches any number of others," Freyja said softly, "like an insect plucks the web of a spider and sends its killer toward it. You will kill many yet, won't you, Wolfe?"

"As many as I can," Wolfe said, low and rough.

"Is that to be your legacy, then?" Freyja asked, after only a moment. "Will that be how you are remembered—after you die?"

"I will not be dying," Wolfe said, and rose, looking down at her. "Death is a friend of mine. I have nothing to fear from him."

"Wolfe," Freyja called, just as he was about to leave the hall, to plunge into the snow and let it cool him of this anger, this reckless anger, before he turned it loose within the bounds of Odin's home, "just because you know Death…" and he realized what she meant, "…doesn't mean you'll be ready…for death."

"I will never be ready for death," Wolfe said, turning just enough to look back at her. "For I serve strength. And strength…will ward me against any comers, and see me through more years than you…witch." And with his teeth bared in a smile, he left the meadhall, certain in his heart that he would see more days than anyone else within, save for perhaps the strongest woman he'd ever known, who waited, lingered somewhere within the walls, filled with ecstasy for herself, while Wolfe only churned inside with rage.

4

1.

Reed

Eden Prairie, Minnesota

The windows of the agency exploded in a shower of glass and fire as everything left within the office building lit off in a giant blast. The parking lot was covered in flame that rolled slowly across the pavement, little glittering fragments of glass running ahead of it like earthbound stars racing across the ground. The concussive blast was deafening, a hazard to one's hearing, and it sent little tingles running across my skin, which was already chilling from sitting outside in the October wind.

I wanted to feel mournful as I watched the agency I'd worked so hard to build disintegrate in a blast of fire and thunder so loud it'd probably wake everyone between Eden Prairie and Minneapolis, but...

Unfortunately, I'd known this moment was coming for months now.

And I was ready for it.

"Eyes on target, repeat, I have eyes on target!" Augustus Coleman's shout rang in my ears, crackling in my earpiece as the fire receded back into the agency building, the explosion mostly done. It settled into a steady fire, the kind that would burn the building down eventually if someone didn't—

"Moving to suppress the fire," Scott Byerly said, flat,

almost monotone. "No need to deal with a building collapse while we're fighting the biggest battle of our lives."

"Oh, you're such an innocent little sweetheart," Veronika Acheron's snide, all-knowing voice issued forth in my ear. "I'd let it burn and see if I could throw chunks of it at the enemy."

"I don't have eyes on the enemy yet," Jamal Coleman said, cutting in on the radio frequency. "Where is she?"

"Jamal, she's at your six o'clock high," Abby's voice crackled in. "Turn around."

"Uh, thanks," Jamal said. "Oh. There she is…"

There she was.

Red hair glowing like it was about to join our office in bursting into flame, hovering over the parking lot like a damned avenging angel, and throwing fire down on everything I'd freaking built over the last year, there she freaking was.

Rose Steward.

Succubus.

Scot.

Asshole.

God, I wanted to kill her.

"All right, team," I said, "let's put this bitch in a coffin. For Sienna!"

I shouted it like a battle cry, and launched forward from my hiding place—

A thousand feet above, I was hiding in a low cloud bank. At the call, I came spiking down at the head of a tornado the likes of which every trailer park in Oklahoma feared to high hell.

But I didn't come at her alone.

The parking lot below exploded, as though someone had planted a massive bomb beneath it. Which we sorta had, spending the last three months working on defenses for the agency, because…

I knew this day—technically night, I guess—was coming.

Over a billion fragments of rock launched upward into the sky and toward Rose like a funneled shotgun blast of earth, enshrouding her in a cloud of grey that closed in around her.

I saw movement from below and then a glint of bright red; Rose lasered her way through the cloud of rock in seconds, cackling in the night like a crone.

"That's not good," Augustus muttered into the radio.

"Option Alpha is ineffective," J.J.'s voice sounded through my earpiece. "Reed?"

"On it," I said, and my tornado wrapped up Rose in a gust that blew something like five hundred miles an hour, sustained winds strong enough to annihilate any structure man could build. I was about three hundred feet behind it, figuring she might try and—

She looked around, eyes glowing, trying to find me in the dark but not having a lot of luck. She blasted at the wind around her, hands glowing plasmatic blue, superheating the air.

I killed the tornado; I'd seen what happened when plasma blasts were combined with a tornado earlier this year during a mission in Orlando. The effects…were not pretty.

"Veronika," I said, almost pleading, "see if you can dispel her—"

"You know my powers don't work at long range," Veronika said. "Fortunately, there's a lap-dog for that." There was a pause. "Get it? Like an app, except—"

"Terrible," Augustus said. "Rock armor ready to go in five seconds. Artillery in ten."

"Fire's out," Scott Byerly said. "I'm ready to pull out Option Gamma in thirty seconds."

"Good to go on Option Gamma," Jamal said.

"Good to go on—do I have to say it like that?" Taneshia French's high voice came through the earpiece. "Y'all so geeky."

"You date Augustus and have the nerve to call us geeky?" J.J. asked, umbraged to the nines. I couldn't see his face because he was safely parked several blocks away, him and Abby leading the comms effort from there, but I could imagine it. I imagined it was faux angry, red as a tomato.

"Come on, lap-dog," Veronika said, "throw me, you big wuss."

"I am not a—" Guy Friday sounded super pissed.

7

"Shut up and throw me!" Veronika shouted, and then I saw her.

"For Sienna!" Friday had heaved Veronika from one of the rock blinds Augustus had created for us. He'd bored a tunnel system interconnecting the building and the various berms in the parking lot over the last few months. It seemed like a little thing, really, moving earth and rock around under the surface so we could go from our office to anywhere in the area. It had about a dozen exits, every single one of which was currently hiding our people. All except—

"She's a little high for a shot," Phinneus Chalke said in his low, gravelly voice. "If I let loose now, the bullet has a lot of room to overtravel."

"Hold your fire, Phinneus," I said, keeping in my position above Rose as I watched Veronika launch toward her from her hiding place below. Friday had thrown her like she was a softball. She was coming up fast on Rose from behind, hopefully gonna catch her unawares—

"Hi, bitch!" Veronika shouted as she reached the apogee of her arc and slammed into Rose, grabbing hold of her and burying two glowing blue hands into her back and pushing straight through her skin and out the other side. Gravity caught hold of her and she started to dip, her hand just sticking through Rose at the chest and the lower back, bright blue in the night. "Bye, bitch!"

Veronika fell, arms tearing right through Rose's center as she dropped.

I could see the damage and it wasn't pretty; Rose was shaped like an upside-down V now. Uh, more of one than humans normally are, I mean, like her crotch had been extended to mid-chest. She was bowed right up the middle, too, split nearly in half, and I felt the need to exploit this situation.

"Gravity! Tear her in half!" I ordered, hoping that said order would fall on the right ears at the right moment, which was obviously now.

"Dude, what if it makes two of her?" J.J. asks. "Like a worm?"

"People don't work like that, sweetie," Abby said. "Not

even super succubi."

"I...I can't really do that..." Jamie Barton's usually steady voice sounded a little...flustered. "I'm not—I don't really kill people..."

"Gravity," I said, using her preferred superhero name, "we didn't ask you to come here because this lady wanted a stirring game of tiddlywinks; if we don't kill her, *Sienna is dead!*"

My own words hit me right in the feels, blurted out in a scream in the night, much higher than I'd intended it to be or it needed to be in order for Gravity to hear it through the earpiece.

The truth was...Sienna might already be dead.

"Screw it; I'll do it myself," I said, and let loose of the winds beneath me, launching toward Rose, aided by a tailwind I was adding second by second. I'd cut the thousand feet between us in heartbeats. "Option Gamma, go."

"Go for Gamma," Scott Byerly said, and I saw a hard stream of water glitter in the night as it launched into the sky, aiming for the nearly bisected Rose. It hit her right in the face, like a clown's flower, drenching her.

And then it lit up like a strobe as Jamal and Taneshia both applied lightning to it.

The water blasting Rose in the face acted like a perfect conduit for the lightning, which traveled the couple hundred feet from where Scott, Taneshia and Jamal had combined their powers, and zapped the living hell out of Rose as she hung there, suspended above the wrecked parking lot, lit by the flashing lightning as it wrapped around her.

She hung there, unmoving, for just a second, and then the split that started at her chest began to shrink, pulling back together as she healed, completely, her shredded clothes the only sign that she'd even been hit.

"That was a refreshing dip," Rose said, and I couldn't see her face from where I streaked down from above, but I could imagine the smile from the thousand surveillance photos and vids I'd studied over the last three months.

I wanted to wipe it off her face, along with all the skin and fat and other tissue, clean it off all the way to the damned

9

bone.

Then I wanted to shatter that to pieces.

"Uh, Option Gamma is a failure," Jamal said, like we all hadn't just seen it.

"Epsilon go," I said, and I was almost to her.

She must have heard me a second before I hit, because she turned, movement streaky and fast. Her eyes lit up, and I had a quarter second to watch them go from surprise to pleasure before I landed on her with an F-off-the-scale tornado, wind speeds in excess of a thousand miles an hour.

I'd never done anything so powerful before, but the tornado reflected my absolutely pure fury. This bitch had taken my sister, captured her, imprisoned her in Scotland, maybe even killed her—I didn't know.

But I was going to find out.

"WHERE IS SHE?!" I shouted over the winds, ripping at her face, her body, at everything else around her. Her clothing shredded in a second as particulate dust within the whirlwind was sped to velocities that would turn it into a kind of granular blender in seconds.

Rose just grinned at me as streaks of blood appeared across her face, little pieces of dust and sand ripping her skin. I was dragging us to the earth, her cheeks flapping so hard that she had jowls as her eyelids ripped off in the fury of my storm. Her answer was nonsensical, lost to the wind, and I settled for riding her to the earth, dragging her down to the ruptured parking lot below.

Augustus's rock armor sprang up from beneath us, built over him to the point where it looked like a twenty foot tall golem of solid stone. I parted the winds to allow him to take hold of her, and he did not disappoint. He ripped both of Rose's legs off, which I imagined would have caused her eyes to widen in surprise if, y'know, I hadn't already ripped her lids off. Her face was streaky with blood, looking like the first phase of it melting off, as though someone had opened the Ark of the Covenant nearby.

But the wrath of God here was being provided by the small "g" gods, every single one of us pissed off about what she had done to our friend.

Augustus's golem tore Rose's arms off next, just plucked them clean off and threw them wide, and now she was nothing but a torso and head. If she evinced surprise at this turn of events, she didn't show it, her grin bloody but still present, shocking in the fact she was able to maintain it with her face as shredded as it was. The golem wrapped its arms around her, snugging what remained of her to its chest and holding her there as I descended from above, staring her right in her bloody eyes and face.

We had seconds.

"Where is she?" I asked, still yelling but having dialed it down a few notches as I addressed the half-skinned, limbless thing in front of me. Augustus was piling the rock around her, driving gravel into her limb stumps in a bid to shred any potential healing. It looked like a rock polisher operating at high speed, shavings of bone being chipped off as quickly as they regrew, blood sluicing down from each stump as he kept her healing at bay.

"Wouldn't ye…like to know?" she managed to get out between grunting squeals of pain.

"Uh, yeah," Jamal said, and I heard him clearly through the earpiece even though he was now less than fifty feet away. "That's why he's asking."

Rose let out a screech, and I thought it was of pain, but then it turned into a long, high laugh. "Is that Jamal Coleman I heard?" Rose's head twisted, and she seemed to be trying to look around. "Augustus has me in his loving grip, I can tell. And Reed, the loving brother, he's right here, o' course…I saw Veronika earlier, as she got a bit handsy with me…lovely Scott put out the fire and tried to give me a shocking with the others…" She laughed low. "Surely J.J. and Abigail dear are near at hand. The gang's all here, it seems…just what I was hoping for, of course…"

"Of course," I said. "Did you doubt we'd all band together to stop your sick ass?"

Rose laughed, and it was a hideous sound. "I fucking counted on it, Reed m'boy."

She blew up, shattering Augustus's golem without any warning. Blue plasma lit the night as the dust cloud from the golem flooded over us, and I braced, blowing the particulate matter away as quickly as it appeared, rechanneling it into a tornado above her head. If she didn't want to answer my questions, I'd just kill her, and without her to guide me, I'd spend the next month, year, decade, thousand years—however long I lived—overturning every single stone in Scotland to find my sister.

Because she had to be there.

She had to be.

"It's so funny that you think you're going to trap me!" Rose said, her limbs replaced by writhing blue tendrils of plasma, as though she'd suddenly become some sort of plasmatic octopus. She sent one of them my way and Veronika jumped in front of me, diffusing the energy away as though she were carrying a shield. "I'm the one that did the trapping here, my lad. And you fools went and stayed right here in it rather than run. Do you even know what I am? What I can do?"

"You can shut the hell up," I said, and brought the tornado of particles down on her like an infinite sandstorm, dropping it upon her head and all the rest of her, ready for it to be over. She'd die taunting us.

She'd die before telling us anything.

"This is going nowhere," I said. "Let's finish her. Go Zeta."

"Wait, which is Zeta?" Guy Friday's voice crackled in my ear.

"It's where we kill her to death, you idiot!" Veronika shouted over the fray. "Pull out all the stops and execute!"

Lightning flashed as Jamal and Taneshia both poured on their fire. It diffused over the sandstorm I'd caused, the tornado I was bringing down on Rose's head right now, playing through the storm and lighting everything with a frightening aura. Veronika had halted her assault to play defense on catching Rose's plasma bursts, and the others were joining in now—Augustus was hurling boulders at Rose's back, which she was fending off with one hand, lightning absorbed into her body like it was a small tickle, wrapped around her naked torso and flashing as she absorbed it without noticing.

Rose flared into fire, and I reversed the tornado, sucking the heat up and into the sky, turning it into a bellows for removing the flames from the fight. It lit up the Eden Prairie night in a way that the lights in all the corporate parks and malls didn't, turning our battlefield into brightest day.

Guy Friday came at Rose with a length of fallen light pole, smashing it against her without effect; Augustus's golems kept throwing themselves in the path of Rose's red energy walls, erupting into a million pieces of stone and then coming back a second later. Taneshia and Jamal were still pouring it on, and steady gunfire was running, Phinneus Chalke firing a machine gun from the covering rooftop nearby.

And none of it was doing a damned thing.

"Chase, Friday, Kat, Gravity—let loose! Theta option!" I called in the thunder. Well, technically we didn't have thunder, but they were our second team, and I was calling them in.

Chase leapt out of one of the nearby berms, appearing out of the dirt, and coming at Rose on her blind side. She extended her glowing red lightsaber and sprung at her, ready to bury it into Rose—

Rose turned, and another rocking explosion of force sent Chase flying, Veronika flying, Friday flying—anyone who was close to her. It rattled through me like a sonic boom, shaking me down to my bones and teeth, causing an ache in my molars from the force. I suspected it might even have done a little damage to my internal organs based on the sudden stomachache and the extra thuds my heart produced.

"Nice shockwave," I said, gathering my tornado back together. She'd taken it apart with that one move, and shattered every one of Augustus's golems.

"You can't beat me, Reed boy," she said with an airy giggle. "You were dumb to stand here and try. And for love, no less? Love of yuir little sis? You're lucky I'm here to take you alive, so I can flay you in front of her—"

"You think I don't know that, dumbass?" I stared her down, ready to whip a wind shield in front of me if she threw something. I could dodge if she went the route of using an energy beam. J.J. and Abby had done months of analysis on the powers she'd displayed in prior fights, ones we'd accessed and downloaded before we got locked out of Scotland's systems.

Months of game film, readying for this moment.

And she was still pulling out surprises.

"You're the one who chose to stand and fight with the most powerful meta on the face of the planet." She let out a raw cackle that split the Minnesota night. "Who's the dumbarse, really?"

"Still you," I said. "I've had months to prepare for you."

She let out a long laugh. "There's nothing you can do to prepare for me, darling." Her eyes glowed. "And all this time, I've been getting ready for you as well—"

Rose's eyes exploded into fierce laser beams and a rock golem jumped up to take the hit for me. I dodged left at the last second, aided by a hurricane gale of a wind. I used the cover of the ensuing explosion to circle around and start picking up plan Omicron.

Which involved hurling steel pipes into Rose's body until I hit enough vital organs that she stopped moving.

I peppered her with lengths of steel that shot through her like toothpicks through an hors d'oeuvre, a half dozen that struck her torso, burying themselves in the skin. I aimed for her head, but she moved blazingly fast, twitching just out of the path of anything but a glancing blow. "Jamal, Taneshia!" I shouted. "Ground her!" And they lit her ass up.

She jerked and sparked, the lightning smoking her skin. "You think that can—" she started to say.

"Gravity, please!" I said, my grip on the pipes pretty weaksauce. I couldn't apply torsion the way she could, and I needed Rose to be ripped apart right now; I didn't need to shove little pieces of pipe through her and out the other side, which was what my powers could do.

"I can't kill her," Gravity said, causing me to curse, loudly, not under my breath. "Language," she said.

Jamie Barton was a good person and we were in the middle of a really bad fight, which was not where I needed her. I cursed the fact that I thought that kind of heroing was worthy of admiration, that I thought it was something to aspire to for all these years. Jamie Barton had never killed anyone; she'd been the bright, shining hero New York needed.

But right now, I needed a dirty-fighting Sienna Nealon who'd tear this bitch apart so I could go save the real Sienna, and I didn't have that on my team.

"You can't hurt me," Rose said, the lengths of pipe pushing out of her as she Wolfe-healed through the wounding we'd given her. She sent three of them back at me with gravity powers of her own, and I could feel a slight tweak as Jamie Barton dispelled them, saving my life by curving them off and burying them in a nearby building.

"I don't want to hurt you," I said, looking right back at her. "I want to kill your ass and splatter you all over the ground so I can go find my sister."

Rose laughed. "What do you think you'll find if you do go look?" Now she was mischievous, playful, taking the time to taunt me at the failure of my plans. "It's been three months, lad. Do you think there's even anything left of her at this point?"

"Chase," I said, ignoring Rose's awful jibe, one that played to my worst fears.

"On it," Chase said, and leapt out of the ground hole beneath Rose again, aided by a wind burst from me.

She caught Rose right in the back, seemingly unawares, lightsaber lancing up in a streak of glowing red that hit Rose from mid-hip all the way up through the center of her head. She hung there for a second, the calm eye in the center of the storm—

And then she lashed out, smashing Chase once more into a nearby tree, which deftly caught her the moment Rose turned her back. It set Chase down gently.

Rose cranked her neck to one side, then the other, as if experimenting to see if she'd hold together after that splitting attack from Chase. She did, and opened her mouth. "I think I'm done taking pain now. Noble effort, all."

A tree branch extended behind her as Rose was talking,

then slammed into her back, jerking her forward harshly enough that Rose actually frowned.

Then she turned around and lit the damned thing on fire, branch to root, in less than a second. And when she turned…

There was no sign of blood, no sign of injury from the strike.

She'd just…taken it.

"May I suggest," a calm, soothing voice came over my earpiece, "we finish running down the list while in retreat?" The voice was commanding, long familiar, and also—really, really strained.

And when Dr. Quinton Zollers, the most powerful telepath on the planet, sounds strained, I start to worry.

"Zollers, are you holding her off?" I asked.

"She is dampening everything with an incredible amount of empathic effort," Zollers said. "I'm keeping her out of your minds, but I can't do it much longer. Her mind is powerful, but she doesn't appear to have telepathy on her side. That said, if I have to fight her much longer, the sheer amount of despair she's blanketing the area with is going to start affecting you."

"So you've got a pet telepath," Rose said, eyes narrowed, "helping you. Is it Sienna's little favorite? Because I'm looking for him, too. I'll have to thank you properly if you've brought him to me. Maybe drain you in front of Sienna, the fun way—you and me." She looked me up and down appraisingly. "I'd thought about it anyway—insult to injury, you know? Really give her a show—"

"First of all, I'm taken, and second—scary, ginger, and crazy is not my type," I said, as Friday leapt at her again from below, this time carrying a freaking car. He planted it right in her back and she shrugged it off, even though he had to have been doing forty or fifty miles an hour at impact. The car and Friday came crashing back down into the trench where the parking lot had been before Augustus blew the lid off of it in the first attack.

"Not Italian enough?" Rose's eyes glittered. "I'll absorb both of you. All of you. In the worst ways possible, right in front of what's left of your sister. I don't know if it'll make much of an impact at this point, but I'm going to do it, going to take every last drip of you, an inch at a time, dirty like—"

"Angel, it's time to go," I said. "Augustus—you know what to do."

"Oh, so scary," Rose said, interrupting her monologue to show her disdain. Her face was twisted in a blighted sort of rage and sneering contempt. "You think you can just get away from me? Everything you've done so far—"

"Has basically gone to plan," I said, drifting closer to the ground. I hit her with the wind and forced her down. She grunted, frowned, bared her teeth, but drifted lower. "We get it. You're strong." The parking lot was reassembling around me, concrete and stone reforming into a solid surface held up over the empty tunnel below by Augustus's will. Guy Friday, Chase, Jamal and Taneshia all leapt into the ground and vanished as Augustus pulled it over them.

"Stronger than you," Rose said, buffeted by my winds, dragged down even though I could feel her tugging to break free. It was a contest of will versus wind, and she had the power to go supersonic.

But I had the power to drag down airliners, and so pulling her?

Difficult. But doable.

I was straining, sweating. She was almost on the ground, hovering about three or four feet off the surface of the reassembled parking lot. I had her almost positioned...

The garbage truck slammed into Rose at a hundred and fifty miles an hour as Angel skidded the back end and swung it around with an assist from Augustus's rocky efforts. All that momentum had to go somewhere, and the garbage truck functioned like a baseball bat, with Rose as the ball—

Rose flew into the office building, smashing through the second floor, right into the core building supports, and blew out the back. I heard her hit the building behind it, and the building behind that as I swept in and ripped the door off the garbage truck.

Angel was sitting inside, dazed. "Did we get her?" She blinked her eyes, dark hair made even darker by the sudden lack of light for a mile around us. The entire electrical grid had gone out, and all the light from the meta powers flying around had gone out now that nearly everyone was underground and retreating.

"We got her," I said, "but we're still heading toward Beta outcome." I couldn't hide my frustration. We'd had plans upon plans to kill Rose, and so far we'd only achieved the secondary goal, which was not to let any of my people get killed. "Phinneus? Jamie? Are you out?"

"We're in the ground," Chalke's rough voice came through. "Hitting the extraction point now."

"I've got them," Scott said. "You, Kat and Angel are the last ones out—except for the rear guard team."

"One last surprise," I muttered, dragging Angel bodily out of the garbage truck and leaping into the nearby hole that Augustus had left for me. It sealed as soon as we were through, and now I could only see shadowed figures ahead as the warrens below the reformed parking lot guided me to one place—our last exit.

Scott was waiting with one other person as Angel and I staggered up. "Take her," I said, shoving Angel toward him, and he did, pushing her into the waiting pipe without word or ceremony.

"This didn't go so well," Scott observed.

"Could have gone worse," I said, waiting, counting it out. One-one-thousand. Two-one-thousand. "You sure everyone's out?"

"They're gone, dude," he said. "Miles away. J.J.?"

"Can confirm," J.J.'s voice rattled. He was with them by now, rolling along down a pipe of his own, in his little airtight watching pod. "We have every single one of the team, from Abby to Zollers, in motion, except for you three."

"Scott, go," I said, nodding at him, and he hesitated a second before leaping into the pipe that was half-filled with water, waiting for me and our last party member. He vanished a quarter second later, carried off by his own waves that slopped through the pipe like the waterslide it was. He was traveling at several hundred miles an hour and would emerge halfway to the Dakotas at a point we'd chosen but that Augustus had never unearthed the entry to. He'd crack it once we were all there, and we'd decide what the next move was after this...debacle.

"You ready for this?" I asked our last waiting teammate. She was here as a favor to me, and she looked...nervous, to say the least.

"I've never really done anything like this," she said, voice warbling slightly. "At least...not really intentionally, other than that, uh...one time."

The "one time" she was talking about was the time she'd sent a steel pipe through a serial abuser's chest at several hundred miles an hour, turning the momentum of the weapon against a man who'd tormented her for most of her life.

Her name was Olivia Brackett, and earlier this year, in Florida, I'd helped save her life from the people who'd tortured and kept her in captivity for most of her adult life.

"You're going to do fine," I said, touching her gently—really gently—on the shoulder to avoid having it come flying back at me at face-breaking speed.

Because that was her power, to take the momentum of other objects, accelerate it, and turn it loose in another direction. This had worked very badly to her disadvantage in an Orlando park in January, when a pedestrian had gotten too close to her and been flung into a tree.

Now, though...I had a use in mind for it.

The ground shuddered as Rose blasted her way into our tunnel. Now all that was left by Augustus, per my instructions, was a single path leading from where I'd gone into the ground, straight to the pipe where Olivia and I waited. It was as close to a funnel as I could create, a direct path for Rose to come at us, pissed off and angry and unthinking, ready to pulp me into near nothingness.

And I could tell by the look in her eyes...she was feeling it.

Rose was bleeding—or at least had bled. Trails of it were working their way down her forehead, and her eyes blazed with fury at us. "Hey," I called out, waving at her. "Gotta admit, I thought that last one was going to kill you, finally." I kept my tone even. "But it's okay. At least you, you Scottish witch, you haggis-eating clownfish with glowy limp hair, finally know what it feels like to eat a beating the like of which most people can't imagine. I mean, it's funny that you think you can attack us on our home ground and think we'd just roll over and die for you—"

"Your stupid whore of a sister couldn't beat me," she said, eyes flaring up. "Hell—she's barely alive at all anymore." And now she was taunting me. "She couldn't beat me—why would you think you could?"

"Because I've got a lifetime of experience dealing with angry, skanky Eurotrash?" I asked. My goad worked, and she launched at us, straight on the path. I felt Olivia suck in a quick, fearful breath as Rose streaked toward us, accelerating so fast she broke the sound barrier in mere feet—

She hit Olivia's personal bubble, and time seemed to slow for a second where I stood within it. Rose's face was contorted with fury, then gave way to surprise in the frozen moment of time that she hung there—

Then she was thrown through the roof at five times the speed at which she'd been coming toward us, crashing through the stone and rock, which showered down and was reflected off in a spattering of grit and boulder by Olivia's bubble, as Rose streaked into the sky and out of sight.

"She's at Mach 5," J.J.'s voice cut over the earpiece. "Mach 10—holy hell, I think she just set a new speed record in Earth's atmosphere. She's still holding together, though, which means—I don't think she's dead, Reed. Better—"

"I'm on it," I said, and gently I put a hand on Olivia's arm. "Time to go," I said, driving a hard wind against the tunnel roof where Rose had entered. It started to wobble and collapse as I worked to bring it down.

"Okay," Olivia said, sounding a little shell-shocked at what she'd just done. She ducked into the water pipe, and a second later I heard the rushing of water carry her off, a little gasp her only sign of passage as she sped up to several hundred miles an hour on Scott's water.

I brought down the tunnel to the edge of the pipe and leapt in, the shock of cold water drenching me even as it thrust me forward, seizing me tightly like some sort of aqua seatbelt. It repositioned me to sit upright and carried me off into the darkness as the tunnel collapsed behind me, sealing me off from the hardest enemy I'd ever fought.

And one who still, somewhere—had my sister at her mercy.

2.

Sienna

My head bobbed with the gentle sway of the room, staring at the glass bottles straight ahead. They were backed by stone, amber liquid within staring back at me like vials in a chemistry lab from their wooden shelf. My temple pressed down on a hard surface, uncomfortable, woozy, off-kilter and off balance, my brain drifting like I'd taken a concussive hit to the skull.

I should know. I've probably taken more of those than anyone else alive.

Strong alcohol assailed my nostrils like a pungent cleaning solution. It made me want to gag, to heave, to throw up my guts and get on with it, overwhelming my sense of smell almost like the noise was doing to my sense of hearing.

Oh, the noise.

Chatter was all around me, an endless bevy of conversations where people were airing their stupid, useless opinions while my head ached and I wanted to do nothing but sleep, still pushing my temple against the firm, unyielding surface beneath me, my cheek cool against its grainy wood.

"Hey, wake up." Someone pushed my shoulder. Roughly, like they didn't realize I was a delicate little flower. I ignored them.

A few seconds later, another shove, right on the trapezoid, which sent a little dose of pain up my neck. "I said wake up."

"I heard you the first time," I said as I sensed the hand going toward my muscle again, intercepted it, and applied a little pressure. I heard the first hint of a crack in the bone, my cold hand against this warm, rough, calloused one, and I shoved it—and its owner—away from me without a lot of grace.

The shelves I could see dimly through squinted eyes shattered and came crashing down, the hundred bottles coming down with them in shattering wreckage. The guy I'd thrown landed in a heap, all that detritus raining down on him. Around me I heard another sound, something that might have been terrifying to most, but to me sounded like the dinner bell being rung: barstools scooting back, and slightly drunk men standing up. Probably not in fear either, since I didn't hear anyone bolting for the door.

"You cannae do that," someone said over my shoulder.

"Lighten up, Francis," I said, slurring, not really sure I was calling him Francis. It felt like an instinct, to say that, but I couldn't remember where it came from. Some movie, maybe…?

Someone reached for me, and I sensed their movement a second before they landed a hand on mine. I grabbed them, slower than usual, less fluid, a little clumsy, and yanked. A cry told me I'd probably pulled one of their arm bones out of socket. Probably the elbow. That was always a good one. I lanced out with a kick without even raising my head and there was an "OOF!" as they went tumbling back.

"Don't touch me," I said, trying to project my warning to the rest of them, but probably slurring pretty hard in the process. I wasn't sure, but it was possible it came out as, "Dun tich ma." Which a Scot should be able to understand, because they could somehow comprehend their own whack-ass speech.

"I think you've had enough," came another voice, and I waved them off with a broadly flopping hand. This voice was clear, loud, and its bearer was keeping their distance.

"I'll decide when I've had enough," I said, lifting my head off the bar to look at a woman who was standing about ten feet from me, hands folded behind her. She was dark-haired, dark-eyed, and less fair-skinned than most of the Scots I'd met. "Who the hell are you?"

"Rose sent me," she said, watching me with a ghostly, ghastly smile. "She said to tell you…she's on her way, and to hold tight right here until she arrives."

My blood ran as cold as if someone had just given me a blood transfusion straight out of a Minnesota lake in January. I almost fell off my stool lifting my head, but caught myself just in time. I looked past the shattered glass and the bartender lying in a heap beneath the stone-backed shelves and looked for my glass of Scotch, which the bartender had apparently taken away before deciding to invade my personal bubble with his hand. "Shit," I said, when I looked again and still couldn't find my glass.

"What's that?" the woman asked, still standing politely a few feet away, hands tucked behind her, stiff and straight, like some Stepford assistant right out of one of those robot movies.

"Took my drink," I said, grousing all the way. I looked to my left, seeking the end of the bar so I could thread my way around it and get a bottle. I judged the distance to be about twenty feet, i.e., a little too far in my current condition.

"Don't you think you've had enough?" she asked me.

Yeah, don't you think you've had enough, you pathetic little shite?

The voice in my head was like someone had dripped a couple of drops of cold water down the back of my shirt, and I sat up stiffly, almost falling off my stool. "I'll have as much as I damned well please," I said.

"Are you sure that's wise?" the woman asked. "Are you sure you won't make her…mad?"

There was a throbbing in my head as the pressure increased. *Oooh…you wouldn't want to make her mad, now, would ye?*

"No," I said, and the pressure subsided a little. "I wouldn't want to make her mad."

"That's a good lass," the woman said, and beckoned me toward the corner, where she made her way to a table and pulled out the nearest seat, then circumnavigated to the other side of the table before sitting herself, stiffly, seriously, and then putting a hand out in obvious invitation: *join me.*

As invitations went, it wasn't much of one; it carried the force of her command—not this her, but the much worse her—

Rose.

I staggered up, my balance a struggle, and drunkenly sashayed my way across the bar until I nearly collapsed in the chair. When I was safely in it, the woman clapped in what the folks of old would have called "gaily," before that word took on another meaning. There was nothing sapphic about her clap; it was just kind of a happy clap, but saying happy clap made it sound like a joyful case of gonorrhea.

"What's that look for?" she asked, staring at me. She waved someone over from the bar. "Scotch on the rocks for me. Water for her. Still, not sparkling."

I explained my thesis about the sad death of the word "gaily" in other contexts. I think. I might have slurred a few words. Not the bad kind of slurred, the kind that makes me hard to understand. "Words don't mean what they used to mean," I finished, as someone set a glass of water in front of me.

The woman stared at me. "This is the problem that troubles your mind right now?"

I stared back at her. She was staring me down, like a challenge. "Well, I don't have many others to work on presently, see?"

"I suppose not." She leaned forward. "You don't even the slightest urge to fight anymore, do you?"

I stared at the wood grain of the table. The top was less than an inch thick. For all I knew, it had been sanded and refinished a hundred times or something, starting out the thickness of a hand and now down to this. "They used to make things to last," I murmured.

"You dodging my question?" she asked, and I raised my head to look at her, but instead saw stone walls behind her as she leered at me, almost smiling.

It probably wouldn't do to dodge a question from Rose's envoy. Rose was the rough disciplinarian type, always looking for a reason to "punish" me.

She didn't have to look far…at least for the first month.

But it had been three months now, and after learning of the special bonus pains that "punishment" entailed…I'd toned down on some of the obvious defiance, bit by bit, and things had gone…well, a little smoother, I guess.

"Why do you ask?" I put it out there in a soft voice, trying not to sound so full of piss and vinegar as to provoke an immediate reaction.

"Oh, I don't know," she demurred, sitting back straight again, perfect little robot. She raised a hand and a little crackle of lightning ran over it, sparking as it jumped to my water glass before diffusing into the glass and table. "I suppose I was just thinking…you used to be so fearsome, and me? I'm spoiling for a bit of a fight." She leaned in again. "See…these days, working for Rose…I dinnae get to fight much anymore. Not many people willing to raise a hand against her in these parts…but you?" She smiled. "I know you. The world knows you. You never shy from throwing a punch. And I thought…if you can beat me…" She sparked her hand again. "…you can have my powers. Well, you can have me."

"Now you're starting to sound like the other definition of 'gaily,'" I said. "Which is cool…but not for me."

She grinned. "Don't pretend you don't miss having powers other than what you've got right now. Don't pretend you wouldn't like to be able to throw a surprise in Rose's face the next time she comes at you to collect her little tax." She almost looked hungry, leaning forward. "What do you say? We have a little throwdown right here, and if you win…you get a nice little surprise for the next time you meet her?"

"Which should be soon, since you say she's on her way." I picked up my water glass with shaking hands. Some of it slopped over the edge, dripping in great puddles on the table.

"We have time," the woman whispered. "She's coming back from Minneapolis, so she'll be a while. Which is why she sent me to keep you here."

I dropped my glass and it thumped on the table, spilling the remainder of its contents over the side in a dozen little waterfalls. It reduced to dripping shortly, the volume already gone over, and I sat there, dimly aware of the tapping it made. Nobody in the bar said a damned thing about it; I suppose after the number I'd done to the bar, the bartender and one of the patrons, nobody had the guts to call me out for spilling water.

"She's got news for you," the woman said, pretending to think about it. She had a sly grin, almost certainly fully aware that I hadn't dropped my glass by sheer coincidence. "But you'll have to wait until she gets here to find out what it is. She said something about a…gift?" She looked at me questioningly. "Might you like to have one for her, as well?"

She leaned closer and stood, putting her face halfway over the rounded table. I could reach out and seize her by the cheeks, have her halfway to drained before she could pry me loose. A few punches and she'd be out, no lightning for me to deal with as I pulled her soul from her body as easily as I could strip an oyster out of a shell. A little in-head beating to add some seasoning, and I'd serve her electrical powers cold to Rose when she arrived, hit her so hard she'd think Thor himself had come to fry her ass back to the Scottish equivalent of Valhalla.

I was standing and I didn't even realize it, swaying gently from side to side, across the table from the grinning Scotswoman who was trying desperately to get me to fight her. I stared and stared, and finally, the voice again:

Who are you kidding? You're so damned worthless, you'd probably get your arse kicked by this little dish.

I sat down heavily, thumping back onto the chair, and stared at the tabletop.

"That's the reasonable choice," the woman said, returning to her own seat. "Good for you."

"Thanks," I said, haggard, drawn, and feeling like my chin was about to collapse on my breastbone, then that the rest of me would follow all the way to the ground, like some great chain reaction. "You saying that means absolutely nothing to me."

She feigned a hurt look. "Why would you say such a thing?"

I looked at her, my head still hung, the last ounces of my

defiance coming out in a spearing, angry look. Up-eye, you could call it. "Because I don't set much store by the opinion of random servants of *her.*"

"Tsk tsk," the woman said, almost sadly, "you should set great store by my opinion." And she grinned again, and then the grin morphed from that of the woman I'd been talking to…

…into a more familiar one, hair shifting in shade as though clouds had blown through and replaced the darkish-brown with a bright, fiery red, and her skin tone lightened to a milky pale. Her eyes went from dusky brown to green, sparkling like emeralds, and the grin…

The grin morphed into that of a Cheshire cat from hell, so delighted, so pleased, and yet the mere sight of it recalled a hundred tortures and pains inflicted upon me, and I flinched visibly as I took it in.

"…after all," Rose said, shaking her head, loosing her hair as though she'd had it up for a long while, that grin—that evil grin—pointed at me, "I am your goddess now."

3.

A quiet fell over the bar room, and I looked around. There was no one here; they had left or been cleared out, and I hadn't even noticed. "When did you do that?" I asked, chucking a thumb over my shoulder to indicate the empty bar.

She just smiled. "I could do it anytime." She nodded her head, and suddenly the room was filled to the brimming with people, loud, a party going on. The ragged old bar with its low beams of old wood and stone walls had suddenly become a boxy modernistic room, straight out of the Hollywood Hills. "Do you feel more at home now?"

I stared at the people. They looked…vaguely familiar. I turned back to her, and she was still grinning. "No," I said.

"I know," she said, and it disappeared. "I took that little sliver from your memory of your California trip a couple years back. You met a nice boy on that one, didn't you?"

It only took me a second for me to realize who she was talking about. Steven Clayton, movie star and overall nice guy.

"I see you know who I mean," she said, watching me shrewdly. "Lucky for you I'm not looking to cause too loud a stir. Also…you don't seem to care that much about him, which makes him a bit of a poor target."

"You using telepathic powers now?" I asked, watching for her reaction.

It didn't satisfy. "I could be," she said, utterly neutral. "But

29

I don't need them with you, now, do I, Sienna? I know the inside of your head as though I were seeing into my own. I've carved off enough little slices of you now, haven't I? Enough memories to see you for who you are, inside and out." She nodded her head at me. "Though you're changing, I suppose. Wearing a pretty barrette today, are you?"

I felt for my hair self-consciously. I did have a barrette in, holding my hair out of my eyes. "Well, you know," I said, "you need be able to see in a fight."

"And you are just getting in fights left and right, aren't you?" She chuckled, sitting much looser than her fictional Stepford Thor-type character had. "But not with me, and not with my supposed servant?" She tsked again, very matronly. "You used to be willing to fight anyone. Now you're beating up pitiful human bartenders for the crime of cutting you off, you drunkard." She leaned in and whispered, "It's almost sad to see you like this. A once-mighty lioness reduced to pacing her cage, unable to take a bite of anything satisfying. Having to have her meat thrown to her…and even then, when I practically put a meta with lightning powers on a silver platter for you…you still won't take a bite." She laughed to herself, so amused. "You're well trained, I guess. Still, it's sad."

"This is what you wanted," I said, drifting left to right, still drunk and feeling it more now than I had a few minutes earlier. "Remember? For me to feel…trapped in Scotland? Well…I'm trapped in Scotland." I leaned against the back of my chair, fearing I might take a tumble if it didn't support me. "Nowhere to run."

"You've been running all over, though, haven't you?" She raised an eyebrow at me, leaning from neutral toward darkly amused. "I'm having to work to keep an eye on your pretty little arse as you crisscross my country."

"Just pacing my cage, *darlin'*," I said, giving her a little more defiance than I intended to. "As a lioness does in captivity."

She seemed to be trying to decide whether to smack me down for that sarcasm. She must have landed on, "No," because instead she leaned back and crossed one leg over the other, tightly, a real lady, this one. "There's no fight left in you but a few stray, angry words." She smiled, but there was no pleasure in it. "I like that you know when you're beat."

I hung my head sullenly. "Well...you've beaten me enough that I think the message has sunk in."

She sighed, deeply and fully. "Indeed. We're just waiting on a few last...party favors...and then you and I can conclude our business." She looked at me soberly, which was more than I could have pulled off at present. "I'm sorry it's dragged on this long. I'd meant to be done with you long ago, but..." She smiled thinly. "Your friends, they're more difficult than you are."

I wondered if she knew how much hope she'd just given me. I felt a surge, almost a glow in my heart, hearing that. "Well..." I said, as she watched me for reaction, "they are my friends, after all."

"Aye, they are," she said, "for a wee bit longer." She looked past me, pursing her lips, and then she stood, so abruptly that it was almost like she'd been sitting illusory all along and just finally dissolved it so I could see her standing. "Well...let's get on with the evening's business, shall we?"

I started to open my mouth to protest, to scream, to move, but she was on me in less than a second. My chair tipped over and I hit the old wooden floor with a thundering clatter as Rose overwhelmed me, keeping me from slamming into it full force but pushing me down all the same. I struggled, futilely, as she pushed her hands against my face and put a hand right in the center of my chest. It felt like a ten-thousand-ton weight rested on me, not crushing me, but not allowing me to move past the point of it.

I bucked, but only for a second, a last spasm of resistance as I tried to kick my legs free and she—almost gently, except for the ten-thousand-ton weight of the resistance—thumped me in the chest hard enough to knock my breath out of me. "There, there," she said softly, keeping her hand on my cheek and anchoring me in place with the other. "Don't make me weigh down your legs."

The pain started a few seconds later, where her hand rested against my face. It reached a screaming crescendo seconds after that, or years; it was hard to tell. I wanted to cry, wanted to scream, wanted to be anywhere but here, on this bar floor in Scotland, as Rose ripped some unknown memories out of my head, but instead the pain grew and grew, a balloon of anguish expanding inside me to the point where I simply couldn't bear it anymore, and I faded into the darkness of unconsciousness instead.

4.

Roberto Bastian

Mexico City
2009

Life seemed like a dusty haze these days to Roberto Bastian. He took a sniff of the air in this high-class hotel, one of the finest in Mexico City, and found it...wanting.

There was a glass of clear liquid sitting in front of him, on the in-suite bar. He'd poured it for himself. He probably could have rung up a servant to do so for him, paid someone more than enough pesos to keep him company while he went through this one, the next one—hell, all night long. It wouldn't even have made a dent in his wallet.

But as he took his second drink of the tequila, that smooth, almost biteless liquid sliding down his throat, he realized...he didn't want the kind of company you paid money for. Not now...

Not ever.

He sniffed and ran his fingers over his grizzled chin. He hadn't shaved in days. When he'd come into the hotel lobby with his crew, he was pretty sure he looked like what he was—a merc that was on a job, watching the back of the man they'd escorted in with them. Because even here in the heart of Mexico City, a drug kingpin couldn't be too careful. He had bodyguards on him every hour of the day. Someone was probably standing behind him while he took a piss even now.

Bastian had done that. He took another drink as he considered how far he'd fallen in his own estimation, but...he'd done it.

And tomorrow morning, when he was back on watch...he'd probably do it again. Stand in the same room as that soulless bastard when he took his morning deuce.

Because that was what Bastian was paid for.

He stared at the clear liquid in the glass. The scent of agave was strong, almost enough to make Roberto want to put it down, forget about it, write this off as a bad idea before the night even began, really.

But he didn't.

He took another drink instead.

The knock at the door surprised him; if his boss needed him, he'd have someone call. Bastian stood, on his feet in an instant, hand on his gun less than a second after that. "Who's there?" he called, then walked twelve feet to his right immediately, in case they tried to kill him by shooting through the door.

"My name is Erich Winter," came the voice, strong, projected through the wood between them. "I have to come to make you an offer."

Bastian frowned. He'd been guarding a drug kingpin for getting close to a year now. The only offers he got were the kind that ended in inevitable betrayal and death for someone.

"What kind of offer?" He shifted position again, this time moving almost against the wall to his left. He resolved not to speak again. This Erich Winter—if that was even his real name—could be trying to triangulate where he was standing to make a shot.

That'd wipe his boss's strongest bodyguard. Smart move if someone was looking to make a play.

Of course, the way Bastian thought of his boss, he might have actually respected somebody who killed the bastard, provided it was done for the right reason. Pretty unlikely, that. Anyone who wanted to kill his boss was probably just the same sort of scum looking to replace him.

"I want you to come work for me." The voice was that of an older man, Bastian realized. Accented, too. European, somewhere? Had to be Eastern, maybe Germany?

No. Bastian had served in Germany in the eighties; this wasn't that accent. Norway? Sweden, possibly?

Bastian couldn't tell. And he didn't like uncertainty. He stayed quiet, listening, waiting for this Winter to expound on his offer.

"I know you are sitting in your room in your time off," Winter's voice came again, a low rumble filled with that accent. "Drinking alone. I can smell the tequila through the door."

Bastian sniffed. Only a metahuman could smell something that sharply.

"Yes," Winter said. "I am like you. It is why I want you to come to work for me. I run a group dedicated to catching the criminals of our kind."

Bastian let out an unintended snort. "Look, I don't know what you've heard about me, but…" He put his head against the wall. It had started to swim. "But unless you're coming after me as one of your targets…I think you've got the wrong guy."

"You were not always bodyguard to a drug lord," Winter said. "You are a decorated war hero. The first Gulf War. Afghanistan. Iraq. You have shown bravery, loyalty, duty—"

"That was a long time ago," Bastian said, under his breath. He had his pistol in hand, ready to counterfire, but his finger was off the trigger now.

"Not so long ago," Winter said. "You remember how you felt in those days, do you not?"

Bastian felt a cold, creeping sense of disgust run through his body. "Are you an empath? You making me feel things right now?"

"No." The voice was followed by a rush of cold, and Bastian looked over to see ice covering the door handle. With a click, machinery in the guts of the lock shattered, and the door opened a crack to reveal a tall, wrinkled white man with eyes that were blue as ice.

"Frost jotun," Bastian murmured, taking a step back as the

tall meta brushed into the room, slowly, and closed the door behind him, never taking his eyes off Bastian. Norwegian after all. Those eyes were shockingly blue, and Bastian felt completely transfixed.

"Indeed," Winter said, without expression. "My surname is not some random thing."

Bastian exhaled slowly, and his breath misted the cold air. It was a hundred degrees outside. "What do you want?"

Winter's eyes sparkled like frosty grass on a sunlit morning. "I want you to come work for me."

Bastian let out a low laugh, devoid of any joy. "I doubt you can match what I'm making here."

Winter just stared him down. "Do I need to?"

Bastian frowned at the man, then looked back at the windows, which offered a commanding view of Mexico City's skyline. "Why would I leave all this behind?" he asked, finally deciding that this Winter *probably* wasn't a threat.

He didn't put his pistol down, though. Or turn his back on the big man.

"Because you're sick of drinking alone and feeling sick in your stomach at the end of your day's labors," Winter said, and it was like he'd applied ice to Bastian's spine.

Bastian froze mid-step, on his way to pick up his tequila. He kept his head down, but raised his eyes to look at the Mexico City skyline, sun-tinged as the light of day faded. "You don't know what you're talking about. I—"

"You work for a man that you hate, in a field that you hate," Winter said, standing like a forbidding statue in the middle of the room. "You feel as though you might as well be injecting the poison your boss makes into the waiting veins of his customers far at the other end of this long chain that you protect. You can almost feel your humanity slip away as you do your business, day by day." He cocked his head at Bastian. "How did it feel the first time you pulled the trigger on someone who wasn't an enemy of your country?"

Bastian swallowed heavily. "I'm f—" He couldn't even finish the sentence. The lie would be so obvious…

"You don't have to feel this way anymore," Winter said, taking a step toward him. "Afraid to open your eyes in the morning for fear of what you'll have to do this day. You could wake up and feel…alive again. As though you were making a difference. Being the shield of decent people instead of the sword of a terrible man." Winter's eyes glinted in the sunlight, cobalt, frightening, as though they saw into Bastian's very soul.

It was a hard sell, but he'd hit Bastian right in the heart from the jump, and what the hell was he going to say?

No, I like killing people that haven't done anything but piss off an awful human being!

I love the way I feel when I wake up in the service of a capricious bastard who's slept more times with teenage girls that he's kidnapped than with his wife!

It's so much fun to work for a guy who runs narcotics into my country as we ponder the complex problems of supply chain and mercilessly wiping out not only his enemies, but also any unfortunate citizens that get in his way!

Bastian ran his fingertips over his stubbled jaw, and knew he'd been beat. No strategic withdrawal for him, though, because surrender was for losers. Instead he looked up at the victor, considered one last time how much he was leaving behind—and knew the choice wasn't even close. He didn't even have any questions, save one:

"When do we start?"

*

"God, you were naïve," Gerry Harmon said, almost cackling in the small Scottish village where they seemed to live—or not—these days. "How long did it take you to realize he was lying to you?"

Bastian's jaw tightened as the world of his memory faded away and deposited them back here. The grass was swaying in a late autumn breeze, cold chills like the kind Winter had foisted on him rolling over his skin. He was dead, had been for years, yet he still possessed the capacity to feel chill? Bastian turned his head away, looking out over the round-mountain vistas of this Scottish purgatory. Grey clouds hung overhead, from horizon to horizon, and Bastian was about tired of that.

They always came back here.

"It took a while," Bastian answered at last from his place in the little circle. This was how they sat, like a bad habit formed over time that you just couldn't seem to break.

"Probably the night we killed Sienna's loverboy," Eve Kappler said, casting a sidelong glance at Zack, who was sitting, silent, staring at the pebbled ground in the center of their circle.

"He wasn't the only one that died that night," Bjorn said, his low, rumbling voice like a peal of thunder from the Scottish sky. This was closer, though, and more menacing, like a dog's growl.

"Yes, and some of us followed shortly thereafter," Bastian said, flicking his gaze to Aleksandr Gavrikov, who sat curled up, arms wrapped around his knees. "Or came before."

"And some of us came long, long after," Harmon said, voice raised like the loudest, drunkest guest at a party. "Seriously, though—why would you pick this memory?" The former President cocked his head. "Is this your secret shame, Roberto? Because I suspect you've had lower moments."

"Probably not more fateful lower moments, though," Bastian said quietly.

"Well, this was hardly thrilling," Harmon said, looking at the Scottish boy next to him. Graham was sad of eye, even for this sorry lot, and he didn't raise his head. "Does anyone have a better memory we could dive into? Something with a little—oh, I don't know—*joy*?" Harmon put a spike of emphasis on the last word, like it was a cudgel he wanted to drive into all of them.

"Do you feel joyful, Gerry?" Zack Davis asked, raising his head from where he sat in the circle, low as the rest of them. "Has there been a lot of cause for celebration of late?"

"No, there hasn't," Harmon said, "and that's the point. Why do we keep dwelling in the darkness, eating more and more of this depressing boredom by the day?" He gestured at the sky. "We've been here for months. We still can't see through Rose's eyes—ever—and we're trapped in here like dogs in a puppy mill. We could be depressed all on our own, just contemplating the circumstances. But why would we want to do that?" He shifted, his suit coat flapping open as he put his arms back, palms down behind him, like he was ready to crab walk out of the circle. "Let's find something we can relive that doesn't make us all want to die. Again," he amended.

"What's the point?" Graham asked. "There's no way out." He looked right at Harmon. "This is life now, whether you like it or not. Welcome to the Scotland of Rose Steward's mind—there is no escape. Not for us—" he looked up, favoring each of them with a glance of pure hopelessness "—and not for your bonnie Sienna."

Zack stirred, looking up at Graham. "Do you still see her?"

Graham waited a moment, then nodded slowly. "Aye, I saw her earlier. Rose gave it to her, but good, again. Carved off another little cutlet from her soul. She'll probably be joining us soon, I'd say." He paused, almost sadly, and said, "Your girl…she's given up. Just lets Rose have at it anytime she wants these days."

Bastian settled into a quiet with the rest of them. No one argued, because…how would they? They couldn't see.

And it had been months of this. Months of being beaten down just by the quiet and isolation. Who knew how Sienna was actually doing, out there, if Graham's reports were correct?

Months of being beaten down actively? Hell, maybe Sienna was broken, giving up.

And Bastian? He didn't know how to feel about that.

He tried to imagine this Rose battering Sienna down, putting hands on her, tearing out little pieces of her memory, of who she was…

Something about it just burned his dinner rolls.

Bastian put a hand over his face, feeling the bristle of whiskers that he hadn't grown since 2012. Seven years he'd been dead, and this was what he'd come to. From prisoner in Sienna Nealon's head to prisoner in this Rose *puta's* mind, and a true prisoner at that. His every moment was spent with these yahoos in this same place, sitting outside a Scottish village by an ever-burning fire, the skies dark around them.

The maddening sameness every day was enough to make his job in Mexico look like heaven by comparison.

Bastian looked at the faces around his, and made a decision. He kept it to himself, but now he knew.

He could not do another three months of this, for sure not another six, or a year, or many years. This was hell, as near to it as he'd ever been, minus the choices that had led him to that desperation in Mexico City.

He was a prisoner here, a true one, and being stuck in Rose Steward's mind was his fate for the rest of his days.

Unless he found an actual way out. Not the little daydreams of one that they'd talked about all this time, or a fanciful vision of an idea of a maybe of a way out...

He needed a way out. Any way out would do. Even a permanent ending would be better than this.

It was a little decision, maybe the only one he had left to make.

Escape was a thing that was far off, a hope he almost didn't contemplate, like being locked in a black, empty box for months at a time. In the dark.

Like she had been.

And he was willing to do whatever it took now to either find a way out...

Or end it, if given the chance.

Because anything, Bastian reflected, looking at the hopeless, quiet souls in the circle around him, would be better than living...without really, actually living...like this.

5.

Sienna

I woke in darkness, in a bed, sheets placed over me, still in my clothes, which, honestly, stunk of Scotch. I moaned, rolling over, wondering if Rose had dragged me upstairs from the bar into the inn above, because underneath the Scotch I could smell what had maybe been fresh sheets at one point, before I'd spent hours tossing and turning in them, as well as a general smell of a very old hotel-like room. It was the cocktail of cleaning solutions and aged building that drew me to that conclusion.

Also...I had to pee, and my head ached like someone had flown me into the ground at a thousand miles an hour.

Someone stirred nearby, and I was instantly on my guard. There was no telling what I was going to have to deal with, other than safely being able to assume Rose herself wasn't lurking in the corner just for me to wake up. She didn't have the patience to do that anymore. She was all about crushing my hopes and dreams and various bones, but she liked to do it on her timetable, not mine.

In other words, she would have slapped me awake rather than waiting in the corner, staring at me like some creeper while I slept, as this person was doing.

I rolled off the bed and thumped against the floor, uneven boards greeting my fingertips as I caught myself. I was back to standing a moment later, crouching defensively and peering into the darkness.

"Ye're awake," a soft voice said, a little thick with tiredness, grog settled over her. I knew it was a her by the lightness, and she didn't sound Scottish. She lacked that thick brogue I seemed to be running into everywhere nowadays.

So Rose had sent a servant to keep an eye on me, make sure I didn't choke on my tongue in my sleep or something. Probably wise. Best not to leave the toddler you want to torture alone in the tub with a toaster next to them.

"I'm awake," I said, trying to decide how best to handle this situation. Rose had sent a few actual servants to taunt and harass me over the last few months, her little ruse with her Rakshasa powers last night notwithstanding. She was a busy woman, and she had certainly made me wait my fair share of times lately for her to come swooping in and rip a little segment off my soul. Helped build the anticipated fear, I was sure, knowing that I was having to wait for my little sliver of soul death to come to me. Hell, she probably thought I was quaking in my boots while I waited.

But I didn't really have boots anymore. I was dressed pretty shabbily at this juncture, since I had no money and what I did scrounge up tended to go for decent Scotch.

The light clicked on across the bed from me, shedding illumination over the room. It was pretty shit, this place probably dating back to the days when armies traveled by horseback and their generals reserved rooms like this to sup in a roadside inn and then get some sleep on a crappy mattress. Not that the mattress was crappy, but it wasn't exactly going to get a 5-star on Yelp from me. Maybe that was uncharitable because I already had a head and neck ache before I started, but dammit, I had standards.

Sitting in the shabby chair across from me was a woman with strawberry blond hair, looking—well, like I'd just woken her up. She was lightly freckled, dressed in the shabby-chic of the modern post-teen/early twenty-something, and she had lots of holes down the front of her jeans. She wore a t-shirt under a thick cloth jacket that looked like a cross between hipster and military surplus. Her face was clean, unlined, and I put her age at around my own, though it was hard to tell because she was rubbing one of her eyes, which was a light green.

She could have been Rose's slightly adulterated sister— lighter eyes, lighter hair, slightly darker skin—but Rose's family had all died, as far as I knew, so this was probably just another Scottish girl repurposed to her use.

Except for that accent. Too light. Maybe she was from Edinburgh. Which was far from here, but...Scotland wasn't a huge place, maybe the size of a medium US state. Nothing was that far from anything else.

My patience thinned by the headache, I decided to get right down to it. "You got something to tell me?" I stood, recognizing this girl was not in a fighting posture. "Or are you just keeping me here for her?"

"No," she said, still rubbing the sleep out of her eyes. She grimaced as she sat up, cradling her neck. "Ooh," she lilted softly, "that chair was not good for the neck."

"Well, the bed wasn't much better," I said. "Next time book a room at the Hilton. We'll both be happier."

She caught my gaze with an irritable one of her own. "We're in the middle of nowhere. I didn't exactly have my fair run of housing options, ye know?" Definitely not Scottish with that accent. It sounded...vaguely familiar.

"What are you? Irish?" I asked, my curiosity overriding my instinct to go crashing out the window without looking back. I'd done that a few times with Rose's servants, and now that Wolfe's healing powers had deserted me, it always ended in blood loss and time spent healing. On the plus side, with reduced blood volume came cheaper drunkenness. Silver lining for when you're a bit skint, as the Brits say.

"Good guess," she said, still blinking her way out of sleep. "My name's Eilish."

"Mm hmm," I said, still staring her down. "And how long have you worked for Rose?"

She squinted at me. "I don't work for Rose."

"Oh, I see," I said, sauntering toward the end of the bed. "So you're...what? A kindly Irish innkeeper, lost in Scotland?" She shook her head. "A good Samaritan, who paid to get me a room at the inn so I could recover from last night's…fracas?" She shook her head again. "Come on," I said, patience wearing thin. "You work for her."

"I don't," she said, getting to her feet. She did it quickly— quicker than human.

"Is that so?"

I came at her in a metahuman lunge of speed, around the foot of the bed and right at her throat. She flinched away at metaspeed, and I had my answer as she almost tripped over the chair she'd been sleeping in, barely avoiding it at the last second. She put it between us, like that would stop me, and held up her hands. "Now wait a second—"

"Do you have a message for me?" I asked, feeling like I'd done my part to move the conversation along.

"What?" She frowned. "What are ye talking about? Message?"

"From her?" I asked, staring her down. I suddenly realized where I'd seen her before—she'd been at the Edinburgh train station when I'd been running from Rose's minions, trying desperately to get to York to meet Reed a few months back. Rose's minions had been within about an inch of rolling me when she'd somehow stopped them with a shout, which suggested to me that she had some authority over them.

Yeah, she was Team Rose all the way.

"I don't work for her," she said, turning up the heat of her insistence.

I rolled my eyes. I'd heard that one before. Rose's favorite game was sending random people at me in various situations, trying to get me to help them or them to help me. It was always a trap, always, without fail, and the prize was me getting ransacked by her, another little part of me ripped asunder and filed away in her psycho-Scottish-brain-files. It happened when I stopped to help an elderly woman change her tire in a downpour, it had happened when I'd tried to stop a very dramatic assault in a park in Edinburgh— everywhere I roamed in Scotland, Rose had servants there, playing games for my benefit, and the prize was always a good hard soul ripping for Sienna.

Of course, I got that whether I participated in the game or

not, but the lesson was not lost on me—she was grinding me down to indifference to the human condition, training decency out of me through moments like this. Everyone I tried to save was a potential attacker, so why keep saving people?

It was kind of a nice metaphor for the world lately, but as much time as I had to think about it, I didn't much appreciate it. Why would I? She was teaching me a lesson—not to trust people, not to help people.

And it was working.

"Sure you don't," I said, to match my eye roll. "So…no message?"

She looked at me, face all crossed up in confusion, like she was trying to work her way through a particularly confusing puzzle I'd thrown at her. "No. I—"

"Cool, later," I said, and headed for the door, ignoring my bladder. I'd relieve myself downstairs, in the bar where I'd gotten my ass kicked last night.

I threw open the door, and heard footsteps behind me, urgent ones. "Wait—" she said.

Sliding through the door, I shut it behind me, hard, and heard her curse in that florid accent. "I said wait!" she called after me, throwing the door open.

Since she'd already denied being Rose's servant, I didn't have a lot of desire to do anything she said. If she'd said she was Rose's servant, I'd have been compelled to listen. But playing the psychological game? Ugh.

I walked with a slow limp from where she'd rammed my leg into the ground last night and I hadn't even noticed at the time, so preoccupied was I with other stuff. Apparently I hadn't fully healed in the time I'd slept, which also explained the wicked hangover. Normally that would have been taken care of by my metahuman powers.

I went down an old, narrow, rickety staircase that looked like something out of a horror movie, passing a window that looked over a faded moor. It was lit by an exterior light and the moon, providing a fine view of endless nothing, probably rocky and ugly and kind of coldly forbidding, at least based on what I'd seen during the ride up here. I was way outside

Edinburgh at this point, bumming my way across Scotland in an effort to shed the city, which I'd grown quickly sick of after my first month or so stuck here.

Rose didn't seem to mind; she'd given me the right to wander, after all, and her games played out regardless of where in the country I was. Last night proved that well enough.

"Hey, wait!" Eilish of the Irish shouted to me from a story above, but I was done heeding anything she had to say. I came out of the staircase into a foyer of rich woods and aged plaster, the inn/bar (I guess technically the same, in old terms) check-in desk an ancient and falling-apart podium to my left. No one was manning it, and the bar waited just beyond, so I shot past it and into the tavern area where I'd gotten my ass thoroughly beat by Rose again last night, looking for a bathroom.

I found it and did my business before Eilish managed to track me down, pulling up my ragged pants as she came in the door to the aged restroom. I popped out of the stall and found her there waiting in front of the mirror, which was spotty and fogged by age. I washed my hands, studiously ignoring her as she glared at me. "Did ye nae hear me?"

I ignored her, figuring if she had a message from Rose that she wanted to deliver now that the sham was over, she'd get to delivering it. I lathered up, then washed my hands carefully, taking great pains not to look at myself in the mirror. Which was greatly aided by the mirror being so damned cloudy, like it had been here since the 1700s. Hell, for all I knew, it had been. I caught a flash of my pretty pink barrette in my hair and focused on that when I looked up, ignoring anything else about my appearance.

"Hello…?" Eilish seemed determined to get my attention. Persistent little annoyance, wasn't she? "I'm—"

I stepped over to the dryer and it clicked on, drowning out whatever she was saying. I looked at her, blinking innocently, and shrugged, making a motion toward my ear as it hit my hands with heated air, and I stared down at the shoddy white tile beneath my feet, keeping only a cursory watch on her out of the corner of my eye for a sucker punch as I waited for my hands to dry. I took an extra long time, figuring I'd really be an asshole and test her patience.

After pulling my hands from beneath the dryer and letting it click off, I inspected them as Eilish said, "Finally. Now—"

"Oops, spot," I said, and stuck them back under the dryer again as it started up once more with world-ending volume. I favored her with a grin, really rubbing it in. This was my sole power over Rose's minions nowadays, and I had to enjoy these moments while I could. The fight might have gone out of me, but the irritating asshole remained.

Until she ripped that out of my soul too, anyway.

I played the dryer trick a couple more times and Eilish just stood there, seething, cut off every time by the sudden WHOOOOSH! of it starting up. She was plainly incensed, and maybe new at being a meta, because if she'd had a reasonable level of experience, she'd know I could hear her just fine over the dryer going.

Finally, I'd had enough, and pulled my hands out, then circled around her before she could do anything but spin in place, and went right out the door.

"Hey!" she said, sputtering, catching up to me halfway out the bar. "I'm trying to talk to you!"

"You're succeeding, more or less," I said, almost to the exit. The bar was empty, the lights dimmed, shut down for the night. I was still limping, but I didn't want to stay here any longer. I glanced at the place where Rose had assaulted me, and where once I might have felt nausea from being so abused…

Instead I just felt this prickle of guilt, like I'd earned this.

Like everything that had happened was my fault.

All the times she'd held me down and ripped out a piece of me—heart screaming, skin on fire, pain like a knife to a part of me so deeply buried it was somewhere behind my heart—had blurred together, this long cycle of times that I couldn't even remember the specific details of anymore. I remembered the first time in the graveyard, the nausea afterward, the sick feeling that I'd been bested, been taken advantage of in a way that had never happened in a thousand fights.

47

And I remembered the second time, in a snowy field that she'd made for me, where she held me down again and showed me just how easily she could beat me—

But after that, they all ran together. Thinking about them made my head go fuzzy, and staring at the spot where she'd done it again, just hours ago?

The guilt was there, the aching in the soul, painful. It surfaced for a second. But those other feelings? The guilt, the sick gripping of my stomach and twisting?

It was ever-present these days, and staring at the spot where it had most recently happened didn't do anything much but stir those feelings lightly inside me.

I walked out the front door of the inn and found myself in a chilly, poorly lit parking lot. There was nothing but inky night ahead, broken by the moon shining down over those rocky moors. In the distance I could see hilly Scottish mountains, those round and bare lumps of land pushed up by time and geological forces I didn't really understand. They could have been done by the Scottish version of Augustus for all I knew of them.

Standing out front of the inn, I tried to decide what to do next. It wasn't a bad night for a walk, the bitter chill starting up to tell me that winter was coming soon to Scotland.

Eilish came bursting out of the inn a few steps behind me. "Sienna!" she said.

I ignored her, still trying to decide which direction to go. North, south, east, west?

Did it matter?

"You don't even know who I am," Eilish said, gushing, a little anger tinging her words. I was pretty sure if I turned around and looked at her, those cheeks would be flushed.

"I know who you are," I said. "You're another one of hers." I said it dully, meant it dully, like a blunt force object I was hurling slowly at her to get her to go away. Like a bottle you hurl at a dog. Well, I wouldn't hurl a bottle at a dog, unless it was the guy who posed as my dog for several months in an effort to spy on me. But people do that sort of thing. Asshole people. Not asshole like me. Real assholes.

You get the point.

"I'm not one of hers," Eilish said, circling wide around me. Smart move; I was less likely to lash out if she didn't make any overtly threatening motions. "I'm here to talk to you. You, personally, and not on behalf of anyone."

"Sure," I said, calm, not believing a word of it.

"You don't know who I am—" she started to say, again, coming around me now so she could look me in the eyes.

I slapped her in the belly, so fast she didn't see it coming. She hit her knees, all the air rushing out of her because I'd targeted it perfectly. She looked insulted, which was good, because I'd meant it as such. "But you know who I am," I said, "and since you do...you ought to know better than to piss me off." I turned away, stalking off, picking my direction randomly.

"Do you even know who you are anymore?" she wheezed. "After all this—these months?" She was still down, clutching herself, fighting for words and to get her wind back. "I came here—I needed to talk to you—I could maybe help ye—"

"I'm fine, thanks," I said, telling the biggest whopper of a lie I'd maybe ever come out with. But it was fine, because she'd been lying to me the whole time, and hit me with the biggest of hers right before I'd fired mine.

"You don't know—" she started again.

"And I don't want to," I said, striding off the path, starting over the uneven moors, a little drag to my step. "I don't want to know you, I don't want to know who you are, I don't want to see your face again—and I don't need your damned help," I called back, not even bothering to turn around. She was still rasping, but thankfully she was no longer following.

I made my way under the dark Scottish night, tracing a path over rough and rocky moors. I stumbled on the rocks, making my own path over the wild and grassy lands, unaware of where I was going, and without any hope...

...just as I had for the last three months.

6.

Reed

Sacred Heart, Minnesota

I emerged from Scotty's turbo waterslide into an underground space the size of a warehouse. There wasn't much light, just a few flashlights or lamps strung here and there, ones Augustus and Scott had transported out here for use when we arrived.

Well, we'd arrived, and used they were, casting a pale glow over the rocky walls. It looked a little like a cave that had never been open to above ground, which…it actually was, albeit one made very recently.

I landed on my feet, using my wind powers to keep from doing a face-first digger that would have probably cost me the respect of my team, stepping off the slide and into their midst in a dramatic and determined fashion.

Go, leader.

Scott was waiting, and ran his hand over me, drawing the residual water off my clothes. I felt good and dry a moment later, staring at my little circle of a war party.

"Well, that didn't go exactly as we hoped," Augustus said, speaking up before anyone else got a chance. He was snuggled up with Taneshia, the two of them leaning on each other pretty good. Behind him I could see Jamal, tapping away at a tablet, which he must have either grabbed and brought with him or else already smuggled through during the build process. Either way, he was apparently connected to the internet and hard at work.

"Agreed," I said softly, before anyone else could add something worse. "But we knew it was a risk going into this fight. Rose Steward is the toughest enemy we've ever faced." Obviously, since she had wrecked my sister.

"I don't want to seem like the ungratefully unpleasant member of this party," Jamie Barton said, looking around our circle, her costume's cowl and mask hanging off the back of her head. It was a new one, added some color over her last iteration. "But...I'm not used to facing unstoppable enemies. How do you even fight that?"

"Yeah, she was like a god...dess," Olivia Brackett said, standing just a little behind me. She tended to stick close to me in these sort of things, probably because she hadn't had much chance to meet, let alone bond with, anyone in the group other than, briefly, Scott.

"Aren't we all?" Angel snarked, halfway submerged in the shadows, arms folded in front of her, body half-facing away, like she didn't really want to be part of this conversation. Which wasn't true, because she'd volunteered for this.

"You do seem to run across the worst sort of supervillains you could," Phinneus Chalke said. He had his rifle slung across him, the chamber open, and he looked like he was performing routine maintenance or something. "Last time the President, a super telepath, this time a succubus who's eaten enough souls to turn her into the meta equivalent of a tricked-out Swiss army knife." He shook his head. "Not sure what you kids are going to do for an encore next year."

"I'm going to Disneyland," Veronika said, elbowing Phinneus lightly, her eyes dancing even in the dark.

"I already did that once this year," Scott said, a little sourly, "and it was not so happy a place, at least for me. Can we just say it?" He paused, looking around. "We can't beat this lady."

"Don't be such a downer," Kat said, slapping Scott lightly across the arm.

"Downer?" Chase looked around the room. "I think the guy spoke some truth." She got a nod of appreciation from

Scott. "This lady is the toughest nut I've ever seen. We just threw everything at her, trying to crack her—three months of strategy; we tossed every single plan into this—and we got nowhere."

"Assuming Olivia's attack didn't kill her," I said, looking for J.J. and Abby in the darkness. I found them all snuggled up in the corner, lit by their laptop screen. What was with all these couples cuddling in my strategy meeting? Ugh.

J.J.'s eyes found mine and he shook his head. "We had her on radar heading back to Scotland. She came back for a quick peek after you launched her, but…she must have tried to dig and decided we got away clean, because she headed home. We lost her once she entered UK airspace."

"And you can't hack your way into—" I started to say.

"Scotland's cyberspace is bottled up tight," Jamal said, similarly lit by the glow of his tablet. "We have no inroads to anything there since she shut us out. This Rose is either a pro or she's working with a serious one." Jamal's face fell. "And I got a bad feeling about who she's using, if she outsourced this."

"Your ArcheGrey chick?" Augustus asked. Taneshia smacked him. "Uh, your ArcheGrey…crush?"

Taneshia nodded. "Better."

"You don't seem to have many angles of attack," Dr. Zollers said at last, quiet from his place in the corner, that deep, resonant voice echoing through our little chamber now that he'd decided to make his voice heard. "Cyberspace is closed. All the things we've tried get turned back."

"There are other options," I said, pretty sure I wasn't just talking out my ass. "Things we haven't tried. This woman is not invincible, no matter what she thinks. She's human—well, metahuman—and she can be killed."

"Did anyone else see that in the last part of the fight, she just stopped taking damage?" Guy Friday asked, shrunk down to his skin and bones self, not an ounce of muscle on his frame. "Like…at all?"

"She's almost certainly absorbed an Achilles," Zollers said, tone even and his eyes intense, "based on her capacity to soak up damage. It makes her skin well nigh invulnerable, though you can still bat her around with a good hit. That makes things...difficult, when combined with Wolfe's ability to heal."

"I watched Sienna burn the skin off an Achilles," I said, staring right back at him. "There are ways—"

"But she's also immune to fire, provided she has that power front of mind," Zollers said. "And immune to telepathy, lightning, to physical damage, apparently—"

"She's not freaking invincible, okay?" I was getting heated. "She can't hold all those powers top of mind at once." *I hoped,* I didn't say. "We can beat her. We're just missing an idea that will allow us to—"

"Oh, man," Jamie Barton said, and sat down heavily on...well, nothing. She seemed to have created a repellent gravity channel under her backside that functioned like a stool. "Look...I did what you asked. I hid my kid, I put my life on hold, all because you said this lady was dangerous, and she'd be coming after old associations of Sienna's—"

"Reed was right," Guy Friday said, and I cringed to hear him say it, looking anorexically skinny but still wearing the mask. "This woman is dangerous, and she is after every single one of us. She's trying to hurt Sienna every which way she can, including by coming at us. Which means...in spite of all our fears..." He looked at me significantly.

"Sienna's still alive," I said, almost under my breath, a sweet trickle of relief rolling in the form of goosebumps over my skin.

"Wow, Friday," Scott said, "that was...well reasoned." He was frowning, probably because Friday didn't do insights. Or thinking in general.

"We're targets," Friday said. "She'll keep coming for us. Be afraid on the day she stops. But she'll milk every single route she can, every association, no matter how tangential, until she rips apart Sienna's life once and for all."

"I think Friday's right," Abby called from her place next to J.J. "This woman's got a serious wide on for Sienna, and she's going to some major extremes to flay her emotionally an inch at a time." She looked right at Jamie Barton. "I know this probably seems stupid to you, given your dealings with

Sienna were over a year ago, and obviously kinda brief—"

"Not as brief as I would have liked," Barton muttered, "especially given that little trip she had me make to DC last year."

"—but your family is in real danger if you go back to just living your life," Abby said. "Even before you got involved in this."

"This is some fine round and round," Augustus said, "but what are we going to do next? Now that plans A through triple Z failed."

"We tug on every thread," I said. "Every idea, no matter how insane or improbable. Every ally, no matter how far removed they might be—"

"I felt like we scraped the barrel pretty hard on that this time," Kat said. "I mean, seriously—you brought in this sheltered, object-flingy-girl you met like a year ago?" She nodded her head at Olivia. "No offense, but it reeks of desperation."

"I—sheltered—what?" Olivia asked, looking a little flummoxed.

"It's okay, sweetie," Veronika said. "You just hurled the earth's biggest badass into the upper ionosphere for a few seconds. You may be tighter than a nun's honeypot but you don't lack for utility."

Olivia didn't seem to know how to take that. "Uh...thanks?"

"By our powers combined," Augustus said, nodding at me, then Scott, "we can just about conjure up Captain Planet. And we didn't make a dent in her."

"I never thought of that before," Scott said, "but with Sienna, we were like elementals. Wow."

"We need to plumb every possibility," I said, clenching my fist in emphasis. "No matter how desperate." I looked at Kat. "You need to try Janus again."

"Ughhhh," Kat said, and she seemed to sink. "All right. But he's going to tell me no, again. He wants no part of Rose, and even more importantly, he doesn't want to help Sienna. I get the feeling there might be some bad blood between them for some reason."

"I don't give a shit," I said. "He owes her his life, several times over. This is his moment to make himself useful, or else."

She raised an eyebrow at me. "Or else what?"

"Or else I'm going to take an active interest in what he's doing over there in the UK," I said, putting on my determined face. It was kind of a glare and a leer combined together. "A very active interest—the kind that he's not going to like."

"I'll tell him," she said. "I'll need a burner phone."

"Talk to Jamal about that," I said, waving her off.

"What do you want me to ask him for?" Kat asked, and as I stared at her blankly, she said, "In terms of assistance? Because if you ask for help in general, and he agrees, he's not obligated to do a damn thing. You need something specific to ask him for."

"We need to get into Scotland," I said. "Undetected."

She cringed. "Not sure I'd trust him for that."

"You want to get into Scotland undetected?" Guy Friday asked. "I can get you into Scotland undetected, no problem. Just say the word."

I ignored him. "We need material support. Intelligence. Eyes on the ground, since the only place we're catching glimpses of Rose right now is when she crosses out of Scotland into the greater UK. If he's got any of that—"

"That's a good ask," Kat said with a nod. "He might go along with that. But…you won't get him to offer much more."

"I'll take what I can get," I said, shifting my attention away, back to Jamal. "Have you had any luck with—"

"ArcheGrey?" Jamal shook his head. "I've been searching for her for months, and she's still ghostly as ever. I can't even tell if this thing with Scotland's cybersecurity has her fingerprints on it or not. She's good. Pretty much the best."

I narrowed my eyes at that. "She's close, at least."

Scott seemed to be watching me out of the corner of his eye. "You're not thinking about knocking on a certain door in Richfield again, are you? Because Cassidy was pretty clear about what it would cost to get her help, and about what it'd cost if we tried to come at her without paying."

"I could really use the biggest brain on the planet on our side," I said, burning inside. "And I don't have access to Sienna's bank accounts, which means Cassidy isn't going to be helping us unless someone's got a cool million or two to burn." I looked around. "Anyone? Should I take up a collection?"

"Doubt my dad would throw any money in on that," Scott said, a little tightly. "He doesn't like Sienna. At all."

"Didn't Sienna work with people over in the UK?" Chase asked, kind of a bolt out of the blue. We all looked at her, and she stiffened, like she hadn't expected the attention. "I mean, she was over there a few years ago on some murder case, right? Wouldn't she have made some local contacts?"

"She did," J.J. said. "At least one of them got killed in York." He turned his laptop around. "Foreign Secretary Wexford, found dead in a hotel by the train station. We have footage of Sienna fleeing out the window moments later, pursued by Rose."

"Exit, pursued by a bear," Phinneus Chalke said, chortling under his breath. We all heard him. "Shit."

"So, other than that," J.J. said, spinning the laptop back around—personally, I didn't see what was on it—"we could maybe try and nose around for who she dealt with, but…I dunno."

"I got the feeling she ruffled some feathers over there," I said. "Just based on our conversations. Help from the UK strikes me as a dry hole. I'm guessing that Wexford guy was her primary contact, and he's dead."

"He's the one who offered her to come over there for asylum," Friday said, kind of helpfully. For once…twice, now, actually. What the hell? "Said it came from the Prime Minister, though?"

I raised an eyebrow. "That's…interesting. Did she tell you this?"

Friday shrugged. "Maybe. I don't remember. I totally eavesdropped on their conversation anyway."

"Nice," Chase said, sour. "So, uhm…while we're beating every bush—"

"Hehe, bush," Friday giggled.

She gave him a look of laser death, like she'd shot her lightsaber powers out of her eyes, but went on: "—for possible help, can I just say…not a huge fan of the idea of continuing this fight. I get that you all think she's still alive, and I'm super excited for you, but…" She looked around, taking the temperature of the room. "Okay, no easy way to say this, so I just will—this lady seems to want to kill or harm all of us. All of us." She grimaced. "Including probably me, now that I'm on her radar—yay for taking crazy jobs, with crazy people. Should have kept working at saw mills." She stopped talking, seemingly a steadily lowering mutter to herself, and raised her voice once more. "You guys seriously think she's not going to stop until she kills us all? Captures us all and then kills us in front of Sienna?"

I stared right back at her, even, and hit her with honesty. "Yeah. I think that's exactly what she's going to do. She'll kill any one of us she can at this point, just to have somebody to show Sienna to keep—not hope, I guess, but—desperation alive." My eyes lit up as I found the right word. "She's been after us for months, from York to now. Preparing, making sure she was ready. We ripped victory right out of her hands last night, so—yeah, I think she had a plan to make a display out of us to Sienna, and now that she didn't get any of us, or our families—" because I'd made sure we hid them all, from Isabella all the way down to Abby's grandmother "—she's going to be—I don't know. Lashing out in any direction, I guess? We'll see what happens." I let out a long sigh. "But someone's going to die because we're not there to, I suspect."

"That's kind of sad," Augustus said. "Like a human sacrifice."

"Another question you should be asking yourselves," Zollers said, stirring himself back into the conversation again, "what's Rose's endgame?" When no one responded to his dramatic question, he went on. "Because…what do you think happens when she finishes with Sienna? Torments her to the levels of her satisfaction, however she's doing that? Finishes killing all of us in front of her?" His eyes were serious, probing, and they found me. "Do you think she's just going to be done at that point? Go back to living a normal life, after killing thousands of people and carefully tearing apart the most powerful metahuman guardian of the Earth?"

I swallowed heavily. It was a thought that had lingered in the back of my mind, a worry that Zollers had just given voice to. "No, I don't think she'll just go quietly into the sunset," I said. "And I don't think she'll be looking to pick up where Sienna stopped, either."

He shook his head. "You're right. I can't see inside her mind, but I know a megalomaniac when I see one. This girl...she's traumatized, she's damaged, but she's so powerful and so sure of herself...killing all of us, hurting Sienna, killing Sienna...this won't be the end for her." Everyone was listening in silence, and I heard Olivia speak for all of us when she gulped, audibly, next to me, as Zollers finished:

"This...is just the beginning for Rose."

7.

Wolfe

"This is just the beginning for us, darling Wolfe," Rose said, smiling.

They sat in a palace of opulence, mahogany everywhere, bookshelves filled with leather volumes, a snifter of some deeply rich alcoholic beverage cradled between Wolfe's long, clawed fingers. He raised it to his nose, smelled the notes of wood and peat, wrinkled his nose.

It stunk.

The whole place stunk.

It reeked of old power, British power, and Wolfe's eyes slid over the room. It reminded him of a drawing room of an old manor house, or some country club filled with endless bald heads and old men, plotting pointless things as they spun the wheels of power.

Wolfe almost felt his stomach growl, but he didn't have a stomach anymore. He cupped the snifter in his hand, though, unwilling to part with it.

The redhead who sat across from him smiled, as though she could detect his unease. "What's the matter, my Wolfe?" She leaned in, across the padded armrest of her seat, which mirrored his own, a comfortable throne in the middle of this opulent room. "What's wrong? I can feel the unhappiness radiating off of you. Tell me what vexes you, my dear, and I'll fix it."

Wolfe kept his eyes down, the luxury around him like a reminder that he didn't live in a world like this anymore.

That he didn't *live* at all, anymore.

"You can't bring me back to life," Wolfe said, sullenly, snifter still cradled in his clawed fingernails, clinking against them.

Rose stared at him, those green eyes almost aglow. "You're right," she said finally. "I can't. No doubt. There's not a thing I can do for you in that regard, but…" The green glittered. "Maybe I can give you a little something to make up for it? A little…facsimile of life?"

Wolfe stared at her suspiciously. "How do you mean?"

The world changed around them. Gone were the wood panels, the rich alcohol, the smell of wealth, and the plush seating. Now they were sitting on a rock in the woods, Rose almost upon him, close enough to brush his arm, and she did, reaching out and touching him, gently. She leaned in, breathed in his ear. "I know what you want."

"Do you?" Wolfe didn't growl. He kept it low, though, close to one. He knew who was mistress here.

"I do," she said, warm breath washing over his ear. Almost like the real thing.

A twig snapped in the distance, and Wolfe's ears perked up. He stared through the thick branches, sniffing—

He caught it. A scent on the wind.

Prey.

A man came walking through the trees, a backpack on his back, paying little heed to anything. He was whistling, some happy tune, and it jangled in Wolfe's ears. He was dressed in the clothes of a hiker, shorts and boots, parading himself along, looking down rather than up.

"It's not real," Wolfe said, turning his head away sullenly.

Rose ran a finger along his jaw, bringing his face back up. "It's real enough. Not perfect, but…" She smiled slyly. "You miss the hunt, don't you? The run, the beating of the heart, the taste of the kill? I can feel it, that desire from you. I know you want it." She looked at the man crashing his way through the woods with significance. "He's yours. Do whatever you want with him. I don't mind. There's a real soul in there—one of mine. He'll feel real pain." Her eyes glittered with excitement. "You can do that to him. Real screams. Real fear." She brushed a finger down his arm. "Come on. What do you say?"

Wolfe looked over at the man, still making his way past them on a circuitous course. He didn't see them. Wouldn't see them. He was already making a turn to show them his back, striding along with purpose, his little hike in mind.

Running him down would be the easiest thing in the world.

"Come on," Rose said. "You can taste the meat. The blood." She was dripping words in his ear like honey, like sweetness, warm and wonderful. "I want to hear him scream like you do. I want to hear you tear him apart piece by piece, listen to you cackle in joy as he cries in agony." She licked his earlobe. "Give it to him good, Wolfe. Let the beast run free." She ran a hand down his back and goosed him.

Wolfe sprang to his feet and after the man, no more encouragement needed. His feet crackled in the grass and underbrush as he loped along on all fours, in a mad springing sprint toward his prey.

The man looked back, saw Wolfe. He registered confusion, cocked his head, trying to decide what he was seeing.

By the time he started to run, it was far too late.

Wolfe brought him down with one solid bite, and the screaming began. He did his thing—playful, furious, leaving scratches and scars, pain and tears—and it lasted for hours. Hours and hours. Bitter tortures that ranged past the sundown and the sunup.

And Rose watched him the whole time, licking her lips, whispering encouragement in his ear, joining in, touching him…until there was nothing left of the prey at all.

8.

Sienna

I came out of the moors near daybreak, crossing onto a road that was utterly desolate, winding off into the distance in both directions without a hint of human activity. It was cold and windy, and I was sick of being chilled to the bone. The sun was hanging in a completely empty sky of blue, not a cloud to be found. Bitter, brisk autumn winds swept across the moors, bouncing off the rocky crags and acidic water to find me over the miles, freezing my ass out.

I stood on the road, deciding my direction at random. West seemed sound, so I turned that way and started hiking, rubbing my hands against my arms, crossing them over my chest to hold in heat.

My ears felt as though they'd been dipped in ice. Fun feeling. I was not nearly adequately dressed for Scotland in fall, and definitely not for winter, which I could sense was over the horizon, thundering down on me. It'd be here soon enough.

But would I live to see it?

The changing of the seasons was almost like a metaphor for my life. Autumn was slow death, and I was in the midst of that. Winter was the end…and it was coming.

The blacktop ran to the horizon, mountains rising out of the rocky ground at random intervals. The mountains here were different than I'd seen before. They looked like boobs, just sticking up out of flat ground, no gravity to pull them off center. No foothills, just a randomly placed, giant, rounded mountain. I felt like I should avert my eyes every time I saw one, those torpedo protrusions. Scotland had clearly been enhanced, because there was no hint of anything leading up to it, just a giant mound of earth boob that fell right back to flat ground again on the other side. Gradual elevation changes were for other lands, I supposed. Here it was moors and boob mountains, and nothing else.

Lonely and forbidding, isn't it? that damned voice started again. *No one about for miles and miles.*

"Shut up, Rose," I said, feet thudding dully against the road as I hiked. "Nobody likes you."

You don't like me because I speak the truth and your tender little ears can't handle it anymore, can they?

"My tender little ass has had enough of you kicking it too, while we're on the subject," I said. "My tender little face has had enough of being punched. And if you're going to roost in my head, I demand you start paying rent, because you're the worst tenant I've ever had, way worse than even Wolfe or Bjorn." That was kinda true. She hadn't gone out of her way to show me grisly imagery, but frankly, those two had taken most of the shock value out of life in their mad rush to expose me to the horrors that they'd done, which was a huge help when I started doing criminal investigations. There wasn't a desecrated corpse I'd come across in the years since that could make me heave, thanks to those two.

You're going to die here, she whispered, making me roll my eyes. *You're going to die in pieces.*

"Blah blah blah," I said, in lieu of something wittier. "Don't you have something else to be doing? Maybe go wash your hair in human blood to maintain that coloring? Pinch your cheeks and spray on the SPF 500 to make sure you don't burn?"

You should talk.

"I should talk," I said, seizing the opportunity. "I should talk lots and lots, because frankly, you can't carry a conversation to save your flat ass." That's right, I took a shot at Rose's ass, mostly because she wasn't actually around to hear it. "I mean, really, it's all 'Sienna' this and 'Sienna' that every time we're together. I'm trying hard to figure out whether you hate me or you secretly want to have relations with me. I mean, it could maybe even go both ways, because you are clearly obsessed—"

There's a thin line between love and hate, but I can tell you which side I'm on, darling—

"I'm not your darling."

Oh, but you are. You're mine. I own you. You don't like my arse? Well, that's okay, because I own yours, too.

"Come and get it, then. It'd be nothing but an improvement on what you've got in the trunk right now, if you can figure out some way to transplant it."

I will come get it. I will come get you—again. Soon. You know it. Every minute we grow closer together, closer to another…moment. Our souls have touched so many times, Sienna. I know you better than any lover you've ever had.

"Really? I don't find our encounters as satisfying as even the worst of them."

I've touched your skin more than anyone else has. Touched you. I'm in your heart now. In your head.

"Well, you're in one of those," I agreed. "So long as you're not trying to get into my pants, which, trust me, would just balloon on you, flat-ass."

You think you're so funny—

"Other people think I'm funny, too," I said. "I made a bartender crack up the other day in some backwater Scotland town. I had them rolling in the floor in that place."

I make them roll on the floor, too. In—

"Death, yes, you grim wench, I see where you're going with this. You have a one-track mind."

I could make another track just for you, Sienna dear. You'll be all mine by the end. All this sauciness? It's fading, like you are. You can't even say these things to my face; you have to say them to—

"To your empty soul presence, yes. I'd say them to your face, but I'm usually too busy turning around and grabbing my ankles in your presence, oh august ginger from hell."

I'm not from hell—

"Disagree. Strongly disagree."

I'm from where you're from—

"Minneapolis? You've got the wrong accent. And you'd need to say, 'Dontcha know' at the end of a lot of your sentences. Also, 'Uffdah' is a valid exclamation."

I own you, she said, voice rising in frustrated intensity.

"You're beating me," I said, walking the roadside, still nothing on the horizon. "Don't confuse the two."

You will surrender your will, yourself, to me. Every day we grow closer together. Every day we get closer to the point where listening to me will be the sweetest thing you could do. Where you'll beg for me to take a little more and a little more, where you'll desire nothing but to be close to me, to hear me sing my song in your mind—

"I'm guessing your singing voice is ass, Queen of the Rasp. Sultry doesn't even cover what you've got going on; it's more like 'digesting ashtray remnants.' Which would explain that hair, too."

You'll be mine.

"Worst valentine evah," I said. "But I'm sure that'll be a banner day for you, making me your little lapdog. Making me do your bidding. I'd say 'over my dead body,' but I think we know that's the point, anyway—"

That's not the point.

The pain is the point. Death is just the end. Getting there...

...that's the pleasure.

"I don't share your kinks," I said, shielding my eyes from the glaring sun overhead. It was surprisingly bright given I was walking with it at my back. A few seconds of shade were nice, and then I kept on hiking, letting my arm drop to the side.

Well, there is no safeword...because you're not safe. You'll never be safe again. There's only you and me, Sienna. The two of us, alone on the board—

A horn honked behind us, and I turned to see a car approaching. I hadn't even heard it. In the driver's seat was a man who was waving, a little uncertainly, as he slowed.

"Alone except for this guy," I said, shading my eyes, "and seven billion other people. Other than that, it's totally just the two of us."

Dammit. Rose's internal voice swore in my head, sounding a little pissed that this interruption had come along.

The guy pulled his car alongside me and rolled down the window. "You look lost," he said, in a deep Scottish accent. Like hill country, can-barely-understand-him, took-ten-minutes-and-three-Scottish-to-English-translators-to-puzzle-out-what-he-said thick.

I looked around, as though he could be talking to someone else. The woman in my head, maybe. "Uh…well, I don't know where I am."

"American?" That was even more jumbled, but I got it.

"Is it that obvious?" I asked, a little droll. Of course it was obvious.

"Hop in; I'll give you a ride," he said, and for just a moment I thought he'd said something else entirely.

I hesitated, thinking of Rose's little traps. This was a prime one, sending me a guy in my hour of hiking need. We'd get down the road a little ways, and he'd be revealed to be a metahuman with siren powers or something, and terrible things would ensue that would make me feel like even less of a person and more of a human carpet in a high-traffic area. I was starting to get paranoid about the things Rose would do to wreck me, to break me. I was having nightmares about her sending human beings after me to die en masse against my skin, giving me zero additional power but a boatload of tortured souls to keep me company.

She'd never done any such thing, of course, but my imagination liked to run wild with invented possibilities for how she could mess with me.

Sending a human man, compelling us to have sex while he died in the act? Pretty torturous. Right up Rose's alley, except that suddenly I'd have company in my head. Would she want that? Maybe, maybe not. With her, it was hard to say.

And that was just the beginning of the evils I could imagine her perpetrating. This was a woman who was cutting apart my soul and drinking it like pineapple juice, a little squeeze at a time while she tried to track down my friends and family to torture/murder them in front of me.

I'm not that bad… she said in my head, then proceeded to follow it up with an evil cackle.

"I'm fine, thanks," I said to the guy, almost morbidly curious as to where he'd go from here. If Rose had an escalation plan for him.

He raised an eyebrow. "You sure? Because you look a little like you're waiting for Tilda Swinton to come along and offer you some Turkish delight."

I stared at him blankly. "I…have no idea what that means." Reed probably would have gotten it.

Oh, how I missed Reed.

He blushed. "Doesn't matter. It's a long way out of Rannock Moor. You sure you don't want a ride?"

That settled on me. A long walk? I hadn't eaten in a while—days, maybe. Hadn't had anything to drink but Scotch, which was not a great way to hydrate or get my calories. I was aching for more, though.

Oh, come on, Rose's voice compelled me. *Just get in the car. What's the worst that can happen?*

I don't even want to think about what the worst that can happen is, I answered back. *Because I'm still stuck back on all the horrible things you could do that aren't the worst.*

She laughed, a great, horrifying empty sound. *This is how it's going to be from now until the end.*

You won't know who to trust.

I stared at the man in the car, his face broad and inviting. He didn't have an ounce of deception or guile there—which meant exactly nothing to me now, since neither had Rose when she conned me harder than anyone else in my history.

"I'll be okay, thanks," I said coolly. I didn't want to take a chance with this guy, that was the simple fact of it. I'd stumbled into too many of Rose's traps to bite down on the bait here. Just like the first time she'd fooled me, pretended to be my admirer, my friend, and then turned on me, this time I could almost detect another impending betrayal, faint and in the distance, this guy turning from friendly to vicious just over the horizon, pawing at me, trying to kill me, and me being forced to kill him first with my bare hands—

"I'll just walk," I said, finally decided.

He looked up at me from the car, and shrugged. "I think ye're making a mistake, but I hope ye do all right." He reached down to shift his car back into drive, and—

Something popped out of his neck with a whistling noise, and there was a wet slap as something hit my hip.

The pain came a second later, a screaming, deep-to-the-bone pain, and I wondered if I'd been shot. But there hadn't been a gunshot, and no suppressor on Earth was that quiet. I hit the asphalt like a ton of rocks, my not-flat ass absorbing most of the impact as I drove my hands toward the source of the pain.

I was bleeding, profusely, from the hip. Whatever had hit me had nicked an artery, and I was spraying wildly. I thrust my hands on the wound, sticking a finger in it like a cork. It wasn't small either, like a bullet had gone in. It was bigger, like someone had thrust a PVC pipe into my skin.

Looking up, squirts of blood geysered out of the window. The guy, my knight in shining car, was there, the top of his head, from the middle of his nose and his eyes, disappearing behind the door. But I could see his eyes, and they were wild, panicked. I could tell that whatever had gone through him had left him, well—

Dying.

His fingers were coated in blood, hanging over the edge of the window as I stared up at him, writhing, trying to get myself under control from the spearing pain in my hip. His eyes faded as the life left them, and he sagged against the door.

"Such a shame," a cold voice came from behind the car. Shoes on the asphalt made noise, a squeal of rubber pushing against the pavement.

I didn't know the voice, but it sounded way too gleeful in the face of tragedy to be someone good.

There was movement through the car windows. Two guys, their heads appearing as they circled, one to either side, using it as cover against me.

I tried to stand and failed, waiting to see what was coming my way. I had a suspicion...

That was confirmed a moment later when a shock of blond hair appeared from my right, and Colin Fannon strolled around the front of the car on my left, his familiar beanie and hippie gear long ago shed in favor of a black suit and white shirt beneath. He looked like a good lackey, and wore the uniform of one.

Mr. Blonde squatted a few feet away from me, grinning, soullessly, while Fannon stood back and employed a ten-thousand-yard empty gaze. "A real tragedy, right?" Blonde asked, still grinning. He looked at the guy who he'd killed with one of his metal projectiles, and shrugged. "After all…if he hadn't been talking to you, he'd still be alive…now come on." He punched me in the face, and I just blinked at him. He hit like a three-year-old boy, with every knuckle, diffusing the power of the blow across his entire fist. I just stared back at him, flatly, so he tried it again. "She wants to see you," he said, and punched me again, a third time, like a complete and total pansy. I just sort of adjusted my jaw and kept looking at him as though he'd done nothing, his calm steadily fading as he stared at me, realizing he wasn't doing a damned thing to knock me out—which was probably what he'd been ordered to do.

Finally, Mr. Blonde looked over at Fannon and shrugged his shoulders, a very, "You want to try?" look that was more command than invitation. I looked at Fannon, Fannon looked at me.

There was a flash, and that was all. Something cracked me in the jaw so hard that my lights went out instantly, and my gut knew what had happened just by sheer instinct—Fannon had used his speedster power to land a punch on me that lacked none for power and had better form than Mr. Blonde's pathetic efforts.

The bright, blue Scottish sky faded to black as I passed out—once more in the clutches of Rose's servants.

9.

Gavrikov

Outside Kirensk, Russian Empire
1906

Aleksandr's hands shook as he held the cup of water. It had been carefully boiled to eliminate any of the sicknesses that might have come drinking it. Wine was not a luxury they had much of, and Father tended to hoard it for himself whenever possible.

For himself...and Klementina, whether she wanted it or not.

The water had a smell to it—slightly rotten, like a putrefied animal. Aleksandr ignored it, as he ignored so many adversities, and pressed the cup to his mouth, the hard metal threatening to bite into his lower lip. It wasn't sharp, but his hands carried his shaking anger, the warm water touching the cracks of his lips and burning them.

"You look terrible," Klementina said, easing down into the seat next to his. They were pitiful chairs, made by someone in Kirensk, bought for a pittance as they'd seen some use for many years before they had made it to this house. The surfaces were all scuffed and scratched, and one of the legs on Klementina's had been replaced by one slightly shorter than the original. Consequently, the chair rocked against the wood floors of their house, the uneven nature of which made things slightly worse. She reached out a careful hand, past the metal cup, and touched him beneath the eye.

Aleksandr cringed; it was blacked where Father had hit him last night. It had not even been a true argument. He had merely raised his voice and Father had slapped him down, bringing such pain that Aleksandr had hit the ground and not gotten up for some time, cradling his face. His father had mouthed words about defiance, about respecting his authority, and Aleksandr had scarcely listened, for he had heard them all before and grown quite tired of them.

"I feel fine," Aleksandr said, trying to spark a smile for his sister. However much Father had hurt him, it was minimal compared to what he did to Klementina—and nearly every night, too.

"I doubt that very much," she said, her lips pursed tightly. Her blond hair flowed over her shoulders freely, a surprising sheen to it that the village girls in Kirensk lacked. Her eyes were vibrant as well, in a way he wondered if they should be, given all that happened to her—to both of them, really, living out here with Father.

"I will be okay," Aleksandr said, brushing her hand with his. He looked around; Father was somewhere outside, but the walls here were thin, and terrible for the winter. They were forced to huddle together for warmth during the worst of those days, and more than once Aleksandr had been cast out by his father for defiance, for his words—or even simply because his father wanted him away from Klementina. "I worry about you."

Klementina's lively eyes flickered only briefly, then fell as she looked at the floor between them. "And I worry for you more than myself."

Aleksandr stared at his sister's pretty face, and a feeling rose in his chest like a dragon of imagination, afire with hope. "Someday I will protect you," he said. "Someday I—"

"Aleksandr," Klementina said softly, raising her eyes to watch him, raising a hand to touch him, once more, softly, upon the cheek, as the embers of the fire died inside him at her words, "you cannot even protect yourself." She took the cup from his hand, staring down into it. "I will get you more water," she said, and stood, dress swishing around her. He watched her go, the dirty cloth moving before his eyes in a swaying motion as she went to the outside cook fire to refill his cup from the pot.

*

Gavrikov watched the memory with a strange detachment. He had not seen the old hovel where they'd lived outside Kirensk for many years. When last he'd laid eyes on it, it was falling down, forgotten by time and by the Soviet Union that had risen, a cruel replacement for the already cruel Empire and Czars of his youth.

"Your sister was still a pretty young thing back then," Bjorn almost purred. "I think she might have improved with age. Now she has that artificial look, though, that seems to give her the appearance of one of those made-up starlets. It is a step backward, but…still, she is pretty."

Gavrikov listened sourly. There was little point in arguing with Bjorn. He had made piggish comments since before Gavrikov had made his acquaintance, and it stood to reason he would be doing so for as long as his soul still existed upon this plane, whether Aleksandr cared for them or not.

"What do you think is going on out there?" Roberto Bastian asked, quietly pensive. He'd been silent for a while, lost in his own mind perhaps, as Gavrikov had.

Graham, the quiet Scotsman, was the one to answer them, stirring from his place by the fire, as it crackled and popped almost as if real. "She's bringing in Sienna again. Got a…surprise for her." His face shifted uncertainly. "It doesn't look good."

"It's never going to look good for Sienna again," Harmon said, shaking his head. "The end is nigh."

"I don't know about that," Bastian said quietly, then looked around the circle when silence fell at his words. "She hasn't been beaten yet."

"He's right," Zack said, the fire dancing in his eyes. "She doesn't quit."

"She's quit," Graham said, staring back at Zack. "She's

submitting to Rose now. Just…gives up when she sees her. It's all over now."

"No, it's not," Bastian said in that same low quiet. "Nothing's ever over with Sienna."

"Death will probably fix her up in that regard," Eve said, a little nastily.

"She ain't dead yet," Bastian muttered, like one last stab of defiance as he mentally left the conversation.

Gavrikov listened to the quiet as the talk subsided. That was how it went, coming and going in spells. Someone would pipe up again soon, and they'd be back at it, talking about only one thing—this one thing, the thing that continued to be ever present, that consumed their days.

Rose and Sienna. Sienna and Rose. The present mistress and the former one.

So much of it was down to the uncertainty. They hadn't seen Rose since they'd arrived, couldn't see what she was doing, had only the weak commentary of Graham to inform them of the outside world.

It did not sound good, of course. None of it did. Gavrikov wondered why it bothered him, this small nitpicking at his soul every time poor news came along…

And it did bother him. Hearing about some setback Sienna had suffered…it was like a punch to him as well, and he could feel it, soul-deep.

"Rose tried to get the brother and his friends," Graham said, staring into the fire. "Awhile ago."

Gavrikov's breath caught in his throat. "Which friends?"

Graham just shrugged. "All of them."

Gavrikov held his breath, breath he didn't even draw anymore, in truth. He held the illusion of breath, only. "And…?"

Graham still stared straight ahead, into the fire. "It didn't go her way. Next time, though. They were waiting for her this round. Next time, she'll catch them unawares." He looked up at Gavrikov, indifferent. "This time she walked into a trap they'd set. It didn't kill her—obviously—but it held her back long enough for them to escape."

"All of them?" Gavrikov asked, mouth still dry.

"Yeah," Graham said with a nod. "This time."

Gavrikov kept the air from rushing out of him in relief. Klementina was surely among them…

Someday I will protect you.

And he had, in a roundabout way, for years, with Sienna as white knight in his place.

But those days…they were drawing to a close, weren't they?

Who would Klementina—Kat—have to watch out for her now that Sienna was nearly out of the picture? For it sounded as though Rose would happily go after her.

What care did Rose have if she killed Klementina?

None. Gavrikov was no Wolfe to her; his value was limited, at best. He was a cast-off at worst.

Which meant…soon there would be no one to protect Klementina, if Sienna died.

And Rose was after her…and was the most powerful metahuman in the world.

If Sienna died.

"She's never quit yet," he muttered under his breath, but no one seemed to notice him.

It was true, of course. That was perhaps the most irritating thing about her, that stubborn refusal to leave the fight even when she should. He did not know exactly what she'd gone through since he'd been dragged from her, but…

He knew her head.

He knew her heart.

And however badly she was hurt…she surely had not surrendered all hope.

It was an easy decision, when he considered what the alternatives were. On one side was Rose, who was furiously seeking every one of Sienna's friends, including Klementina, in a bid to kill them, probably in the worst ways possible.

And on the other was this girl—this woman—in whose head he had lived and fought these last years, whose spirit he could…admire.

Whose will…would never be broken.

Only one person would protect Klementina…and it was not Rose.

His decision made, Aleksandr Gavrikov nodded once, in the darkness, the fire lighting up the cool night around him, and his mind started to work, trying to figure out the most optimal path—or any path—some way he might be able to actually help Sienna Nealon should the moment come.

10.

Sienna

I woke with a headache, another one, not a huge surprise given that Fannon had punched me at superspeed. My jaw ached as though it had been plowed into, full-force, by a speeding ScotRail train, and my eyes wanted, desperately, to remain closed, as though they had never wanted anything else in their lives, the whiners.

Squeezing them open was a task of Herculean proportions, and one I set to work on with only marginally more gusto than I would have had while attacking a sink full of dirty dishes. (Not much; I'm a terrible housekeeper.)

It took a few minutes of steady effort, but I finally got them open, and there before me were the two yutzes responsible for my headache.

Fannon and Mr. Blonde.

"Well, if it isn't Tweedle-blazing-fast and Tweedle-blazing-dumb," I said, squinting against harsh industrial lighting overhead. I could see the metal beams and support pillars of a warehouse around me. My hands were neatly bound behind me, and I rattled the metacuffs at my back. They were solid, not ordinary handcuffs, which I probably could have ripped apart with steady effort, even in my weakened state.

These were super strong, meant to contain people with powers, and…they were definitely containing me, I thought with a grunt as I pulled—carefully—against them. There were ways out of them, but none I wanted to use at present.

Mr. Blonde walked over to me and punched me again, no less effectively than the last. I blinked at him once he was done, and sighed. "I don't even have an iron jaw anymore and I barely felt that, you big wuss."

Rage flushed its way through his ovoid face, and he walked over again and hammered me three times in succession. I took one on the forehead—hard enough to barely break the skin—one on the nose—hard enough that it cracked the cartilage—and one on the jaw, which didn't do squat except pop the joint and annoy me.

I moved my face every which way I could the moment he stepped back, still glowering. I twitched my nose, opened my jaw up and down, and twisted my neck. It hadn't felt good, any of it, being blasted by a meta, even one with as poor form as Mr. Blonde, but I was running out of patience with this bullshit. "You know," I said, stopping my absurd facial stretching exercises, "maybe you could take lessons from some little girls. Because I think they could do more damage than you just did—pansy."

His eyes were lit, and he started toward me again. I glanced at Fannon, but he didn't even emote so much as a whiff, just stared straight ahead like an automaton. I knew that nobody was home in there, but it was starting to look like the lights weren't even on anymore, like he was one of those blue-blooded robots from *The World's End*, except his head probably wouldn't go back on if it got, uh, "accidentally" popped off.

"You little—" Mr. Blonde started to say, advancing on me with a clear windup.

I brought my head back, pretending to flinch away from him, as though I were trying to avoid my comeuppance. Chained to a chair, unable to move much, I probably didn't register as much of a threat to Blondie.

Which was a stupid mistake on his part.

As he stepped closer and raised his fist, I accelerated my head forward to meet his punch. And meet it I did, my forehead greeting his fist with an almighty headbutt.

I caught him flatly across all his knuckles, transferring the force of my attack into his fist. It hurt me, no lie, but I pushed through as it split my forehead open and sluiced blood down into my eyes. I hammered on, driving my head as far as it would go, my neck cramping its way into a locked state, my spine all lined up.

With my eyes closed I couldn't see Blonde's fist shatter, but I could hear the bones make noises like Rice Krispies when you poured milk on them. He let out a gasp of surprise, and then everything went silent as he staggered back.

I opened my eyes and ignored the blood dripping over my brow. I was greeted with such pleasant success.

Mr. Blonde was holding his hand up, except now it was grossly misshapen. Every one of his fingers was horribly broken, and bones were sticking out of his wrist like pebbles beneath the skin. Even worse (for him; I got nothing but joy out of it), the shock of my blow had gone up his radius and ulna, causing them to jackknife out of his skin mid-forearm. Finally, one of them also jutted out from behind his elbow, and Blonde was regarding the whole spectacle with increasing horror, eyes wide and mouth open, little gasps escaping him with every breath.

"Looks like your tennis game just went straight to hell," I said, and Blonde's head juddered sideways to look at me with utter incomprehension, as though he were just responding to the stimulus of sound. He stared at me for a moment, uneasy, eyes unfocused—

And then he keeled over backward, fainting dead away.

Slow clapping came from behind me, and I turned my head to look. I sort of knew what I'd find before I turned all the way around, but...

Rose was grinning madly, bringing her hands together with such force it rang through the warehouse. A little blood seeped into my left eye, blinding me out of that one, and I squinted to keep looking at her. "That was bloody brilliant," she said, with something approaching genuine glee. "I love it."

"I just busted up your dear and faithful servant," I said, "and this pleases you? I could have been breaking these assholes for months now if I'd known you were cool with it."

Her emerald eyes flickered. "I'm not exactly 'cool' with it, but they're so...fungible. It's hard to get too mad, especially when I see you get a little bit of that fighting spirit back." She walked right over to me, heels clicking against the concrete. She was all dolled up today, black pants and a crimson blouse, open-toed shoes that didn't really fit the weather. Her hair was windblown, but that was hardly a shock. It was a sign she'd been flying, one I knew all too well.

And missed. God, how I missed flying. The wind in my hair, against my skin...

It had been three months, and of all the things I missed, flying was top of the list.

"Been anywhere fun?" I asked.

Rose grinned, and I felt a little sick. "I have been somewhere fun, actually. Made a little trip, picked something up just for you."

I shrugged, trying to play it cool. Given her stated objective of destroying me personally, it didn't do me a lot of good to freak out at her words anymore, her veiled and not-veiled threats. I had to wait until she had something solid, tangible, a real danger before me to bring out the good stuff—panic.

If then, even.

"Oh, but we'll get to that." She nodded, and then looked at Fannon. "Colin...be a dear and break her left hand, would you?"

I felt the pain almost as soon as she said it, the joints in my left hand howling at the feel of the bones shattering. Colin shattered my entire hand, every single finger and bone all the way up to the wrist. I don't recall how many bones there are in the hand, but I was pretty sure he got them all, and speedily, too.

Gritting my teeth together didn't do a lot to defray the pain, but it kept me from crying out, which felt important. Rose stuck her ugly face in mine and smiled. "That was for him." and she nodded to Mr. Blonde. "I was just kidding before about letting you get away with it." She laughed in my face, then spat in it. "Can't have you hurting my minions.

You might get the idea you can just get away with that sort of thing and it's a no—no—no, little girl." She put a hand on my head and tipped me over.

I tried to curl up, and the impact on the back of the chair spared my head from a hard hit. It did not, however, spare my broken hand, which—holy shit—this took it to a whole new level of agony, because it was pinned behind me, between the back of the chair and the ground, and I landed right on it.

If I was in agony before, this was anguish, pain, suffering and the sun exploding all at once. It was like every bone was poking its way out of the hand all at once.

This time, there was no controlling the scream. I let it loose, and Rose cackled, drowning it out. I couldn't tell whether that was in my head or in real life, the gleeful sound bouncing off the warehouse walls, but holy hell, it was bad. And loud.

It took a few minutes to compose myself, at which time Rose resolved into view before my eyes again. I'd had them closed while trying to get myself back together, but now they were wide open and staring at her as she stared down at me.

"Do you hate me, Sienna?" she asked, watching me from above, standing astride my torso.

"Hell yes," I said, a little too agonized for tact.

"That's all right," she said, stooping over me, then dropping her flat ass on my belly without warning, knocking the air out of me. She leaned down, so close to my face, and breathed garlic breath right up my nose when I managed to inhale. I almost gagged, hoping I could vomit right in her eye to show her what I thought of her. "Because I hate you, too. Hate you soooo much." She stuck her fingernails in my face, arranging them from the thumbnail at the top of my forehead, digging into the cut Blonde had made with a punch, then sticking the others in a semi-circle down my left temple and cheek.

Not gonna lie, the pain was intense, and she wasn't even doing much; just disturbing one already-open wound and clawing into my face to create four more. There was no skin to skin contact, either; she was just gouging at me, slowly.

"Do you know what happens when you hate someone so much?" she asked, still digging in, increasing her grip slowly. "When you think about them all the time? Twenty-four seven? When you're thinking about how to—to just hurt them all time? Hm?" She dug in harder, hit bone with the tips of her nails, and I couldn't escape, because she had my head pinned against the floor.

I was making a series of strained grunts because damn, it hurt. But I pulled together the conscious effort to taunt her, because doing so while she was trying to cause me agonizing pain seemed like a swell idea. "I dunno, Rose," I said, straining to keep my voice level, "but I'm starting to think that you don't hate me so much as you love me. Maybe some feelings sublimated in there. I'm not calling you sapphic, just saying that your tendencies might be below the surface—"

The bitch took my left eye straight out of my head, and she did it so fast I didn't even get a blink in before she did it.

I squirmed and heaved and probably screamed and cried, but I didn't really hear any of it, wasn't really conscious of any of it. When I kind of came to again, Rose was still straddling my abdomen, holding my eyeball by the optic nerve and staring into it like she could see the secrets of my soul.

Which she could. But not by staring into my plucked eye. It was dead tissue now, after all, and she had a much better method for getting to the heart of me.

"You have pretty eyes," she said, and tossed it over her shoulder. "I'm sure it'll be just as lovely when it grows back."

She got down in my face, and since I was still cuffed there wasn't much I could do to stop her, especially since she had all her weight on me. I mean, I maybe could have thrown her off, but maybe not. She was stronger than me and could fly, had control of gravity—I was pretty sure I'd tried to buck her after she'd taken my eye, and without a lot of result.

"You're probably not wrong," she said, breathing that garlicky stank right in my face. "I started out *really* hating you. You were everything I lost, see? And it was your fault, too. I looked at you and saw everything I hated every time I looked in the mirror." She moved her head around in front of my

81

remaining eye, trying to get me to look her right in hers. "I had a mam who hated me too, see? I was an outcast. I watched lots of people who'd wronged me, but that still I cared about, die—somewhat like you have."

She leaned in and licked my cheek, which made me want to heave. "But the more of you I take, the harder it is to just hate you. Because now that we're past that surface meanness, that hard front you put up to throw everyone off...I'm seeing you—the real you. The one everyone else doesn't know. And you're just a scared little girl who doesn't think her mam ever loved her, and who never knew her dad." She patted herself on the chest. "That's like me, too. We're mirror twins, you and I."

"And I'm your scapegoat," I said, glaring at her with the eye I had left. "You can just...pile up everything you hate about yourself and stick it on me and...feel good, I guess."

She seemed to give that a thought, then punched me in the stomach. It was short, it was sharp, and it took my breath away worse than her landing that flat ass on me. "If I want a psychological analysis, I'll drag it out of your friend Zollers when I catch up with him—which will be soon, by the way." She was totally even keel, just flat, still staring me down. "This is your time to listen, so—*shhhhh.*" And she laid a finger over my lips.

It smelled like blood and rancid meat, and I wondered what she'd been doing with that. I shuddered to wonder, then I remembered—plucking out my eye.

"Hurting you doesn't make me feel good because you're my scapegoat, Sienna," she said, looking up, pensive, really thinking it over. "Hurting you makes me feel good because...you're such a shite person." And she spat on me again. "Have you ever met anyone you didn't look down on and make fun of, at least in your head?" She spat on me again, and it got in my surviving eye. "Any man who showed interest in you that you didn't turn away after scorning him, or sleeping with him once? Or worse. I mean, think about what you did to poor Scotty." She put her hands over her cheeks like she was scandalized. "You don't like him thinking for himself, so you just sapped those independent thoughts

82

right out of his head."

"Like you've done to everyone around you—" I started.

She knocked the wind out of me again with another body blow, but less gently this time. "Still talking," she said, way too chipper, the sadist. "See, I don't play the heroine. I'm very clear about who I am. I'm your fresh hell." She winked at me. "I'm your worst nightmare. I'm the consequences of your shitty actions come back to haunt you like Catherine to Heathcliff—"

"Screw you, and to hell with *Wuthering Heights*," I said, and she punched me again, even harder.

"You're just a savage, aren't you? No appreciation for the classics." She got right in my face, mouth an inch from my nose. "I see you clearly now. See you all the way through. We're close in a way no one else ever has been with you, not even your brother. I'm picking off every secret you've got, taking them one by one. We're going to be very tight by the time this is all over. I still hate you, but there's less of you to hate all the time, I'm finding." She licked my cheek and laughed. "Mmm. Your tears. So sweet."

I hadn't even realized I'd been crying, but my cheeks were wet. I'd assumed blood, but...

"I hate you, I love you," she said, singsongy, "I don't want to be you, I can't stand to see you this way..." She slapped me in the stomach and then grabbed the back of my chair and lifted me up. "Anyway. That was tough, I know. I'm going to take my little tax, and then I have something for you. A gift." She set my chair down and steadied it, then looked me in the eye. "To make up for—well, I know I had to be harsh here. You need some discipline in your life, my dear." She smiled. "Isn't that what Mommy used to say?" Hearing her pronounce "Mommy" in a near-American accent was a little disturbing.

She undid the top few buttons of her blouse and pushed the top aside, which made me look at her like she was crazy with my surviving eye. She grinned, laughed, and said, "Hang on. There's a reason for this. It goes with the mommy theme, see?" And she grabbed me around the neck and pushed my cheek right to her sternum.

I writhed against her, off balance, still cuffed to the chair as she rubbed my face madly against her chest, my cheeks pushed against her breastbone up to her clavicle. Her chin came down and was like iron against the top of my head, anchoring it in place. I could feel the top of my skull bow under the pressure and she said, "Settle down, little baby. This will only take a few seconds…"

The screaming pain in my cheek under the socket where my eye used to be started seconds later. It was like that whole side of my face was on fire, and she was gripping me impossibly tight to her. I squirmed, and I burned, and felt my soul catch fire and—

A few seconds later it was over, and Rose was pulling away, buttoning her blouse back up. "Whew," she said, fanning herself, "that was warm. You're like a little furnace."

I felt like someone had taken a good ice cream scoop and jellied out part of my brains. Like I just wanted to drool and stare for a while until the fog in my mind passed. I just blinked, my cheek still burning from the contact with her skin.

"While I'm thinking of it," she said, fastening her top button, "did you just not have a childhood at all? I mean, you have no memories of that time. Like they're all repressed or something. Nothing before your mum locked you up." She shook her head. "I mean, most people don't remember much, but they remember something, at least." She made a semi-satisfied noise. "So…this time, I took a little gem, I must say. Turns out your mam once fixed a picnic dinner in your living room, and it made you feel all special and nice, because it was a break from the monotonous routine of 'Be ever-vigilant in your preparation for fighting off whatever bad people came along to do you harm.'" She said it very straight-faced, and then cackled again. "How's that working out for you?"

"It was going pretty well until some flat-ass psychopath drained five thousand people to create a designer shopping list of superpowers she could draw from," I said, more than a little dazedly and way outside the bounds of my good judgment, which felt like it had been sucked out of my head with whatever memory she'd just taken. I looked up at her, and she looked down at me, and I figured, why not go for broke? "How'd you get the serum, Rose? To give them their powers?"

"Same place as anyone else got it," she said, adjusting her blouse, and straightening it where it was tucked into her pants. Because she wanted to look her best for whatever she was about to do to torture me, I guessed.

"Revelen," I muttered, feeling a trickle run down my left cheek. Was that the side she'd licked? The one that she'd plucked the eye out of? Because that probably wasn't tears, that was—

Oh. Gross. As though I needed another reminder that Rose was a complete nut.

"Yeah, Revelen," she said, finishing up her tuck adjustment and giving her ass a look over her shoulder. She frowned, and I hoped I'd really hurt her with that flat-ass comment. "I wouldn't worry about them, though. They'll never get around to you."

"Who are they?" I asked, distant, feeling like I was barely conscious. Still asking the big questions, though, because why not?

Her eyes burned when she looked back at me. "Doesn't matter. You'll be nice and dead before they become any concern of yours. Although—" and here she lightened a shade "—once they found out it was you I was going after, they fell over themselves trying to help me."

I tried to process that, again, dazedly. "Why? Why do they hate me?"

"I'm sure you gave them a reason," she said, and she scuffed her heel on the concrete. "Not that it matters anymore." She beckoned over my shoulder. "Come on, now."

I tried to look back, but she kicked me in the shin and that put an end to my sneak peek, because she didn't do it anywhere approaching gentle. By the time I got my head up again, she was standing there in front of me, signaling to me to look at her, and she pasted a big smile across her face as I did.

Standing next to her, tightly gripped by the arm, was…someone. Someone tall, someone male, who was clad entirely in dark clothing, and had blood that I could smell but not see, all over their sleeves. She held them tightly, still grinning, a black bag over their head so I couldn't see the face, and Rose said, brightly, "I told you I had a gift for you…and now…" She leaned in, and my heart sank as she finished with, "Now we can bond while I kill them right in front of you."

11.

Reed

Sacred Heart, Minnesota

Augustus opened up the shelter and let us out shortly after our talk. We had plans, things we needed to accomplish, and also, we each had a task we were set to.

Some of these things would be easier than others.

We were in the middle of a cornfield that lay fallow for autumn, nothing but dead stalks cleared all the way around us. Ubers were starting to show up at the nearest road, about a quarter mile away across the field, courtesy of Jamal creating a bunch of fake accounts for us, and off we were going to do our respective things.

Important things. Very important things.

"You look lost," Dr. Zollers said to me, appearing almost soundlessly at my side.

"I'm not lost," I said, "I'm in western Minnesota."

"I meant at the thought of sending all these people out to shake their respective bushes," he said, probably reading it all right out of my mind.

"You can smell my fear, huh?" I didn't look at him. Zollers was an okay guy, but I didn't want or need headshrinking right now. "What's it like? Does it have a lemon-fresh scent?"

"It's like a man thinking this might be the last time he sees some of his crew," Zollers said, so seriously.

"Well," I said, a tenseness in my shoulders that seemed to be giving my neck a twinge, "you have to admit—it is a possibility. Rose could be anywhere, at any time, since we can't really track her all that well."

"I know this," Zollers said with a ghostly smile. "And you're going off-point."

"She could take any of our people at any time if she finds us," I said. "Think about Fannon. We didn't even see that coming until he betrayed us. Hell—we don't even know how she got him to betray us. Was it money? Mind control powers of some stripe?"

He frowned. "Not as such, no, I don't think. She's doing something else. I think you know it's not Siren powers at work."

"I wish I shared your confidence," I said. "But I don't have enough of an idea what she's doing to guess—"

"If she has Siren powers," he said, giving me a knowing smile, "she would have used them by now. In this battle or one of the ones she's obliquely attempted before." He stared at me. "The other schemes she's—"

"I know this wasn't her first attempt at us," I said, nodding along. Because it wasn't. It was probably her fifth or sixth, but…it was the first time she'd come at us directly, herself.

"You've got a lot of awfully dark circles under your eyes, Reed," Zollers said. "If you need to sleep—"

I closed them, briefly. "It's not—" I ran a hand over my forehead. "It's not that I'm tired, tired—" My shoulder was still twinging in pain. "You've been monitoring our sleep for months. Has she been trying to get to us through the Dreamwalk?"

"Regularly," Zollers said with a nod. "I've been blocking her from any of the people you have here, but…only once they've joined the team. Anyone could have been affected before they got here."

"She's good at that, messing with your mind," I said. I knew firsthand. The night after we got back from York, Isabelle had woken me out of a nightmare where Rose was…doing things to me. I felt gross, dirty and abused afterward, afraid to even go to sleep for days. I'd called Zollers immediately, and he'd been with us ever since. "It only gets worse from here, I'd guess."

"You need to prepare yourself," Zollers said. "For this and other contingencies."

"Contingencies?"

"You're bound to lose someone in this fight," he said, leaning closer, whispering. "This woman is serious and dedicated, and no matter how much you plan with her, it is entirely likely that she will overwhelm you at some point, catch us by surprise."

I pushed my fingers into my face, massaging the bones and tissue around my sinuses. "Did you not see that battle? She already has. I thought we'd have beaten her by now. I don't know what else we could have thrown at her."

"I'm sure you'll think of something," Zollers said, putting a soft hand on my shoulder, squeezing once and nearly dropping me to my knees from the pain. Then, suddenly, it faded, and I was left with a blissful clarity in my head where a screaming muscle ache had been before. I dropped my hands from my eyes, and he was smiling. "I've got you covered."

I tested my shoulder experimentally; it was perfect. Headache gone. "Thank you," I said, as Zollers started to pull away.

He waved over his shoulder, and headed off, pulling his phone out of his pocket, one of the untraceables that our tech team had been handing out. He walked off a little ways to where Augustus and Taneshia were getting into an Uber and started to talk to them, saying…something. I couldn't tell what, because they were speaking low. I watched them talk to each other, so casually, and my stomach turned at the threat to us all.

Thinking about putting people in real danger—not battle danger, but separated from the herd where Rose could get at them danger—almost gave me a headache again.

"Can I talk to you for a minute?" Jamie Barton was suddenly at my shoulder.

"Sure thing, Gravity," I said, going extra formal. "Can I guess first, though—you want to go home?"

She looked at me steadily. "I want to go home."

"You can leave anytime you want," I said, a little tautly.

Her face fell. "But?"

"But Rose might come after you," I said, shrugging. "I mean, it was always a risk anyway, but…if you head back to your life now that she knows you've fought with us…" I just laid that out there, figuring she'd get it.

Her shoulders slumped. "So now that I agreed to do one favor for Sienna, I'm in until—forever? Like the Mafia?"

"I hope not," I said, my own voice straining. "But come on. You saw what happened at our office earlier. Rose came at us, and she came hard. She's going to continue to, at her convenience—until she gets us. Probably all of us."

"It so stinks to be stuck in a situation like this that you didn't even create," Jamie said, putting her fingers in her long, blond hair. "My daughter and best friend are in hiding, and—"

"I understand," I said. "My girlfriend is completely stuck in an unfair position as well." Which was true, though I hadn't told anyone exactly how unfair. Isabella was riding clouds right now, somewhere over the Southwest, out of the flight path of the airlines, and with a parachute on her back in case I happened to get killed. It wasn't a perfect solution, but she had enough food and water to keep her going for a few months, albeit probably quite unhappily, and I was regularly bringing her more supplies via the currents of wind, so…

Still, I was going to be in the doghouse for a long time when she got down. She'd agreed to do it, but I couldn't imagine spending a month or two in the clouds by yourself is very good for your health and sanity, even if your boyfriend visits regularly-ish.

Though I was just about to find out how badly that sort of prison sentence messed with someone's mind.

"This just…it stinks," Barton said, shaking her head.

"Life's not fair," I said. "It wasn't fair when Sienna got accused of things she didn't do, it wasn't fair when this Rose decided to make herself the most terrible enemy ever, and you're right, it's not fair that you got dragged into this. But imagine if we hadn't pulled you in when we did."

She looked up at me with soft blue eyes. "I wouldn't even see her coming, would I?"

I thought about the conversation Rose and I had in my dreams after I'd fled York. It was the worst nightmare I'd ever had, and combined with just enough...other elements...that when Isabella woke me I couldn't recall a time where I felt more helpless in my life. "No," I said quietly. "That's not how she works."

Jamie sort of nodded, once, then again. "All right," she almost whispered, and started to totter off.

"We're going to win this," I said. "And then...you'll be back home before you know it."

She looked back at me, and smiled tightly. "I hope so." And shuffled off, joining the part of the team which was about to move to the next rendezvous point.

I hoped I was right, but...it was hard not to have doubts. I looked back to find Olivia Brackett just standing there, ghosting my steps as she seemed to do since she'd gotten here. I waved her forward, and she almost seemed like she wanted to ask, "Who, me?" as though I'd chosen her by mistake. She got over that quickly and came forward, cheeks red. "Yes?" she asked.

"I needed to talk to you for a second," I said. "Because...I'm about to do something...desperate. And it affects you, so..." My voice trailed off.

"What...what is it?" she asked, looking genuinely like I'd hammered her with a bolt out of the blue.

"I'm bringing Tracy down out of the clouds for a talk," I said, and watched her eyes widen.

Tracy was a meta that had been raised in the same crazy cloister as Olivia, but instead of being one of the putative prey animals, like her, he'd been up in the hierarchy. Son of the leader, Tracy had acted as an enforcer and all-around sick son of a bitch for the place, keeping the "prisoners" in line for Roger, their leader.

Which was a bad enough job, but...having met Tracy, fought him, dealt with him...I knew another detail about his job that bothered me.

He'd enjoyed the hell out of every minute of it.

When we'd fought back in January, I'd found him a tough one to deal with. He could kill momentum around him, just drag it down kind of like Gravity setting up a well around something. He could also charge like a rhino, harnessing a massive amount of momentum to himself, like a freight train. Which made him perfect for dealing with Olivia, because his was almost an opposition power to hers; his moved himself and stopped others, while Olivia's moved others but didn't really work on herself. Try and hit him with a car, it'd do nothing. When he charged, he was unstoppable.

But the last time we'd fought, I'd found something he couldn't stop.

The wind.

I'd lifted his ass off like Isabella, but without the regular food and water, and just sent him out to orbit the Earth at five thousand feet for the last ten months. It was not, upon reflection, one of my kindest punishments ever. In fact, for a guy who'd long argued against Sienna's incarceration methods when I'd been actively helping shove people into the Cube—the government metahuman prison—this was probably me at my most hypocritical.

Still, Tracy had orbited the Earth for ten months because I couldn't think of anything else to do with him, other than kill him. Which I hadn't wanted to do.

So he'd had ten whole months to really consider life, hunger and thirst (seriously, I only remembered to feed him about once or twice a week, and I'd give him water on about the same schedule), being an asshole…

I'd hoped that it had taken some of the defiance out of him, but…

Well, we'd find out soon enough, assuming Olivia didn't break down in front of me.

"Wait, you've still got him…?" She pointed into the air.

"Yeah, he's, uh…been up there the whole time," I said, nodding.

She blinked at me. "Yikes."

"I'm sure he's thinking something similar."

"What do you think he's going to be like when he gets down?" Now she was whispering.

"You know him better than I do," I said. "How do you think he's going to be?"

She stared into space for a moment, really churning those thoughts. "I don't know. I know how I'd be after a few months isolated, alone. Did—did he eat while he was up there?"

"I sent him food and drink…some of the time," I said, feeling a little guilty. It hadn't been on the regular, maybe two or three times a week. And it wasn't super quality food, either, because I didn't like him at all. I hated him, and wanted him to suffer, if I was being honest.

Yeah. I'd become everything I'd railed against in my conversations with Sienna. I was running a private prison and mistreating my one inmate. At least I wasn't doing it for profit, though if anyone had wanted to pay me to keep his dumb ass aloft, I would have taken it.

She made a face. "Well, I don't think he's going to be happy."

"If he gives me one ounce of lip or assholery, he's back in the sky," I said. "But…I felt like I should tell you in case you wanted to clear out while I meet with him. If he hasn't changed, he's going back up. But if he's, uh…humbled…"

"You're going to ask him to join us?" Olivia almost looked amused. "Wow. We really are desperate. I should have known when you wanted my help that things were dire."

"You were already on my list, even before this," I said. "But I knew you'd already said 'no' to Scott when he asked for the FBI."

"Scott didn't bail me out of a jam like you did," Olivia said, drawing a deep breath. "No, I…I'll stand right here while you bring him down. I want…I want to look that sonofabitch in the eye and see if he's really changed. And if he hasn't—"

"You tell me, and up, up and away he goes," I said, motioning with my hand in a quick down-up. She nodded, and I took a breath. "Okay. Here we go."

I dispelled the winds around Tracy, who was currently about a mile above us, just drifting. I'd changed his course and put the wind at his back on my journey through the pipe

93

to Sacred Heart, Minnesota, and he'd been in a holding pattern up there for the last few minutes while I worked things out.

Now it was time to get serious, and find out if he was a useful idiot in this quest, or just an idiot.

I wasn't kind about bringing him down; he fell out of the sky like a wingless, engineless plane, screaming all the way. His clothing was ragged, his mouth was open and noise was coming out, and he was headed for the earth at terminal velocity.

When Tracy got a few feet from the earth, though, he just...stopped.

He opened his eyes, looking around, wild-eyed as I'd ever seen any human being. I'd created a cushion of air beneath him, catching him about six inches from the ground. And there he hovered, in silence for a few seconds, as I stared at him with my arms folded across my chest.

He'd been bald when last I'd seen him; now his hair was long and black, a beard matching that look down his neck a few inches, like a really unkempt and totally white bread version of Jason Momoa. He looked like he'd been stuck in the clouds for a decade, scruffy, disgusting, and the smell...

I took a step back and pinched my nose. I couldn't imagine my meta senses were making it any better.

His mouth was open, and he was breathing in gasps, eyes wild and flicking around.

"Hi, Tracy," I said, a little warily. "Did you enjoy your time away?"

He looked right at me, and I could see tears forming in my eyes. "Ohmigahhhhh..." was all he got out.

I nudged Olivia. "He doesn't seem to be, uh..."

"Eloquent?" she offered.

"Please don't send me back up there," he said, hiccuping the words out. He had big tears in his eyes. Big tears. Epically huge, Guy-Friday-swole-to-the-max tears, and they were dripping down his face. "Please. Pleeeeease." He pulled his hands together and bound them, interlacing the fingers. "I will do anything you want, just...please don't send me back up there."

This time, Olivia nudged me. "Let him down."

I dispelled the last gusts of air, and for the first time in nearly a year, Tracy touched ground. It was a soft landing, his knees and elbows catching him before he ate dirt. He sat there on all fours for a moment, just frozen, eyes closed, waterworks still dripping from his face—

And then he buried his face in the soil.

His shoulders were heaving, big, racking sobs muffled by how he'd put his face in the dirt. He lifted it up and his lips were covered in black soil, which—I mean, this was a farmer's field, so I imagined manure was in there somewhere.

Tracy didn't seem bothered by it. He squeezed big handfuls of black dirt and got onto his knees, a look of relief like he'd just emptied his bladder after holding it forever breaking over his extremely bearded face. "Thank you," he said, and it sounded so pathetic, a little like a foghorn, like he'd forgotten how to speak. "Thank you," he said again, still crying, shuffling on his knees toward me.

"Whoa!" I said, but he reached me before I could stop him, wrapping his arms around my midsection. He was crying into my belly button, crying, this grown man, and squeezing me tight.

"Please don't send me back please don't send me back please don't please don't—"

"I think he's probably changed," Olivia said, a few steps back. She was eyeing him—and by extension me—with a rather heavy amount of distaste.

"Tracy?" I asked, and he raised tearful eyes to me, lips still stained with black…which he was rubbing into my shirt. "Do you want to tell Olivia you're sorry?"

He blinked at me, swallowed deeply, and his gaze drifted drunkenly over to her. "I am so sorry," he said after only a brief moment, during which he did not let me go. He wasn't crushing me, but he was definitely holding on like I was a lifeline and he was adrift at sea, about to go under. "I am so, so, so sorry," he said, voice quivering like a sine wave. "I was wrong. So wrong. I wronged you—and it was wrong—"

"Okay, that's good enough," I said, putting a hand on his shoulder, trying to stop his ramble.

"I didn't realize," he went on, still rambly, "that we were doing this kind of thing to you—" he pointed at the sky "—and I—I—I just…" And he broke into sobs again.

"Yeah, I think he's changed," Olivia said, evincing distaste as Tracy buried his face in my stomach again, still sobbing. "You're all good here." And she started to walk off.

"Hey—I—" I called after her, but she quickened her pace to get away.

I couldn't blame her. There was a big, hairy, sobbing guy attached to me at the waist. I looked around for help, and found Zollers, who was smiling at me a little benevolently. I pointed to the top of Tracy's head in question, and Zollers nodded, once, still smiling. Almost a smirk, actually. I guess he was sincere.

"Score another one for our team," I said, looking down at the sobbing and broken man that I'd made, so desperate he was practically willing to be my slave. And apparently oh-so-in need of a hug. "Yay for us." I could only hope my team was finding as much fortune as I had so far.

And that they were avoiding the very real danger that was Rose.

12.

Sienna

I stared in horror at the black-masked figure Rose held at her side, her leer like a knife right through to my heart.

She'd caught someone.

Someone important to me.

I swallowed heavily, so loudly that I feared it might echo over every surface of the empty warehouse where I sat, chained to a chair, one of my eyes plucked out, the pain from that and my other injuries rendering me almost insensate.

But not nearly insensate enough to fail to grasp that something truly horrible was about to happen.

The smell of my own blood was heavy in my mouth, in my throat, in my nose, and I felt like I was going to choke on it. Rose was grinning madly—as though she grinned any other way—as she held the hostage, all dressed in black from top to bottom. "Well?" she asked with a hint of glee. "Do you want to unwrap your present?"

"No," I answered honestly, even though, obviously, in sick horror, I did want to know who she'd grabbed.

"But this is my gift to you," she said in mock outrage, as though I'd insulted her. "This is going to make us closer." She jerked the figure around, and they wobbled, on unsteady legs. She dragged them up to me and got right up in my face, right up to my remaining eye. "I did this for you."

I raised my head back, recoiling from her, and then

brought it forward in a headbutt like I'd done to Mr. Blonde only a few minutes earlier.

The difference was night and day. I'd caught Blonde in the middle of a lousy punch, completely unprepared for my attack.

Here I caught Rose in the jaw, seemingly unprepared for me—

But Rose…Rose was always prepared, now.

There was a flash of light and pain across my entire head, and my head whipped back. I blinked at the shock of ramming my head into a steel girder, and when I managed to pry my eyes open and the world came swimming back into focus—

Rose hadn't moved an inch.

She was still there, still grinning like a madwoman, unmoved.

I'd hit her right in the jaw, and she hadn't even felt it.

"I absorbed an Achilles a couple weeks ago," she said, smiling. "It took a while to track down the bloodlines to make one of those. Serious work on an ancestry search. Distant relative of an old friend of yours, Anselmo. Latent genes…but we managed to get them unlocked just fine, didn't we?" She put the hostage in a headlock and rubbed their head through the bag, giving them a noogie. "Life's so much fun when you've got things to look forward to, isn't it?"

Pain rattled through me; I didn't know quite what to say to that. I was pretty sure I was concussed, my head ringing like a bell from my failed attack against an invincible target. Still, she had a point.

I had nothing to look forward to but torture and tears, and having a little piece of my soul sliced off any time Rose felt like taking a nip of the '94 Sienna. It was a bad year, heavy, lingered on the tongue, overwhelmed the senses.

"No idea what you're…talking about," I said through the pain, unable to even cradle my poor, beleaguered head.

"You make me sad," Rose said, all false pouty, "and happy at the same time. Back to that love/hate thing." She took a couple steps back, presumably to allow me to breathe without her stankass breath in my face. "All right, I know just the thing to cheer you up—let's unwrap your present!"

And she ripped the mask off the figure, leaving me to gape, slack-jawed and in horror, at what lay beneath it.

13.

"Andrew Phillips?" I asked, looking into the blinking eyes of my old boss. He still had that double chin, that round face, the shaded, blond hair, though he was pretty pale.

"It's you. This is your fault," he said in that deadened voice. "I should have known." He seemed pretty calm about it, but then, he seldom showed much emotion.

"Do I look like I'm in a position to orchestrate your kidnapping?" I asked, rattling my metacuffs furiously. "Asshole! I'm a kidnappee too, and you should be doing something about it, because you're supposed to be in the business of solving metahuman crimes." I threw all that out there out of reflex, mostly, because obviously he couldn't have done shit to help me, now or ever.

Not with Rose.

Rose, who was taking all this with a deep measure of amusement. "So nice to see two people reunited after a long stretch apart." She was really breathing it in, enjoying her moment. "Do you have anything else to say to each other?"

"I'm glad you got fired," Phillips said. "You were an obnoxious pain in the ass to work with, and you caused me more problems than any employee, ever."

"Thanks," I said. "Pretty sure you put that on my last evaluation, maybe slightly more in bureaucratese, but I got the message."

"When we catch up with you," Phillips went on, just staring straight ahead, refusing to even look at me, "you're going to spend the rest of your life in jail. However long it lasts."

"I'd love to," I said. "Any chance you want to call the boys in blue to come get me right now?"

"Oh, the bobbies aren't going to get my lovely Sienna," Rose said, dragging Phillips forward a step to pinch my cheek, and not gently, either. Like a pissed-off aunt. Like my aunt, actually, because Charlie had been a shithead and a succubus. "She's all mine, forever. Or as long as she lasts." Rose cackled. "Which—" she turned her attention back to Phillips "—is more than we can say for you, boss man." She looked at him, he looked back at her. "How do you want it?"

"How do I want what?" Phillips asked, like he'd missed a step.

"Wait, you're going to kill him in front of me?" I stared at her, disbelieving. "But...I hate him."

"I know that," she said, looking at me like I was an idiot. "That's why he's a present, see? Not a torture. I know you hate him, and I'm going to kill him in front of you, like a gift." She stared at me blankly, waiting for me to get it. "See?" As though I were a simpleton for not seeing.

I was exhausted, beaten, lacking an eye, my hand screaming from being shattered, mentally fatigued, and now probably concussed, in addition to the other pains of torture. Three months Rose had been batting me around like a cat with a plaything. I couldn't even think straight. "Uhh..." She stared at me, expectantly, and I tried to scrape around for some residual emotion, trying to figure out how I should feel about this moment.

Rose was going to kill a man who'd made my life a complete hell. Who'd spearheaded a manhunt against me for mostly political reasons, who knew I was innocent and was a huge douche to me anyway. Who'd nearly killed me on several occasions, through his own efforts, and aided in several others.

And Rose, who I hated (not anywhere close to loved, because she was crazy as hell), was holding him in front of me, saying she was going to kill him.

How was I supposed to feel about this?

Shouldn't I be doing the touchdown dance, on unsteady legs?

I sighed. "Please don't," I said, almost too low to be heard, even for a meta.

"What's that?" Rose asked.

"Please don't kill him," I said, almost completely resigned. She was either going to kill him or not. I didn't hold out much illusion that she was going to take my request to heart one way or another; if she thought I really wanted to spare him, she'd kill him anyway to spite me, I thought. If I acted like I really wanted him dead…well, she might jump all over that and kill him anyway, so we could bond or something, like she'd said.

So I kept my objection right up the middle in terms of emotional engagement.

"Excuse me?" She wrinkled the skin around her eyes, almost squinting at me.

"I have a moral objection to you killing him," I said. "He's a giant dick, but…I don't want him dead."

"That's a compelling case you just laid out for me, thanks," Phillips said.

"Oh, shut up," I said, right back at him. "You've done more than anyone other than Gerry Harmon and the Clary clan and whoever runs Revelen to make my life hell these last few years. I should want you dead, but I don't. That's about as much as I can offer right now." I nodded my throbbing head toward Rose. "Besides, she's going to do what she wants to you anyway. I'm just laying down a marker to ease my conscience because I wouldn't have killed you myself."

Rose giggled. "You want me to spare his life?"

"Sure, why not?" I asked, a little airily. I may not have actively wanted Phillips dead, but if she thought I was going to weep to see him ripped apart in front of me, well…I'd seen worse happen to better people. This was the least of the things I was going to have to live with, even if it was putatively done in my name.

"Even if I drain him and put the blame on you?" Rose dangled a finger above Phillips's temple, and he eyed it, about as wildly as I'd ever seen him look at something.

"What's another murder on the back of all the ones I've already been accused of?" I shrugged my shoulders.

"Please," Phillips said, and I sensed the first hint of disquiet from him.

Rose looked him in the eye. "Please what? Please me? You couldn't if you tried, darling." She put a hand on him, and within three seconds he started to jerk and spasm, until she removed it. "Your soul is thin, like melted butter. You've got so very little will, you pathetic little man. I could eat you like a tattie scone, all in one bite."

"Maybe it'd help fill out your ass," I said.

Rose's eyes flashed annoyed for a tenth of a second, and then she smiled. "You keep talking about my arse. I'm staring to think you like it."

"I prefer my asses a bit more manly," I said, looking right at Phillips. "Which is another reason I don't like him."

"Oh?" Rose asked. She pushed Phillips out in front and looked down. "He does seem a bit lacking, doesn't he? His is an old man arse; just drops right off, doesn't it?"

"Yep."

"Is this a Chippendale's show or my execution?" Phillips asked, annoyance flashing across his face. Like he wasn't about two seconds from dying.

"Can't it be both?" Rose asked with a smirk.

I was trying to read Rose, trying to figure out the direction I needed to move things in order to spare Phillips's life. It was a pretty thin thread I had to hold onto. If I begged, she'd kill him to spite me. If I told her to do it...she might, just because she was crazy.

But if I acted like I didn't really care, didn't emotionally engage with her torture...

Hell, she might kill him anyway.

Andrew Phillips was probably going to die in front of me. And soon.

Yet I couldn't help trying to seize on that thin thread of hope...in order to save his asshole ass.

I couldn't seem too needy, though, so I changed the subject. "Gah...I so need a Scotch."

Rose was up in my face a second later. "Thirsty?"

I looked her in the eye with the remaining one of mine. "I have a headache. And an empty-socket ache. And—"

"You don't need to list your injuries off for me, Sienna dear," she said. "I gave them to you, remember. How's the hand?"

"Broken into about a million pieces," I said. It had, thankfully, gone mostly numb. Mostly. "Just like you wanted, I'm sure."

"It'll heal," she said, thinking out loud, staring over my shoulder into the space beyond. "And you'll be just as strong as before. That's the thing about metas—we don't develop scars on our skin, like humans. So we miss the lessons that scars give them." She grabbed Phillips by the hand and used her fingernail to scratch a deep cut in his wrist.

"Owww," he said, looking all offended that she'd gouged him.

"If he lives long enough, this'll make a nice little reminder for him," she said, letting the blood drip down through the pale blond hairs on his forearm.

"Of what?" I asked. "I mean, seriously, what lesson does he learn from that? 'In the future, I should really avoid getting kidnapped by psychotic Scots'? Because I don't think he intended to this time—"

"Oh, please. I seduced him," she said, rolling her eyes.

I looked at Phillips; he suddenly got a little cagey, not looking at me. "This is your type?" I asked, cocking my head at Rose. "Really? Pale, crazy redheads?"

"He's got an eye for a flat ass, I suppose," Rose said with a grin.

"It was more the legs," Philips admitted, and she scratched him again. "Ow!"

"Now that, he might learn something from," I said. "Maybe."

"Metas miss the lessons because we don't form scars…outside our bodies," Rose said, acting like the conversation hadn't diverged wildly from where she thought she was leading it. "But we do form them, don't we, Sienna?" She leaned in on me again, breathing stankly—probably Phillips's breath or something—right in my face. "The way our mothers treat us…our past loves…it's all scarring, just…not of the flesh."

"Which is good, because earlier someone told me I had nice eyes," I said, "just before she ripped one out. I'd hate to disappoint you by not growing that back."

"What does that have to do with scars?" she asked, frowning at me.

"I don't know," I said. "Wounds…scar tissue…blah blah blah. I'm in a lot of pain; it's a miracle I make any sense at all."

"Or that you're half as lippy as you are," she said, now without the smile.

"I mean, you could take that away, if you wanted to," I said, in a pretty calm acknowledgment of the fact that three months into this, Rose hadn't completely made a vegetable of me yet, or done much to neuter my smartassery, "but I'm pretty sure I'm done at that point." She stared at me in fierce concentration. "You take that away, and there's not going to be enough left of me to even care when you do something horrible that's meant to torture me."

She glared at me through narrowed eyes. "This is true. It's too much a part of who you are. I figured the beatings…the pain…the broken bones, the constant ripping out of memories like I'm rewiring a circuit board…badly, I might add…I thought this would do something other than make you less reticent to come at me, but…there you went a few minutes ago and crashed your head into mine. After injuring one of my servants." She sighed. "I think we need to step our game up."

"My game's just fine, thanks," I said, but that wasn't true. If my game was fine, Rose's head wouldn't have been attached to her body any longer.

My game was in the toilet, and it had been since she'd ripped my damned souls out of my body and stolen my effing groove.

Actually, it probably predated that, since I'd been on the run from the law for months before that happened. Almost a year now, in fact.

But that had more to do with the man she was holding

hostage than Rose herself.

"How do we pick up the pace of things here...?" Rose murmured to herself, seeking an answer. I worried about who she was asking, but...

...I kinda got an answer a moment later.

She brightened, the response clearly coming down that she liked. "You think big, Wolfe. I like that."

And with nothing more than a nod as warning, she tore Andrew Phillips's head right off, tossing his body aside. Just ripped it clean off with one good tear.

His eyes stared at me, blinking, but no words came out of his mouth although his lips moved. Whether it was the twitch of death or he could actually still control them...I didn't know.

Rose gently set it in front of me, at my feet, and patted it on the thinning blonde hair. "Now...you just sit here and look at this...and think about what you've done...and know it's the first of many to come. M'kay?" She stared at me, all bright-eyed, as though she were a parent disciplining a child, then got up and patted me on the head, a little harder. She got the spot where I'd slammed into her invincible skull earlier. "Really think on it," she said, driving the pain into my head by tapping me on the wound. "We'll talk again soon. Oh—and before I forget—one for the road—"

She touched me on the face, just for a few seconds, enough to get my skin burning, and I blacked out for a second. When I came back to, she was pulling her hand off my cheek. "Ooh, that one was good," she said, fanning herself. "Erotic. You're quite the little vixen for a girl who doesn't like to eat her lovers, did you know that? I hear it's rare for a succubus to restrain herself so. Anyway...what's that weird thing you Americans say? 'Toodles'?" She used another horrific American accent, and turned her back, waving at me as she walked her flat ass away. "Enjoy the gift."

And I looked down at my feet, into the dead eyes of Andrew Phillips, and my stomach sank, again, as the pain throbbed through my body—my face, my cheek, my head, my eye, my hand—and a dozen other spots where it flared like fire.

I looked from the dead eyes of Colin Fannon back to the deader ones of Andrew Phillips, then watched Rose as she pushed her way out of a door at the far end of the warehouse. I wondered, idly, as I sat there, how long it would be before I saw her again.

However long it was…it wouldn't be nearly long enough for me.

14.

Wolfe

"Och, these are good times, Wolfe," Rose said, cackling as he made his way into her little lounge, the smell of wood filtering through his nose. She was touching him on the shoulder, brushing against him again, and it felt...

Wolfe's voice was low and quiet, seeping with the pleasure he could feel running through his body from her contact with his arm. "Yes...good times."

"Aye, little Miss Sienna has earned this," Rose said, draping herself over one of the chairs in the middle of the room, sitting sideways with her legs hanging off one side while leaning her neck against the other side. It looked... uncomfortable.

Wolfe just sat down normally in his. Maybe a little uncomfortably, because the chair was too small for him.

He brushed against the soft, velvety upholstery as Rose stared at him, her lips a smile that seemed barely hidden, as though it might grow bigger at any moment or simply disappear. "Do you know what?"

Wolfe was hunched over in the uncomfortable chair. "...What?"

"I think I'm paying her back for what she did to you," Rose said, and she sat up abruptly, leaned in, and stroked Wolfe's face. "All the bad things she did to you."

Wolfe took that stoically, as he did with her touch across

his face.

"Miss Rose?" A small voice stirred Wolfe out of the feeling she was projecting across his body.

"Ooh!" Rose made a little noise and stopped touching his neck, and as the pleasant feel seemed to crawl off his skin, Wolfe felt himself wanting to growl as anger squirmed up to replace it. He opened his eyes to find Rose on her feet, hugging some man.

Wolfe took a closer look; she had him wrapped up good, hugging him, but he could see the fellow somewhat. He was tall and well-apportioned, tanned and dark-haired, with a confident pretty-boy smile and model good looks. When he'd spoken, Wolfe could hear the twisting sound of his Italian accent at the end of his query.

"Wolfe," Rose said, breaking from the man, "I simply must introduce you to another of my dear friends—like you. This…" She was flushed with a kind of pleasure of her own. "…is Mario."

The growl escaped him automatically, without any effort on his part.

Mario broke into a laugh. "Oh, a funny one, I see." It made Wolfe see red.

"Oh, Wolfe," Rose said, lips puckered and pouty. "Mario is my very good friend. Can't you just…treat him nice? For me?"

Wolfe kept his head down, looking at Mario out of thinly slitted eyelids, like he was a prey animal. He started to respond, but a low growl made its way out in lieu of words.

"Wolfe," Rose said, a little like she was disappointed, and on the verge of commanding him, "this man is important to me." She had storm clouds over her eyes. "As you are." She moved a little closer and brushed against the side of his face. "You love me, don't you…?"

The stir of pleasure ran along Wolfe's cheek, then all through him, and he felt almost as though he were being lit up. "I…"

Rose frowned. "You *do* love me…don't you?"

"I respect your strength," Wolfe said, almost grudgingly. "It's everything Wolfe has sought in life—from the days when he—I—served the great Hades."

A twinge of dissatisfaction presented itself atop Rose's brow, which was lined as she frowned at him. A moment later, it lightened. "You've had a hard life, Wolfe." She touched him again. "Come now. Sit with us." And there were suddenly three chairs. "You're both so important to my plans. Come on, then." And she beckoned him forward, to where Mario was already seated.

She put herself between them as Wolfe dragged himself back into the uncomfortably soft chair, and Rose cackled with pleasure at being here, where she wanted to be. "I've got two brave, strong men beside me," she said, practically glowing in her smile. "Who wouldn't want to be me?"

"No one," Mario said, almost gushing as he leaned over to take her hand. He kissed it gently with his lips.

Wolfe watched the whole thing, and Rose looked to him a moment later, and offered her other hand. Wolfe took it immediately, kissing it carefully, avoiding his teeth. He felt the surge of pleasure that mere contact with her skin produced here, in this place, and he said, "No one, my queen," and watched that smile blossom out upon her lips, and he felt…so unbearably good, that even with the blight that was Mario, he never wanted this moment to end.

15.

Sienna

Fannon ejected me from the van without a lot in the way of words or worry for my good health. I hit the ground at the side of the road and rolled, landing pretty roughly on my shoulder. It didn't feel great, but it was kind of a minimal thing compared to the busted hand, the missing eye, the vicious headache that made me feel like some brainworm had clawed into my empty socket.

I lay there in the stubby grass, darkness all around me save for one spot on the horizon about a hundred yards away, and watched my breath puff in the moonlit night. It was a seeping cold, sneaking in around my ragged clothing, which would have surely marked me as the bummiest bum of all time. Like I gave a shit at this point.

Eventually I heaved myself to sitting position, and regretted it immediately. All the blood seemed to leave my head as soon as I did it, and I wanted to tip right back over and hit the dirt, which was somewhat soft and yet rigid, like it had settled where it was sitting a few thousand years ago and was reluctant to move. There were ridges in the earth, little ones, like tire treads made in mud and hardened by the sun. I pushed against them with my good hand and they crumbled as I stared out over the ground around me.

Back on the moors. I could see the rocks, the rushes stretching into the distance, and the occasional acidic pond.

And there…a hundred yards away was the inn that I'd stormed out of just this very morning after my confrontation with that servant of Rose's.

Every part of my body ached, even the ones that Rose hadn't broken, and as I heaved myself to my feet, I reluctantly admitted that I might need a little bit of heal time.

I looked down at my hand, at all the bones protruding from the skin, and realized I'd had to turn my head in order to even see it, thanks to my missing eye.

Okay, maybe a lot of healing time. At least an overnight somewhere.

"Asshole," I said to no one in particular and Rose in absentia, and started wobbling my way on unsteady legs toward the building, its strangely Addams Family house-ish structure (but boxier) seeming to sway with my every movement.

And I wasn't even drunk yet. But we'd fix that soon.

I wandered toward the door, and it opened as I was about ten feet away. A guy came stumbling out, clearly a little too deep into his cups. He met my eyes and let loose of the door, his keys in hand. I could smell the alcohol on him from here.

He staggered a step, and I sized him up quickly. He did the same to me, looking me over with obvious distaste.

Now I thought of him as an asshole, because I could clean up like a damned champ, if, y'know, I had decent clothing and a place to bathe and maybe some makeup and also the desire not to brutally beat him for looking at me that way.

I steered his way, hard, and bumped into him. Not a meta bump, more like a gentle one, as though I'd missed a step or he had—not hard to believe in his current state.

"Oh, sorry," he said in a thick brogue, raising his eyes to me in surprise. The bump had happened pretty fast, after all.

"My fault," I said, recoiling quickly, like I was horrified to have been this close to him. "I think I'm already feeling it, y'know?" I grinned at him stupidly, and, I hoped, a little drunkenly—or at least that it'd be perceived as such.

That was exactly how he took it, splitting into a wide grin. "I know just what you mean," he slurred, and then stumbled past me. "Have a good night!"

I waited until he was way, way past, and then I lifted up the keys and wallet I'd pulled from him with my meta speed. "Oh, I will," I called over my shoulder as I pocketed them both and made for the door. I'd return them to the lost and found at the end of the night, the wallet a few pounds lighter.

Welcome to the 234th brokeass metahuman drinking games! May the sots be ever in your favor.

I made my way through the lobby quickly, ignoring the lady at the podium waiting to check in poor unfortunates. Hopefully the guy I'd just left in my wake would be one of them, soon enough, because honestly, he did not need to be driving in his present condition.

Stepping into the dark bar, I found the lights just a little dimmer than they'd been last night, and slid my broken hand as deep in my sleeve as I could, almost burying it up there. No one needed to see my bones sticking out, after all, not even me. I squinted my lost eye tightly closed as well, though I doubted there was much I could do for that other than pick a seat all the way at the end of the bar and keep my face perpetually turned sideways. It was already itching and aching in the socket, which either meant I was still experiencing the after-effects of the pain or things were growing back. I suspected the latter, but looking to check would have probably made me lose my lunch, so I just squinted it closed as best I could and plopped down at the end of the bar, sitting sideways so the bartender wouldn't see the horror of my face.

"Good grief," the bartender said as he made his way over to me, brow puckered in mild concern. "What happened to you?"

"It's been a hell of a day," I said, taking out the money I'd pulled from drunkie boy's wallet. "Give me a glass of the fifteen-year-old Glenfiddich?"

His eyebrows recoiled up his face in surprise like leaping mountain climbers, but he saw the cash, so he nodded and went off to get my drink. He didn't go far, because it wasn't exactly a sprawling bar. The room was about the size of my old living quarters at the Directorate, or the Agency back when I was actually a federal employee. There was room for maybe fifteen four-person tables; not a huge drinking area. Over the smell of the alcohol was the scent of deep-fried pub foods, and it made me a little queasy, contemplating that much grease on my empty stomach.

If Rose was going to continue to try and break me, I was going to demand some kind of a meal plan, because it felt like losing my eye and getting my ass kicked on an empty stomach was really sending me to the dietary woodshed. I mean, a few months ago I'd worked myself into peak shape, tight shoulders and everything else, and now I was seriously thinking about eating fried cod with my dinner of Scotch. As an accessory to the main course of alcohol, no less.

"Man, my life sure has turned to shit," I said to no one in particular. I realized at that moment that because of the shitty way I had to sit, my back was facing the door of the establishment.

I sighed in annoyance. What the hell did it matter, anyway? If someone came in with a yearning to kill me, they could do it, right now, and it'd be a hell of a lot more merciful than what Rose had in mind for me. And if the US government by chance sent in a hostile bunch of badass Seal Team Six types, then…again, they could kill me, or bag and drag me. Who gave a shit at this point? Rose would probably rip me out of their grasp at the expense of their lives, but that wasn't my problem, was it?

I doubted the government would send anyone though; I had a feeling they might have learned their lesson after their last op crashed and burned a few months ago, costing them beaucoup lives after Rose had blown up their helicopters while I ran for my frigging life. I know I would have gotten the message from that one, loud and clear—leave Sienna alone.

It was kind of sad that I was thinking that life in a government prison would beat the living hell out of this torturous existence as Rose's human chew toy. At least in prison I'd get three squares a day. And probably experience just as much solitude and desired sexual activity. Downside: I'd miss the scenic vistas of Scotland, but, frankly, I was pretty sick of that shit at this point. If I never saw another boob mountain again, I was cool with that.

"Your drink," the bartender said, putting a little half-glass in front of me, filled with amber liquid. No rocks, which was how I had wanted it. He probably figured, without me even asking, that watering down my drink was a poor idea. I threw some pounds at him, and he wandered off to get my change, leaving me alone—again—with only my thoughts and my booze, which was the most I could expect out of life at the moment.

You don't even have the will to seriously fight back anymore, that damned voice came and interrupted my sweet silence just as I was taking my first sip. I swallowed abruptly, probably drinking down a quarter of my most excellent beverage without even savoring the oaky awesomeness. What a waste.

"Doesn't seem a lot of point in it, does it?" I asked, probably looking to the room like I was talking to my Scotch.

You had so much fire in you, once—

"Well, I used to eat burritos a lot more frequently. Your Mexican cuisine here is pretty lacking."

—it's almost sad to see this. Like a lioness long-caged, who's lost her desire to hunt. To stalk. To—

"Yeah, yeah, synonym for hunt. I get it."

But you're just…adrift. So pathetic all the time.

"Like you wanted."

When are you going to get off the mat and throw a punch? A real one, not some idle defiance?

"When are you going to buy me another drink to make up for making me swallow the first quarter of this one without giving me a chance to swish it around in my mouth first? Huh? Never, that's when, you freeloading headspace asshole. If you'd just pay me the rent you're due for that space you keep expanding in my head, I wouldn't have to—" I looked around to make sure no one was listening to me "—lift wallets in order to get money to buy booze."

"And who taught you to do that?" A soft voice from behind me caused me to spin on my stool to see who'd spoken.

I hadn't heard her come in, but I heard her now as she sunk onto the stool next to mine, her strawberry blond hair looking more blond than strawberry in this dim light. She looked…wary, as though she thought I might spring on her. She looked to be keeping herself ready to spring away if it came to that.

It was that girl again, the one who'd brought me upstairs last night after Rose shellacked me. "Eilish of the Irish," I muttered, raising my drink to her as I came all the way around.

"Jaysus," she muttered, eyes going huge like baskets of fried bar food as she took in my appearance.

"Not quite," I said, taking a long drink. Actually, I drained it, then raised it up to get the bartender's attention. He saw it and nodded, finishing off someone else's drink and hopefully coming to service mine soon. My head drifted slightly, and I realized she'd asked me a question. Out of politeness—and probably because the Scotch was starting to do its fine work—I answered. "I learned how to lift from a friend of mine—one of your people, incidentally—" my head swirled "—who was a…a hell of a thief. He taught me a few things." I looked at my empty glass. "Until his luck ran out."

She was quiet for a moment. "So you did know Breandan."

I looked up at her, scalp tingling. I hated the fact that one of Rose's servants knew that name. But of course they would; they knew everything about me, thanks to her strip-mining my memory.

"I don't want to hear that name come out of your filthy-ass mouth again," I said, looking up at her dangerously. "I know I look bad right now, but…I will rip the skin off of you and leave you bleeding for her to find if you say his name again…you hear me?"

"Fuck you," she said, and almost spit in my face if not for a last minute adjustment to the side. She was fired up now, cheeks rosy red, and the start of tears appearing in the corners of your eyes. "I'll say his name all day long if I want; you didn't own him, Sienna Nealon." There was a real anger there, and it almost made me sit back, but I stayed neutral, still listening, trying to figure out the angle, the game.

Then she hit me with it, and it almost knocked me off my barstool. "Because he was mine," she said, fiery, cheeks red, eyes turning that way, "before you went and took him off to America and got him killed."

16.

Eve Kappler

Stuttgart, Germany
1986

"I hate you all," Eve said, staring at the faces around her with the dismissive lack of giving a care that came so easily to her. It was like a second skin since she'd come here, to this academy where she'd thought she would learn so much about herself, her powers, her—well, everything.

But at seventeen now, all Eve had concluded was that she thoroughly disdained every person here.

Karl laughed at her from a small distance away. "But you seem to enjoy our company so much, Eve!" He was a hideous bastard; older than her by a year and bald already, by choice, like a skinhead. He grew a mustache and beard, as anomalous a look as she could have imagined, it blending together with his milky-white skin to make him look quite the fool. He and his little gang.

"I would rather have a long sit on an electric fence while urinating," she said, leaving them behind as she walked off from whatever class they'd just finished. Physics, perhaps? She couldn't recall; she'd been stewing the entire time.

They were all so juvenile, her contemporaries. Certainly there were a few exceptions, lights in the dark of this place. Jan was one. So was Ava.

Eve smiled to herself. No surprise it was the females. None of the boys that inhabited this place were anything other than fools. She'd seen that much for herself.

She stalked along the concrete path beside the green grasses of early autumn. Winter would be here soon enough, following autumn, whose breath was already in the air. Eve was ready to be done, and was close now. She'd followed this path about as far as she cared to, all the way through the incessant stupidity.

Eve didn't belong here, and she knew it. She didn't feel like she belonged anywhere, though, and that was the probl—

*

"You're boring me," Gerry Harmon said, looking her dead in the eye as he said it. "The others…they certainly take a stab at it every once in a while, but this is the single most boring memory you ever had. It's like some self-indulgent arthouse indie film, some narcissistic reflection of your own soul that no one else gives a damn about."

Eve blushed, staring back at the former President. "You would know narcissism, wouldn't you?" She leaned forward, the fire crackling in front of her. "You'll never be on a dollar bill, will you, Harmon?" He stiffened slightly. "Does that bother you?"

"I'd have been on every piece of currency if I'd succeeded in my plans," Harmon said, brusquely. "Or—actually, no. There wouldn't be any more need for money if I'd succeeded. We would be free from want."

"Also free from will and life," Zack said. "Just tossing that out there."

"Everyone would have had a place in my world," Harmon said, snapping back at the boy. And that was what Zack was to Eve; just a boy, a loyal little dog to follow Sienna Nealon around. Yap yap.

"I have no place in your world," Eve said, certain of nothing else.

Harmon just stared at her. "Of course you would."

Eve blew air out between her lips. "I'm not a joiner, ja? If you'd watched the memory all the way through, you would have seen it for yourself. I am my own person, not some adjunct personality meant to be taken over by the virus of Gerry Harmon or stuck in the depths of Sienna Nealon, some cog in her machine."

"You spun pretty well for her these last few years," Bastian said, adding insult where none was needed.

Eve felt her cheeks flash red. "She provided entertainment. And substance to a life that would be otherwise…unfulfilling." She looked around. "I mean…really take in what we're doing here. Nothing. Three months we've been in Rose's head, and…nothing. All we can feel is the slow, deteriorating passage of days, with no windows to the world outside save for what loverboy here wants to tell us." She pointed at Graham.

Graham stared, dazed, at her. He lacked even the passion to object. "That's true," he said languidly.

"I want out," she said, looking at Harmon. "Your plan was sound, to take us away from this place. I want my own body again. To pursue my own aims again."

Harmon stared at her shrewdly. "Something you have to keep in mind…"

"Is that he's going to betray you." Zack's pronouncement was casual and effortless.

Harmon rolled his eyes. "You keep thinking that." He looked back at Eve. "Once I'm in a new body…unless it's a telepath…my powered days are done."

Eve felt a little stunned in her place. "But…with Sienna you could—"

"Succubi are different," Harmon said. "She took our souls. I can transfer our minds, I think—but I doubt our powers will come along for the ride unless the body, the physiology, is set up like a succubus to accommodate additional metahuman powers. If we transfer to a normal human…we're going to be normal again."

"I was never normal," Eve said, staring him down. "Even before I manifested."

Harmon put up his hands in a kind of seeming surrender. "As you say. But your powers…will be gone, most probably."

Eve didn't have to think about that for more than a moment. "I don't care. I want out. I want to be gone from this place." She dripped loathing, disdain, lashing out and kicking a stick in the fire, sending ashes skyward in an upward rain of embers. "And I never want to have to look at any of your faces ever again."

"So much love," Gavrikov cracked with a weak smile.

"I hate you all," Eve said, sinking into silence again, as did the rest of them. She felt like she meant it—though perhaps not as fervently as she had in the days when she was in school, and surrounded by Karl and the other morons.

17.

"Bullshit," I said, looking at the strawberry blond on the stool next to mine as the bartender set her up with shots. Three of them, in rapid order, plopping them down in front of her one at a time. He'd approached in silence, and with but a word from her—"Me first"—he'd taken her order and forgotten all about me.

Me. My ass sitting on this stool, with a missing eye and an effed-up hand, and the bartender…ignored me, and was totally transfixed on Eilish, who sat like a sullen black hole next to me as the bartender lined up her shots, then stood there, holding the bottle expectantly, waiting for her to—I dunno, kiss him or something. Just standing, waiting.

Eilish lifted the first shot. I'd seen the label; the whiskey was Irish (big surprise), and she took it down in one good gulp. She made a little face, the taste pinching her lips, face pale and yet burning, her cheeks aflame like the rest of us super white people in this cold place, hidden from the sun's rays. "Not bullshit. Truth."

I blinked. "I doubt I even know what that is anymore." I offered my empty glass to the bartender, but he didn't even look at me. He was too busy staring lovingly across the bar, which bore signs of extreme age, at Eilish, who bore signs of extreme not-age.

"I've been trying to catch up with you for months. Years."

She lifted the second shot and downed it, right down the hatch, as I watched her somewhat enviously. She looked straight ahead, right through the bartender, as if he weren't in the path of her heat ray vision. "Gathering my courage, trying to decide if I wanted to meet you or not. Figured I'd wait for you to come back to the UK, figuring sooner or later you'd pass this way—missed you last time in London, then you went and made yourself wanted—"

"You could have come to America," I said, eyeing the bartender again. "If you're really a Siren."

She froze, hand on the third shot. "He told you about me, did he?"

"He told me what his girlfriend was," I said coolly, my sense catching back up with me, breezing past the Scotch. "She died during the war. She was killed by Century—"

"I was pinched by the Metropolitan Police Service," she said, staring sullenly at that last shot. "Taken by them when he and I parted ways for the last time. Arrested by a female officer—" she lifted her shot in salute "—questioned by a female detective, locked up by female prison guards, and didn't get a chance to be alone with a man for about two months to effect my escape, by which time…Breandan was long gone." She looked at me. "Gone with you."

"Yeah," I said, my voice scratchy. My mind was racing. I didn't believe a word of it…but somehow I simultaneously believed every word of it, which was maybe driving me even crazier. It would have been no big deal for Rose to get this information, right? She had nearly unlimited access to my memories, could tap stuff out of my head with greatest ease, including the knowledge that my old friend Breandan had a girlfriend who disappeared in the war with Sovereign and Century, who just happened to be an Irish Siren. Hell, even if she hadn't lifted it from me, surely there were records in the US, maybe in the UK, that she could have tapped in order to set this all up.

It was well within the realm of possibility that Rose was pulling another fast one on me. The girl sitting in front of me didn't even have to be a Siren. She could be a telepath, casting a delusion on me. She could be a legit person, but with a telepath for backup. Or a Rakshasa, again with the illusions. Or an empath, or anything, really, even one of Rose's countless, eponymous plants. The bartender could have been a plant too, to play along, and Eilish might have had zero powers.

There were a million ways to slice this so that Rose could monkey with my head.

And unfortunately, I realized, as I sat there next to Eilish, watching her down the third shot, a little tear streaming down her cheek, her eyes red and the bartender falling all over himself to offer her a hankie…

It was working.

"Listen, Eilish," I said, and she looked around at me again, and shuddered at the sight of my face. "I don't know what you think is going on here—"

"You're in over your head," she said immediately, cradling the empty shot glass.

I froze. "You think so?"

"You're missing an eye and your hand is beat all to shit," she said, "and I'm thinking there's a host of other problems ye got too, but…those are the worst, obviously."

"Obviously."

"I don't much care what your deal is," she said, looking away from me again. "I just want to know…" And here she turned once more, sadness deep in her eyes in a way I didn't think anyone could fake until I met Rose…and she faked me. Her voice came out hushed, but strong. "How did he die?"

"Bravely," I said after only a beat. "Saving lives."

She stared at me for a moment, and another tear ran down her cheek to her chin. She swallowed hard, and said, "Good, I guess. I—we never talked about how we'd want to go out. It seemed…a pretty far-off idea, us being meta and all." She looked hard at the bar. "But things surely did change fast when that Century bunch showed up on the scene." She looked up again. "Did ye know they got our home? Our cloister?"

"Yeah," I said softly. "We heard about it at the time."

"I just hung around London afterward, hoping he'd show

back up. Our flat was—well, torn up, of course—"

Of course it was. I'd been there when the tearing up was done. By a group of assassins seeking out Breandan to kill him, just as they had countless other metahumans during the war.

"—and I was left at loose ends," she said, still holding that shot glass resentfully. The bartender leaned over, holding his whiskey like he was waiting for nothing more than a, "By your leave," from her to pour another. She nodded, and he filled up the two glasses on the bar lickety split. "I know a little about you. Well, everything public, anyway. You know what I mean when I say that, don't you?"

I did a little flushing of my own. Anyone who wanted to take the basic effort of hitting up Wikipedia could have checked out my bio, including some nice suppositions about the loves and losses of my life. There were some actual book versions out there too, annoyingly enough, which I hadn't bothered to read. None were flattering, I was assured. "I know what you mean, yes," I said, figuring she was referring to the big one—Zack.

Oh, I missed the sound of Zack in my head. He would have cut through the spinning, drunky bullshit I was experiencing right now and told me the hard truth about Eilish that I was wavering on.

She was almost certainly a plant for Rose. Because that was everyone I met lately. And if not…she'd end up being dead, another tool for my evil mistress to enforce her inevitable will and abject hopelessness upon me. Honestly, I figured any day now she was going to start kissing me in order to drain me. It felt like it was heading that way, like she was drawing ever closer to some bizarre line of obsession with me that ended…well, nowhere I particularly wanted to go.

Oh, you'll love me before the end, Rose's voice rang in my head, all faux-injured at my thought rejection.

"I doubt it," I mumbled, and looked up to find Eilish frowning at me. "Sorry. Voice in my head."

"Oh?" She looked at me with a cocked eye. "Do you still have those?"

"Why wouldn't I?" I asked, freezing. Was this the slip? The

one that told me Eilish knew more than she should? It sure seemed like it.

"Something strange is going on in Scotland." She cradled her shot glass. "Even I notice that." She nodded at the bartender. "You're the most famous meta on the planet, and you're walking around here like no one knows you." She glanced at me, but only quickly, like she couldn't stand to for very long. "But everybody knows you. You're Sienna Fooking Nealon. So how are you walking around Scotland with everyone ignoring you? And don't tell me it's because of your diet, or that you look like shite. We've all seen you looking worse after your various misadventures. Maybe not the diet part."

"Thanks," I said, having only a vague idea what she meant about the diet part of that.

"Don't mention it," she said. "Also, you're lacking an eye, your hand's a mess, you're bruised like a spoiled fruit and you're mighty casual about it, considering you supposedly have the power to heal instantaneously. That'd be tied to your voices—the souls in your head—wouldn't it?" She looked at me and her eyes shone, keenly. There was none of the dull emptiness of Fannon's, which meant jack shit. She could be a willing servant for all I knew. It's not like Rose didn't have anything to offer.

I have so much to offer, Rose's voice sang out in my skull. I caught a flash of red, full lips and made a sour face, inadvertently, because—seriously, she was either leaning toward that kissing thing or playing on my distaste for it. Not cool.

Eilish was looking at me funny. "Bitter drink on your tongue? You know…from five minutes ago, when you actually drank it?"

"Bitter thoughts on my mind," I said, shaking my head. I'd rather have kissed a wookie, or a really shaggy dog, than Rose. Girl dog, boy dog, didn't matter. Anyone but that hateful cow.

But I love you—

"Shut up!" I said, bopping myself on the side of the head. When I caught Eilish's gaze again, I figured we could get the charade out of the way; she was either on Rose's side or she wasn't. "Yeah, my voices are gone, all save for one. The most annoying, aggravating one I've ever had, sending me visions and witless prattle of a flat-ass ginger all day, every day. It's hell."

Oh, you'll pay for that when next we meet.

"I doubt it. I'm pretty skint, as you UK-vians say." I looked up at Eilish, who was still giving me this look that was crossed between pity and worry. "Pain in my head. Sorry."

"So Breandan did die in the war," she said, staring straight ahead. "I guess I can stop wondering now. It was never very clear, you know? In all the books. Just that he was with you for a while. Some of the government reports, they listed him among the dead, but…" She shook her head. "It never really told me what happened."

"It was quick," I said, somehow torn into playing along, even though I doubted she'd ever laid eyes on Breandan Duffy, even though my stomach gave a sick quiver at going along with this. "He was shot while protecting some of the other metas in a sneak attack by Century. He didn't even have a chance to feel it," I said, and watched another tear streak down her cheek. I really didn't know why I was telling her this, my gut at war with the storm of emotions in my head, the ones she was tugging on.

I'd been betrayed so many times in my life, and Rose…Rose had done the jumbo giant super duper extra best of them all—

That's because I am the best, darling.

She'd twisted me hard, made me—against my instincts, against my paranoia—believe that she was someone who really thought of me as a hero, someone worthy of help and saving and—and all this other crap that I guess I'd started to miss, having been on the run for so long, hated for so long. Rose…Rose had tapped into that loneliness at the feeling of loathing that I bathed in every day I watched the news, and she'd just slipped in past my defenses even as I knew she could have been trouble, ignored the warning signs, and let her sideswipe me like a silent, electric bus doing fifty.

I couldn't do this again.

"It's good to know for sure," Eilish whispered, then tipped back another shot. She took a hard breath, and I knew it had burned.

"You should get out of here," I said, no idea why I was saying it. "Before we're…seen together. Before word gets back to—"

"To whom?" came a dry voice from just behind me. I turned on my barstool, and there waited—

Rose.

Her hair was all fixed up nice, wavy and curled, shining under the dim barlight. Her green eyes were sparkling, and she was dressed to the nines, her push-up bra doing yeoman's work at holding those puppies up and giving me a PTSD flashback from when she'd pressed me against her cleavage earlier in order to burn a memory or two out of me. She looked like she was ready for a night on the town, skirt and leggings and high heels all working to give her a look like she was DTF, and I hoped like hell it was for the sake of somebody else and not for me, because she was so not my type.

She sauntered over and draped an arm over my shoulder. I barely repressed a shudder, and she popped gum right in my freaking ear, which, once upon a time, would have been a killing offense. She looked at me, gave me a long, gross kiss on the cheek, and then hung on me, like one of those assholes at parties that occasionally thought they could just hang on whoever they wanted—until I broke a bone or two to convince them that no, this was not okay behavior.

With Rose…there was not a damned thing I could do.

She studied Eilish with a long look, then looked back at me, grin spreading wide. "So…who's your friend?" And for some reason—maybe because I wasn't entirely convinced Eilish was a liar—my stomach started to sink, heavily, again.

18.

Reed

Richfield, Minnesota

I overflew the city of Richfield, looking for one specific house. When I found it, I paused overhead, the winds keeping me aloft, a gentle push beneath me that immediately diffused off at my sides, keeping me from having to deal with that rushing sound of wind as I lifted my phone to my ear.

It rang, then was picked up. "You're good to go," J.J. said. "Trace scrambler is in place. She'll think you're calling from Western Canada—at least for the two minutes or so it takes her to crack through, so—make it snappy."

"Thanks," I said, and hung up.

Then I dialed another number.

It rang four times, and then a somewhat tired and crabby voice answered. "What do you want, Reed?"

"You know what I want, Cassidy," I said. "I want eyes and ears in Scotland. I want Sienna's enemies denied the same. And…" I smiled. "I kinda want a burger."

"Good luck with the first two," she said, "as for the third, I recommend Fuddrucker's at 494 and France."

"You know you could help me," I said.

"And you know the price," she said, all dull and dead inside, so very transactional these days. "I don't do pro

129

bono."

"I'm perfectly willing to pay you," I said, "and Sienna would be willing to pay you, too. Probably not quite as much as you want, but a pretty damned reasonable rate. Five million, ten million—a good chunk of change."

"Also a fraction of what I make now," she said, patiently explaining it to me like the dullard I was, in her mind.

"There are factors other than money involved here, Cassidy," I said. "Sienna showed you mercy at a time when she didn't have to."

"She also has wrecked my life in every way possible," Cassidy said, like she didn't care about anything anymore. "But I try not to hold a grudge, which means I also don't consider past favors—at least not beyond the one I did for you during that whole LA thing. So...we're square."

"That's your final answer?" I asked. "Sienna's life is in danger, and you will only help us if we pay you an extortionate amount, hundreds of millions of dollars, for your continued time?"

"That'd be the rough shape of things, yes," she said. "I trust I don't have to tell you what happens if you come knocking on my door trying to forcefully convince me otherwise? You do recall what happened last time you tried, right?"

"I know you think we're all idiots compared to you, Cassidy," I said, smiling tightly from above her house, looking down, "but I don't think you really know us at all."

"Oh, I know you," she said. "You're probably dreaming about busting down my door right now, using some physical threat of violence to try and compel me to act." She sounded deadly serious. "I'm just warning you—you come for me, you better be ready for—" She paused. "What was—"

The roof ripped off her house, and the four walls followed. It disintegrated in gusts of wind so powerful that they'd never been seen before in nature.

But me? I wasn't nature.

I was hell's own fury at this point.

And Cassidy was about to bear the brunt of my displeasure.

I ripped her house up by the roots and sent every piece of

it skyward, soaring past me. Entire walls shot by in the darkness, shadowed against the million lights of Minneapolis and the suburbs below. A concrete block foundation wall went zooming by, then a few traps, as I sent them into the atmosphere, disassembling Cassidy's house a component piece at a time, until finally—

Cassidy herself went shooting by, screaming into the wind. I halted her, moved her aside toward me, then sent the rest of her house back down, down to the earth, reassembling it a piece at a time, but…well, not very well. It's not like using the wind at that level of fury is a precise thing. As soon as I was done bringing it down, it immediately collapsed in on itself.

Her eyes squinted tightly shut, Cassidy just sat there, gripped in the winds across from me, sitting like she was in a chair. I blew a good few bursts past her, making sure she wasn't concealing any weapons. She jerked and shivered in her nightgown, and said, "Did you just use the air to cop a feel on me?"

I rolled my eyes. "No. I used the air to make sure you weren't hiding any weapons on your person. You're not my type, Cassidy, and if I had any other way of getting through this problem, I promise I wouldn't be here now, talking to you."

She just oozed with annoyance, breath rasping with the hints of her asthma, dark hair rustling in the night. She looked at me with a rough sense of disgust coupled with resignation. "How did I not see this coming?"

"You assumed I'd play nice," I said, "that at worst, I'd get somewhat violent and come charging in on you. You underestimated the level of my desperation, and the depths I'd sink to." I leaned in closer to her. "Well, Cassidy…I'm desperate. And I'm sunk, because my sister is missing. She's been kidnapped by—"

"Rose Steward. I know," she said, shaking her head like a petulant child, her voice about what you'd expect from a pissed-off six-year-old being forced to sit at the dinner table until they eat their cabbage.

"Then you know I'm assembling a team?"

She curled her lips in disgust. "Yes."

"If you join up, you'll get paid nicely. Not as nicely as you're used to, but you have to understand—you don't just get to work and eat and buzz around like an annoying locust helping third-world dictators maintain their tyrannical grip on power—"

"I also help megacorps raid their competitors," she said, "and people spy on their spouses—whatever, it doesn't matter. If I unlock Scotland for you, you'll let me get back to my life?"

"I would have," I said, "before you made me play 'Tornadoes and Trailer Parks' with your house. Now you're coming with me, because when you've already kidnapped someone, you might as well transport them across state lines or even internationally."

Cassidy blinked. "What? That's dumb. The penalty for transporting across state lines is—"

"I don't really care," I said, and the wind threw her forward, almost into my face so I could look her in the eye in the dark. "The thing you missed in your calculation about what I would do to you is—there is nothing I won't do to save my sister. *Nothing*. Right up to killing you and letting your body drop into the Atlantic so the fishes can enjoy a ten-second meal before you're nothing but bones."

Cassidy drew a deep breath. "So…if I open up Scotland for you…and come with you…"

"And don't betray us to Rose."

She swallowed heavily. "I don't betray you to Rose…"

"And you do everything—EVERY EFFING THING—in your power to help me get Sienna back," I said, staring her down, "I will promise you that I will never knock on your door again if you don't want me to, and I'll even owe you a favor—beyond the payment from Sienna that I promise."

She licked her lips. "And if I don't…I take a sudden dive?"

"The dive won't be sudden," I said, "but I promise the stop at the end will be very abrupt. The same goes for if you betray us. The last thing I do will be to make sure you die in the worst way I can." A small swarm of roofing nails blew past to illustrate my point. "I think bleeding to death is right at the top of the list, but I can also pull off drownings, blunt force decapitations, etcetera…"

She didn't even think about it for a full second. "Okay, deal. Millions from Sienna's offshore accounts, you never ask for my help again unless I permit it, you owe me a favor—and one other thing." She looked like she was in over her head and bluffing, but I listened anyway. "You keep Sienna off my back."

I thought about it for a second. "I can't make that promise and you know it. If you do something bad enough, my word isn't going to bind her."

She made a face, emotions warring through. "Damn." Cassidy looked up. "Okay, deal. Under those conditions. I'll unlock Scotland's electronic network to your people and help you through it." She looked down at the shattered remains of her house beneath her feet. "I really did not see that coming."

"You still don't know shit about people, Cassidy," I said, sweeping us off to the west on the winds, accelerating us to several hundred miles per hour. *And,* I didn't say, *you clearly have no idea the lengths people will go…for love.*

19.

Sienna

My breath was caught in my throat, and it felt like I was choking on it.

Rose stood next to me in the bar, her hand lightly on my shoulder, the promise of force and violence as she stared at Eilish, who stared right back at her. "Who's your friend, Sienna?" she asked again.

"Just some stranger in a bar," I said, turning away from Eilish. "You know how it is. People recognize me."

"Aye, people recognize you," Rose said, still staring at Eilish. "Though I'm a bit surprised. You're a bit out of sorts. Hair's all a mess." She tousled it, then stopped at the barrette up top, and gave it a yank, causing me a mild amount of pain. "Then there's this. A bit ostentatious, isn't it? I mean, pink? Not really your color."

"It's a disguise," I said. "No one could imagine me wearing one like that."

Rose laughed lightly. "Aye, that's true. And the rest of you!" She ran her hands down my shirt. "I mean, you look like absolute hell. This is what happens when you spend all your money on drink."

I looked down at my ensemble. It was dirty, matted with blood, and—well, I hadn't changed it in a week or two due to lack of clothing to change into. I'd pilfered this off someone's clothesline, the unsuspecting bastard. Who hangs out their wash in October? Still, a thick shirt and heavy pants to go with the worn boots I'd purloined when I'd been running from Rose the first time.

And every piece of my ensemble looked like it had been through a war. Lots of holes and tears. "I guess when you're busy getting your ass kicked around Scotland," I said, "fashion falls to the bottom of the worry list."

Rose sniffed me theatrically. "And so does bathing, apparently."

"I did notice that," Eilish said quietly, into her empty shot glass.

"What's your name, love?" Rose asked her, leaning in a little closer, her hand like a claw around my upper arm.

"Eilish," came the answer.

"That's a pretty name," Rose said. "You're from Ireland?"

"Aye," Eilish said. "Me mum's da is from Scotland, though."

"Lots of back and forth here," Rose seemed to agree, looking at her with a kind of veiled suspicion, before turning back to me. "You need to be prettied up, Sienna. This is simply unacceptable."

"Oh, fuck off," I said, ripping my arm out of her grasp. "I'm not your prom date, okay?"

Rose got a wide smile. "You belong to me."

"You gonna drag me back to your cave, man?" I asked her, still waiting on my damned Scotch refill. Dumb hypnotized bartender. It would have been nice to be drunk for this. It always made it hurt less when Rose started to beat me when I was drunk.

Yeah, that's right. My drunkenness was actually a pain mitigation strategy. Not looking so stupid now, am I?

A phone rang in the tension, and Rose said, "Excuse me just a tic," and pulled it up. "Hello?"

I could hear the conversation on the other end of the line, and it chilled me. "Augustus Coleman just showed up in Atlanta, Georgia. We've got him under surveillance at his mother's house."

"That's wonderf—" Rose started to say.

I spun on my barstool and went for her ankles. Invincible

she might have been, but she was hardly immutable to the laws of physics.

I swept her legs before she realized what was happening, and followed her to the floor to land atop her.

She looked mildly surprised as her head thumped against the wood floor. "What do you think you're do—"

I smashed her phone into a million pieces, driving it right out of her hand to shatter against a nearby table leg. I was only going to get one shot at this, and that meant I had to be quick.

With vicious intensity, I drove my elbow into her face, aiming for the tender eye socket. Anywhere else on her would feel like I was driving my bone into a steel door, and probably numb my whole arm for the rest of the night.

I hit, hard, like a runaway train right to her eyeball. I ripped a grunt out of her, an actual admission of pain. Even though I knew this wouldn't last very long, I needed to drag it out every second I could.

Because…keeping her from taking off was Augustus's only chance of escape.

And I was going to buy him every millisecond I could, no matter how much I was going to pay for it later.

"Why is it always the eyes with you?" Rose managed to sputter out as I raised my arm and unfurled my fingers, driving them both into her face again. She blocked them with a slap, smashing every single finger on my good hand and rendering it another shattered mess. I wasn't going to be playing any piano recitals for a day or two, that much was sure. Or after that either, because I didn't know how to play piano.

I went back to the elbow, trying to drive it into her face again, make her recoil, make her jar her brain. It wouldn't do much, especially with Wolfe working behind the scenes, but it was the most susceptible part of her body. If I could hit her hard enough, ram against an object at a few hundred miles per hour, I might maybe be able to turn her skull into a blender and destroy her brain—

"That's enough of that," she said, and hit me with a short punch right to the ribs as I reared up to hit her again. It felt like someone shattered that entire side of my body, broke at least four ribs, and neither gently nor cleanly, either. I could feel bone fragments protruding through the skin and others poking into the meat of my side as I went sailing through the air and came crashing down on a table across the room. It broke my fall, but not softly, and I went over backward to crash on the floor.

I came to a moment later, dazed. The wooden ceiling beams swayed overhead like they were in the middle of an earthquake, about to collapse on me. It took me a few seconds to realize that they weren't actually moving, that I was probably just concussed again. I'd tried to rock Rose's brain into a mush state, but of course she'd turned around and done the same thing to me with very little effort, maybe even by accident.

Her face flared into view above me and I felt the pressure of her weight as she dropped on my stomach, knocking the wind out of me again. She slapped me across the cheek and I opened my mouth to gasp in pain at both those events. Pushing a hand against my face, not very gently, I felt the burn start at my cheek.

A second later, she ripped it clear of my face, and looked behind her. "Eilish, eh? Breandan's girlfriend?" She had a ghastly smile on her.

For my part, I couldn't remember Eilish's name or why she was here until Rose said it. Then it felt like one of those names that was on the tip of your tongue, and suddenly, boom—I knew it again, as natural as if I'd known it all along. I couldn't recall our conversation just now though, but the fact that she was Breandan's girlfriend—that was interesting news, again, that I felt like I'd known at one point, but completely forgotten.

That was the power of a succubus to steal memories.

"Come here, my little Irish dove," Rose said, beckoning her over. "Come here," she said again, voice iron. "I won't hurt you—unless you run. Then I'll flay you alive and listen to your screams as my lullaby." This she said with only a trace of menace. "That's it…right over here."

Eilish popped into my view, which was still somewhat

tunneled by the concussion. She shuffled on tentative feet as Rose reached out for her, beckoned her forward. When Eilish was close enough, Rose grabbed her by the front of her blouse and dragged her down, wrapping an arm around her shoulders and hugging her close, like they were old friends.

As for Eilish…she looked like she'd just been seized by someone she hated, squeezed in a python's grip around her shoulders. She didn't fight back, though.

"You were trying to hide her from me," Rose said, grinning madly. She didn't look any the worse for the wear considering I'd just tried to pop her eyeball like a balloon through overpressure. She was fine as frog's hair, a little madder than she'd been with me when she walked in, but unaffected by my stunt, save for the time it had cost her. Hell, if I was lucky, maybe I'd made her mad enough to forget all about Augustus—

"It didn't work, obviously," Rose said, leaning in, dragging Eilish like a captive along with her. "I know everything about you. Everything. There's no secrets between us, Sienna darling." She brushed my cheek with her fingers. "And pretty soon…there'll be nothing between us at all." She got to her feet, dragging Eilish up with her like she weighed nothing. "I have some business to attend to in Atlanta, it sounds like. Don't think you can distract me from that." She got stone serious, and then released Eilish, snapping her fingers. "Take this one, too."

Fannon stepped into view behind Eilish with a pair of metacuffs, snapping them down on her wrists, pulling them behind her. He wasn't gentle, but Eilish looked like she knew the routine, a sullen veil falling over her face, which was red at the cheeks and ears.

"Don't even think about using your power on my dear Colin here," Rose said, resting a hand casually on his neck and rubbing it. "He's mine, all mine, and your powers won't work on him." She leaned in toward Eilish. "You can try if you'd like, but there's not enough left of him to respond to you. You understand?" She put her face right in Eilish's. "You get me?"

"I get you," Eilish said, turning away.

"You'll try anyway, and that's all fine," Rose said, like iron, "but it won't work. You should learn from this little darling here." She used her toe to give me a nudge to the thigh, and it didn't hurt too much, probably because I was already a crumpled mess of broken human. To Fannon, she said, "Cuff her, too."

And he did, getting right to work on me, rolling me onto my face and putting it into the barroom floor. I could smell the wax and old varnish as Fannon pushed my empty socket into the ground, sending radiating waves of pain through my whole face where Rose had grabbed and throttled my forehead earlier, and across my cheek, too.

That was nothing compared to the ribs, at this point, though. Those were going to be an issue.

"Have one of the girls pretty her up for me, will you, darling?" Rose whispered in my ear, though I was sure Colin was diligently taking mental notes of her commands. "Get her in a nice dress, clean her up, have them do her hair. We've got a special date when I get back from Atlanta, and I want her at her best for the occasion." She nibbled at my ear, then laughed softly. "It's going to be a banner occasion, Sienna my dear, so you best enjoy yourself when I'm gone, because when I get back…"

She leaned in closer, practically kissing me on the ear as she whispered, just for me, like she was singing sweetness into my ear: "When I get back…we're going to take a big step forward, you and me. I'm going to start really taking your will…and pretty soon here…you won't have anything left to fight me with, you won't have that smart mouth to snap off sarcastic comments with…and soon enough, you won't fight anymore…I'm going to take your last drops of will, like I did with Fannon here…

"No more hateful defiance…

"Then we'll be together for as long as you last…no more Sienna Nealon…

"Just you and me…

"…but mostly me…because there won't be hardly any of you left next time…after we're done."

20.

Colin tossed my ass unceremoniously in the back of the van along with Eilish, who didn't make a sound as she hit the rubber floor—and my legs, thankfully, not my ribs—other than a grunt. Fannon slammed the door shut, leaving us in the dark, my face pressed against the stinking, sweaty rubber, which was, unfortunately, a place I was all too familiar with.

"Get off me," I said, trying to push Eilish away. She was draped across my legs, hands cuffed behind her, which did not make for the easiest mobility.

She stirred and rolled over, her weight leaving my legs. "Shite," she muttered under her breath, the Irish accent more pronounced than earlier. "What the hell am I going to do now?"

"Like you've never been cuffed and put in the back of a van before," I said, rolling over onto my back, being very careful with those ribs. Oh, they ached, but they weren't screaming, a feeling I was dedicated to continuing.

"I've nae been put in the back of an empty van before, at least not without being offered candy or something first," she said, slurring slightly. "Especially not going with some Scottish bird and a drunk American."

"I'm not drunk, you're drunk," I said, lifting my legs carefully in the air and then bending my knees. "Miss Seducing-the-bartender-for-shots. I couldn't get a refill if I shook my ass at him."

"Have ye seen yourself lately?" Eilish stirred, sitting up against the wall of the van as the vehicle started with a rumble. "Also, there was nothing sexual about how I got those shots—unlike what's going on between you and that Amy Pond lookalike."

"Ugh," I said, pulling my knees close to my chest and then hugging them, gritting my teeth against the pain as my ribs emitted a large wave of agonizing protest which I ignored. "Her name is Rose. And I assure you, if there's an attraction, it's all one-sided. I don't even think she really feels that way; I think she's just dangerously obsessed in a weird, Single-White-Female kind of way, except she's not stealing my fashion choices or my life—yet."

"Well, I can understand the first part. You're not exactly making Tom Ford proud, are you?"

"Oh, screw you, Irish," I said, finally getting my cuffed hands up underneath my heels. "She ripped the memories of whatever conversation we had out of my head, by the way, so if you told me something important, I don't recall."

She was quiet for a moment. "You know I'm Breandan's girlfriend?"

"Got that by her mentioning it," I said, letting my legs unfold now that I'd managed to get my hands in front of me. It had been no easy thing with that agonizing pain in my ribs.

"Well, you told me how he died, so there's that," she said.

"Did I accuse you of being a plant for her?" I asked.

"No," Eilish said, hackles rising. "I wouldn't work for that See-You-Next-Tuesday if she promised me all the whiskey in Galway."

"A woman after my own heart," I muttered as I unfastened the barrette in my hair.

"Yeah, she seems like she's after your heart and all else," Eilish muttered.

"Well, she's not getting any of it if I can help it," I said, bending the barrette until it snapped, leaving me with the smaller, inside piece of it, two lengths of flat metal about an inch long, bound by a small hinge in the middle.

"What in the hell are you doing?" Eilish asked, listening in the dark and silence, the only other sound the van rattling down the road.

"I don't know how much of our conversation you heard at

the last there," I said, straightening the hinge so that the barrette was now just one long, thin piece of metal bound in the middle by the hinge, "but Rose made me a promise just now—that when she gets back, she's going to turn me into a human vegetable, like the guy up front in the driver's seat." I pointed in the direction of the small, covered-over window to the cab that had only faint traces of illumination bleeding around its edges. "I'm not down for that, so…I'm going to deprive her of that victory."

"How are you going to do that?"

"With great aplomb," I said, shoving my improvised barrette shim into the teeth of the handcuffs. I ratcheted the action, feeding the shim in along the length of metal that girded my wrist until I heard it stop clicking. Then I pulled—

And the handcuff came off, pretty as you please. Or pretty as Rose would have had me. One of those.

"What the—oh," Eilish said, face appearing in the darkness as she peered at me. "The barrette."

"You know about that?" I asked, repeating the trick on the other side to open up the other cuff. It came loose in seconds, and I was left rubbing my wrists gingerly.

"I'm a thief; of course I know how to get out of handcuffs if I'm given the chance," she said, like it was obvious. "Good luck for you your ginger stalker didn't."

"She's not a criminal," I said, then amended, "or at least hasn't had to think like one. She's been in control for so long she just assumes everything is going to go her way—by force."

"Well, that's wonderful," Eilish said, then pivoted, thrusting her hands, still stuck behind her, at me. "Now do me."

I hesitated a second. "Well…how about this, instead—" And I lunged at her.

She cried out as I planted a hand over her lips and pushed her down. I didn't really want a fight right now; my plans for escape and what came after didn't involve another person, but…

I had to know. For sure.

And as a soul-stealing succubus, I *could* know for sure.

She struggled pretty hard, but with her hands stuck behind her, Eilish was easy to physically overpower, even absent the fact I was stronger than her by a lot. Pressing my hand against her face, I tunneled into Eilish's mind and took a quick overview—

There were no signs of Rose's penetration here. One thing I'd gotten familiar with—and that I wondered if Rose had picked up on, given how thoroughly she had Colin and Mr. Blonde whipped—was the feeling it made in someone's mind when Rose started playing Jenga with their intellectual tower. Colin's brain was riddled with holes, massive ones, the biggest being the blocks that control personality.

Those had been pulled out last, but there were other holes from earlier, which had told me, when I'd assaulted him about two months ago…Rose had been working on him for a while.

And not just via her succubus powers up close and personal, skin to skin. She'd dreamwalked to him, messed with his mind, made him crave her to the point where he willingly walked into her arms in York. Happily, even, like he was going to meet a longtime lover so they could consummate their relationship after months of buildup.

Needless to say…it did not work out well for him.

I saw none of those fingerprints in my look around Eilish's mind. Hers was clear, free of dream influence, holes, and…

Brushing past her childhood memories, I saw hundred and hundreds of them that included a scrappy little Irish boy that looked…oh so familiar.

Breandan.

I pulled my hands off her with tears in my eyes, both because of what I'd seen and because of what it meant. I popped the shim into her handcuffs and loosed her, and she moaned as she stirred back out of the pain and daze I'd just inflicted on her.

"I'm sorry," I said as she sat up. I'd already moved to the other side of the van cabin from her, plopping down on the rubber mat.

"What the hell was that for?" she asked, holding her neck where I'd pressed my hand against her. I was sure it had burned.

"I had to make sure you weren't a spy for Rose," I said somberly, trying to figure out what to do next. I'd had a plan for when this moment came…and Eilish had just blown it right to hell.

"I trust now you're satisfied?" She leaned against the van's wall as it thumped over a bump in the road.

"I saw inside your mind," I said, shaking my head. "You're not with her. And…you are who you say you are."

"Glad we're on the same page there," she said, then thumped her head against the metal side of the van. "So…we're out of the cuffs now. What's next in your plan?"

I took a deep breath, and it hurt because of the ribs. "Escape the van, of course." My voice sounded hollow, even to my ears.

"And then?"

"Escape farther."

"Well, that's a bit less clear than the first part of the plan," she said. "There a reason for that?"

I swallowed. "Yeah. It's because that part's improvised."

"But the barrette was planned?" She sounded like she had a headache. "Why would you plan, in the face of an unstoppable enemy who's been kicking your arse since— what, Edinburgh? Your appearance a few months ago, when the city went all to hell? Am I right?" I nodded in the dark, and she must have seen it. "She's batting you around like a cat since then, just dominating you, and your plan is to get out of your handcuffs—and that's it?" She was still slurring her words. "Well, that's helpful. What were you going to do next, sit about wherever she put you? Stand around until she came back and—" Eilish's voice trailed off.

"No," I said softly. "I wasn't going to sit around until she came back for me. I knew…" I swallowed heavily. "She's been getting closer to this for a while. Getting louder about it. It was always coming, but…I've been trying to put it off, hoping…"

"For a way out," Eilish said.

"Yeah," I said, nodding.

"Jaysus," she said, and thumped her head against the side

of the van again. "Of all the days to catch you. I should have let that question go unanswered."

"It would have been better for your health," I agreed.

"You were really going to do it, weren't you?" Eilish asked, and now she sounded...scared.

"How did you know?" I knew she knew. The how was a mystery.

"I thought about it myself when they caught me, and I kept getting blocked by having female guards," she said. "I know what it feels like to get...low. To feel like there's no way out."

"I bet," I said, humoring her. "But...nobody has gone through what Rose is putting me through."

"Are you...are you still going to?" she asked.

"I wish," I said, and choked off the emotion that wanted to follow. "I can't really leave you at her mercy."

"How were you going to do it?" she asked. "I only ask because...it doesn't really look like there's a good way out for either of us."

"Shoelaces," I said, thumping my foot down. "Make a noose and hang from a vent, something like that." I nodded at the small window to the passenger cabin. "Or my clothing would work, in a pinch. It's strong enough. I made sure of that."

"Jaysus," she said again. "Figures I'd catch the world's strongest woman on the worst damned month, worst damned day—worst hour, no less—of her life."

"Yeah..." I said, a little scratchy, feeling it all hit me—that lack of hope, that desperation that had been closing in for so long, that Rose had blanketed me with until I barely dared to think of what I was willing to do to escape it—

To escape her.

"And if you hadn't shown up, trapping us both," I said, finishing my thought, my voice dead, hollow, broken, "it would have been the last month...the last day...and the last hour...of my life."

21.

Wolfe

Atlanta, Georgia

Rose broke down the door with a shattering kick, sending it flying off its hinges in the manner that Sienna had adopted so many times. "Honey, I'm home," she said, announcing herself with the most peculiar—somewhat shitty—American accent, as though she was newly arrived from some fifties TV sitcom.

Wolfe watched through the windows of her mind, seeing through her eyes, feeling the air on her skin as she strolled in, looking for her target. "Where am I looking, Wolfe?" she asked aloud, voice echoing down the entry hall.

Searching his memory of his travels with Sienna to this place, Wolfe said, "Bedrooms ahead down the hall. Family room and kitchen to the right."

"Hmm," Rose said, sticking her head through the open archway into the family room. "Looks like nobody's in here. Where do you reckon he stashed his mam?"

"You've had her under surveillance for months, haven't you?" Mario asked, sharing the space behind Rose's eyes with Wolfe. Wolfe looked at him sidelong; Mario wore a small, confident smile, watching the scene unfold with the certainty that it would go their way. "Surely she could not have escaped!"

Wolfe was less certain. But he kept this to himself, because in the face of Mario's endless enthusiasm…Wolfe had nothing but the desire to taste his brains and see if they lacked as much in flavor as they did in wit.

"Hellooooo!" Rose called as she strode down the hallway and kicked open one of the bedrooms. It was filled with geekery, posters of engineering schematics of electronic devices, one of a blue telephone booth, and enough components of computers that Wolfe felt a little disgusted just seeing them all in one place.

"Don't be such a technophobe, Wolfe," Rose said. "There's nothing to fear here."

"I'm not afraid," Wolfe growled. "I just don't like their little toys."

"Welcome to the twenty-first century," Mario said, chuckling at him. Oh, but his meat would be sweet to peel from the bones.

Wolfe just kept his counsel to himself. An argument might upset Rose, and right now she needed to be focused to catch Augustus.

"Augustus lad," Rose said, loud, taunting, "come out, come out wherever you are!" She waited in the silence of the hallway. "I won't hurt you…yet." She giggled.

Wolfe waited too. He'd dealt with Augustus through Sienna for years. The earth-mover had become dangerous as he'd grown, especially once he'd gotten the serum from Harmon that had boosted his powers. Before, he could throw boulders and make little rock statues.

Now he could move tectonic plates if pressed hard enough. Not the sort of thing Wolfe would have walked into feeling invincible, but then, he was never an Achilles.

"This is going to be marvelous," Mario said, just oozing that suck-up feeling.

"Stick to your job and it will be," Wolfe growled. He could just see Mario failing, Rose being injured beyond easy repair. Which was exactly what had happened countless times that Sienna had walked stupidly, arrogantly into danger.

The ground exploded, hardly a surprise. "Oh!" Rose cried, clearly caught by it. Pebbles of aggregate spanged off her legs and tore through her ensemble, prompting her to giggle as she sprang forward down the hall. "You're a feisty one, Augustus! I'm going to make you pay for that!" She laughed, gleeful.

Wolfe felt the thudding movement of her sprint down the hall, springing like a tigress into action. "Get him! Get him!" Mario crowed, as though riding the shoulder of a giant and egging her on.

"Don't distract her," Wolfe said, growling, "and pay attention to your—"

A blast of lightning arced at them, catching them right out of the blind side and running wildly over Rose's skin. She let out a gasp of surprise, and suddenly someone else was there with them, a pale shadow of a person that Wolfe saw for only a second.

Then Rose let out another laugh and said, "You won't get me that easi—"

The stone smashed into her from behind and Wolfe heard the crack of Rose's skull. Mario gasped, his eyes wide, and Rose hit the ground.

"Idiot!" Wolfe said, lashing out at him, gently, smacking his shoulder as he tried to assess the damage. "You just failed her!"

It had been no small hit. Rose's face was planted in the carpet, her cognition slowed by the damage she'd just taken. There was a skull fracture, Wolfe could feel it by touching the silken inputs flowing in from Rose's mind at large. He could feel the sudden slowing of his own thoughts, though considerably less than they might have been had it been his skull that had been fractured like this.

He summoned up his power, trying to concentrate on the area before him. The back of Rose's skull was caved in, brains crushed and mushed, and more was coming. "Make her invincible again!" he shouted at Mario, who nodded, a little stiffly, as Wolfe closed his eyes to concentrate on fixing the problem.

One thousand one.

Her body was being pelted endlessly by small stones. Now a large one—

One thousand two.

They were bouncing off her skin, raining from it like matters of no consequence.

One thousand three.

"Wolfe…" she moaned, stirring back to herself.

One thousand four.

"Working on it," Wolfe said.

One thousand five.

The skin stitched itself back together, bone unfolded from where it had crumpled, and within the next few seconds, Rose had floated back to her feet.

"Thank you, darling Wolfe," Rose said, cracking her neck as she realigned it, rocks raining off of her in a fury of an earthen storm.

"Go, go, go," Wolfe said, and she was off, springing forward after her prey, the perfect huntress.

"I don't know what happened there," Mario said, hands shaking as he sat before Wolfe, his face warm red like blood lingered just below the surface, waiting to be let.

"You got distracted by lightning," Wolfe said, and batted Mario across the back of the head, prompting him to scream in surprise and pain. "And you failed." Wolfe drew closer, pushing his face into Mario's. Mario did not blink, but he did try and withdraw, and Wolfe reached up and caught him by the chin. No escape.

"I…I…" Mario said.

"Focus," Wolfe growled, low. "This woman is the greatest huntress on the planet, and the strongest metahuman. You serve her now, and if you fail her…I will spend the last moments of your existence as a disembodied soul snacking on whatever remains of you that can feel pain." He leaned in, breathing right in Mario's ear. "You can feel pain…and you will feel pain, more of it than you would have thought possible…so…don't…fail."

He pulled back, and Mario nodded furiously. "Okay, okay," Mario said.

Wolfe growled and spun away. He'd dealt with these sorts of idiots before, in Sienna's head. That was all he dealt with in Sienna's head, actually. Losing six and picking up one didn't seem like such a terrible trade. Just another way in which his present situation was infinitely superior to the previous.

"And," Wolfe muttered to himself, "I have the satisfaction of knowing that the bitch who killed me is about to be flayed while I get a front row seat." He forced a smile as Rose pursued Augustus into the bedroom, and found them both—Augustus and Taneshia, holding on to each other, standing before the bed, the entire floor ripped up and bare ground waiting for them.

"Don't be hasty," Rose said, looking at the earth beneath Augustus's feet. "If you come with me now, I can promise you a nice, clean—only mildly torturous death. If you make me dig you out of the earth…" She let the threat hang.

"Oh, that's a compelling offer," Augustus said. "Painful death, or slightly more painful death." He made a show of choosing, his hand wrapped around Taneshia's waist as they stood there, just a few feet from Rose's tender grasp. If she reached out now, she might catch them before they could flee, but…the earth beneath his feet suggested he had an easy escape route—dive into the ground and roll through it quicker than Rose, with her unboosted earth powers, could pursue.

"I'm generous that way," she said, buying time. Wolfe could see what she was doing, as the shadow of another power appeared in her mind. This one was some sort of laser, an energy projection ability that would hurt Augustus badly enough that he'd be hampered, impaired, in using his powers.

And making his escape. Giving Rose time to…well, crush him.

As she did all her enemies.

"Hey, Rose?" Augustus asked, staring at her sincerely. "How about we make a different deal, you and me?" Taneshia turned her head to look at Augustus like he'd gone crazy, but he just smiled at her. "It's okay, baby. How about…you give back Sienna…and get your ass off the continent of North America forevermore, and we won't come to Scotland, take away all your toys, and help Sienna murder your sorry ass?"

Rose just stared at him for a moment, then broke out laughing. "Oh, Augustus...you sweet child. Your poor Sienna...there's not enough left of her to do me harm," she said, though in her mind Wolfe could read the truth she left unspoken, *Or at least there won't be after the next time I see her.*

Augustus's face got pinched, tight, and he just shook his head. "I don't think I believe you."

"Believe what you want," she said, "but you look at your man Fannon, you'll see the truth...I can own whoever I touch." She wiggled her fingers. "I can make things easy on you..." She clenched her fist. "But it seems like you don't enjoy easy."

"I prefer a girl who's not easy, no," Augustus said, squeezing Taneshia tight to him. "Also, if I was going to go for a white girl, I'd pick a less psychotic one who's got, like, a bodacious ass, not one that looks like it got hammered by a meat tenderizer for a few years. Blonde, maybe. Good stems—"

"Okay, yeah, that's about enough deep description, my dear," Taneshia said.

"One you'd never see coming," Augustus finished, and suddenly, Wolfe realized—

"KAT!" he shouted, but the vines were already springing out of the rich earth and snaking their way around Rose's ankles.

The slab beneath them burst in another shower of rocks and concrete, and pieces of root followed, wrapping around Rose's chest, her arms, hauling her down, fighting against her attempt to fly away, to rip loose.

"WOLFE!" Rose screamed in her head, her mouth covered over by a thick root that had sprung from—well, who knew where. Some neighboring tree, presumably.

"I can't cut you out," Wolfe said, trying to impart his calm to her. "Use fire."

"Fire," Rose said, and another shadow of a figure appeared before them for just a moment as the world turned hot around them, and when the flames died down...

The earth where Augustus had stood was covered over

with rock like a crusted-over volcano, the entry sealed. Rose stuck out a hand, and another shadowy figure appeared for a moment, as she tried to move it—

But nothing happened. She lifted a hand again, trying to—

It failed.

She stood in silence there, for a moment, Mario standing with her, Wolfe a little ways back, watching the whole scene unfold as though projected onto a massive screen before them. She breathed, shoulders rising and falling, then slowly turned around, lost in thought.

"I need more infrastructure in America," she said, "I can see that now. I need metahumans. Politicians. Agency heads. I need to spread out my tendrils of control through this place if I'm going to close the net on these lot."

Mario nodded along sycophantically, saying, "Yes, yes. Of course."

"I should have done this months ago," she said, still lost in her own thoughts, "instead of trying to branch out in the UK. What need have I of influence in London when these little sacrificial lambs are running around in America?" She stirred out of her reverie. "Yes…yes, this is the next thing. I wanted to keep Sienna dear whole until I could sweep up these lot and rip them apart in front of her, but…they're a lot more prepared than I thought they'd be. Not nearly strong enough to do anything but ambush and run, but in a country of this size…" She looked right at Wolfe. "Thank you, Wolfe, my dear. That would have turned out much worse if you hadn't taken up the helm at a critical moment. I'll reward you richly for this."

Wolfe felt a small tingle of pride—and something else, warmer, more passionate, stirring in him as Rose reached out and brushed his cheek, a flush of emotion and pleasure rolling through him from the face on down. She was right there next to him now, smiling at him, looking him in the eye, and Mario…was gone.

"We have a long flight home," she whispered in his ear, fingers doing just the opposite to him as they did to any living soul she came in contact with in the real world. The screen of her outside world faded away, and Wolfe was left with her, alone, in a kind of pleasant darkness, nothing but the pretty redhead and her smile. "How would you like to spend it with me?"

22.

Sienna

I heard Fannon's phone ring from the back of the van, and it made me wonder two things—one, how much of our conversation could he actually hear and understand?

And two, why was Rose's ringtone the Johnny Cash version of "Personal Jesus?"

No, scratch that second one. I understood that one within seconds.

He talked in a low mumble, nothing easily understandable, but I could hear her aggravating tones on the other end of the call, and I knew from the time elapsed that she probably hadn't gotten past the coast of the UK yet, on her jaunt to Atlanta to deal with Augustus. Probably making one last call to be sure he understood all that was expected of him while she was out of contact for a while crossing the Atlantic. He agreed quietly with whatever she told him, which was more than I'd been able to get out of him since York.

"What do we do?" Eilish asked me, meta-low.

There was only one option now. "Overpower him when he opens up the van, beat his ass, and escape, quickly."

"Simple," she said, mulling it over like she was pronouncing judgment on a fine wine. "Straightforward. I like it."

"Good," I said, "because he's super fast and I'm probably going to need your help to subdue him."

She raised her eyebrows to that. "My help?"

We waited until the van stopped, until Colin put it in park, and got out, footsteps a strange, crunching noise as he circled around to us—we handcuffed ladies he'd left in the back.

Boy, was he going to be surprised when he opened the doors...I dearly hoped.

He pulled open the door and was cast in shadow, lamp light from the building behind him rushing in. I saw him in silhouette and lunged for him, Eilish following just a second behind me. We'd both been perched right at the edge of the van, and when Fannon opened that door, we were already moving.

I hit him in the midsection and drove the air out of him, following with a punch to the face that I hoped would stun him. He gasped for air as I took him off his feet, driving him sideways. Eilish followed a moment behind, smacking him with an elbow as she came out just on the other side, to his left as I took up his right.

The trick to beating a speedster was restraining him. Easier said than done since they could typically move faster than even a meta eye could easily detect. But we'd caught him flatfooted, partially brain-dead from Rose's efforts, and I suspected Colin's utility as a zombie was much reduced. As I swept him off his feet, I realized I was right, lifting him by the midsection off the ground and holding him horizontal until Eilish joined me, grabbing his left foot and arm and breaking them both as she treated him a little roughly.

"Keep him off the ground!" I shouted as I dragged him forward, Eilish taking up my slack on that side of his body. I wrapped my own arm around one leg and then broke his right arm at the elbow. He swung it at me and it flopped freely, probably causing him an inordinate amount of pain which, in his brain-dead state, he seemed not to notice. He was swinging at Eilish too, without any effect, the occasional blow from his broken limbs doing little more than drawing a cringe from her.

We pulled him over to the side of the van as I took in our surroundings. We were parked behind a warehouse, probably the same place Rose kept using as her base to torment me. There were no houses in sight, no suburbs, no cities; just flat, dark ground that I couldn't see very well because the moon was tucked behind a thick layer of clouds.

Once we'd gotten him out of sight of any doors, we paused. I'd half-expected him to shout, to cry out, to do anything to draw attention to himself, but he just kept thrashing, pointlessly, the only effect on us a steady, lurching drag back toward the side of the van. We were still a good few feet away though, and it wasn't like reaching it was going to give him a magical ability to escape our grip, so as he bucked, we kept stepping that way.

"Hold him a sec while I drop into his brain," I said, grabbing his exposed forearm where his thrashing had rolled the sleeve up. He thumped my fingers as I tried to catch him, and it hurt, but I managed to grip on nonetheless. A few seconds—and flimsy escape attempts later—

I was in his mind.

There was not a lot of the substance of Colin Fannon left inside there. I was expecting—well, anything, really, and what I got was almost nothing. His memories? Gone. Emotions? Mostly gone, because every one of them he'd felt prior to Rose ripping the pieces out of his head were all sucked away.

The only thing left of Colin was this interesting thread of desire rooted around Rose's promises to him. I could see how she'd turned him, touched him, used her skin as a weapon and torture tool that somehow—somewhere in the process of draining him—had become something Colin…actually enjoyed. Like the pain released endorphins, some torturous version of the runner's high that people into bondage reported.

Personally, I'd had the hell beaten out of me quite a bit and never felt anything but pain, but…Colin had found something in Rose's tortures that had captured the lone spark of desire she'd left him with.

"How's it going in there?" Eilish's voice came to me as I started to withdraw from that slow-mo, hazy thing that happened whenever I leapt into someone's mind.

"This guy is a mess," I said, coming back to myself in the cold parking lot in Scotland, skin chilled, arms hurting from where Colin was trying to super-speed writhe out of my grasp. He'd jerked us another foot or two toward the van, but that was it. Now he was about a foot away from the side panel, for all the good it would do him.

"He's a fighter, this one," Eilish said as Colin jerked violently once more, dragging us another step closer to the van.

"Let's get him away from this," I said, not wanting to see what he'd do when he got in range of the panel. We were close now, his head brushing it.

"No," Colin said, in a whisper, and violently bucked again, jerking us both off balance with the power of his spasm. I stumbled a step closer to the van and Eilish followed, but neither of us lost our footing.

"Colin, this isn't going to work," I said, trying to steady him. He paused, like he was listening. "I'm not going to let you—"

He looked right at me, dead eyes on mine, and I felt a shuddering chill unrelated to the cool night. "For her," he said.

Before I could react, he raised his head up and threw it back as fast as he could. For most people, that would be pretty quick. For a meta, murderously fast and hard.

For a speedster, though...

Colin's head hit the side of the van at several hundred miles per hour, and his head simply exploded. Blood, bone and brains dashed out everywhere like someone had popped a balloon filled to the max with gore. Eilish and I both dove away at the last second, letting loose of him and dodging most of the splatter.

I rolled to my feet through long practice, coming up ready to fight, this shadow of my old habit coming back to me now. I looked at what remained of Colin; it was like he ended just above the ears, simply ceased to be above that line. He twitched once, then twice, glassy eyes staring in different directions.

"Jaysus!" Eilish said, getting to her feet and hot-footing

because of the splatter on the cuffs of her jeans. "Who does that? Really!"

I just stared at the remains of Colin Fannon. We hadn't been close, but I'd known him, and he was the least of the people I could have lost if Rose had managed to snare someone else, someone closer to me the way she'd gotten him. "Someone who's been brainwashed by the most dangerous meta on earth," I said, finally giving voice to a hard truth.

Rose really was the most dangerous metahuman on the planet. Which was a shame, because...

I remembered when the most dangerous meta on earth had been me.

23.

"Where are we headed?" Eilish asked once we were in motion, driving along the Scottish highway, away from the warehouse and the gross remains of poor Colin Fannon, who'd died for not a damned thing.

Eilish was at the wheel, steering the old van, because I figured assaulting the warehouse was a terrible idea. Mr. Blonde could have been lingering inside, and all I needed right now was to get bushwhacked by him when I was still buzzing and healing. I didn't even have my eye back yet, and my hands, while painfully functional, were not exactly tip-top.

"The biggest nearby city," I said.

"Scotland's not that big," she said. "Every city's probably only a few hours away."

"I don't want to go to Edinburgh," I said. That place had left a bitter taste in my mouth. Like the blood from the ass kickings and betrayal Rose had laid on me there.

"Glasgow or Inverness, then," Eilish said. "I suspect given that we didn't travel that far, Glasgow's going to be closer." She was white-knuckling the steering wheel. "You're picking a city because—"

"Easier to hide among people," I said. Which was true, but...

There was the little problem of Rose likely having some kind of lock on the camera systems in Scotland. With that tended to come access to facial recognition software, and

159

then the ability to come thundering down on us like pinpoint artillery fire.

But...if I could hide my face, trying to blend in among the people of Glasgow was probably a solid move. Because there were a lot more of them than in any country town.

"Ah, here we go," she said, the van's lights illuminating a road sign. It was written in some kind of language I'd never seen.

"What did it say?" I asked.

"It's Gaelic," she said. "We're on the right path; that's the long and short of it."

"You read Gaelic?" I asked.

Eilish shrugged. "Some. Enough to get by."

I leaned my head against the headrest, which was desperately uncomfortable at best. Also, I was sitting in the wrong side of the car to be a passenger. THE WRONG SIDE. Always, in this country. But at least this van had enough leg room I didn't feel like I was riding in a portable trash compactor.

"Do you have a plan now?" Eilish asked, pretty tentative.

I took a breath. "Well...get the hell away from Rose and her minions is the starting point, so...yeah. That comprises a plan, I suppose."

"That's more an objective," Eilish said a little weakly.

"It's what I've got," I said, shrugging as best I could, y'know, as limp as a cloth in the seat.

I didn't even realize I'd drifted off until Eilish was shaking me awake. I looked around, darkness still surrounding us on all sides, and she said, in a hushed whisper, "We're in Glasgow."

"Great," I said, looking out the window onto a street that wouldn't have scored any points for style. "Why are we here?"

"Because you said you wanted to go to Glasgow!"

"I meant on this street," I said. There was a massage parlor behind a dirty window, but of course it was closed because it must have been the middle of the night. Down the road I could see a towering apartment block, and on either side we were surrounded by decaying three- and four-story buildings of what I considered the standard European variety.

"About that," Eilish said, suddenly going for nonchalant. "Turns out that I forgot to fill up last time I passed the petrol station. Also, I might not have a credit card, and there were no station attendants to pay, so…" She just shrugged.

It took me a second to detangle what she'd said there. "You mean you don't have any money and you always use your powers to get men to pay for things."

"When you put it like that, it sounds worse than it is," she said, shrugging once more. "I mean, I also usually ask the men for their wallets too, being as you can't every time count on running across a man at a checkout lane, but I'm a bit skint now, yes. Coming over from Ireland drained my funds. There were only lady ticket sellers—imagine that."

"As you may imagine," I said, pulling out the cash I'd pickpocketed the night before, "I could have helped, had you woken me at a gas station. As it stands…" I thudded my head against the van window and looked out. The street was pretty well abandoned. "We needed to get rid of the van anyway. Now we just need to make sure we get way the hell away from it ASAP."

"How are you going to hide your face from the cameras?" Eilish asked.

"I didn't know we were in the city already or I'd have found a way before we got close," I said, a little crossly considering she'd driven me exactly where I'd asked. "I'll just pull my shirt up to obscure the bottom of my face for now, and look for a scarf or something." I pulled it up to the bridge of my nose, then tried to bind my hair back. Without a hairpin or something similar, I failed. "Do you have a—" She handed me a rubber binder wordlessly. "Thanks," I said, and made a quick bun. It wasn't pretty, but it also wasn't the sort of thing I normally wore, so for disguise purposes, it plus the shirt weren't terrible—for the cameras.

I'd look like a real weirdo to anyone we passed, though. Lucky it was the middle of the damned night.

"Okay," I said, opening the door, looking like I was set for urban siege, or maybe just weathering a really bad burst of flatulence by somebody else, "now…where do we go?"

Eilish shut her door and circled around to join me on the sidewalk. "Hell if I know. First time in Scotland, see?"

"How did you find me, anyway?" I asked.

"You weren't exactly hard to track down," she said, looking at me almost pityingly. "Seems you weren't hiding your whereabouts."

That was true. Why would I? Rose was keeping the US government off of me, and I couldn't seem to shake her, so… Though the difficulty of keeping a roof over my head might have been part of it, too. When you're sleeping in the great outdoors, a lot more people are likely to notice you coming and going because you look…well, peculiar, I guess. Scornworthy? Pitiable? Something.

"Town's back that way," Eilish said, throwing a thumb behind us. "I did notice as we were driving through."

"Okay, this way we go," I said, and started hiking back the way we'd come. Casting a look behind me, I saw a sign declaring that the "GLASGOW NECROPOLIS" and some other landmarks lay the way we'd been going.

Eilish fell into step beside me, and we settled into a companionable silence. "You know," she said after a few steps, misty breath steaming out of her mouth, "people see you with that shirt up, they might just think you're hiding your face from the cold."

"I doubt it," I said. This wasn't cold. Scots wouldn't think this was cold, because this Minnesotan didn't think it was anything to write home about. This was pitiful late summer weather where I came from, and I suspected the Scots were probably of the same opinion.

Meanwhile, Eilish had her hands thrust into her pockets and raised the front of her shirt up like me, breath still steaming out of it like she was a turtle and someone had poured scalding water in her shirt shell. "Brr," she said. When she caught me looking, disdain in my eyes, she said, "What? London acclimated me to a little warmer standard, all right?"

I shuffled along beside darkened, and seemingly abandoned, buildings. There didn't seem to be much in the first floor of these places, like the tenants had vacated.

Maybe the upstairs had some things going on in them, but it was hard to tell from down here, looking up.

We passed a sign that told me I was on George Street, for whatever that was worth; unless I got my hands on a touristy map, probably nothing. A thought occurred: "Do you have a cell phone?" I asked Eilish.

"Sure," she said, handing it to me. "You need to make a ca—?"

I smashed it into a million pieces on the street, and her eyes widened. "Sorry," I said. "They could be tracking us by that."

"But all my numbers—oh, who am I kidding?" She just shrugged. "It was stolen anyway."

I cocked an eyebrow at her. "Do you have anything that's not stolen?"

She got pretty clouded around the eyes right then, and shrugged off my inquiry. "Doesn't matter."

I took that to be a hearty yes, but in evasive body language talk. Deciding not to press, instead I headed forward again, my face still buried inside my shirt. Which smelled. Oof. Eilish fell in beside me once more, and we lapsed into another silence.

The night air was chilling my skin, and we were making progress toward…uh…well, into the city. I still had no idea where we were going, but dammit, we were making good time.

We passed into a city square beside a big government building. It was hard not to know it was a government building just by the sheer design of the thing. It practically cried out, "I am for handling municipal business and mountains of paperwork and red tape!" I mean, it didn't, because buildings don't make those kinds of noises, preferring to limit their sounds to creaking and groaning from their supports, but…it was plainly a government building.

It faced out onto a pretty ambitious square. We were skirting the edge, following George Street, because I saw park benches, and where there were park benches, there would almost certainly be vagrants sleeping. Nothing against them, but I was trying to be antisocial at the moment, and stopping to chew the fat with someone sleeping on a bench meant I'd be leaving a witness behind. Or a corpse. Probably the former, because I wasn't really down with killing innocent people. And the press would probably figure out a way to turn that into some sort of ten-thousand-word indictment of how Sienna Nealon hates the poor.

"I'm becoming concerned about the lack of a plan," Eilish piped up when we'd made it through the far side of the square. "We're just sort of…walking."

"Yes," I said, swaying my arms as I walked along, just trying to keep my internal heat high so I didn't get cold. Okay, so it wasn't cold, but it was chilly.

"And where are we walking?"

"I don't know. Maybe we'll pull a Proclaimers and go five hundred miles or so."

"Hah," she said without mirth. "Because they're from Scotland, right?"

I frowned. "The Proclaimers are from Scotland?" With a shrug, I said, "I did not know that."

"But seriously," Eilish said, "where do we go?"

"Well, I'd say we need to look for shelter, but you're the only person in this town I trust."

"Oh," she said, then puffed up a degree. "Well, that's rather flattering—"

"It's because I browsed through your mind and made sure you weren't betraying me."

She deflated a tick. "Oh. That's less flattering."

"We could try and get a hotel room," I said, looking around. It wasn't exactly a booming commercial strip through here; more of the same when it came to apartment buildings and shops, it seemed like, with the odd parking garage thrown in. "You charm the desk clerk, I wipe his memory after?"

"Sounds like a winner," she said, glancing around nervously. "So long as our faces don't betray us to the cameras, because I think every hotel has one behind the desk nowadays."

That let a little of the air of enthusiasm out of my plan. "Welp…we could try and barge into a private home, I guess?"

There was a church up ahead right in the middle of the street, the avenue bending around it in either direction. We walked in silence and followed the road around it, and when we came around the back, it opened back up to George Street, as though the church hadn't obstructed it, and also a wider, fairly massive pedestrian avenue joined it here as the cross street.

"Huh," I said, looking down the pedestrian street. It seemed to be closed off to vehicle traffic, which…could have been good or bad. I wasn't sure which just yet. I saw a lot of high end shops; you could tell because they had fancy signage and lighting, whereas a mom and pop Greek restaurant would stick with a painted window and something simple. These were brand name stores, but I didn't see any obvious hotels.

"Looks like we found the shopping," Eilish said, stamping her feet and still steaming out hot breath from beneath her collar. "Not going to do us much good at this hour though, is it?"

I was so tired. I was surprised that the limited naps I'd taken the last two nights hadn't cut short my ability to think at all. Actually, scratch that; it probably had, because normally I would have had a plan by now. Though, in my defense, being disempowered and having my ass whooped for three months was new ground for me. Even Mom hadn't been quite this cruel, and she'd been pretty bad.

My eyelids drooped, and the cold wasn't doing much to prop them back up. I looked left, then right. The pedestrian road seemed to be called Buchanan Street. Though I doubted it was named after the US President, that was the association that came to mind.

I looked down at all those retail shops, staring at the few of them that still had lit signs at this hour. "What time is it?" I wondered.

"I don't know; someone broke my phone," Eilish said a little crossly. In her passive aggressive mode, she reminded me a lot of Breandan, who I'd also once been on the run in a UK city with.

"Then the answer to that question is, 'Time for you to get a watch,'" I said, and favored her with an idiotic, punch drunk smile.

She made a face. "Could you…close that eyelid? It's a bit…" She shuddered.

"Rose catches us, seeing my empty socket is going to be the least of your problems."

"Oh, it's not empty anymore," she said. "Empty, it'd just be dark in this light. You're growing an eyeball in there, and it looks gack-worthy, let me tell you."

"Lovely," I said, and started to walk down Buchanan. Something stopped me.

Tires squealed faintly in the distance, and my entire back stiffened like every muscle contracted at once. The sound came from somewhere across the city.

It was followed by another set of squealing tires.

And another.

Then another.

"Shit," I said under my breath, releasing a cloud of fog. "I hear trouble."

"I heard it too," Eilish said, and she, too, was stiff next to me. "What…what do you think it is?"

I swallowed, but it didn't get rid of the lump of fear that was lodged in my throat. "I think…it's some servant of Rose, either Police Scotland or metas under her control…" The sound came again, closer this time. "And I think they're coming for us."

24.

Bjorn hated that Rose bitch. Hated her with everything in him. If her head had rolled across the ground toward him, he would have kicked it from Norway to Russia without even worrying where it landed…

*

"You're a very useless person, aren't you?" Harmon asked.

"Shut your mouth, mind gamer," Bjorn said. "I am the son of Odin—"

"Hasn't he been dead for several hundred years? Because if so, you should stop treading on him at some point." Harmon's eyes gleamed with irritation, and he spat out his reply with over-the-top frustration.

Bjorn shut his mouth. Not because he didn't have anything else to say, but because he was tired of dealing with these people. He lapsed into silence and stared at the fire. He may have hated Harmon, but Harmon was hardly the source of his problems at his point.

It was that bitch, Rose.

"If I get a chance to put a dagger in her head," Bjorn said, glaring, as the others just sat around the fire, useless, staring, "I will do so—over and over again, you may be assured."

He would have gladly gone back to the last one—Sienna—

167

if he could. At least there, he didn't hate his host. Occasionally dislike, but not hate.

Not anymore.

Not now that he had met Rose.

Gods, but he hated her...

25.

Sienna

The squealing tires were a concern, less for the disquieting noise itself tearing through the Glasgow night and more for what it heralded. I couldn't tell if they were headed in our direction or just doing a general sweep of the city—

And I didn't want to find out it was the former as they rode up on me, either.

"Should we—should we run?" Eilish asked, frozen at my side.

"We should definitely run for the shadows," I said, and sprinted for a nearby alleyway.

The cold choked my nasal passages, creeping in like I'd taken a good huff of frozen air. Which I sorta had when I breathed. It prickled along my skin, finding the gaping holes in my baggy clothing and crawling up my flesh like icy spiders. My lungs hurt, though not as bad as if it had been below freezing, and I pelted along, Eilish just behind me, and dove into an alley off Buchanan St.

She was right behind me, dodging in just after. The squealing tires were getting closer.

"You think they know where we are?" she asked.

I looked across the street and saw there a dome camera hanging off the side of the building. I was sure we'd passed countless of them before now, probably without paying them any attention. "Probably," I said tightly. This was my fear of being in Glasgow, that even with my shirt up over the bottom of my face, they'd still figure out where I was.

"What do we do?" she asked.

I stuck my head out of the alleyway. Damn, I needed a map. I needed some idea of where I was going. Some place to hide from the cameras. I needed a bazooka and Rose to turn her back and drop her guard long enough for me to plant a round right up her ass.

"Well," I said, "we could wait right here in full view of the cameras, or else—" I turned, and found the alley just…ended. It backed up to another building, and there was no way out. "Shit. We run down Buchanan Street and find a more viable place to hide or fight, that's what we do."

"Ooooookay," Eilish said, and we bolted back out onto the street, heading downhill on a long slope. I wondered if the river this town was built on—I vaguely recalled it being the Clyde—was in this direction. It hardly seemed likely it'd be uphill from here.

We passed luxury shops, fancy places that would have kicked me out if I'd wandered in right now as I was presently dressed. I pulled my hand out—the one Rose had busted all to hell—well, the first one she'd busted all to hell—and found that my bones were at least back inside the skin, which was a good sign for healing, of course. It still ached, but it wasn't totally useless. It'd probably splinter some freshly healed bones (and some still-healing ones) the first time I threw a punch with it, but it wasn't completely useless. I checked the other; it wasn't in great order, but we'd get through if a fight came. I mean, I'd managed to subdue Colin with them, at least.

That eye, though…it wasn't seeing anything, which left me with a big honking blind spot on my left side. Never a fun way to go into a fight.

My feet slapped against the cobbles as we fled downhill. Buchanan Street was dead, utterly, not a shop open and not a person in sight. The fine people of Glasgow either had enough sense to be indoors at this late hour or else they'd been systematically co-opted by Rose over the last few months like Edinburgh had, to the point where she'd sliced off enough pieces of people's souls to turn them into complete mental eunuchs, the way she'd been—slowly—doing to me.

That's right. I have ears everywhere. Eyes everywhere. Unlike you.

"That's pretty ableist," I said.

"What?" Eilish asked.

"Voice in my head, sorry," I said.

"I thought you lost those!"

"Hard to explain."

It's not that hard to explain. You and I...we're becoming closer all the time, darling.

Wish you wouldn't call me that, I said. *It really adds a creepy, unasked-for element to our whole relationship.*

By the end...you won't just be asking for me to take more of you. You'll be gagging for it.

I blinked. *I'm already gagging.* Then I realized: *Oh, you meant "begging."*

Yes, the voice said, slightly confused. *Do you not say that in America?*

No, gagging is the thing that precedes vomiting in the US.

Oh, I'm sorry, Rose's voice sounded in my head, the most contrite I'd heard her since she'd dropped her facade. *Yeah, I meant begging. You'll be begging for me to take more by the end. For me to touch you again—*

I think you had it right with "gagging." Still, again, getting into that creepy territory, Rose. No means no, not that you'll listen.

Your will says no. But when I take your will...all you'll ever say is, "Yes," and you'll say it to whatever I want.

Not helping your cause there. Aloud, I said, "I really need to get this crazy bitch out of my head."

Eilish was huffing behind me. "This b—wait, you can hear the Scottish loon? *In your head?*"

"I'm not crazy," I said, ducking into another alley, this one across the street and not in full view of a camera. I wasn't winded, exactly, but neither was I full of breath and eager to continue my endless run. I paused at the mouth of the alley, looking farther down Buchanan Street. I looked behind me; here the alley did open up, slightly, but...it was pretty dark back there, and I could hear the squealing of tires in that direction. "She's actually pouring herself into my head, or has been these last few months. Drinking a little of my memories, pouring a little of herself into me in return somehow."

"Can…can you do that?" Eilish asked, hands on her knees, breathing in big gulps. Of air. Not soda, like Big Gulp. Damn, I was thirsty.

"Maybe," I said. "Another, more powerful succubus did it to me once upon a time, without taking my soul in pieces." Days like this, I really missed Andromeda/Adelaide. Who wouldn't want an awesome quasi-sister to team up with against the really, really wicked one that had decided to destroy me? Deus ex machina, I would have gladly taken a badass succubus goddess with infinite powers on my side right now.

Unfortunately, all I had was me and a gasping Irish girl with the ability to charm men with her mouth. With her words, I should say, because "with her mouth" kinda makes it sound dirtier than it was.

"Well, this isn't really turning out how I thought it would when I came to find you," Eilish said, expressing clear regret for her life choices with her tone.

"This is how it always turns out whenever anyone decides to come talk to me and they've got metahuman powers," I said. "We either fight, or they get drawn into some conspiracy and battle. Every time." She gave me a horrorstruck look. "Okay, not every single time, but enough that I'm starting to think I should just avoid talking to people. And being near people…maybe just avoid people in general, I dunno…give in to the Scotch and become a hermit…with booze as my only companions…"

"Those squeals are getting closer," she said, alarm rising in her voice.

"Yeah, I didn't lose an ear; I hear them," I said, sticking my head out of the mouth of the alley again. I estimated Buchanan Street came to a big cross street intersection in about five blocks or so, some sort of descending glass transit station shaped like a horn of plenty waiting there. Between here and there was nothing but lots of shops, the occasional tree, and a statue of a woman positioned right in the middle of the street. "Come on."

We broke from cover and started running, me wondering the whole time if I was just headed for more trouble. It wasn't like I knew where I was running, so running in general wasn't exactly a proven strategy at this point.

Still, I hustled down the hill and toward the transit station, hoping I'd find another path that'd lead somewhere safe before those cars that were in such a hurry to get to their destination found me.

"That's an interesting place to put a statue," Eilish said, huffing along behind me.

"Uh huh," I said, half ignoring her. My lungs were not as resilient as they'd been a few months ago when I'd started this whole Scottish hell, probably because I hadn't been running for—well, any of them. That's what happens when you lose all hope of survival; your cardio game just goes all to shit.

"I mean, there's not even a plinth. It's just standing on the road."

I glanced at the statue she was talking about. It was true: there was no plinth, no base. I would have even thought it was a person because it was life-sized, but that sucker was frozen in place like no human statue I'd ever seen. They could get pretty still, don't get me wrong, but the meta eye is more capable of spotting movement than the human eye, and I could always tell when I was dealing with a human statue. "And yet here is where they put it."

"I mean, who the hell is it, even?" she asked, still huffing.

I stared at it for a second. It was garbed in robes, wrapped around it, and it took me a second to recognize it. "That'd be a statue of the goddess Diana, the Huntress."

"Wait, how'd you know that at this distance? You read the plaque?"

"I don't see a plaque," I said, doing a little huffing of my own. "I recognized her because I've met the lady in question." Man, breathing was not getting easier.

"Oh?"

"Yeah," I said. "Last time I saw her, she liplocked with my brother on a runway in Italy, possibly the most cringeworthy thing I've ever seen in my entire life. With the exception of that brief period where everyone seemed to think dancing Gangnam Style was some kind of awesome—"

We were almost to the statue, almost to the intersection, and she suddenly sprung to life, causing Eilish to shriek a truncated, "AIEEEEEE!" that hit some high notes previously undiscovered by anyone but dogs, and me to stop so fast that I was pretty sure I exhaled every breath I'd ever taken and possibly my entire lungs with them.

"I've seen worse than that kiss,'" the goddess Diana said, rounding on me meta-fast, eyes glaring at me in the dark.

"Gyahhhhh," I said, trying to keep it low but nearly goose-stepping into the atmosphere in surprise. One minute you think you're staring at a well-made statue, the next, she's speaking to you and glaring. Suddenly, I wondered if my undies had just passed my ripped-up shirt for worst condition clothing I wore, because seeing her jump out at me had surely affected bladder or bowel control. "What the hell are you doing here, Diana?"

Her taut face broke into a hint of a smile. "Your brother called me and said you were in great peril. And he's a good kisser, so…" She looked really predatory as she grinned. "I came to help you."

26.

"Oh, good, we have another friend," Eilish said, sounding like she was coming out of the early stages of a heart attack. I looked back and found her again with her hands on her knees, sucking in air in great gasps. "Someone else to die with. Lucky us."

"We're not dying today, fool," Diana said, frowning at Eilish. She shed her robes, which I thought was kind of a funny fashion choice for modern day—at least when you're not pretending to be the world's most epic living statue—and beneath it she was...

Holy crap.

She was loaded for not just bears, but bears that had been kitted out like Navy SEALs.

A British SA-80 bullpup assault rifle hung from a strap around her shoulders, and she had two pistols—I couldn't tell for sure in the dark, but they looked like CZ-75 family weapons to me—on her belt, as well as a variety of knives.

"Diana," I said, looking her right in the eye, "this woman after me...she's a full unleashed succubus. Thousands of powers at her disposal. She's got Wolfe, she's got an Achilles—"

"Yes," Diana said with a curt nod. "Your brother has told me all this."

I exhaled, shoulders slumping. "Wait, Reed knows that? How?"

"They have had clashes." And she nodded toward the

intersection ahead. "We should go. I have a safehouse nearby. Reed and his nerd squad guided me to your location."

"Reed and his what?" I fell in as Diana turned to stalk off, and heard Eilish happily—with an actual gasp of happiness—do the same behind me. "Wait, how did they know where I was?"

"They are watching," Diana said, pointing at one of the cameras mounted on the side of a building. "They have gained access to the system."

"How the hell did they manage that?" I asked, my shoes thumping against the cobblestones with renewed vigor as I followed Diana. "Does this mean Rose is locked out?"

"Her soul slaves can no longer watch your every movement by camera, no," Diana said, so matter-of-fact and brusque. She was setting a decent pace. "But they are still in this area, in the flesh, on the streets, so we will need to exercise care should we come across anyone."

"Oh, whew," Eilish said, behind me. "Thank goodness." When I shot her a look, she said, "We've run across someone with a plan. I can't describe the level of relief I'm feeling."

"I had a plan," I said, only a little wounded.

"Sure you did," Eilish said, not even bothering to sound reassuring. "I'm sure it was a wonderful plan, and it would have paid great dividends any minute now."

"Once we're in the safehouse," Diana said, "we will lay low for the night, and into tomorrow. Once darkness falls, I will procure transport to remove us from this city, and we will rendezvous with a plane or ship that your brother sends."

I blinked as we darted down another alley on the left side of the street, this one actually having an exit. We stalked between the brick structures and I listened for anything like tires squealing behind us. The sound was strangely...absent. "Wait, he doesn't already have transport?"

"As I understand it," Diana said, still tightly, "air traffic control and military radar remain under this Rose's grip. They are not easily taken over by the powers we have at hand."

"Huh," I said, thinking it over. Had Jamal, J.J. and Abby finally managed to get into the Scottish camera system on their own? Or was there more being unsaid because Diana either didn't know about it or didn't have cause to tell me?

Either way…my brother had cooked up a rescue plan three months after I'd told him to abandon all hope and let me die from Rose's tender mercies.

I maybe felt my eyes get a little misty. Just a little. Could have been the cold, who knows?

He didn't give up on me, even when I gave up on myself.

Nope. Wasn't the cold.

"I love you, Reed," I whispered.

Diana stiffened in front of me. "And you call me awkward."

"I guess we wouldn't catch you saying any such thing to your brother," I said, sniffling just slightly.

"Absolutely not." In this, she was firm.

"Can't say I blame you there," I said. "He's a huge tool. I just saw him a couple months ago, in fact."

Diana paused, turning her head slightly to look at me out of the corner of one eye—and that was it. "Oh?"

"Yeah."

"How was he?" she asked after a long moment of consideration, like she was trying to decide whether she should even ask.

"He's fine," I said, answering first with the part she probably wanted to hear. "Also, still a huge tool. And probably engaging in escalating acts of criminality, though I can't be sure of that."

She stood statue still again for a few seconds, then nodded once, and I thought I caught a hint of either satisfaction or simple acknowledgment of his personality. "That is Janus, all right. Always a schemer."

"No doubt," I said, following her lead as we snaked our way up an alley and crossed a main street. Two more streets of careful stealth later and we entered an alley door into the back hall of an aging hotel. Diana led us up a staircase filled with cracked and peeling white paint, Eilish looking at everything like a wall was going to burst and Rose was going to come flying out. I didn't see any surveillance cameras on the walls, which was unusual for hotels these days, and she'd used a keycard to access the place.

Diana opened the room door with the keycard, and in we went, the sound of the tires squealing in the streets of Glasgow long ago left behind. She shut the door behind us and we all just stood there for a second in a room with double beds covered in maroon diamond-patterned bedspreads, an entry to a small bathroom, and a beaten-up walnut desk and dresser. The TV hung silent on the wall, overlooking the whole scene.

I stared at Eilish, she stared at me, and Diana stared at us both. We all three just listened, waiting to hear something—anything.

When the phone rang, I thought we were all going to shit ourselves.

"Jaysus!" Eilish said, almost dancing. "I gotta pee." She disappeared into the bathroom. "Let me know if we have to go fleeing out the window or something." She didn't shut the door, which most people would have found distressing, but I found oddly reassuring. It meant she wasn't making a phone call in there.

Diana picked up the ringing telephone. "Pronto." I thought that was a little weird. Then she thrust it at me. "It's for you."

I stared at the white plastic telephone as though she were handing me a bomb, but after a second, I took it. "Hello?" I asked, you know, like a normal American.

"Hey," Reed's voice melted into my ear, relief infusing his tone like reassuring coffee notes in a Starbucks Mocha Frappuccino after months of drinking bizarre British flavors.

"Reed," I said, almost doing a little melting myself.

27.

Reed

Hearing my sister's voice on the other end of that line was like finding out a family member was going to live after sitting in a damned hospital waiting room with no news for months. "Sienna, are you okay?" I rushed it out, hurrying to get my number two concern out of my head and mouth now that I knew she was at least alive (concern number one).

"I'm...still alive," she said, and she sounded pretty haggard. "Reed, she's been draining me. A little at a time."

That caused my brow to furrow hard. "What do you mean?"

Sienna took a ragged breath that sounded like she was breathing into a ripped paper bag. "I mean she's been using her succubus powers to rip memories out of me. Just...she's...I don't know how to say it. She's been proving she's stronger than me."

"No, she's not," I said quickly.

I heard Sienna take a long breath, and then her tone took a turn toward rueful. "Reed...she completely dominates me in every encounter. Anytime we come face to face, she kicks my ass."

"That's being more powerful than you," I said. "Not stronger. There's a difference."

She kinda laughed, but there was no joy in it. "Oh, yeah?"

"Yeah," I said, lighting up about the subject. Sienna

sounded more down than I'd ever heard her. "Power is the ability to force your will on others. And in this case, strength—I'm talking about resilience, Sienna—is something different. She may have you outclassed in terms of powers, but guess what? So did Sovereign."

"I lost my souls, Reed," she said quietly.

"I know. But you haven't always had them," I said. And then I looked around the cave-like hollow in front of me, where the gang was all huddled, watching me on the phone, listening intently to one side of the conversation—hell, maybe both if their ears were especially sharp and the volume was high enough. "And you've got a lot of people in your corner here, cheering you on." I held the phone up and a round of whoops and, "Yeah, Sienna!" and "We're with you!" echoed off the cave ceilings as Augustus and Scott and the others let out a round of every noise of support you can imagine. "ROAWWWWWR! KITTEEEENNS!" was Friday's contribution, for some reason. "The gang's all here," I said. "And we're coming to get you."

"Reed, this Rose…" she said, and the tension ratcheted up in her voice. "She's…so dangerous."

"Yeah, I know," I said. "We've gone head to head with her a few times now."

I could hear Sienna's gulp on the other end of the line. "Is everyone…?"

"Everyone's fine," I said. "We clashed with her at the headquarters when she came to destroy it, and we all came out fine. Augustus, Taneshia and Kat went up against her in Atlanta earlier today and they say they actually managed to knock her down somehow. She's not invincible. She's just…really tough. But we've got brains and brawn at work here, and we're coming over there. We'll meet up with you, and we'll all kill her together."

The painful silence told me everything about Sienna's worry in this case, and when she spoke, she did it so low the microphone on the other end of the line almost didn't pick it up. "Reed…if you lead the team over here…she could kill someone. She could kill…everyone."

"Oh, I hope that she doesn't kill me," came a voice with an

Irish accent on the other end of the line. "I'm so new. I'm expendable, you know. She could just wipe me out and so long as you killed her after that, you'd barely even notice me gone. I'd be like a skidmark as you celebrate your flawless victory. Never mind the poor Irish girl—"

"I'm starting to see how you and Breandan got along so well," Sienna said, only a little crossly.

"Wait, what?" I asked. "Who is that?"

"Breandan's girlfriend," she said. "Eilish. It's a long story."

"Did she say that was Breandan's girlfriend talking?" Scott asked, face all afrown. "Because he told me she was dead."

"She's very much alive," Sienna said, answering him. "I can confirm beyond doubt. She's the real deal."

"Oh, that's cool," Kat said, and she was—I shit you not—powdering her nose, not even looking but listening to the conversation. "Breandan was funny. We could use somebody funny around here again."

"Yeah, I'm tired of carrying all the comic relief on these shoulders," Friday said, swelling slightly in the shoulders to emphasize the point. "This chick sounds totally kittens." He lowered his voice. "And Euro girls are easy, you know?" Chase walked over and slapped him in the back of the head. "Owww."

"Interesting," Zollers said. "Sienna…are you sure she is who she says she is?"

"Is that Zollers?" Sienna asked.

"It's me, Sienna," he said, a very slight smile crossing his lips.

"Man, the gang really is all there," she said, and her voice sounded a little husky for a second before she answered. "I took a page out of your book to be sure she wasn't lying, Doc. She is who she says she is."

"Hey, Sienna?" J.J. called. "I can't really hear you, but I know everyone else is talking to you, and I know you can hear me, so—we've got control of the surveillance systems in Scotland now—"

"Way to go, J.J.," she said.

Cassidy cleared her throat loudly, face buried in three computer monitors. "Yeah, that was not J.J. that did that."

"Who said that?" Sienna's voice registered all the confusion I expected.

"That was, uh—" I started to say.

"Cassidy Ellis," Cassidy said, not looking up. She rasped slightly, her asthma marring her voice.

"The hell?" Sienna asked. "How much did that cost you?"

"It cost *you* about ten million," Cassidy called back.

"I said five to ten," I countered, "at Sienna's discretion. And some other…favors that shall remain unspecified."

There was a long silence on the other end of the phone, and then Sienna said, "God, I hope they weren't—"

"Sexual," Cassidy finished for her. "Really churlish, Sienna."

"—sexual in nature—dammit, Cassidy, you're gonna get five million and no more if you interrupt my jokes. I live three months in hell and you can't even give me this?" Sienna was quiet for a moment. "I guess I should worry that you were able to finish that sentence, though. You never have known people that well before now."

"I'm learning," she said, still looking at the computer. "All the time."

"That's…slightly threatening," Jamal said. "Sienna, Cassidy has the system on lock—for now. Rose isn't going to find you through the camera nets in Scotland, but that's hardly the only method she has at her disposal."

"Tell me about it," Sienna said. "She's made zombies out of a lot of people in this country. Do you have control of the radar and—"

"No," Cassidy said firmly. "That's way out of reach. Not impossible, just…really difficult." Without looking up, she nodded to Abby.

Abby just sort of blinked. "Oh…am I in this one-sided conversation with a phone that I can't even hear now?" She looked around for a few seconds. "Uhm…well…a theory we have is that, uh…before the metahuman revelation a few years ago, some of the major world governments with a deep interest in Infosec rounded up some of the top people like Jamal and Cassidy and put them to work developing high-level encryption for their really sensitive systems. And then promptly hoarded those secrets to themselves, using some…uh, outsourcing where occasionally necessary to shore up any weaknesses in that system." She finished, then looked to Cassidy, as though for approval. "Is that what you wanted me to explain?"

"Yes," Cassidy said. "I'm using my brain power elsewhere, so if you people could keep the distracting talking and breathing to a minimum, that'd be very helpful."

"She's having to work really hard to keep the system open to us and closed to Rose's people," Jamal said, "who are probably those high-level metas that Abby just mentioned, the ones employed by the UK government, which…Rose has fully penetrated. It's a lot of deep tech talk, but suffice it to say, there's a lot of folks in a military installation somewhere in Scotland right now that are crapping their pants and sitting in it because they're at the cyberwar equivalent of DEFCON 1."

"Wouldn't it be DEFCON 5?" Scott asked.

"No," Veronika said. "The lower the DEFCON level, the worse it is. DEFCON 1 means you're in the middle of a nuclear war. DEFCON 5 means calm seas and vagina all the way to the horizon."

Olivia was sitting next to me, and suddenly reddened visibly even in the dark of the cave. "Uhm…I don't think I like the sound of DEFCON 5."

"It sounds pretty inappropriate," Jamie Barton said, blushing like she wished she had her mask on.

"I have to tell you guys something else," Sienna said. "Colin Fannon is dead."

That quieted the cave-room. "Damn," I said.

"Rose got him early," I said. "She'd almost completely ensnared him via dreamwalk before you even came over here. Once he showed up in York, she drained the important parts and left him a shell of a servant."

"Damn, Fannon," Phinneus Chalke breathed in that aged, old man pissed off way he had. His beard stirred. "Hell of a way to go out."

"Did you hire Phinneus Chalke?" Sienna asked.

"Gang," I said, "all here." By way of explanation.

"Who else did you dig up? Did I hear Jamie Barton in the background?"

"Reluctantly," Jamie called out.

"Yeah, don't even mention me, Sweet Cheeks," Veronika said.

"Veronika, you're gonna love Rose," Sienna called out. "She makes me highly uncomfortable in many of the same ways you do."

"I love me some fiery hot redhead," Veronika called back. "She loses points for the soul-sucking, though. That's not my bag, but it's not like I have enough soul left to really give much of a damn, so if she's worth it, I guess maybe…"

"We're coming for you, Sienna," I said. "I'm working on arranging transport right now—"

"Reed," she said, in a knowing voice that was like a brick wall that she probably expected would stop me, "if you don't have control over Scotland's radar systems…how are you going to get into Scotland? Safely, I mean?"

"There are ways," I said, a little tensely, because I was—well, not lying, but delaying, since I didn't know what ways I was talking about.

"You want to get into Scotland?" Friday piped up. "I can get you into Scotland. I can get you into Scotland faster than any other way. You'll be there in hours. And out again, too, if you want."

"Right," I said, glazing right over that comment, "we're working on coming up with something—y'know, sane, with chances of survival higher than negative five hundred percent—"

"Wait," Sienna said. "Friday…are you thinking about… Greg Vansen?"

"Yeah, girl," Friday said. "He owes us. Big time."

There was a long pause. "You know…" she finally said, "he's actually got a completely valid and very workable idea there."

It was like every muscle in my body seized up at once, and I almost cough-laughed at the absurdity of it, but held on to it at the last. "Who? Friday?"

"Yeah," she said. "He does know a guy. We both do. And

he's right...Greg Vansen can get you into Scotland. And out again, under the radar. If Friday knows how to find him...you should go with that. It'll be the safest way to do this thing." There was a pause, another swallow, a tentative, "You know...if you want to do this thing."

"Sister of mine," I said, putting heavy emphasis on that title, "the cavalry is coming. We're going to come get you, we're going to bring you safely home, and once we're here...we're going to set up the biggest, most explosive ambush on the face of the planet, and we're going to bring this Rose Steward down. And once she's down, we're going to dose her with suppressant, and you're going to take back what's yours."

Her voice crackled a little. "And then?"

"And then..." I let my voice trail off. "We'll figure out 'and then' later, okay? For now...we're going to save you, then we're going to stop her...and so on. One problem at a time until they're all gone."

"That could be a while," she said, but I caught the hints of a shaky smile over the phone. "I don't know if you've noticed, but...I've got a lot of problems."

"It'd be hard not to notice," I said. "But you're safe now. Get some sleep. We'll work on getting this Greg guy and getting over there. We'll bring every weapon in the arsenal, and I've got doses of suppressant already stocked in case things go bad while we're extracting you, but...we're going to set down, we're going to pick you up, and we're going to get the hell out of there. That's all. Once we're back over here, we'll really plan the next battle. The big one. We'll figure out this Rose's weaknesses, and we'll take the fight to her like she's never felt before. She's going to understand the difference between power and strength, trust me." My voice was like hardened steel. "Get some sleep. Because tomorrow...the cavalry is coming to bring you home."

28.

Sienna

I actually did sleep, to my surprise, some combination of days of exhaustion coupled with relief at my brother's efforts to save my ass from annihilation at the hands of the angry Scottish ginger quelling my fears enough to allow me to pass out. I woke up a couple times during the night to find Diana on watch by the window and Eilish snoring lightly in the other bed, and always found my way back to sleep without issue, until I woke for the last time to find sunlight streaming past the curtains and Eilish and Diana...

...playing cards?

"I think you're a cheat," Eilish said, eyeing Diana angrily. Her voice was raised, and her cheeks were red as the bedspreads, flushed way past her strawberry blond hair.

Diana regarded her cards with near indifference. "I have lived over two thousand years. What you ascribe to cheating can better be put down to simply understanding the rules of the game at a level which you could not fathom with your flyspeck life." She laid down her hand. "Also...full house. Aces over twos."

"How is that even possible?" Eilish threw down her cards without even turning them over. "I say it again—you're a cheat."

Diana looked at her indifferently. "Are you always this sore a loser?"

"Only when I'm being cheated," she said, standing there, steaming.

"Didn't you have a boyfriend who can change the luck to be in your favor?" I asked, and Eilish's head snapped around and she glared at me. "Because I'm guessing that got used in a game a time or two."

"It's not cheating to use your natural abilities," Eilish said, looking away quickly. "It wasn't like I was ever doing it. It was all him, and if he wanted to…y'know, 'help,' who was I to turn down an assist?"

"An honest player, if you did," I said, running my hand over my tangled hair. It was bad; I didn't even need to look in a mirror to tell. A barrette was not going to fix this problem. Besides, now that trick was probably played out. Unfortunately. Because I needed all the tricks up my sleeve I could get against Rose.

But maybe those days were over, I started to hope as I got out of bed, stretching, wearing the bathrobe I'd taken out of the closet in lieu of, y'know, sleeping in my filthy disgusting clothes.

"Reed had something delivered for you this morning," Diana said, nodding at a shopping bag on the dresser. "I had to go down to the front desk to pick it up."

I paused on the way to the bathroom and poked through the bag. It was fresh clothes—t-shirt, jeans, boots, socks—all in my size. Some toiletries too, and snacks. I dove right into the package of granola bars, inhaling two of them before coming up for air. "Oh, man," I said, not shamed at all about how I looked scarfing hard.

Diana was smiling at me thinly. "You eat like you have never seen food before."

"I do feel like it's been a while since I had a good meal," I said, taking down another granola bar. "Does this place have a minibar? Because I could use a nip."

Eilish eyed me with a little concern, then shrugged. "I could use a shot myself."

Diana looked at each of us a little smokily, through slitted eyes, then seemed to give up. "There's one in the corner. Might as well make use of the liquor within."

"Cool," I said.

"The hotel has a pool as well," Diana said, moving off toward the minibar with precise movements, "in case you want to take a swim later."

I made a mental note of that, for reasons other than swimming, and headed off to pee, taking my new toiletries and clothes with me. Unlike Eilish, I closed the door, and when I was done, I didn't look at myself in the mirror. It wasn't pretty, so I avoided even glancing, closed the curtain and heated up the shower, peeling off the last of my clothes and stepping in.

Warm water washed over me for the first time in what felt like ages. Dirt and grime and sweat that I hadn't even known was on my skin came off with a good scrub, and as I blinked my eyes I realized—hey, I had eyes again, plural. The left did feel a little sticky, but it was good, and I tested my vision. Back to better than 20/20. I flexed my broken hands, and they were all back together again, good as new. Both legs were good, though I realized as I looked at them—they looked bonier than I'd ever seen them in my adult life. They'd always been thicker and more muscular than the international beauty standard average, because, uhm, I enjoyed eating under normal circumstances, but I'd lost a lot of the muscle tone I'd put on after I'd started working out heavily, and it had been replaced with...nothing.

I looked bony. My hips were still wide, because that was just how I was made, but...I pulled the shower curtain back and...

Through the steam-covered mirror, I could see the truth I'd been ignoring for months.

I just looked sick.

Sickly thin. My skin was tight because metahuman skin was elastic like nobody's business, but my neck was thin, my arms were thin, my ribs stuck out—thankfully all knitted together now from the breaking I'd experienced at Rose's hands, but I could just about count them in the mirror. My hips were still wide, but my hip bones were protruding in the reflection, and that slightly circular double chin I'd always found so annoying, the one that I'd almost but not quite gotten rid of when I was exercising hours a day—it was fully gone. My neck was like a giraffe's compared to how it used to be, and my face was so narrow it didn't look like it belonged to a living person.

The mirror was fogging over to the point where I couldn't see myself anymore, so I shut the curtain and got about finishing the work of scrubbing myself clean. My hair was thin and came out in chunks as I washed it. Not enough to give me full bore alopecia, but enough to tell me that I was apparently losing it at a vastly accelerated rate. It washed down toward the drain in clumps as I worked scrubbing off the gross feeling that weeks without a shower had brought.

No matter how much I scrubbed, I didn't know if I was getting it all. The hot, warm smell of humidity flooded my senses, and it was like the stink of failure hung on me in that shower. I eased down to sit in the tub, letting the hot water wash over me, and closed my eyes. I pulled my hair back and leaned my neck against the tub.

"She's killing me," I whispered to no one in particular.

Oh, yes, but that was the point though, wasn't it, love? Rose's voice rang out in my head.

I sat up like someone had fired a gun beside my ear. I could almost hear her laughter.

You're so very lovely now, darling, Rose said. *You've lost so much weight. Your looks are much improved.*

"I look like I'm already dead," I whispered, not wanting Eilish or Diana to hear me. "I look like a skeleton, like I'm ready for burial."

Noooo—well, maybe a little. But I like that lean, hungry look on a girl. Especially on you. You look...properly haunted. Properly hunted. Like you've been chased around a bit. Like someone finally put the fear in you after so long you've been putting the fear in others. I've been eating you alive, Sienna dear. Did you really expect to keep all that meat on your bones while I was cutting it off?

I just stared at the white tile, water washing down all over me. "I didn't expect...this."

You should have. You should have expected—

A knock sounded at the door, heavy and hard. "Hey," Eilish said. "We've got shots. Come on out. We're waiting on

189

you, but we're not going to be waiting much longer."

I sat up in the tub, the warm water still washing down me, the curtain hemming me in on one side, the dim light a pleasant retreat from the bright light of day. It was a nice little small place, somewhere I could safely fold in on myself for a few minutes. "Yeah," I said, voice a little shakier than I might have wanted. "I—I'll be right out." I picked up the body wash bottle; I'd emptied it entirely and I still didn't really feel clean.

I wondered if I ever would again.

Turning off the water, I got to my feet. With great care, I dried off, leaving my hair wet and tangled. I put on a fresh bathrobe and felt the soft terrycloth against my skin. When I opened the door, steam rushed out, and I didn't even bother looking in the mirror, for fear of seeing myself—my skeletal self, whom I barely recognized—again.

When I came out, I walked past the door, almost tripping over a white envelope. I frowned at it and scooped it up, walking out to find Eilish and Diana sitting there, staring quietly at anything but each other—or me, and I knew instantly that no matter how quietly I'd whispered, they knew I'd been talking to myself.

Or that I'd been talking to Rose.

Liquor was sitting out there in little bottles, and without ceremony I walked over and scooped one up. I took it down in seconds, loving the rich, peaty flavor as it sluiced over my tongue and down my throat. I felt a little quiver of relief after it was down.

"What's that?" Eilish asked, nodding at the envelope in my hand.

"Note from the front desk, I assume," I said, tearing it open. "It came under the door."

Eilish frowned. "It wasn't there a minute ago when I tapped on the bathroom to roust you out."

I shrugged and flipped it over to remove the paper within, and froze right there.

It said, "*Sienna,*" in handwritten scrawl.

While my heart was busy stopping, I hurriedly pulled out the little card within. It was blank on the outside, and when I opened it, a simple message was written, by hand, within:

Meet me at the Glasgow Necropolis in one hour, alone, for our date…or I'll come to you.

Love, Rose

P.S. If you make me come after you, your little friends will die a much more painful death.

29.

"Are you sure about this?" Diana asked, leaning over the center console of her car just outside the gates of the Glasgow Cathedral, a classically huge European cathedral with a green metal roof. Her dark hair hung around her face, and she seemed ready to hop out with me.

"Just go," I said. "I have to do this alone."

She gave me a reluctant nod. "If you change your mind..."

"We're on the course now," I said, and shut the door. "No turning back."

She didn't answer, but she did rev the engine and drive off. She was in a beautiful Jaguar, which she'd had in the parking garage of the hotel. It had been a pleasant change from riding around the back of a smelly kidnapper van, the kind you normally see workmen or pedos use.

But now she was driving off, taking that brief illusion of security I'd felt along with her.

Now I was back to being Sienna the hounded, Sienna the skeleton, just a bony ghost of her former badass self.

You'll never be entirely yourself again, darling, Rose's voice came to me, *because I'm taking you—your self. I told you, you belong to me. All of you. You just don't quite seem to feel it yet, in your heart.*

But you'll get there.

I looked up at the church yard. I stood in the towering shade of the cathedral, stone and dark and forbidding. The necropolis lay ahead, across a bridge, but first I'd have to walk down a long street to get to it.

The weather was cold, brisk, chilling me as I started forward, the unease pervading me as it had since I'd first read the note. My heart had sunk, my stomach had gone down with the ship, and my mood had followed. That sense of breathless, hopeless despair had rekindled immediately like a new fire sprung from old ashes, easily brought back out by nothing more than a simple reminder:

That Rose did own me, and I couldn't escape her no matter what I did.

I walked down the street toward the bridge, the church looming just past the trees on my left. The hillside necropolis rose ahead, all sorts of graves and monuments sticking out of the hill like…I dunno, like tombstones out of a damned hill. It was a serene place, the cemetery ahead, not quite one of the boob mountains that Scotland seemed to have in steady supply, but close. Asphalt paths snaked their way around the green hillside, plenty of trees providing cover for the countless monuments and mausoleums.

I started to cross the bridge and paused to look down. There was a modest amount of traffic below, a few cars here and there, cooking along at a fast enough speed that if I were to just jump over and let my face lead as one was coming, I'd go splat pretty good—

"Oh, don't go thinking on taking the easy way out, darling," Rose said, slipping her arm into mine and steering me—not quite gently, but not with overwhelming force, just a steady hand—away from the bridge's edge. "I'd have to come save you." She grinned at me, her bright red hair all dolled up and straightened, beautiful and glistening. "And then I'd have to punish you. But I suppose you've already got one of those coming, now, don't you?"

I just walked along where she led, across the bridge and up the hill, past a sign that held a map of the graveyard.

"Dinnae be like that, pet," Rose said, still steering me with her arm locked in mine. It was a gentle pressure, because she didn't need any more. That was Rose; she didn't use any more force than she felt was necessary to push me along up until now.

But she'd done so much damage while still holding back so

much. It was probably what terrified me most about her.

"How should I be?" I asked, my voice matching my look, so dead.

"People are going to die because of you," Rose said, and here she lost the charm, the brightness. "Your friends are going to die because of you. Your old ones—and the new. That Eilish girl, she'll suffer some. Not as much as if you hadn't shown up, but…I can't just let her off Scot free." She chuckled. "'Scot free.' You get it? Because we're a fearsome and proud lot, see?" She snugged me closer. "Do you remember when I asked you about your lineage?"

My feet dragged along, soles of my new boots scuffing against the asphalt path as we passed a yew tree. "Yes."

"Och," Rose said, letting out a little burst of disappointment. "If you're not going to participate in the conversation, what's the point in me giving you a little more time before I suck your will right out of your soul?" She pushed her palm against my cheek for a few seconds, long enough for me to cringe away as the burning started. "Talk to me out here, or I'll make you do it in here." She tapped the side of her head with her free hand.

"Yes, I remember," I said, a little louder.

"Better," she said, but she sounded gruff, like she was on guard for me to be intransigent. "Well, I took the liberty of having one of my little slaves do some research into your name. Nealon. Do you know where it comes from?"

"No," I said. "Some guy named Simon, that's all I know."

"Aye, Simon Nealon," she said, "but that's not where it comes from; that's just the beginning of your limited understanding of your name. It's originally 'Niallan.' It's Irish. Means 'descendant of Niall.'"

I looked over to find her waiting expectantly, so I asked the question she was clearly hankering for me to ask. "Who was Niall?"

"I'm glad you asked," she said, smiling again. "See, this is why you get to keep your will a little longer, this back and forth thing. Niall of the Nine Hostages was the High King of early Ireland—not the whole island, mind, but a king nonetheless, and a god, as they think of these things."

"A meta," I breathed.

"Almost certainly." Rose was getting all excited. "My grandfather used to tell me stories of the days in which metas were gods and ruled the world. Exciting tales, they were."

"Did you take them as an instruction manual?" I asked as we hit a curving switchback and she pulled me in that direction, leading me up the hill.

Rose let out a light laugh, and I wondered how much it'd take to set her off in just general smartass conversation. She seemed content, happy even, to have me talking to her, and I wondered why the hell that was since she love/hated me.

Maybe the love side was winning. Which was a worrying thought all on its own.

"I took them as what they were—a tale of halcyon days," Rose said, and she'd gone quietly pensive. "He talked about the armies that rose up to fight them, how metahumans could crush anyone that they came across—until World War I, and the advent of tanks, machine guns—all that."

I listened in silence, taking it all in. She sounded wistful, and I realized as she paused, she probably expected me to comment. "I hear it was a real awakening for our people, that war."

"I think it took the heart out of him, and others of his generation," she said, still steering me up the hill toward the summit. The path was dark asphalt, greyed by exposure to the weather but probably black when it had been poured. "You might know a little something about that, losing heart—or at least I thought you did." Here she was smirking at me. "Every time I give you a little rope, you get a little cheeky, don't you?" She reached over and pinched my cheek, quite hard. "I understand why you did what you did. Your friends? You fight harder for them than for yourself. But this doesn't end in a win for you, Sienna girl. No way, no how. I lost everything. Now you have to—"

"Why?" I asked, turning toward her. She raised an eyebrow at me, but I went on anyway. "What did I do to you, other than fail to come up to Scotland because I was busy protecting people in London? I didn't run the war against metahumans. I tried to save as many as I could. If I were dead—something that clearly excites you now—if I had died the day before your family, your village was hit, the same thing would have happened. Weissman and Raymond would have killed them all. Seems to me your beef should be with them, with Sovereign, for running the war. I lost people too—my mom, my boyfriend. Eilish, she lost someone in the war with them. You're blaming people who had nothing to do with your loss for—"

Rose grabbed me by the face and pulled me close, almost bonking her head to mine. "I blame you…because you're set up as this big hero—"

"I'm a criminal, Rose. Get your head out of your ass. I'm an international fugitive, not a hero."

"—and you let it all happen—"

"I was as powerless against them as I am against you now," I said, as she readjusted her grip to my hair and put an inch of daylight between us, presumably so as not to rip my soul clean from my body in the middle of our spat. She was staring at me with those intense green eyes and I was staring right back. "You don't want me to fight you, but you fault me for not fighting them? I hate to tell you, but back then, Weissman was as scary and impossible to me as you are now. He could control time itself, stop it and appear behind you without you even knowing it. He killed the entire Omega council of ministers, the most powerful metas in the world, all by his lonesome, in front of me. Couldn't do a thing—"

"But would you have done a thing, if you could?" she asked. "Didn't you…fight them? Leave them crippled and bleeding?"

"Yes, I would have done something—if I could," I said. "I wasn't quite as dead inside then as I am now." I looked away from her, those green eyes burning holes in me. "As dead inside as I was even before you started taking pieces out."

"Oh, you poor sad soul," she cooed, the mocking hitting a high note, plainly disingenuous. "I know just what'll cheer you up." She left that alarming assertion just hanging there, waiting, almost expectantly, for me to guess, before finally answering herself. "I have a gift for you."

"Oh, boy," I said, trying to mute that worried feeling that

was crawling cold slivers all up and down the back of my neck. "Another gift. I just...can't wait to see who you kill this time."

She pulled me along, wordlessly, up the hill a little farther, where, under a tall, nearly bare tree sat an open grave, leaves surrounding the ground around it, blotting out the browning grass. "You're not going to believe it when you see," she said, her eyes practically dancing, her smile so mischievous and...well, evil. She still had her elbow crooked in mine, and she led me right up to the edge of the open grave. "Here you go."

I looked into the darkness of the open pit for a second. It was definitely empty, a headstone sitting just above it. My gaze rose to take it in; the headstone was a simple grave marker, nothing fancy.

The name on it, though...caused my breath to catch in my throat.

It read:

SIENNA NEALON.

30.

"Do you like it?" Rose asked, her voice all high and atwitter. The sun was glaring down on us from behind a blanket of clouds, an impossibly bright spot in a whitened sky, shining down right on me.

And my grave.

I stood on the grassy hill, looking into the black depths of my own grave, Rose's arm still linked through mine. She seemed like she was bulging with pride or self-satisfaction, maybe both. Either way, she was definitely happy to be here, showing me this, like a cat bringing a dead mouse to its master and expecting reward.

"You know," she said, still smugly smiling, "if you didn't like it...I think I'd be just devastated. Why...I don't know what I'd do if you were...ungrateful."

"Push me into it right now, I assume," I said. This feeling of fatigue, of being so tired of dancing to her tune, fell over me like a thick, suffocating blanket. I looked up at her with both eyes—now that I had both again—and I knew I was reflecting pure disgust.

I was so tired of this bitch. She'd hounded me for so long, so many months, from her traitorous start to this—this ignominious finish she had in mind. She'd showed me her endgame, and looking at the lines carved into the tombstone, I felt...

Revulsion.

Disgust.

Not at the thought of dying, but at the thought that I'd let her push me for this long without ripping her face off every single day of the last three months, the way I had when we'd started this painful journey of self-annihilation together.

"I take all the time and trouble to make this nice gift for you..." Her words dripped with menace.

"You had some poor saps under your command carve a stone and dig a grave," I fired back.

"The sheer ingratitude," she said, with rising heat.

"Oh, thank you for digging a grave for me," I said with mocking reverence. "It's so nice that I know where I'm going to land at the end of all this. I'm so—what's that word you people use over here? Oh, right—I'm so *chuffed* that I get a grave of my very own. Yay me."

"I do all this for you, and the—the sheer ingratitude—" She was just spitting anger now, the fury rising within her as she tightened her arm wound around mine.

"So sorry I'm not happy about you bringing me to my own graveside," I said, "you anti-social whore."

She just froze, eyes bulging, wide. "What...did you just call me?"

I gave her the heat vision, staring her down, defiance in my eyes. "You heard me." While she glared at me, my free hand crawled its way down to my front pocket, casually, hooking around the shampoo bottle I'd stashed there.

She jerked me closer, to look her right in the eyes. The greens were like a plasma fire, burning bright emerald. "I've given you everything—"

"Pain, agony, fear; yeah, that's a real embarrassment of riches—"

"—and this is the reward I get—"

"Do you have mommy issues, too? Because I'm getting a deep and serious whiff of mommy issues from you. Like, enough to make mine appear minuscule by comparison. If mine are a bass boat, yours are the QEII—"

She unhooked her arm from mine and pushed me off her, disconnecting very lightly from touching me. "You...you're supposed to love me."

My eyes widened, mostly theatrically, because Rose was

crazy as a loon by this point. "Who was that cartoon character that tried to pet Bugs Bunny, but ended up actually crushing him to death? Because that's your spirit animal. That's you. You're so broken inside, Rose, you don't know what direction you're facing anymore. You're so…starved for love…" her eyes flashed pure venom at me "…but I get the feeling something broke in you a long time before your family died. You're pure crazy, lady, and—"

She came at me, and I saw it just barely in time. She had her hands on me inside a second, eyes blazing, looking—not even daggers, fricking full-blown claymore swords—at me, murder in those eyes. "I—I'm going to—you won't—I've had enough of your bloody cheek—"

"I've had enough of your glares," I said, and uncorked the shampoo bottle in my left hand. A stink of chlorine wafted up from where I'd filled it after a quick trip to the hotel pool, one hundred percent pure chlorine—

And I threw it in Rose's eyes.

She howled and let me go, plunging her hands toward her own face, as though that would do anything for them. She'd get Wolfe on that problem shortly, but it wasn't like his powers could make the damned chlorine go away once it was in there. Sure, he could heal it, but it'd just burn her again, and continue to do so until she dealt with the underlying problem.

Oh, and until then, I wanted to give her something else to worry about, so I kicked her right into my open grave.

Screw you, Rose.

She landed in the depths with a thud, but I was already off to the damned races, plunging down the hill at a furious run. I didn't want to be caught out of place when she recovered, and I was fairly certain it wouldn't take long.

I went for the big shortcut, dodging tombstones and passing them like mad, blocks of big marble and granite streaking down the hill as I made my run. To hell with paths; I just charged right off the top of the peak. I was racing for the bridge over the highway below, and it was still a hundred feet away or so when I heard the tormented scream ring out over the hillside like someone had unleashed a banshee from a fresh grave.

Which, uh…kinda sorta happened, actually.

I was running faster than I could ever recall running before as a vanilla meta, bereft of other powers. A succubus was fast, but not supersonic fast. The bridge was thirty feet away—

—then twenty—

—then ten—

Her shriek of pure anger was almost behind me when I leapt over the edge down to the street below. It was a good thirty-foot drop, and I hit and rolled, the road on a natural hill. I diffused the impact over a couple of rolls and came back up as Rose hovered behind me, a few inches off the ground, her eyes red and angry, the skin around them still mottled from where the chlorine was probably still working at her, albeit mildly.

"Find an eyewash?" I asked, as calmly as I could muster. If I'd miscalculated even slightly, I was about to end up in that damned grave.

"I'm a bloody Poseidon now, aren't I?" She squirted herself in the eye with a shot of water out of her fingertip. Once it cleared, she doused the other eye, for what I was guessing was at least the fifth or sixth time. It was almost certainly still burning, because chlorine was not gentle to that tissue.

"Figures," I said, trying to pretend I hadn't suspected that. It would have been a lot more fun and effective if she'd somehow missed getting a Poseidon in her soul collective.

"I'm looking forward to adding another Poseidon," she said, just burning, and I could tell she was about to say something entirely predictable that was probably designed solely to shock me. In fact, it was the only reason she hadn't yet seized me and started peeling the last of my soul out of my body. Or worse, peeling the flesh from it before ripping away the soul.

"Oh?" I played into her repartee, counting the seconds.

"Your old boyfriend Scott," she said, almost spitting rage. "I'm going to get my hands on him, and I'm going to get to know him—intimately—in ways you never dared risk—"

I frowned. "I stole his memories. I think I knew him pretty intimately."

"I'm going to take everything from him," she said, almost sputtering, "and your brother? I'm going to take him, naked, over and over, a little at a time—unlike Fannon, I'll make it last for months—"

"Reed's not really a crazy redhead kind of guy. Neither's Scott, when you get down to it. Blondes, sure. Brunettes—" I flipped my hair a little arrogantly "—obviously. Crazy gingers? But I repeat myself—"

"I'm going to take them and take them—and you'll watch and beg for mercy on their behalf that will never come—"

"Rose, show me on the doll where I stuck a pike in you?"

"I hate you!" she screamed, just losing it, seething in midair, then calming back down almost immediately. "I hate you so much, my head clouds with you—"

"A minute ago you sounded like you wanted me to spend the rest of my days rolling in the hay—"

Her fists were clenched, but she didn't respond. Her muscles loosened very gradually, and I could see her making a decision. "I...need to take you now."

"'Take me'?" No, I didn't like the sound of that. Also, I didn't like the sound of quiet Glasgow streets with no real ambient background noise save for the distant hum of cars, somewhere...not close.

She started to drift toward me, and it was...ominous, like a ghost floating toward you. "I've let you go too long, hoping to...to break that last bit of defiance out of you, to show you the things...things that would hurt you...like your brother, suffering...your friends, breathing their last...but you can watch that from within me, at least for a while longer...before you get dissolved...before you become part of...of me..." Her face tightened. "And I will...make you...love me..."

"I'm going to kill you, Rose," I said, calmly, taking a couple steps back. In the distance, I finally heard it. Sweet music, and I just needed to wait a little longer...

She didn't quite snort, but it was a noise of disdain, a "Pfffft," that made its way between her lips. "You, darling?"

She shook her head at me. "What's that you Americans say? 'You and what army'?"

The first sound of tires squealing in the distance made her stiffen like she'd heard the footsteps of approaching doom. She spun, looking up the slope behind her and seeing—

About ten garbage trucks rampaging down the hill at a hundred miles an hour, three across. It was a flotilla of death, a stampeding herd of metal buffalo churning toward us at high speed.

And Rose stood before it, hovering, jaw about touching her navel.

I crept up behind her, seized her around the neck and kept her looking at it as she drew up her strength. I only had a second or so, but that was all I needed. "*That* army. Though, I guess, technically, it's more like an armored cavalry—" I tightened my grip around her neck, bracing her chin against the crook of my elbow and cranking her head around slightly.

"I'm invincible, you dunce," she said.

"Your skin certainly is," I agreed. "And your bones, too. But the cartilage between your vertebra?"

I cranked her neck as hard as I could. It took a lot of strength to break a normal human's spinal column, and even more to break a high-power meta's. She was definitely channeling an Achilles, and I'd faced one of those so mean and nasty that I never dared to get close enough to him to find out if the soft tissue at his joints had any vulnerability. Besides, his skin was so resistant that quick-strike pressure was instantly rebuffed.

But I had Rose solidly by the neck, and that didn't require quick-strike pressure. I used the slower kind—though not too slow, because I didn't want my soul vacuumed into her like she was a Hoover and I was a dust mite. I just turned it around, putting as much strength into it as I needed until I heard that satisfying—

SNAP!

She went limp in my arms, and I tossed her as I hard as I could at the incoming garbage trucks, then leapt for the side of the embankment, the concrete drop leading down from the necropolis above. I caught the wall about halfway up, and scrambled, gaining handholds until I was fifteen, twenty feet off the ground.

I heard Rose hit one of the trucks before I saw it, bringing my head around in time to see her pinball off the garbage truck at a hundred miles an hour or so. She went thudding down the slope into a parked car, and every one of those garbage trucks steered for her, bouncing off each other in a competitive mad dash to run her over, which they did mere seconds later, the red hair disappearing beneath the wheels of the middle one as they ran her over with a thump, then another got her, and another, and she ended up buried somewhere beneath them all.

Behind the trucks came another squealing of tires, that of a Jaguar, and I leapt down to land on the sidewalk just as the car drifted, with perfect control, into a one-eighty turn, facing back the way it had come when it came to rest. I did a *Dukes of Hazzard* slide over the hood and jumped into the passenger side, slamming the door behind.

"Did it work?" Eilish asked from the backseat. She looked a little pale.

"Like a charm, albeit a little late. I had to stall her."

"Sorry," Eilish said. "Do you know how hard it is to find that many garbage truck drivers all together?"

"I would have checked the nearest pub to their work site," Diana said, hitting the gas and causing the Jag to peel out.

"Well, I did that," Eilish said, "but they had a female supervisor with them, so I had to—well, club her to get her out of the way."

"Is she dead?" Diana asked, looking at me over her shoulder as we raced around the corner, leaving the pile-up of garbage trucks behind, Rose buried somewhere beneath them.

"I kinda doubt it," I said, though I knew deep within there was no chance Rose had gotten killed by my little maneuver. Hurt, definitely. Probably knocked even further off her rocker? Almost certainly. Trapped for a while? We could hope. But dead?

I didn't dare hope for that one. Not a chance.

"Guess I'd better floor it, then," Diana said, as though she didn't already have the pedal to the metal. The Jag rolled through the streets of Glasgow under her pinpoint control, as we hurried to get the hell away from the crazed goddess who was certain to be after us soon.

31.

Wolfe

The chlorine in the eyes had been insult enough to send Rose into a maddening frenzy. The flotilla of garbage trucks had made things oh so much worse, another insult calculated to make her madder, more furious, a slap to her face to create even so minor an insurrection against her control here in Glasgow, the heart of her land.

But the breaking of the neck?

That had plunged her right over the edge.

Wolfe had listened to the snap with surprise. Sienna had fought an Achilles before, had beaten him, bested him, had threatened him with a neck breaking, but this time she'd followed through at a moment when Wolfe had been sure she was all but beaten.

It was not, altogether, a pleasant surprise.

"You idiot!" Rose screamed in her own head, the very light around them turned blood red. She was howling at Mario, screaming and spitting at him with ineffectual spew, little flecks streaking through the air before her mouth. "How did you not know this was a problem?"

Wolfe could have answered—Mario hadn't been an Achilles in life for any longer than it had taken for Rose to drink him up, but Mario wasn't answering for himself.

The garbage trucks hit and the world went sideways, dark, heavy tires thumping over Rose's body, jarring them all within. Everything cut to darkness for a spell, and Wolfe wondered where the light had gone.

Oh.

He strained, pushing against the bounds of unconsciousness. Rose needed to be healed; that was an ironclad thing, one that needed to be done. Wolfe strained against the injury he felt but couldn't see, shrouded in the darkness as he was. She was down, that was sure, heavy pressure on parts of her body. He could sense the trouble spots, pushed against them, focused on them.

Rose came screaming back to wakefulness and her senses drank in all that had happened. She was crushed, pinned beneath a garbage truck, her spine broken at the neck. She'd been bounced off a garbage truck, smashed into another car, then run over. Every one of these blows had exacted a price, every single one doing its own damage.

"What...did she do to me?" Rose asked, halfway between a gasp and a pained screech.

"Broke your neck," Wolfe said calmly, healing the spinal cord and aligning the vertebrae back together. That done, he focused on the abdomen, where the internal organs had split and broken when the garbage truck ran over them, tissue torn asunder. "Had one of her little friends hit you with a garbage truck. Bounced you off another car. Run you over and left it on you."

"That...bitch," Rose said, and she heaved against the weight of the truck parked on her abdomen. It did not yield.

Wolfe just focused on putting her stomach back together. It had split open and spilled its contents into her abdominal cavity, something which would cause problems later. "You'll need to perform some minor surgery on yourself," he said as she struggled to lift the truck again—and failed.

"I want this damned thing off of me!" She had her hands buried into the frame, pushing against it.

Wolfe took one look and knew what the problem was. "You're not just trying to lift one truck. You're trying to lift nine."

Rose's face swam into his view. "What do you mean?" Her voice was low, quiet and hostile. Mario's screams were audible somewhere in the background, out of Wolfe's view. The Italian was not having a good time of things.

"When she had them crash into you," Wolfe said, still focusing on healing that stomach wound. When it was done, she'd have a belly of iron. "The mechanisms for garbage pickup rammed into the truck bodies when they crashed, hopelessly interconnecting them. So you're not trying to lift one—you're trapped beneath all nine."

"I...when I find her next, I'm going flay her soul," Rose said, and there was no pretense. "I don't care if she has to sit on the sidelines of my mind as I rip through and torment all her friends. I wanted to her to see it with her own eyes, but I'm not married to that idea anymore. I'll bring her in here and make her watch, digesting her slowly over the next ten years as I ruin this world she loves."

Wolfe listened impassively, not offering so much as a nod. "Of course," was all he said, but in his heart...he had his doubts. "You should call for trusted help."

Rose just seethed for a moment, then fumbled to find something, anything. She came up a with a cell phone that had a cracked screen, and thrust it against her ear, the garbage truck tire still resting on her abdomen, but rising as Wolfe healed and strengthened it. Metal squealed around them, the joints where the trucks had crashed together tested as he lifted it with her belly. "Shelton," Rose snapped when someone answered. Wolfe could hear the conversation; it was the metal controller that Sienna called "Mr. Blonde." "Sienna Nealon just dumped a fleet of garbage trucks on me near the Glasgow Necropolis. Get something out here that will haul the damned things off of me." There was a pause as Shelton spoke. "No, just send a construction crew with a crane or something to get me out. I want you to go after her. She went racing off, probably in the same car she was dropped off in. Get the police to put a helicopter on her, get cars full of our Mafia friends after her, and you get your arse after her. By the time I get out of here, I want you to have her for me, gift-wrapped, you understand?" She hung up without waiting for his acknowledgment.

Rose just stared into the distance, pinned in the darkness

under the garbage truck, light streaming in around her. Wolfe watched, still fighting the battle against the tread of the truck that was buried in her gut, but very slowly working its way out as he lifted it up. Finally her gaze snapped to him. "What do you think about her strength now?" she demanded.

"Minimal," Wolfe answered, honestly. "She's weak. You overpowered her easily whenever she met you straight on." He lowered his voice. "But she won't meet you straight on anymore. She's too canny for that. She knows she's the prey, and you're the hunter."

Rose was suddenly in his face, and she smelled...wonderful, like sweetness and meat, and everything he liked. She breathed in his ear, put a tongue in it, tickling him in his favorite ways, as the sensation spread all over his body—or soul, since he didn't actually have a body. He felt as though he did, when she touched him, though. "How do I keep this from happening next time?" she asked, still breathing in his ear. She nibbled at him, and he almost purred. "How do I make sure it's her screaming in pain next time, and not me?"

"Come at her with everything you have," Wolfe said without reservation. "All your strength is greater than all her strength. You need to overwhelm her, not be distracted by her tricks...because all she has left are tricks. That's what prey does...it distracts the hunter, tries to win through deceit what it can't win through strength." She touched him, everywhere, was upon him, all over him, kissing him, and he sighed. "She's weak, you're strong...but you can't beat her if you keep playing with her. Taunt her once she's inside your head. For now...just end her."

"Yesss," Rose breathed, into his very soul. "I will end her. And bring her in here...make her watch." She touched him, and Wolfe almost melted with joy. "Maybe she can be your next meal in here...and you can relive that...over and over...do whatever you want with her...however long she lasts..." Rose smiled, and it was like her happiness filled him. "What do you think of that?" And she leaned into him, the joy seeping through every fiber of Wolfe's soul.

"It sounds...wonderful," he said, because without a doubt...it did.

32.

Sienna

"We have a tail."

We were crossing the bridge over the River Clyde when Diana said it. We'd made it through downtown Glasgow without drawing too much attention, and were now on a freeway-style road, high above the river when she made her announcement to those of us in the audience who'd been thinking we might have gotten away clean.

Eilish turned around, looking out the Jag's back window. "I don't see anyone. What are y—"

"There's a helicopter," Diana said, nodding out her window. "High above us. It would be difficult for you to see." Her eyes narrowed. "It would be difficult for anyone to see—but it is there, I assure you."

I looked up through the sunroof. There was a faint dot up there, but it had to be pretty high up. "Are you sure it's covering us?"

"Very sure," Diana said. "We will need to deal with it."

Eilish's voice rose a couple octaves in the back seat. "Uhm…forgive me; I know I'm new to this whole…ahh… being a really aggressive meta criminal, but…how do you 'deal with' a helicopter? A police helicopter, I assume?"

I squinted up at it. I couldn't have judged whether it was a police helo, not at this distance, but Diana's power was muscle control, and when I thought about it, it'd sort of make sense if she could focus her eyes a little more intensely than a normal meta. "There are ways," I said. "But we'll have a more immediate concern than dealing with the chopper pretty soon, I'm guessing."

Diana nodded. "It's the dog that will sniff us out." Her accent was that bizarre Euro mix that I couldn't quite place, probably an amalgamation of all the places in Europe she'd lived in her many years. "The hunters follow behind." Her gaze flicked to the rearview. "Ah. Here they come."

The sound of engines revving caught up to me a couple seconds later, and sure enough, here came a couple cars loaded with…guys with guns? They were white Land Rovers that had been done up all fancy, an Overfinch logo on the hood that I read in reverse. The windows were down, I was guessing cool air was blowing in, and not one of them looked like a cop.

Rose had apparently co-opted some local mafia to her cause.

"Oh, this looks like fun," Eilish said as Diana switched lanes, pushing us behind a big truck with a big cargo trailer.

The first Overfinch came along a moment later, passing the truck and back into view just behind us.

"Ah, he—" I didn't even get a chance to get that out before Diana jerked the steering wheel hard to the side. The Jag swung out, back end skidding, and lightly smacked the Overfinch in the front end.

It must have hit just perfectly, because I only heard a light THUNK! from the back end of our car. It rang out like a shot in the interior.

The Overfinch went sailing sideways, knocked off course—

—into the concrete wall that lined the side of the bridge—

—and disappeared over the side, the mafiosos inside so surprised they didn't even get a shot off.

"Wow," Eilish said.

"Hold on to your arses," Diana said, and she stomped on the accelerator.

The Jag surged forward, blasting out of the way of the truck behind us, which had swerved madly after Diana's little collision technique. Probably thought it was an accident.

Diana wove past a Ford, then a Vauxhall. Then she smoked by a BMW.

"Uh, that helicopter isn't going to be outrun," Eilish pointed out.

"Not at this speed," Diana seemed to agree with a tight smile.

Coming down off the bridge arch, we'd left our pursuers behind—for now. Diana kept the speed nailed at unfathomable heights. She wove in and out of traffic, missing the bumper of a Peugeot by about an inch. Then she skipped past a Toyota by less than a sheet of paper's width.

Buildings were streaking past as we burned through whatever of Glasgow hung on the other bank of the river. The sun was high overhead, but I was pretty sure we'd turned west. Diana's expert control at the wheel made it so that we didn't see a single pursuit car until a few miles later...

When we saw more mafioso Overfinches rolling out onto the street off a freeway entrance ahead.

"So helpful that they're all the same kind of car," Diana said, as we approached. There were two of them up there, both white and gleaming in the day's sunlight.

"Uhm, how do you plan to get past these?" Eilish asked as we shot forward, still weaving through the traffic and nearly kissing the bumper of a black Nissan.

"I'll think of something," Diana muttered as the Overfinches ground to a halt ahead.

Traffic stopped with them, a dozen cars between them and us being forced to a halt as they just stopped in the middle of the M8. The doors opened as Diana coasted to 0 Mph from staggering heights, and we were left without much in the way of a shoulder on either side of the road.

"Okay," Eilish said, seeming to try and retain her calm. "How do we get out of th—"

Diana jerked the wheel to the left, toward the concrete barricade that separated the side of the motorway from a slight embankment below. It bumped, making a grinding noise as she whipped the wheel hard in the other direction.

And the Jag's left side left the ground—

The tires bumped against the concrete barrier on the side of the road, resting there for a second. We all sat in the car, now tilted at a forty-five-degree angle, the left tires off the ground.

"Hold on," Diana said, and gunned the damned engine.

"Holy shite!" Eilish said, and thumped both hands against the seats ahead of her, one on Diana's and one on mine. She was braced, face white as a Scottish snowfield, and her eyes as big as the Jag's hubcaps.

Diana squealed the tires and the Jag lurched forward, still cradled by the road barrier, with the left side a good two feet or more off the ground.

We thundered ahead toward the parked Overfinches, where the mafiosos were just waiting for us. They seemed very surprised when we shot through the neat gap they'd left between their cars and the barrier. Once past, Diana zoomed off the wall and the car thumped as it hit the ground. Then we burned through the nice empty space of cars they'd created ahead of them when they'd stopped, blazing past as they scrambled to get in their vehicles and pursue.

"Everyone okay?" Diana asked, almost perfunctorily.

"I'm fine," Eilish said. "My clothes are fine. Except my knickers. I think they might be a casualty of this battle."

The traffic thickened in front of us, and Diana was forced to slow as an off-ramp presented a chance for our pursuers to catch up. They had an unbroken field of road in front of them, after all, and we were stuck with traffic. She tried to slide into a gap only to be rebuffed by a hostile driver who shot her a two-fingered salute.

"Speaking of shite," I said as we got stuck in a forty-mile-an-hour traffic clog.

The Overfinches were after us, probably only a couple hundred yards back now. I turned and could see the men inside, one car a good hundred yards ahead of the next.

"That…is not good," I said, like this was some massive revelation.

"Oh, hells be fired," Eilish said, and she hit the rolldown switch on her window, but it did nothing. "Really?" She sounded irate. "The child lock, Diana?"

"Hm?" Diana looked back at her for a second, almost frantic in her attempt to find a path forward. An Audi sports car was pulled slightly off the road, as though they'd seen us coming and wanted to do us a bad turn. "What? Oh, fine." And she hit the rolldown switch.

"Thank you," Eilish said, and stuck her head out as one of the Overfinches started to pull alongside us.

I started to yell at her to get back in and seek cover, but she was already shouting out the window at the first Overfinch, which was skidding up beside us as Diana started to inch forward. "Hey, you there," she said, and I realized she was talking to a man hanging out the window with an AK-47. "Would you kindly do me a favor and shoot your friends?"

I jerked and ducked into my seat as the discharge of an assault rifle at full tilt rang beside us. I half expected the sound of bullets tinging against the Jag's exterior, but it didn't come. Instead I saw blood splatter against the Overfinch's windshield, then in the back seat.

"Very impressive," Diana pronounced, mildly, as she leaned forward to look out her window. The mafioso was leaning out the window now, pointing his weapon back at the Overfinch behind him. Another deafening round of shots rang out, and I saw the Overfinch that was skidding up to us from behind take the hits. Its windshield spiderwebbed with cracks, and a splatter of blood flew all through the interior, tinging it with red.

The Overfinch plowed into the one carrying our co-opted gunman, and he was thrown like a ragdoll from where he was leaning out the window to shoot. He ended up three cars ahead, ass hanging out the back of someone's British idea of a minivan.

"This is going to take forever to clear," Diana said, impatiently, and gunned it for the off-ramp instead, bouncing off a Mercedes and clearing enough space to force her way down the empty off-ramp. She jerked the wheel as we entered a cloverleaf exchange, with a reasonable amount of surface traffic just below.

"Stop under the bridge," Eilish said, and Diana did just that, parking the Jag just beneath the overpass, looking at

Eilish questioningly. Eilish started to jerk the door open and it failed to move. She looked up at Diana. "Really, still with the child locks?"

"You act as though I had anything to do with setting them," Diana said, giving her a fair amount of glare. But Diana opened her own door and got out, hurrying, to let Eilish out of hers.

Eilish sprang out of the backseat and jumped in the middle of the road, prompting a Honda driver to skid and come to a stop about a foot from running over the Irish girl. "Hey, hi," Eilish said as the guy rolled down his window with a face full of spleen he was ready to vent on her. "Would you kindly get out of your car and take ours for a joyride at about a hundred miles an hour that way?" She pointed in the direction we were facing. "Quickly, now."

The guy bolted out of his vehicle in a heartbeat and hauled ass for ours, jumping in the driver's seat almost before I had time to grab my shopping bag from the back. He was off and blazing a second later, zooming away as Eilish beckoned us to the shoe car that she'd co-opted on our behalf.

I squeezed into the passenger seat as she and Diana quickly entered the other side. "Drive normally," Eilish said, getting down in the back seat. "Sienna, get in here with me. We don't want it to look like she's got a passenger."

"Right," I said, and slithered my ass back there with her, huddling down as Diana put the car in drive and headed us off down the road at a reasonable speed. "Hopefully that gets the helicopter off our ass, then." I didn't chance a look behind us, but Diana was calm at the wheel, taking us off down a slightly country road. "The question I've got is—where do we go now? If we lost them?"

"The helicopter is heading the other way," Diana said. "For now. They may discover our ruse soon."

"We should switch cars again up ahead," Eilish said. "In a couple miles. We can do it at a petrol station for greater ease. Then maybe again a few miles later, make the track go really cold. But—yeah, I don't know where to go after that."

"I...might know of a place where we can...lay low," Diana said, as though experimenting with the word. "But we will still need a final destination, a place where Reed and the others can extract us from the country."

"Yeah," I said, wondering what kind of place would be best for that, and my stomach still churning at the thought of bringing Reed and my friends into Scotland…and all the dangers—or at least that one, red-head demon—that waited here for them.

33.

Harmon

Boston, Massachusetts
1999

"You should have seen the speech," Gerry Harmon said, almost sadly. He sat in a dim room, in a hospital, with his best grieving face on. The television flickered silently in the background, the volume turned all the way down. "It's a shame they don't carry the public access channel for politics here. I really lit up the chamber." He looked, briefly, at the small figure in the bed next to him. "You should have seen it."

Elizabeth Harmon was a pitifully frail figure, down to a fractional amount of her weight. He didn't want to look at her, because starvation did funny things to the body—a body he knew all too well, until recently—but he did chance a glance, and found her looking back at him, as she often did these days.

And her eyes burned with defiance.

Harmon looked around the dark, shadowed hospital room. All the shades were drawn, night lingering just outside the window of Massachusetts General. Elizabeth didn't have a roommate, and that was all to the better. He checked the call button speaker to make sure it wasn't on, to make sure they had privacy, and then he leaned in close to her ear.

"I know you hate me right now," Harmon said, brushing against her strawlike hair. Once, it had been full of vitality and life. That had been a long while ago though, before a few dozen utterly missed diagnoses, before she'd fallen into this…torpor that mimicked organ failure and brain shutdown.

Once, though, even further back, Harmon could remember a time when she didn't look at him in moments like this with utter loathing.

That was a very long time ago, though. At least when he wasn't controlling her directly.

"I don't blame you for hating me," he said, leaning in, letting her ragged whispers of breath stir his hair. "If I were in your shoes, I would hate me, too." He could read her thoughts, of course, the few he allowed at this point, rattling around in her brain while he shut down her higher motor functions. "But you have to understand, Elizabeth…this is for the greater good." He swallowed, a tightness manifesting itself in his throat. "That's why I wish you had seen the speech. Then…you might know what…this is all for."

She croaked, just a little noise, trying, straining against his blocks on her speech and failing to make an appreciable dent. "I know, I know," he said, picking the thought out of her mind, "but hating me—it's not going to fix the world. And the world is such a mess. We've seen it, haven't we? You remember, don't you? We toured the hospitals where people suffer needlessly while prescription drug companies dicker over their profit margin. We've seen the devastation and fallout from pointless wars, the harm that comes from all these endless fights. From the problems that could be solved if we only harnessed our power to think and work together toward common goals instead of madly seeking vain glory for ourselves, security for ourselves, image for ourselves…and nothing for humanity. Well, I won't have it." He brushed her hair back from her ear. "I'm sorry you have to be the sacrifice upon which this turns, but I don't have it in me to fight the battles ahead while fighting you behind me. You simply…know too much…about me. I let you get too close, and for that, I'm sorry, but…"

He sighed heavily, and she made a rasping noise, trying against the blocks and failing once more. "I know. It would have been better for you if I'd just...wiped those memories and let you go, but..." He brushed at her hair with his fingers again, looking at the strawlike frizz that was so utterly at contrast with the way they'd been when they were younger together. "But I let you stay too long. Let you know me too well. Now, if you were to leave...it would cause a controversy. A milder one than would have been in days past, but...I can't afford any setbacks." He paused, resolute, a feeling falling over him like certainty, a touch from heaven, if he'd believed in such things. "The world can't afford any setbacks. Not if I'm going to fix it."

He stood and gathered his coat, then stooped low to speak into her ear again. "This is the last time we'll talk. You're going to die in just a few hours, once I'm back at the statehouse and have an alibi—just to be sure." He thought of something, and said it, wondering if it would be consoling at all, then ultimately realizing that really, he was just unburdening himself of the emotion. "Being a widower is probably of more benefit to me than being a divorcee, anyway. Your sacrifice makes things possible that might not have been otherwise, so while you hate me right now..." He swallowed. "I do still love you." He kissed her gently on the forehead, letting his lips brush over them, and suppressing her urge to recoil, to screech, to make a horrid noise, just for a moment.

And then he put on his coat, and with a last look back, Gerry Harmon left his wife to die at his hand while he sought out a waiting crowd he could hide himself in, conceal himself in, until the thing was done and he could go home to grieve in his own time.

*

"You killed your own wife?" Zack asked, staring at Harmon across the fire. "To clear the way for your own ambition? I mean...I knew you were a self-serving asshole, but...wow. I mean...just wow."

Harmon sighed, used to the scorn of the classically stupid. "I had to clear the way for my ability to save the world. It doesn't surprise me too much that a pitiful intellect like yours would struggle to understand the price of success. The sacrifice associated with it."

Zack just stared back at him, a little coldly. "Oh, I understand all too well what it feels like to be a sacrifice in someone else's version of saving the world."

Harmon's lips puckered in a twisted smile. "I suppose you do. But I doubt you've been put in a position to choose to make that sacrifice yourself. I had a grand dream to save the world, only to find that this world didn't want to be saved, not really. Actual change requires destruction. Real sacrifice."

"Like the free will of every person in it," Eve said, stirring from where she sat by the fire.

"For a time, perhaps," Harmon said, warming to his subject. "The problem is—"

"All these people thinking and deciding for themselves what they want out of life," Gavrikov said, staring at him with blunted amusement. "You know...I met quite a few people like you when the Empire became the Soviet Union."

"That is not the same thing—" Harmon started to say.

"Are you sure?" Gavrikov asked. "You wanted to be the central planner for the entire world, didn't you? The one who dictated where the needs would be filled? Where the supplies would be allotted? Who would get help and who would be...sacrificed? During the early stages?" Harmon seethed, smelling the conclusion before Gavrikov got there. "The USSR did that. It was called Holodomor, the starvation of the Ukraine. It killed between three and eight million people, plus another million or two in Kazakhstan. China tried it later. It was called the Great Leap Forward. It killed between fifteen and forty-five million, depending on who you ask. Sacrifices are the price of success though, I suppose," he finished with a twist of the knife, looking Harmon dead in the eye. "How do you think that worked out for the sacrificed?"

Harmon kept his lips tightly shut. "I don't think you understand what we're talking about here. True peace.

Freedom from want—"

"Yes, when someone controls every piece of you, every single brain cell," Bjorn said, "you probably don't find yourself wanting much."

"How would you know?" Harmon shot back. "You don't have a brain." None of them could see. "The world was in the palm of my hand before—before she came and snatched it out, preserving the status quo—"

"Preserving free will, I think you mean," Bastian said under his breath.

"—so that people could—what? Starve?" Harmon asked. "Trip over themselves trying to accumulate money or fame or followers on Instagram? Oh, that's a worthy life goal. Plaudits from idiots while the world burns around you and hundreds of millions die senselessly." He thumped his chest; not really his usual way of doing things, but he was so far beyond ticked off, he couldn't hold it in anymore. "I could have saved this world. Yes, there would have been a price, but when I was done it would be remade, the problems solved, the reins handed back to humanity because now they would know how to think, how to approach things properly."

"How to be more like *you*, you mean?" Zack asked, and Harmon could sense the trap even absent his powers.

"Yes, like me," Harmon said, settling back down in the dirt next to the campfire. "I was a governor, a senator, the President. A model citizen—"

"Except for all those people you killed—you know, in the name of sacrifice," Zack said.

"He would have been a model citizen—an excellent informer for the KGB," Gavrikov added.

"If everyone had been like me," Harmon said, "this world would have been a better place."

"You're quite the impressive moral narcissist," Eve said, still not looking up from the fire. "I suppose it would be easy for you if everyone just thought the way you did. If you could pour yourself into everyone else, rather than—oh, I don't know—try and convince them of the rightness of your cause? Persuade them, maybe?"

221

"I made my arguments," Harmon said, still feeling the emotional kettle boiling over. "It's not my fault most of the country, let alone the world, are idiots—"

"You should have opened by telling them that," Zack said. "I'm sure that would persuade them."

Harmon sank back on his haunches. "You're all idiots, too. I've known it all along, but being in Sienna's head clouded things." He stared at the fire, bright, blazing, crackling with a pop as it consumed logs that didn't even exist for a fire that didn't even exist. It was all pointless, wasn't it? "You know," he said, smile twisting his lips at one end again, "I almost— I'm embarrassed to admit this now, but—in her head? I almost bought into it. The myopia of seeing things her way, I suppose. I almost started to think…maybe her stopgap methods of saving the world—maybe they were a good idea. I started to buy into that scheme about free will, about letting people make their own decisions. What a joke." He put a hand over his face, rubbing the hair out of his eyes and mussing it as he did so. "Look where free will and her own decisions have led her. Right into the jaws of a threat she didn't see coming. In my world, none of this would have happened. In my world—"

"We don't live in your world," Zack said coldly, cutting him off without mercy. "And we never will, because Sienna Nealon stopped your dumb ass. You thought you were better than her, and you were wrong. She slapped you down even after you pulled every dirty trick you could to stop her." He glared over the fire at Harmon. "And she's going to do the same here. Just watch and see."

"I don't know about that, boys," Graham said, stirring back to motion at last after just taking it all in. "Things…are not going her way, you know." He wore an impassive look. "She's down."

"She'll be back up," Gavrikov said, and Harmon found a sickening amount of certainty in it.

"She will crush this Rose bitch," Bjorn said, nodding.

"You should put your money on Sienna Nealon," Bastian said. "That's where I'd place my bets—if I still had any."

"You're all fools," Eve said. "Her fight is over. I wouldn't give a warm spit for her chances now." And she spat, all right—into the fire.

Harmon agreed with her, but didn't feel a need to stir the argument. What was the point of bickering with morons? He was still looking for his exit, after all, and to generate excessive anger among the plebes? Well, it didn't seem a smart move, especially given that they might interfere with him when the time came.

The fact that four of the six of them—not counting that Graham, who'd been deathly quiet for a while now, until he'd just spoken—were plainly still rooting for Nealon, and maybe holding out hope of helping her in some way? Foolish. Utterly foolish. The wind had shifted direction, and this was where things had landed.

Sienna Nealon was as good as dead.

And it was up to Harmon to survive her stupidity, to find his own way out—however he had to.

34.

Sienna

We were driving along the shores of Loch Lomond on the A82 when they caught up to us, a scenic, wood-lined route through rural Scotland so different from the craggy Rannoch Moor that I'd spent time in lately that it might as well have been on another planet.

Here we were slipping through rich forests on one side, and on the other we were treated by the occasional break that gave us a view of the Loch, sparkling in the fading autumn sunlight. Clouds hung heavy overhead, and I'd been just starting to enjoy the sensation that we'd just maybe gotten away when a Ferrari zoomed up the curvy lane behind us.

"You think we might be able to pass off as tourists or something if this turns out to be trouble?" I asked, still hunched over in the back seat next to Eilish. We'd swapped out our first stolen car for a second, this one an Audi.

"I doubt it," Diana said, tensing up ahead of us, hand on the stick in case she needed to shift. "You might want to get your seatbelts ready in case I have to…get creative."

"Gulp," Eilish said, actually said the word instead of swallowing heavily. "This thing is a tin can. We'd have an easier time surviving a crash in a plane at high speed."

"They're actually built very safe," Diana said, then, for saucing us with extra fear, "at normal speeds. Which we will not be traveling at, starting…now."

She stomped on the accelerator again, and Eilish squealed as she and I collided in the bump. She clamped a hand on my exposed wrist until I shot her a sizzling look and she said, "Sorry," and jerked it away.

"Don't apologize for my sake," I said. "I could use some more powers at my disposal right now. I'm finding things a bit lonely in this head of mine lately."

Oh, but I'm always with you, darling, Rose said, oh-so-helpfully.

"Die, Rose," I said, not so helpfully.

"Yeah, well, you seem nice and all," Eilish said nervously, "but I'd rather stay in my own body, if it's all the same to you. Little more chance of regular ingestion of food and not whiskey. Longer life expectancy, I think." She gulped, jaw twitching. "Maybe not though, if Rose wants me to die before you, so you can watch or whatever."

"No one is dying," Diana said firmly, like she was the mother watching us kids and reassuring us. It was a very different feeling than I'd ever gotten from her before—not that we'd spent a ton of time together. "Except this bastard." She jerked the wheel.

And the car…did not move at all.

I lifted my head to see a Ferrari coming alongside us, bright and beautiful red, the driver's seat on the side it was damned well supposed to be on.

"What in Tartarus?" Diana asked, jerking the steering wheel and having it resist her back, no movement whatsoever.

"That's…probably not good, right?" Eilish asked, sitting up and rolling down the window to shout out. "Hey, you! Would ye kindly—"

The door ripped cleanly off while she was talking, causing Eilish to let out a sharp scream. It hit the pavement and was gone a second later as we thundered down the winding road. I was given a beautiful view of the side of the Ferrari as it came up alongside as if passing us, and in the passenger seat I could see…

Mr. Blonde. He was grinning, and his hand was extended toward us.

He'd ripped the damned door off our car.

Eilish's seatbelt whipped into release, a click within telling me Mr. Blonde had played with the internal mechanism. Eilish squealed and jerked forward by the wrist, a watch that I hadn't noticed before functioning like a tether dragging her forward. Suddenly I was glad I eschewed all forms of jewelry.

Also, dentistry, of late. Like a true Brit.

With another squeal, Eilish was ripped forward again, almost out the door, the watch dragging her out like an anchor onto the speeding road—

And toward the waiting tires of the Ferrari.

35.

"Hang on!" I shouted, seizing Eilish around the waist and trying to drag her back in. The wind was whipping our hair around us, and Diana was fighting for control of the steering wheel in the front seat. I didn't have the heart to tell her it wouldn't do any good. Diana had been around the block a few times; I was sure she knew what a metal-controlling meta could do, even a low-grade one like Mr. Blonde.

He could kill us. That was the answer. He could kill our asses by pushing our car off course on the next corner and sending us tumbling down the slope into Loch Lomond.

"Hey, hey, hey!" Eilish barked, pain cutting into her voice. The watch's metal links were digging into her hand where Mr. Blonde was dragging her out of the car and I was tugging her back in. "Some of us can't grow a hand back if it's ripped off!" She paused, giving it some thought. "At least, I don't think—you know what, let's not find out!"

"Then let it go!" I shouted, trying with all that was in me to brace against the car and keep her from flying out, under the Ferrari tires. "Because right now, Elsa, it's starting to look like you either lose the watch, lose the hand, or lose your life. You pick, but be quick about it."

"But Breandan gave me this," she nearly whimpered. I could see the pain in her eyes as she stared back at me, gripping her to keep her from flying out. "It's the last thing I have that he gave me."

"It's probably stolen," I said, like that helped.

"Of course it's bloody stolen," she snapped back. "What does that have to do with anything?" She sighed, blood seeping down from where those links were tearing into her flesh. "Oh, all right." And with a deep sigh, she unfastened the clasp.

The watch, now freed, shot off her hand and straight into the wheel well of the Ferrari, which absorbed the hit like a bullet. Eilish stared at the flight path, then looked up at me, blinking. "Yeah, that was going to be you," I said. I could tell she got it.

The watch smacking into the wheel well of the Ferrari seemed to cause Mr. Blonde to jerk in surprise, his face changing slightly behind the wind screen. It made a horrendous noise, missing the tire by inches, and then clanging around.

"Ha!" Diana said, jerking the wheel. Blonde must have been just distracted enough, because the car shot sideways, slamming into the Ferrari perfectly, a fishtail punt that hit the sports car right on the driver's side door and sent it skidding.

The Ferrari squealed tires as it went sideways into a spin. The road curved just then, and it went flying off, spiraling like a Frisbee toward the loch below. It was a sharp drop, fifty feet or so to the water, and I got almost a second to revel in our victory—

Before our Audi jerked, Mr. Blonde's hold on the metal frame dragging us sideways toward the edge of the road. Diana stomped the brakes and the Audi dragged hard against the pavement, resisting the pull of Mr. Blonde.

I chanced a look; Mr. Blonde's Ferrari was frozen in midair, just hanging there, tethered to our own by his metahuman powers. It was sinking, though, as we were pulled nearer and nearer to it—

"Bail out!" I shouted, and shoved Eilish out the busted door with a solid kick. She squealed and was gone, the car pointing toward the overhang and pulling past her as she rolled away. I cast a backward look at Diana and caught her give a sudden nod, tilting the wheel toward the loch and flooring it before she jerked the door open and jumped out.

I hit the ground and rolled as the Audi went surging over

the embankment. I caught a brief glimpse of Mr. Blonde, again frozen in surprise as his brace against the fall came hurtling toward him at fifty miles an hour or whatever Diana had throttled it up to before it leapt off the pavement. It soared, unerringly and inadvertently guided by Mr. Blonde's metallic tether, right into the water after the Ferrari, crashing into the roof of that car as it lingered on the surface for a second.

The sound of the crash was earsplitting, probably bouncing off the water for miles around. I didn't stick around to watch them sink; I was already on my feet and standing in the middle of the road as a small Ford came roaring around the corner and squealed to a stop in front of me.

"Eilish," I said, already heading for the passenger side of the four-door shoe car. "Do your thing."

"Sure, why not?" She was still lying on the shoulder of the road, staring up at the heavens. "Hey, you!" Her voice boomed. "Would you kindly give us a ride?" She sat up, hair a dreadful mess, strawberry blond locks windblown and pushing out in every direction from her head. Her cheeks were a permanent shade of red, either from exertion, the wind, or some combination of the two.

Diana came up the embankment just then, brushing herself off neatly as she strode toward the car parked in the middle of the slightly wooded road. She jerked open the driver's side door and said, "You, out."

"Listen to her," Eilish called. "Like she was your mother, only maybe a little meaner." She caught a hard look from Diana. "What? Manners, that's all I'm saying."

"Manners maketh man," Diana said as the guy hastily cleared out of his car for her. "Do I look like a man to you?"

"In the biceps, you kinda do," Eilish said, popping into the back seat as I got in the passenger side. "And the thighs and calves. You are definitely a lady who does not skip leg day—and I admire that about you, really I do."

Diana grunted, but there was a hint of pleasure in there. "Buckle in, fools. We need to get out of here before he drags himself out of the lake."

"Loch," the guy outside the window corrected in a heavy

Scottish accent. I looked out at him, and—

"John Clifford?" I asked, leaning down to stare at him over Diana between us. He blinked and leaned down to look at me. "What the hell are you doing out here?"

"Well, I'm driving," he said, still staring at me blankly. "Do I know you?"

"It's Sienna Nealon," I said. "Remember? I held you hostage for several hours a few months ago? Ate food from your fridge? Raided your wife Kytt's closet? Stole your car? How's Archie?"

He squinted. "You're not Sienna Nealon. She's—she's not a little wee little thing like you. She's—you know, a bigger girl."

"You know, I'm not sorry we're stealing your car again," I said, eyes narrowing at him.

"But this is Kytt's car," John said, almost a mewling sort of protest. "The insurance company still hasn't replaced mine!"

"I might have made it up to you if not for you reminding me that I'm a frigging human skeleton," I said. "Au revoir, Johnny boy." I waved, and Diana hit the accelerator, leaving him in the dust.

"Should we have maybe offered him a ride to the next town?" Eilish asked, about a mile down the road. "You know, instead of leaving him out there on his own?"

"Nah," I said. "I'm sure someone will be along that knows him shortly. I mean, seriously, what are the odds of actually running into someone I know out here? How many people are in Scotland, anyway? Like twelve? Have I actually met them all already? Because that would explain how Rose took control of the country so easily."

No one seemed to want to answer that, which was fine. We settled into a deep silence as Diana steered the car around the curves of Loch Lomond at about a hundred miles an hour, as we streaked away from our pursuers in hopes of finding open road to wherever we were going.

36.

"Wherever we were going" turned out to be a manor in a little glen that we reached shortly before nightfall. Even at Diana's breakneck, near-psychotic pace, we took a few hours to reach it, the sun far behind the trees that seemed to stretch from end to end of the country as we headed farther north.

"This is it," she said as we turned onto a side road and threaded our way through a thick forest, gravel path leading us through under the darkness of the boughs, and above that, a purpling sky.

The car's heater smelled a little musty, and barely worked to churn out warm air. I got an inkling that Kytt was going to be happy when her insurance company finally paid out for a new car, whenever that happened. On the other hand, I hoped for John's sake he didn't attach my name to the insurance claim, because I had a feeling the underwriting department would kick his claim right out under the whole "acts of gods" proviso, if they had that in the UK. Hell, maybe that was why he still didn't have a car himself.

We rolled up a curving drive, and finally the trees broke to reveal...

An old castle on the horizon, with a sturdy, stone block construction and rising turrets at the four corners, capped by great conic roofs, and decorative crenellations around the perimeter of the building.

"Ooh," Eilish said when she saw it. She shot Diana a look,

leaning between the seats. "Someone's friends with the local lord."

"Laird, in Scotland," Diana said, and a trace of a smile brushed her lips. "But he's actually a duke. And an old friend."

"How old?" I asked, taking in the lines of the castle. It wasn't the traditional kind, with a curtain wall around it and turrets. This was more like a cross between a castle of old and a manor house of—uh, nearer antiquity, I guess. It held none of the defensive breastworks one would associate with a medieval castle, but not a ton of the modern trappings you'd expect from a top-flight manor house, either. It was caught between, full of elegance and glory but also the stone construction of days long gone. "It's tough to tell with you people that have lived thousands of years. Is it, 'I knew him in my formative years, when the crust and mantle of the earth were still cooling and we were slaying Tyrannosaurus Rexes with our meta powers,' or, 'Hey, I met him at a ball a few Christmases ago, and we've kept in touch by email since'?"

"Don't be ridiculous," Diana snapped. "No meta was alive when dinosaurs walked the earth. And I don't have email," she added hastily, as though that one was just as crazy as the first assertion. "Or go to balls," she added, the perfect capper to her statement.

She pulled the purloined Ford up in front of the house, bringing it to a stop and getting out. There were lights on within, and it seemed like there might be something of a gravel car park extending out from where we'd stopped.

From here, I could see the house much better. It was pretty expansive, probably three or four floors, depending on if they had an attic crawlspace. I got out of the car in time to hear the front door open, and someone moved out in silhouette from the front house lights, which glowed brightly in the night.

"The manor is closed for the night," the man said in a thick brogue. "You'll have to come back tomorrow." He slipped out of shadow as the last vestiges of twilight caressed his skin, and I saw a well-trimmed beard streaked with grey, and a receding hairline that came to a widow's peak. "The cafeteria opens at nine for breakfast on weekends." His voice was soft and soothing. "Make sure you try the Scotch eggs." He started to turn to leave.

"Mac," Diana called, "you would turn away an old friend like she was a tourist seeking nothing more than a tchotchke and a 'nosey around' as you people call it up here?"

Mac turned back around, peering at us in the night. "Diana?" he asked, as though he couldn't believe his ears. "Have you left the mainland for the first time in centuries?"

"Probably not keeping in contact by email, then," Eilish said, sidling up to me as she got out of the car. "You know, when your acquaintance stretches back to the days of messenger boys and carrier pigeons, tough to adapt to the new times—"

"I keep waiting for you to join the modern world," Mac said, striding down the steps, "so I can add you to my contacts and hit you with a text every now and again when I'm feeling the need to renew old acquaintances." He was smiling broadly as he came down, and Diana met him at the hood of the car, allowing herself—to my shock—to be enfolded in a big bear hug. "Och, Diana. It's been an age," he said, holding her tight.

"Yeah, and they called it the Mesozoic," I said, prompting Eilish to snort with laughter.

"You're not the sort to travel with friends," Mac said as they broke. He took a couple steps toward us, his arm threaded around Diana's waist. His accent was, by far, the smoothest and most alluring I'd heard since I'd gotten here. His eyes were clear and piercing as he looked at me. "Well, who is this?"

"This is Eilish," Diana said, taking us in turn. "And this…is Sienna Nealon."

Mac let out a low chuckle. "That's good, Diana. Now pull the other one."

"Pull the other what?" I asked. I'd been hearing people say this for months. What the hell did it even mean?

"It's her," Diana said softly, and Mac's demeanor changed immediately.

"It's an honor to have you here," he said, serious once more. He extended his hand, and shook mine, just once, then let it loose. He was strong enough that I knew he was a meta immediately. "You are most welcome in my home."

"Thanks," I said, trying to suppress the surprise that was churning through me. "That's...very generous of you. Especially considering I'm a succubus, and I know how most metas feel about...well, my kind."

"That's because they fear what you can do," Mac said, calm and staid, a little mountain in the middle of the gravel driveway as the darkness compounded minute by minute. He gestured toward the door. "Any luggage?" When we shook our heads no, he led the way. "The old belief was that a succubus would simply latch on to any soul that they could, in order to co-opt the powers that meta might have. It was passed down, revulsion and all, from the days of yore all the way to present, almost becoming a myth of its own in the process. Which was surprising, given how very few people even knew the secret of what your kind was capable of." His gentle lilt was comforting.

"How did you know what we're capable of?" I asked. "Since I'm guessing the big announcement a few years ago didn't exactly catch you by surprise."

His face was slightly lined, and it showed the closer we got to the front door, the lights shining down yellow-orange on him. He was smiling, faintly. "Because I knew your mother, and your sisters, of course."

I froze. "I don't...have any sisters. I'm an only child."

He frowned for a moment. "Right, of course. Sorry. Old brain confused me there for a moment. I forgot you're Lethe's granddaughter, not her daughter. Your mother was...Sierra?"

"Yeah," I said as he opened the front door. That was a weird error, but maybe genealogy wasn't his thing. "She was."

"I met her briefly when she was a child," he said. "Before you were born, I suppose. Her and her sister—Charlie, was it?"

"Yes," I said, and realized what was suspicious about what

he'd said. "But you said 'sisters,' like there would be more of them—"

"I did, didn't I?" He smiled slightly. "I'm just full of misspeaks tonight, aren't I? My old mind isn't what it used to be. Forgive me."

We were standing in a grand foyer, an entry hall that was almost two stories high, and filled to the brimming with photos up both sides, and a few paintings where photos didn't fill the space. It looked like the history of a clan in the modern world, and oh my goodness, did they like their kilts. Every photo, Mac was wearing a kilt.

"Come on," he said, and started walking ahead again. "I didn't exactly know your mother well; it was a brief acquaintance and she was young. But your grandmother..." His eyes sparkled. "Her, I knew."

"Lisa?" I asked.

"I suppose that is what she called herself by then," he said, leading us into a huge, four-story ovoid room with a balcony above, like a turret built into the middle of the castle. Coats of arms and all manner of swords and other weaponry were affixed to the walls, with neat plaques giving detail on them for the tourists. It was almost like a museum, except Mac apparently lived in it. "I knew her as Lethe, and only as a Nealon briefly."

I blinked a few times in surprise. "Wait...her real name was Lethe? Like the river in the underworld?"

Diana just stared at me. "You didn't think there were real rivers in Hades's underworld, did you? It was a cave. The rivers were a metaphor. If you pissed off Styx, you would die, because he was fearsome. Only his lover, Charon, would dare cross him—"

"Nice," I said. "Kinda poetic metaphor. And Lethe—"

"She would make you forget what you knew," Mac said with a smile. He nodded at my hands. "Sound familiar?"

"Very familiar," I said, "especially of late." I cast a look back at Eilish, and she was just taking everything in with a wandering, wondering eye. "No thieving," I said, and her gaze fell.

"I'm just looking," she said, but the level of her huffiness

235

as she said it clued me into her real intentions. "It's all very impressive. But I have to wonder—" and she directed this toward Mac "—why would you open a museum and cafeteria and whatnot—"

"Don't forget the gift shop," Mac said.

"—and all that—here," Eilish said. "In your home. Where you live?"

"It pays the bills," Mac said, beckoning us onward again, into a grand parlor at the back of the house. There was a huge piano, tapestries, old furniture that looked hideously uncomfortable but also probably aesthetically pleasing, if you had an eye for that sort of thing (I didn't). It was a space that was probably perfect for entertaining guests. "The fortunes of dukes are not what they once were, and I failed to capitalize on the industrial revolution as some of my fellow, titled aristocracy did." He wore a look of mild regret. "I like to stay here, you see. I don't like London. Don't care for Edinburgh. I like my lands, like my house, and I don't care to have other interests elsewhere that I need to oversee. So…this pays to keep the lights on, the heat on in winter— which…is necessary, obviously." He smiled. "Come along. The kitchen is just through here. I'm sure we still have a few things from the cafeteria if you're hungry."

"I'm clearly wasting away," I said, running a hand over my skin-and-bones body as I hurried to follow him. My appetite was not what it once had been, but I was still famished.

"Let's get you fed, then," he said with a kind twinkle in his eye.

He took us to the kitchen, where we all fell in upon sandwiches, devouring them as Mac watched, regarding us all with a kind of fatherly amusement. He had traces of black still in his hair and beard, a strong jaw, and some of the kindest eyes I could recall seeing. That's not to say he didn't have an edge; I could tell by looking at him that Mac was a man who'd seen a lot. His fair share of trouble, I would have guessed; maybe death, too. Probably death too.

I was halfway through a roast beef sandwich that was bathed in a horseradish cream sauce when Mac asked, "So, did you know Lethe—Lisa?"

I shook my head and swallowed. "She was dead before I was born, and I, uh...didn't meet any of my other family members besides Mom until I was grown. And then only my aunt, Charlie."

He nodded once, contemplating. "I read about your upbringing in one of your biographies. They didn't mention your aunt."

"They didn't know, thankfully," I said. "You could fill two books with what those people didn't know. But they wrote that crap anyway."

"Isn't that just the way?" Mac asked with a nod. "We make a mad dash to assume the motives and beliefs of others. I would guess if you confronted the person who wrote that biography with all their faulty assumptions, they'd find a way to dig themselves a new defensive earthwork to cower behind rather than face up to losing the pride it would take to admit to change their mind."

"Sad truth of human nature," Diana said from behind a small carton of milk. She had a little mustache of white, and was eating quite, uh...loudly. She'd chosen a whole roast chicken, and it was down to almost bones. Maybe table manners hadn't been a thing in ancient Rome?

Mac tossed a cloth napkin at her, and she wiped her face and hands. "What else can I do for you?"

"We need a phone," I said, looking at Diana, who nodded. "Landline, preferably."

Mac got up, wordlessly, and picked up a cordless phone from where it rested in the kitchen. I nodded to Diana, and he handed it to her. She'd cleaned her fingers, but not that well, and grease streaked its way across the plastic. She dialed a number from memory, then fiddled with the handset until a speaker came on, ringing.

"It's an international call," I said.

Mac frowned. "Well, don't stay on it all night. If I'd known, I'd have said we should Skype. My stupid telecom doesn't offer very beneficial international plans, unfortunately."

"Hello?" Reed's voice answered, tautly, at the other end of the phone.

"Reed," I called as Diana slid the phone onto the wooden

table before us, it finding a rest among a couple of seran-wrapped sandwiches. "We found a safe house with one of Diana's contacts."

"Good," he said, and I caught his exhale a second later, his own relief showing. "We're still hunkered down over here. Friday made contact with Greg Vansen, and he's taken precautions for his family, I guess, before he leaves—just in case. He should be here within the hour. I guess he jumped at the chance to saddle up again, for your sake or something."

"Cuz he knew this was going to be totally KITTENS," Friday shouted the last word in the background.

"Is that some new American slang?" Mac asked, face blank. "'Kittens'?" Diana and Eilish shrugged in answer. "I've been out of circulation a bit too long, it appears. I haven't seen that one on the 'net."

"Rose is still locked out of Scottish telecom," Reed said. "And the camera nets. But she's got eyes on the ground, obviously, as you found out on that bridge. Nice driving, Diana. One of our best people, Angel—she says she couldn't have done it any better."

Diana let slip a very satisfied smile, albeit a thin one. "Thank you."

"Anyway, digitally, Rose is shut out," Reed said. "But... that doesn't mean she's not still dangerous. You left her trapped in a pile-up back in Glasgow, but she's out now, and from what we saw..." His voice trailed off ominously.

"Girl is pissssssssed," J.J. singsonged in the background. "And I don't mean that in the British way either, though she probably needs a drink after you dropped the heavies on her flat ass. She went on a raging tear when she got out. Lucky thing your Irish friend told the drivers to git, because she blew those trucks up baaaaaad." He paused. "Get it, baaaaaad? Cuz sheep. And Scotland?"

"Sheep are more of a Wales thing, I think," Eilish said.

"We have some," Mac said. "But yes, more Wales. Angus cattle—that's our pride."

"Anyway," J.J. said, and I could hear the faint sting of him being wrong—he hated that—sinking in. "I'd count on reprisal, especially since you sunk her metal-hurling boy toy into that lake—loch—whatever."

"Did he make it out?" I asked, wishing for the answer to be a resounding, "NO."

"Oh yeah," Reed said. "He's alive. We intercepted a call from him to Rose. He made it out."

"Damn," I said. "He's a pain in the ass, Mr. Blonde. Not exactly an insurmountable obstacle, but…a pain."

"You have bigger problems," Dr. Zollers's calm voice intoned over the staticky line. "Since Rose failed in her most recent attempt to subdue you, I've been monitoring the group here—mentally—for attack." He got louder, either because he raised his voice or stepped closer to the microphone. "She's trying dreamwalks with us. I've successfully blocked all her attempts thus far, but…she's unlikely to stop."

"Nice," I said, slumping back in my chair. "And we're fresh out of a telepath to watch us here while we sleep tonight."

"You don't need a telepath," Mac said, arms folded in front of him. "We'll sleep in shifts, two at a time. If you find her in your dreams, you have control of your actions—just panic. The watchers will see it out here, and wake you." He wore a satisfied smile of his own. "That's the old way of countering a hostile succubus in an opposing war party."

"Ancient wisdom," I said, and a shadow crossed Mac's face. "Uhm…I mean…thank you for the gift of knowledge." It was a lot more formal than what I'd normally say, but he relaxed his sour look slightly. "That's really helpful."

"You only have to make it through one night," Reed said. "We'll be in flight within an hour. In Scotland in—I don't know, however fast Greg can get us there while keeping us invisible to the radar. But that brings a problem—where do we pick you up?"

"How about right here?" Eilish asked, looking around at us like it was obvious.

Diana winced, dark face surging darker. "That's the rudest thing you've said today. Rose will make a fight of this if she can." She looked apologetically at Mac. "We will find another place; I don't wish to bring trouble to your doorstep."

"A bit late for that," Mac said with amusement, "but I appreciate it. You won't want to land here in any case. Tourists will be thick upon this place in just a few hours. It'll be poor cover for any sort of subterfuge or quiet you wish to maintain."

I thought that one over. We didn't want to do it here, but we needed somewhere isolated, somewhere quiet, somewhere that people wouldn't find us—

A thought occurred to me. "Mac," I said, looking at the duke, "where's the old meta cloister from here?"

"About an hour north," he said. "Caladh Reidh. It wasn't on any maps until Google went and dragged one of their fancy picture-taking cars through the town. Now you can look at it on the internet in all its dead and abandoned glory."

"You can't be serious," Diana said. "You want to leave Scotland via your enemy's old home?"

"There's a certain suicidal poetry in that," Eilish said. "Heavy on the suicidal, I might add."

"It's abandoned," Mac said. "No one goes there anymore. The government cleared out the bodies, so...it's just a ghost town at this point."

"I want to go there," I said, almost a whisper. "Reed...pick us up in Caladh Reidh."

Reed hesitated a long few seconds before answering, and even then, skepticism drenched his tone. "You sure you want to do that?"

"If she's going to come for us...she's going to come for us," I said. "Like you said, she has ways. Scotland is her land. She might not know where we are now—or she might. She's suctioned up enough brains around here that it's hard to know what she's aware of and what she's not."

"That's her home ground, though," Eilish said. "Would we be better off fighting her somewhere—I mean, if we *have* to fight her, if there are no options such as 'scream and run away' available—wouldn't it be better to fight her somewhere she's unfamiliar with?"

I shook my head, staring at my fingernails, all janky from my chewing them over the last months, little hints of dirt stuck between them. "Scotland is Rose's land. She knows this place, the whole country end to end. I don't believe for a minute we get out of here without a last pass, but if we do? It's going to be by doing something she doesn't expect. And while me spitting in her face is a relatively new development these last couple days, I haven't been taking crazy unnecessary chances in the doing of it. If she figures this out, it'll be because she's got eyes everywhere. Caladh Reidh is it. Plan to meet us there, Reed. We'll be waiting."

"Ooooookay," he said, and I could tell he still wasn't sure. "We'll see you there as soon as we can get to you."

"Sounds good," I said, swallowing heavily. "And guys?" I waited, the cough of a staticky hiss through the phone the only signal they were still with me. "Thank you. All of you. For doing this."

"We'll see you tomorrow," Reed said, choking up a little. "Love you, sis." And he hung up swiftly.

"Right into the hornet's nest, then?" Eilish asked, looking a paler than she'd been before the call. "Well, I don't think I'm going to have to worry about Rose in my dreams tonight." She took a deep breath. "Because the likelihood that I sleep? Next to zero now, I'd say."

37.

But sleep Eilish did, amidst her protests, going softly into unconsciousness in a tower room in the corner of the castle, Diana one bed over and Mac and I keeping first watch. A fire burned in the hearth, keeping the chilly Scottish night at bay, and I sat before a fire, cradling a glass of Scotch as I stared into the flames. Contemplating…

Doom.

"How long have you been here?" I asked Mac, staring into the crackling flames. It felt a little funny to be here with a guy who'd been staring into fires since—well—not primordial earth days, but definitely since early man.

"In this estate or in Scotland?" Mac's eyes gleamed in the firelight, and he raised his glass to take a sip of his own Scotch. He hadn't mentioned a name for it and I hadn't asked, but it had that long-aged flavor that I'd come to love in my whiskey. "I moved around a lot between Ireland and Scotland in the early days, shuttling back and forth with my father, Lir. He taught me how to fight." He grew soberly quiet. "It's funny…I've been a man grown for thousands of years…and I still miss that feeling of…knowing someone—your father—is out there, somewhere, and you can talk to them or call upon them for help anytime." He blinked once. "I suppose that sounds foolish from an old man." He sipped his Scotch.

I did a little blinking of my own. "No, that doesn't sound foolish at all. I still miss my mom sometimes, though…I feel like I've been relying on myself and my friends for so long—mostly myself—that it's tough for me to rely on others now." I brushed some hair out of my eyes where it had fallen down there, and realized—I kinda missed the barrette, too. It was really useful. "I guess I don't dwell much on Mom anymore, though."

"How did she die?" he asked.

"During the war," I said. "We were facing off against the Wolfe brothers—"

"Frederick and Grihm?" He made a noise of disgust. "I hope you killed their arses."

"Yeah, I got all three of them," I said. "Hat trick. But while they were kidnapping me, my mom fought a guy named Weissman, a time-stopper, and..." I sighed. "He killed her. She got him first, but...he killed her."

He nodded slowly. "I knew of this Weissman. I never thought anyone would stop him, other than perhaps Akiyama."

I frowned. "You know Akiyama, too?"

"Everyone who's been around for a while at least knows of Akiyama," Mac said, a little dismissively. "He's out there, even now, you know, on that island next to Japan, just sitting there, stewing in his juices. Not a metahuman out there dares to go to that place."

"He seemed nice enough when I met him," I said, quietly.

Mac made an ultra frown, one that wrinkled his forehead all the way up to his high hairline. "Wait, you've actually met him? He's been in seclusion for decades."

"He helped my mom kill Weissman," I said, feeling strangely calm about the whole thing.

Mac sat in silence for a moment. "That makes more sense. A leashed succubus killing a time-shifter—that would be impressively done indeed, without aid. Hell, just about anyone killing a time-shifter would be impressive indeed. Especially when paired with those Wolfe brothers..." He made a small noise of disgust deep in his throat. "I don't envy you, having that one in your head for all those years." He looked up at me. "It does surprise me, though—did he not talk to you about your grandmother?"

I felt like Mac had just taken one of the pokers sitting next to the fireplace and whacked me upside the head with it. "What?" I asked, not sure I'd heard him right. "Wolfe knew my grandmother?"

"He was a guardian of the underworld," Mac said with great amusement. "He knew all of Hades's children—at least the ones that came before he left on his sojourn with your grandmother. They traveled together across the entirety of Europe and Asia, even Africa, the two of them, for hundreds of years. Yes, I should say he knew Lethe—Lisa Nealon."

My head was spinning, as though someone had twisted it around about a hundred times, then meta healing powers kicked in at high speed and unspun it back to its usual position. "He...what the...why would he not tell me that?"

Mac sat in silence for a moment, nodding. "I don't expect it was a very proud time for him. I met them both in Norway for the first time, where Lethe was in Odin's court. She'd just become the first of the Valkyries—"

"What?"

"—and naturally, it was quite the heady time for her, bringing death and horror on the battlefield. She was very excellent at it. I was quite happy we were at peace with Odin, especially after I saw her take on a pack of frost giants...my goodness. That one had the soul for battle." His eyes looked into the distance, and he seemed to be living his glory again, sipping his whiskey. "And Wolfe...Wolfe dutifully followed behind. Oh, he tried to hide it, but anyone who saw him knew."

I felt like Mac was talking almost as much for his own enjoyment as my benefit. It made me wonder if he sat before a fire on nights like this, just talking to himself. "Knew... what?"

"That he was in love with her," Mac said, as though it were the most obvious thing in the world. "You could see in his eyes—all that rage, all that anger—some of it was just who he was, but...some of it was...misdirected, let us say."

"Bullllllllshit," I said. "I'm calling it. Wolfe never loved anybody in his life, unless you count the way they tasted once he'd peeled the skin off them and started to eat them raw."

"Oh, he was, trust me," Mac said. "It was quite the joke among the Nords. He looked at her differently than anyone else in all the world. No one dared say anything in front of him, of course, but…he was. He was completely in love with her. Madly, in fact. And I doubt he ever said a word about it, because, of course…she didn't feel the same."

"Naturally," I said, my head floating about ten thousand miles above my body now, not just from the fatigue of these months of being hounded, but…

Geez.

Wolfe was in love with my grandmother?

That added a creepy new twist to our relationship from the start.

"Can I ask you something else?" I desperately wanted to change topics, now that he'd told me—well, something that had very little applicability to my current situation, but rated high on the "skeeve me out" scale. The fact that Wolfe had carried a stalkerly awkward relationship through at least three generations of my family was giving me goosebumps of the bad variety. Four, depending on how he and my great-grandpa, Hades, got along.

"By all means," Mac said, settling back by the fire. "You can—"

Eilish started to moan in her sleep, jerking around slightly. I was on my feet in a second, grabbing her by the shoulder and rousting her immediately.

She sat up, strawberry blond locks twisted and tangled, falling around her face as she popped up out of the pillow, eyes full and wide. "Wha—what?" A little drool ran down her chin.

"You were moaning in your sleep," I said, my hand smooth on her soft cloth blouse.

She blinked a couple times, like she was coming back to herself. "Yes. You see, I had this nightmare that I went to get some questions answered from this lady who hung about with the love of my life after he disappeared, and I got a bit swept up in some mental Scottish broad trying to kill her." She shuddered. "It was terrible."

I pursed my lips. "I don't think that was a nightmare."

"Yeah, I think I was just reliving my life of late," Eilish said, blinking. "Thanks for waking me up all the same. Not much better out here though, is it?" She lay back down. "Why couldn't I have a nice dream? Something about puppies and a chocolate factory, maybe?" She was back asleep or close to it in seconds.

"I haven't had a night where I slept that heavily in hundreds of years," Mac said, enviously, as I slipped back into my chair beside the fire.

"Guilty conscience?" I cracked, but he smiled tightly, one which did not reach the wrinkles of his eyes, and boy, did I regret asking that question. "Mac…why are you a shut-in up here?"

"I'm not a shut-in," Mac said, stirring slightly. "I walk the grounds. I deal with the tourists every day. Sometimes I even run the cash register, talk to the people as they come in from these exotic lands—China. Malaysia. Phoenix, Arizona—"

"Phoenix, Arizona is exotic?"

He shrugged lightly. "I admired the Old West. I always meant to visit there, but—well, now the west is won. It's mostly civilized these days, I hear."

"Mostly. I mean, the Hot Yoga studios springing up everywhere make me question it, but otherwise…yeah."

He settled into silence for a few minutes. "I was in the great war," he finally said. "I was there when *our* world changed." His eyes glowed like the embers of the fire had sparked out into them. "I watched hope die among our people as our superiority gave way to gods of metal and machine, to tanks and bullets. We'd felt it coming for a while of course, if there is such a thing as a collective psyche for our kind, but…that war…that destruction…it took the heart out of us as sure as anything I'd ever seen. More of us died in that war than anything before or after until the extermination done by Century."

"Which you neatly dodged," I said.

His eyes gleamed. "They tried. They failed. I don't imagine they pictured me being much of a fighter. Too many young people full of passion in their ranks, not enough old hands with the long sight afforded by wisdom. They should have known better than to challenge Manannán Mac Lir. I killed every last one of them that came for me during that time. Mercenaries. Metahumans. I expect they thought I wasn't worth the trouble, after a while. Or maybe they put me down the list. I didn't know what was happening, other than idiots kept coming to my gates and trying to kill me. I didn't find out about the war until later, when I finally joined the world by getting on the internet. Most of my friends went into hiding. Tucked tail and...ran off to a safe haven." He nodded slowly, still staring at the fire, but then he turned to me. "If I'd known...well, I wish I'd joined the twenty-first century sooner. It might have been nice to...go fight a war we had a chance of winning again."

"Indeed," I said, those goosebumps back again for an entirely different reason.

"I've thought about leaving since then," Mac said. "But...I've been here so long. Old habits, I suppose. I'm almost cloaked in this place by now, and like leaving a cocoon when you've lost the muscles to stand...it gets harder every day. I suppose I'll just wait here for death. It wouldn't be so bad."

"It's a different world out there, now," I said. "Television. Internet—"

"I have all those things," he said, dismissing me with a wave. "I'm a shut-in; I'm not cut off from all humanity."

"If you wanted to fight..." I said. "I...seem to have one coming up."

He chuckled, then shook his head. "Even if I did leave, I wouldn't go to that one with you. You have so many cooks already in that kitchen, and ultimately...they may help you, they may not, but if they kill this Rose for you...you'll be filled with this crystallized, deep-seated regret for all the rest of your years."

I sat there, slowly blinking my way through his statement. "What? I want her dead. Why would I regret it if someone helped me kill her?"

Mac laughed softly, and sat forward, his eyes intense, as he looked at me. "I'm not talking about help. I'm talking about someone killing her for you. And as for why...because she's taken more from you than almost anyone else in the world."

"People have died fighting for me before," I said, my ire rising. "I've lost loves, I've lost friends, people who were struck down because of me—"

"Those are terrible losses, I'm sure," Mac said, "but those were other people, taken *because* of you. This girl did something different—she got inside you. Inside your...defenses. She beat you in a way I'm guessing no one else has. She's marked you for a special sort of revenge, a special sort of fight. Entwined herself with you in a way...I don't think you've had happen from any of your other foes. Am I right?"

"You're right," I conceded reluctantly. Everyone else I'd fought, from Old Man Winter to Weissman to Sovereign— they'd all tried to hurt me, to take from me...

...but no one had ripped me apart like Rose.

"One unleashed succubus against another," Mac said, shaking his head. "You might have been best of friends if you didn't hate each other so. Is there anyone who could understand you as well as she could?"

Something about that clicked in me. Was that the reason Rose had dragged me along for so long without killing me?

We'd both lost our families.

We'd lost everything.

We'd been cast out.

And we'd unlimited power come tumbling into our laps by virtue of the succubus secret that had come to us.

Hell...if you looked at our family trees, they were probably interlaced somewhere back a few generations, if even that far. We were basically cousins of some stripe.

Yeah...if not for the fact she hated me with everything in her...Rose and I might have been friends after all.

We are not the same, Rose's voice sounded in my head, faint and distant. *And even if we were...I would have hated you anyway.*

I thought you loved me? I asked, taking a long sip of the Scotch.

She didn't answer.

"She's your equal and opposite," Mac said, like he knew what I was thinking.

"Like a dark shadow me," I said.

He nodded once. "So yes, I could come with you. And not to be too boastful, but...I could probably even kill her for you. But...it wouldn't *help* you, not really. You have others for that. You need to beat her, for the good of yourself. To prove that you can—"

You can't, that voice came again. *You can't beat me.*

"—for your own good," he said, and he looked at Diana and Eilish, sleeping soundly just across the room. "Or else..."

I waited for him to finish, but he didn't say anything for a long while. "Or else what?" I finally asked.

"Or else *you'll* never sleep soundly again," he said, and I knew, sitting before that fire, sadness cloaking his eyes, that he was speaking in the voice of experience.

38.

Reed

Somewhere over the Atlantic Ocean

"Crossing over Greenland now," the nearly mechanical voice echoed through our little travel compartment. It boomed out through the walls, coming in over the whine of the aircraft lancing through the skies at supersonic speed. The speaker's name was Greg Vansen, and he was talking to us from, well...

From far above. From his head. Which was...far above us. Because we were sitting in a shipping container that had been bolted to the cockpit floor, secured tightly and rehabbed into a house, perfect in scale for us.

Because we were tiny. Ant tiny.

"I've finally met Ant-Man," I muttered, "and he's me."

"Isn't this the coolest way to travel?" Guy Friday called from across the living room space we were sitting in. Friday wasn't wrong, but he wasn't exactly right, either. I mean, I was shrunk to minuscule size, riding in a miniature dollhouse—with actual full-sized possessions, plumbing, power, Wi-Fi, its own septic, a full library of Blu Rays, a theater room—I mean, it was the highest style in which I'd ever traveled.

But I was the size of an ant, sitting underneath the pilot seat of an SR-71 thanks to a metahuman with shrinking and growing powers, traveling at hundreds of miles per hour over the Atlantic.

It was also the weirdest way in which I'd ever traveled. And I occasionally flew across the world on the wind and had been carried in the arms of my sister for thousands of miles before. So it's not like I tended to travel conventionally.

"How are you doing over there?" I asked Tracy, sitting in a recliner across the living room. His head was down; he was focused.

"Doing great, sir!" he belted out, nodding furiously at me. He had a haunted look in his eyes, and I had this sense I was going to feel a little guilty about what I'd done to him once this was all over. "Ready to fight whatever you need me to, sir!"

Olivia Brackett was sitting next to me, watching Tracy a little cagily, like she expected him to go nuts any second. I didn't necessarily think she was wrong in this, but Zollers had assured me he was both sincere and mostly stable. The "mostly" worried me. "I'm kind of in awe of how you reprogrammed him."

I let out a little sigh. "Yeah. Well. I was never a fan of behavior modification, and—yeah, I'm still not after seeing him like this. It's like he had a total lobotomy of his id."

She just sat there, staring at me. "I'm waiting for the downside."

I shifted, feeling pained somewhere deep inside. "Training a human with the equivalent of a shock collar seems…wrong. If there's an afterlife with a reckoning, I think this is going to be something I pay for in the long haul."

"I've got no complaints," she said, still looking at him. "And I knew him better than anyone, so…don't beat yourself up. This is all improvement."

I let out a long sigh. "Yeah, but do the ends justify the means?"

She only thought for a second. "In this case, yes."

"You're going to like my sister a lot," I said, clapping Olivia on the shoulder and standing up, leaving the comfortable couch behind me. I was taking deep breaths, a funny feeling since I was in a pressurized cockpit. The air quality did feel different up here. I wondered at our altitude, but I couldn't exactly ask the giant who was sitting somewhere miles above us, by our reckoning.

I wandered over to the kitchen, where Augustus, Scott, Veronika and Taneshia were huddled over a table, playing some card game. I heard Scott say, "Man, Taneshia is going to shoot the moon again," followed by laughter from the others. I decided not to interrupt that good time.

"Can you believe that we have Wi-Fi here?" Kat asked as I wandered by. Her eyes were glued to her phone, and she looked perfectly coiffed, which was, I suppose, her version of being ready for battle. She didn't even look at me, but I knew she was talking to me. "This is way better than flying a private jet. I need to book this guy for all my travel needs."

"It's perfect, if you don't mind traveling smaller than one of those purse dogs you're so fond of," I said, smiling tightly.

Kat threw a hand over her chest, covering her heart. "Oh! They are so adorable. I keep thinking of getting one, but then I remember—so much work."

"You're quite breathtaking, Kat," I said, then shuffled on by. She seemed to take it as a compliment, returning to studying her phone as though it held all the secrets of life. Technically, she held a few of them herself.

"You're going to pace holes in our guest's carpets," Dr. Zollers said, as I passed by a recliner in the corner, where he sat, eyes closed, leaned back with his feet up and his loafers off.

"Very small ones, yes," I said, and the house shook slightly, presumably the result of some atmospheric disturbance. I kept walking, because the last thing I needed right now was to be pigeonholed and psychoanalyzed.

I didn't see Jamie Barton, Angel or Phinneus Chalke; there were fully furnished bedrooms upstairs, and I figured they were probably sleeping. The entire house had a somewhat sterile if lived-in feeling, like the 90s sparsity and love of black and white had been adopted as Greg's ethos of design. Moving into a living room separated from the kitchen by an archway, I found myself in the tech den of our little team.

Which…was getting to be a big team, lately.

"Reed, make 'em bleed," J.J. said, not looking up from his screen, which was lighting his face in the dim room. "It rhymes, and is instruction for what we're going into. See?"

"He sees, dear," Abby said, taking a hand off the keyboard to pat him on the shoulder. Her hair was blue today. I didn't know when she'd dyed it, but it was now blue.

"Admire my duofecta," J.J. said.

"I admire much about you, J.J.," I said. "And you, Abby." She nodded. "In fact, in the manner of all power couples, I shall dub thee—J. Abs."

"I like it better than AbiJay," J.J. said without looking up. "Or just Jabs."

"It doesn't really fit on multiple levels, though," Abby said. "Because we don't have abs, really. We just like cake way too much for those."

"It'd be easier if we had metahuman metabolisms," J.J. agreed. "Do you see how much Kat eats? Or Augustus? And he's got like, rocks under his shirt. Not literal ones—"

"Because you picked the one guy who it could be applied literally to," I cracked.

"—but I mean, you have to eat a LOT as a meta to pack on the weight," J.J. said. "That'd be nice. I'd eat like a hobbit and maintain my prime physique rather than eating like a hobbit and gradually getting closer to the ground, gut-wise." He patted himself. "I have to watch my diet just to keep from overhanging my belt these days."

I turned my attention to the other, silent occupants of the room. "Jamal. Cassidy. How goes it?"

"Sickeningly cute," Cassidy said, not looking up from her triple workstation in the corner.

Jamal took another second to answer. "She's not wrong. It's constant. And wearying. Like, you think maybe they're putting on an act—but they're not. They're like this all the time."

"Aw, you hear that, pwecious?" J.J. asked, leaning in and nuzzling noses with Abby. "We're—"

"Stop, or I will personally scheme a way to tear you apart so viciously that you will hate each other for eternity,"

Cassidy said, still not looking up from her computer. "You will look for ways to extend your lives so that you can hate each other more fully for longer. It will be so personally painful that the only reason you don't contemplate suicide is sheer spite and desire for revenge on each other. So..." She finally looked up, and there was cold, dark malice in her eyes. "Stop it."

Jamal looked at her with something approaching horror mingled with relief, and Abby stood, snapping her laptop shut. "We don't have to take this," she said, taking J.J. by the arm as he stood. "There are other rooms in this house."

"Yes," Cassidy said, turning right back to her computer. "Go. Get a room." She flicked her wrist at them, giving them a limp, skinny hand for direction. "Leave us in peace."

With a huff, Abby left, J.J. in tow.

"I don't really agree with your methods," Jamal said, "but I like your results." And he was back to work.

"Was that necessary?" I asked Cassidy.

She still didn't look up. "It was either get them out of here or take ten minutes vomiting—time in which your little redhead friend could retake all her country's systems, so...yes, it was necessary."

"Okay then," I said, and started to pull myself away.

"You should know," Cassidy said, looking over her shoulder at me. "The Scottish radar is running hot. Really hot. I don't know if we're going to be able to dodge it, even if we shrink. We're probably going to get picked up. I don't think there's a way to avoid it without miniaturizing to the point that even the SR-71 travels at snail speed."

"Dammit," I said. "I should go grab the radio and warn our pilot, I guess." He'd provided us a communication line in case we needed to tell him anything. He'd also warned us— very sternly, because he seemed like a serious guy—not to bother him with idle chatter. "Can you think of any way to avoid it?"

"I'm working on it," she said, "but sometimes you encounter a problem where someone is brute-forcing you, and all the finesse in the world won't stop it. I think you should be prepared for us to be seen." Her jaw tightened. "And I hope that you have strategies enough to beat this Rose when she comes after us, because…" She looked back at the computer. "It seems likely she'll be doing so."

39.

Sienna

When it was my turn to sleep, I drifted off pretty fast. I didn't think it would happen, but it did, Mac's guest bed soft enough that I was out almost immediately, sleep wrapping itself around me as surely as the gentle tentacles of an octopus, dragging me into the deep. Which was probably a nightmare I'd had at some point.

I had someone in mind as I drifted off, someone I wanted to see before tomorrow, and as soon as the darkness closed in around me, I found myself in a quiet place—my old living room, sitting in my old chair.

And she was right there.

She had a crease in her brow, some added wrinkles around her eyes, but there she sat, her red hair showing a few streaks of grey that hadn't been there when last I'd seen her. She had a look of intense concentration about her as she looked around, as though trying to figure out exactly how she'd ended up here.

"Hello, Ariadne," I said, feeling a little tight in the throat for some reason.

She cocked her head at me. "Hello."

"You, uh, probably don't know who I am—" I started to say.

She shook her head. "I know who you are."

I felt a tingle of hope. "You…you do?"

"Of course," she said in those precise tones that used to drive me nuts when she was lecturing. "You're Sienna Nealon. Everyone knows who you are."

That lump in my throat was the size of a charcoal briquette, and I buried my disappointment, though it came out in my voice. "Oh. Yeah."

"This…" She looked around again. "This is a bit of a strange dream, isn't it?"

"Definitely," I said, sounding a little husky. "And it's definitely a dream." I stood, wandering over to the kitchen. It looked exactly as I remembered it, my old house, a benefit of the dreamwalk. It had burned down a year ago, but I could still see it like this, in my mind.

And Ariadne was in it.

"Very strange," she said, rising to her feet. She was dressed in a bathrobe, as she had been so many times when we'd sat in this room, watching TV or talking. It had been a strange time, where she'd been my surrogate mom and roommate and galpal all in one. I'd had an agency all my own, no interference from the government, I'd had friends surrounding me, I'd had a boyfriend…

I'd had it all.

It had been a year since my life had been turned completely upside down, shattered into tiny pieces, and…

…I knew my friends were still there for me.

…I didn't care about having a career anymore. There were more important things.

…I missed my house, but it wasn't the walls and doors and wood and cheap paneling that made it home.

…Ariadne…she made it home.

It was the smell of her heating up apple cider on the stove on a chilly September night. It was the way I'd come home from a mission and find my bed made, my clothes laundered and put away, and a hot meal cooking on the stove.

It was the thousand terrible memories of childhood giving way to the thousand little moments of an adulthood that was making up for those early terrors. It was feeling settled and secure, like someone was there, always.

And I missed it.

"I'm, uh…" I said, turning my face away from her, "I'm…heading into trouble tomorrow. Again."

She seemed to be deciding how to interact with me, since she still thought this was just a dream. "Oh?" she asked, more out of politeness than anything.

"It's…going to be bad," I said. "I'm up against someone who really hates me." That was the easy way to say it. "And…she's powerful. Stronger than me." Ariadne stayed utterly silent, because…what do you say to a stranger who unloads on you like this? "I don't know…if I'm going to make it out of this."

"I'm sure you'll be fine," she said, rather simply.

I turned around. Couldn't help myself. "Why do you say that?"

There wasn't a trace of guile. "You're Sienna Nealon." She must have seen the utterly curious look on my face. "You beat anyone who comes after you."

That one hit me like a spear to the heart, and my shoulders shook once as a violent exhalation of breath came out in the form of a sniffle. I made a little sniffling laugh. "You're damned right I do," I said, once I got it under control.

She just stood there, a straitlaced, slightly uncomfortable expression tight on her face. She put her hands together, looking at me, then looking away, pure Minnesota stoicism in the face of someone…well, ugly crying in front of her. "I'm sorry," I said, "I just need to—"

And I swept in and caught her in a hug, wrapping her up tight. She stiffened in my grasp, and then, after a moment, put her hands around me. "Uh…there, there," she said, less comfortable than maybe any time I'd seen her before. She patted me on the back, and even though it was clear she had no idea why this complete and total stranger was hugging her…

I didn't care.

I held her there for minutes, hours—as long as I could, really, my tears softly falling on her shoulder—until I finally let her go.

40.

We left Mac's house just as the tourists were starting to show up for the day. Clear-eyed, fed with food brought up by Mac from the cafe kitchen, we tromped out the front door just before nine o'clock, as rested as we were going to get on the night before what was probably going to be either an epic escape or—if Mac was right—an epic battle.

For the first time, a part of me was wishing for the latter, even as the rest of me feared it. Not because of me or fear for myself...but because my friends were going into it with me.

"The route is simple," Mac said, handing over a sheet of hand-written directions. It kept us from having to use a GPS or carry a phone, so it was a winning strategy in my view. "Follow that, you'll be there in an hour."

"Thank you, Mac," I said, holding back. I'm not usually a hugger, or a hand shaker.

He nodded, once, as someone drove past us to the parking lot. For the first time, I realized that he'd hidden a small box under his arm beneath the directions. He caught me looking, and pulled it out, handing it to me.

"What's this?" I asked. It wasn't gift-wrapped, and the label was right across the plastic. It was suitcase-shaped, but smaller, like a briefcase or toolbox that you might carry a very basic, very small set of tools in. It was no longer than my forearm.

And it said "Walther" on it.

He didn't answer; just smiled.

I already knew, but I opened it anyway.

It was as sleek as I remembered from when I used to carry one. "This used to be my go-to backup gun," I said, looking at the gleaming, shining silver of the Walther PPK cradled in the foam cutouts within. There was a spare mag, fully loaded, with hollow point ammo.

"So the biography did get that little detail right." Mac's eyes gleamed. "It's not much, but...you can't find much more than that in Scotland without breaking into a police armory."

"I should have done that a few weeks ago," I joked. "Guess I must be off my game."

"Assaulting a police station is no easy feat, even for a succubus," Mac said. "But this is my way of...giving you a leg up, I suppose, in your quest."

"Quest?" Eilish asked. I had a theory she couldn't bear to be left out of any conversation, and would eventually insert herself into it no matter how she had to.

"It seems to this casual observer that you got lost in Scotland," Mac said, a knowing look in his eyes. "Go and find yourself again, Sienna Nealon. Remember who you are."

I know who you are, Rose said, *and I'll find you first, and take you—take all of you—like I have so much of you already.*

"I'm starting to remember," I said, putting the Walther case under my arm. It wouldn't do diddly squat to Rose in her current form, but...it was better than nothing. "Thank you, Mac."

He nodded and started to walk away, pausing for a peck on the cheek from Diana. "Come see me again sometime," he said, looking over his shoulder to wave at us as he departed.

"No," I said, shaking my head. "I'm not coming back to Scotland after this. You're going to have to come see me next time."

He paused for just a moment, then smiled, and nodded. "I'll look forward to it."

And somehow I knew, as we turned away and walked toward the car...

Yeah. I'd see Manannán Mac Lir again.

Over Rose's dead body.

41.

The drive was as promised: an hour of agonized waiting, alternating fear and anticipation coming over me like they were running a circuit, each crossing through my heart in turn.

We passed the time in silence, no one daring to speak. Diana was at the wheel, a stony quiet enveloping her, statuesque as she'd been in Glasgow only days before when she'd jumped out of the night to help save me.

Eilish was a pit of silence in the back. When I looked over my shoulder at her, I found her gnawing her fingernails. They were down to the nubs, and I said, "It's going to be okay."

She blinked at me a few times, as though waking. "You sure about that?"

I drew a long breath, and let it out slowly. "I'd have liked it if I could have had more time to get ready for this, maybe have a training montage while Survivor's 'Eye of the Tiger' played in the background, but…yeah." I nodded. "I'm sure. And I'm ready."

She raised both eyebrows almost to the roof of the car, then shook her head once. "I like the confidence. Wish I shared it."

"You'll get there," I said.

"We may pass beyond these shores without even facing her," Diana said, probably one of the most reassuring things I'd heard the prickly goddess say yet. "For how will she know where we aim to go?"

"She'll know," I said. "It's what she does."

Diana frowned, but didn't argue. I felt a little bad about tossing more nervousness their way, especially for Eilish, but they needed to know what was coming.

They needed to be ready—at least as ready as they might get.

We followed an overgrown, broken-up road that looked like it hadn't been repaved in years, and it wended its way around another boob mountain. When we passed through the other side, I caught my first glimpse of Caladh Reidh.

So, I said in my head, *this is where you grew up.*

Aye, Rose's voice came, almost reluctantly. *And this is where you'll die.*

I took that with a surprising calm. *Like your family?*

The Rose in my head got hot. *You killed them.*

Nope, I said. My guilt was over. My doubt was over.

I'll kill you.

"You'll try," I whispered, and Diana looked at me strangely out of the corner of her eyes. "Sorry," I said.

"Don't go into battle apologizing," she said.

"I wouldn't worry about it," I said. "The apologies are for my allies. My enemies just get the full brunt of my aggravation."

She lowered her voice, as though this would somehow keep Eilish from hearing it. "If you're so sure this Rose is going to show up...do you have a plan?"

"Several," I said, "but they all kind of converge with a general strategy—beat her ass."

Diana raised an eyebrow. "Did you not say she had an Achilles and a Wolfe to aid her?"

"The Wolfe," I said. "She has *the* Wolfe to aid her."

Diana tried to keep a lid on the crazy eyes, but failed, because, let's face it, I'd said something crazy in proposing we fight someone with those powers. "Is there a difference?"

"You ever met Wolfe?" I asked. "Not his brothers, but actually Wolfe."

"A long time ago," she said. "He reasoned his way out of certain death for your grandmother at the hands of my

"Did everyone know her but me?" I asked. "Sometimes it feels like you old metahumans had a club, and anyone born after like 1950 need not apply."

She sort of blinked at me. "Of course we had clubs. They were called pantheons, and we socialized constantly."

"Figures I'd come along after the good clubs went and broke up," Eilish muttered from the backseat, giving more credence to my theory about her.

The village was only a few hundred yards ahead now, a scattering of weathered houses built into the side of the hill. There was a very definite slope down into a deeper valley below, not too far down but enough that if you took a roll down the hill, you'd feel it at the bottom, where a little creek ran over stones. The hills were covered with the brownish grass that seemed so ubiquitous here in Scotland now that winter was on its way. The skies were dark, and I wondered when we'd see the first snowfall.

My guess? Soon.

The Audi rattled over the uneven road, years of winters and lack of tending having taken their toll. We came to a stop just past a house that had its front door thrown wide open, creaking in the wind.

"Let's go," I said, not wasting any time standing on ceremony. I was out of the car a second later.

"I'm having second thoughts," Eilish said. "Now third thoughts, same as the second. Now fourth—yeah, they all say the same thing—this is crazy." She got out of the car nonetheless. "I'm hoping Diana's right, that we just silently steal out of the country and leave the fighting for another day—like never. Never would be good for me."

"Now's not a great time to be afraid," I said.

"It's the time I've got," Eilish said, "and I'm afraid. Because this girl you're pitting us against—"

"I didn't choose this fight."

"—she's got the power of the old gods," Eilish went on, undeterred by my protestation. "How many people did she beef up with that serum you mentioned, and then kill, trying to arrogate unto herself limitless power? This is a woman

263

who's killed more people than a decent number of diseases, and we're walking into her old stomping grounds anticipating a fight. How mad does that make us?"

I stared at the dark skies. "I don't know about you, but…I'm pretty mad at this point."

Diana sidled closer to her. "She means angry, not—"

"Yeah, I got that one," Eilish said.

"I wasn't sure if you—"

"It was pretty obvious." Eilish came up behind me. "Why do you want to fight *that*? Why would want that kind of trouble, right now?"

"Because she took something from me," I said, watching the skies. Reed was out there, somewhere.

With the team.

With more guns.

And with a big dose of suppressant that would render Rose…as powerless as a human being.

She was the stronger succubus?

Pfft.

I wanted to see what she thought of being powerless.

But I didn't dare say that out loud, because if I did…Rose might hear it, and make it a lot harder for me to carry out my devious plan to disempower her and rip my stolen souls, screaming, out of her head.

Along with, probably, a whole heap ton more. Alas. I didn't need the company, but it'd be worth it.

Company's coming, I said in my mind.

I'm not exactly laying out the doilies and the fine china, Rose's voice came, taunting as ever. *I can see your little plans. How do you think it'll feel when they all turn to ashes in your mouth?*

Victory's gonna be sweet, I said, like I didn't even hear her. *Like fresh orange slices on a hot day.*

You're going to be crushed.

People have been threatening that for a long time, I said. *Yet here I am.*

You've never met anyone like me.

"Honey…all I've met are villains like you."

I'm not the villain. But here, for the first time…she sounded almost unsure.

"Talking to yourself, darling?" Rose's voice boomed out over the valley, louder than I'd ever heard it. "That's a sign of serious mental illness."

"Oh, Jaysus," Eilish said, "I always wondered about that. My dad always said, 'Eilish, girl, you talk to yourself, people are going to think you're crazy'—and here comes a certifiable, absolutely definite crazy person, telling me exactly the same truth. Voice of authority, there. That settles it. I must be crazy."

I couldn't help but snicker, especially since Rose was nowhere in sight. Even Diana chortled at that, though I could see she was incredibly wary, her whole body poised to move, jump or run. Maybe all three.

"Thank you," Rose said, and I turned to find her behind me, standing on a rooftop. A couple of the houses nearby had collapsed, nothing but piles of old shingles, broken walls, even some smashed up concrete with rebar jutting out of it. Rose was looking down over all of this, strangely relaxed.

"For what?" I asked. The Walther was in my waistband, tucked in tight, in case I needed it. The moment was not yet though, so I didn't bother to reach for it.

"You're bringing everything I've wanted right to me," she said, eyes dancing under the cloudy skies. "Your little friends here in country…your friends from America, who are on their way right now…"

She came off the roof in a quick glide, not moving at her full speed, but I sensed…she was almost done toying with me. "And you've brought yourself…which is the greatest gift of all."

"I've often said I'm the gift that keeps on giving." I looked her dead in the eyes.

She cocked her head at me. "Where's all that fear I spent months putting into you? Fear for yourself? For your friends?" She seemed to be standing off, just slightly, hesitant.

And suddenly…I knew Rose like she knew me.

"It's still in here," I said, "but I've got a good handle on it now."

"Sounds like I'm going to have to unwrap you to find it,"

she said. "Take your skin off a layer at a time, and I bet you'll find that fear again."

"Promises, promises," I said, just staring her down. "Well, Rose." And I stared back at her, glaring at me, and then beckoned her with one hand.

Not fearless.

Cocky, though. Even when I had no right to be.

"Well..." I said, and cracked a smile, which I did not entirely feel. "Shall we get this party started?"

42.

Zack

Minnesota
October 2012

Sienna lay draped across his chest, breathing slowly against him. She was fully dressed, as was he, all the precautions taken, as they always did. He didn't feel tired yet, but when he felt those first stirrings of fatigue, Zack knew he would roll her off of him to the other side of the bed, so that she didn't accidentally put a hand on his face during the night and rip his soul out of his very body.

"Such romance," Zack whispered to himself.

"Mmm," Sienna muttered. She was already asleep.

He smiled. Her face had relaxed, all the tension bled out of it. She looked different when she slept. He leaned in, played with a lock of her hair, lifted it to his nose. It smelled of very basic shampoo, nothing too strong, because heavy aromas bothered her metahuman nasal sensitivities. She had her cheek pressed against his left pectoral through the shirt, just resting there, a little mushed, but relaxed...

So relaxed.

She definitely didn't look that way when she was awake. There was always a resting intensity about Sienna, a wary look that she sent every direction. Her head wasn't quite mounted on a swivel, but it was close, always seeking the

267

next attack flying at her. It couldn't have been easy, growing up as she had, but this—this look it had produced, something between sardonic amusement and A+ Game Resting Bitch Face—well, she wore it well.

"I love you," he whispered, even lower. He knew she'd hear it.

"Mm." She stirred again, shifting against his ribs. She was using him as a pillow…and he didn't mind at all.

This hadn't started the way he would have wanted it to, had he picked her for himself. He'd been pushed her way by Old Man Winter, but—that was done, now. He was going to tell Winter, and soon.

No, he hadn't chosen this relationship, but now—

Now he couldn't imagine his life without her.

When the hell had that happened?

He looked down again at the relaxed tableau of her face against his chest. It wasn't how he'd ever imagined love coming for him. A woman he could barely touch, couldn't experience any of the other unguarded intimacies with—and yet—

And yet…

"I really do love you, Sienna," he whispered. "No matter what happens, I'll always be in your corner. I—"

*

"—would be throwing up in my mouth right now," Gerry Harmon said, face putrid enough to match his statement, "if I still had a mouth, and had ingested any food in the last year."

"Such a romantic you are, Harmon," Eve Kappler said, darkly amused at the President's outburst.

"I thought it was rather sweet," Bjorn said, sullenly staring at the fire. He seemed to realize that everyone was suddenly staring at him, and his face went through a metamorphosis from shock, as though he couldn't believe he'd said it, to finally, "Yes, okay, I said it. So what?"

"You've changed," Aleksandr Gavrikov said, eyebrow inching up.

"Perhaps," Bjorn said, still staring at the fire, back to sullen. "But if I have…it was none of your doing. It was…" He looked down. "Her."

"'Her,'" Harmon said, dripping with scorn. "What do you think 'her' was doing to you? Brainwashing you, that's what. You all scorn me for wanting to take over the thoughts of the whole world, but look at you—you're all hopelessly dedicated to her, pining after her even all these months removed from her head. You make me sick."

"I'm not pining," Eve said.

"You make me sick for other reasons," Harmon said, and when she stared at him, he added, "German food is terrible. Bratwurst, sauerkraut—it's all nausea-inducing."

"What does that have to do with me?"

"You're German," Harmon said. "It practically radiates off of you."

"I haven't eaten sauerkraut and bratwurst since I was a child—"

"It doesn't matter," Harmon said, lashing out around the circle. "I can feel it wafting off of you all, this hopeless, sad, disgusting regret, this longing—for what? For the good old days when we were the prisoners of Sienna Nealon?" He made a sound like he was going to spit, even though Zack knew he would never do any such uncouth thing. "Where's your motivation to leave? Where's your hope to find a way out?"

"It's all tied up in someone beating Rose," Bastian said. "And if someone's going to beat her, and give us a highway out of here—"

"It is her," Gavrikov said with certainty.

"She's probably forgotten about you all by now," Eve said. "She's been beaten, broken, stripped of memory…there's nothing left of her to fight."

"I don't think so," Bjorn said.

"This is so sad," Harmon said, pacing a few feet, then turning back to the fire, which lit the darkness around them. "You're holding out hope for her to come rescue you, like—like you believe in gods."

"I believe in Sienna Nealon," Zack said, and he stood.

"Then you're a fool," Harmon said, lashing out at him again.

"I believe in Sienna Nealon," Bjorn said, now on his feet, hulking in the light of the fire.

"I believe in Sienna," Gavrikov said, rising, the flames giving his skin its usual cast, the way Zack always thought of him.

"I believe in Sienna, too," Bastian said, and he stood, like the feathered dragon that he could be in life. "We lived with her for years. Inside her mind, in her thoughts. You—you weren't there but a year. You don't know her. She's out there right now—and she's not going to quit. I know this."

"You don't know anything but this sham of a village now," Eve said, still seated by the fire.

Harmon just stared at them, then rolled his eyes. "You're all—"

"Idiots." It was Graham's voice—but it wasn't. It was modulated somehow, crackling with something else, a more feminine softness.

Zack looked down, and where Graham had been sitting only a moment before—

Was Rose.

"You're all idiots," Rose said, shaking her head, sneering at them in the dark. "That's what he was going to say." She pointed at Harmon.

"Yes, thank you for finishing my sentence," Harmon said. "As though I weren't capable of that on my own."

"Your timing is fortuitous, though," Rose said, and she stood. "You believe in Sienna Nealon?" She laughed, and it was cold and crackling, echoing over the hillside. She waved a hand, and a shadowy figure appeared out of the dark, a ghostly version of Sienna, the skin just barely translucent. "Here she is, boys. Worship your goddess in the flesh—or lack thereof." She laughed again. "But don't worry—she'll be solid soon enough." Her face hardened, especially around the eyes, but the smile froze in place. "She'll be with you, here—very soon, now."

"What happened to Graham?" Eve asked, brow puckered.

Rose laughed again. "Here's why you're an idiot, too—

Graham never came to you."

"It was always you," Harmon said.

Rose's eyes danced in the firelight, lively and vivid. "Aye, it was. I wanted to listen to you, at least for as long as it took."

Zack felt a subtle shift around the campfire; even Harmon paused, unsure. "As long as it took...for what?" he asked.

"You asked me—Graham—before," Rose said, dark amusement bleeding out of her, "what happened to the others? To the other souls I've taken? Well, the answer's simple, isn't it? They're here." She raised a hand to the sky, and a thin, reedy howling echoed in the distance. "All of them. Like a Greek chorus, singing the tragedy of my life, and that of those I touch now." She was grinning madly. The clouds were moving above, shifting, like living things. "I've never absorbed a group like you before, see. The fact that you're hanging together this well? It's...poignant? Also, annoying." Her amusement faded. "See...every other soul I ate...they just...dissolved into the crowd like a pebble in a pond. Ripples, then..." She waved her fingertips. "Bye-bye. They became no more than ghosts, they're...gone. Part of the sea of me.

"But you lot..." She shook her head. "Here you sit, three months on, and you're still just...hanging on. Talking about your girl like she's some great lost love." She made a noise of disgust, then nodded at Harmon. "I'm about ready to join him for some retching, the difference being I actually do have a mouth and have eaten recently."

"If you've eaten haggis, you should commence to retching regardless of how you feel about us," Eve said. When everyone looked at her, she said, "It's minced sheep stomach. It's worse than sauerkraut."

"I've been letting this little psychodrama play out because I've had better things to do," Rose said, patience evaporated. She was looking at them all now with dark determination. "I'm sick of you holding out here in your little redoubt that I made for you. It's time for you to get lost in the chorus so I don't have to listen to your stupid prattle about Sienna Nealon any bloody more."

"She's going to kill you," Zack said.

"If she could, she would do it twice," Gavrikov said.

"Three times," Bjorn said. "And hand you your own ass before force-feeding it to you. Which is worse than sheep's stomach for it being so bony."

"You're going to die looking at her face," Bastian said, staring down Rose. "Or worse—you'll never even see it coming."

"I hope she breaks you into tiny pieces," Eve said, standing up at last. "Crushes you like the bony, damaged ginger bitch you are."

"Oh, look at the fire in you lot," Rose said, the flames rising up around them. "Seems you have a hope." She made a motion, and the fire died instantly. "You think I'm going to die to her?" She laughed. "Fine—watch this, then—"

The world seemed to open up, like a curtain rising over a screen, and suddenly, Zack saw her there, standing before Rose, staring her down.

"She's here," Gavrikov breathed.

"In the village," Bjorn said.

"It's daytime," Eve said. "I forgot what daytime looked like."

"She's just…standing there," Bastian said, and the alarm was rising in his voice. "Just…standing there."

"That's right." Rose's voice crackled over them, and Zack could tell, it was ringing out in the real world too, outside her head, because Sienna shifted, subtly. "Time to watch Sienna Nealon die, children…

"Time to watch all your hope die with her."

43.

Sienna

I almost teared up when Rose said, "Time to watch all your hope die with her," because I realized, in that moment, she wasn't talking to me.

She wasn't talking to Diana or Eilish.

She was talking to my souls.

Mine.

"Hello, boys," I said, smiling at her—past her—"and Eve. Did you miss me?"

44.

Zack

"Yes!" Bastian pumped a fist.

"You thought she forgot us?" Bjorn sneered at Harmon. "You think she is out of the fight?"

Harmon just stared straight ahead, blankly, and blinked a couple times. "You heard what she said." He nodded at Rose.

"How could you miss it, fools?" Rose cackled.

"She's going to dissolve us into nothingness," Harmon said, and he looked…ghastly pale. Sounded worse. "We're going to be…nothing." His voice cracked.

"That's right," Rose said, grinning at them.

"All our lives…" Eve said softly. "…to end up…nothing."

"And we will count for nothing," Harmon said, staring straight ahead, dead as a statue. "So…" And he turned his head to look at Rose, and Zack thought, *OH SHIT*, because he'd seen that look before. "Two choices—a whimper? Or—"

"Let's go out with a fucking bang," Eve said, and they all jumped on Rose at the same time.

45.

Rose jerked like someone had pounded her in the face, and I crossed the distance and pounded her in the face to match. My fist met her nose like my knuckles had kissed a brick wall, rebounding, crackling slightly, but I'd done the punch right, carried it through, and while it didn't damage her flesh, Rose definitely felt the impact.

"Are you out of your mind!" Eilish screamed somewhere behind me, but I was already whirling.

I hit Rose with a reverse side kick, planting it right in the base of her spine. Her skin was like forged steel, but I gave it all I had, gave it hell, and I heard the satisfying pop of my contact against her as she tumbled to the ground. I didn't break anything, but I bounced her around some.

"Yes," I said, "I am out of my mind." I raised a fist and hammered her in the back of the skull, aiming for the occipital notch where her spinal column entered her skull. I pulled up my fist and hit her again, then again. "She has driven me out of my—"

She lashed out at me with an elbow before I could break her neck, and it hit me right in the gut with stunning force. I sailed through the air and crashed into a broken mound of concrete, rolling up and out of the landing to find myself standing in a field of broken concrete and rebar.

Rose floated into the air, her smile not what it used to be.

275

"You think any of this matters? Your little souls clawing at me in here, your ugly dog face biting at me out here, nipping at my heels?"

"I'm nipping at your guts, Rose darling," I said, turning her favorite word back around on her. "I'm going to pull them out in a tangle and choke you to death with them."

"That's…nice," Eilish said, drawing attention to herself at a terrible time.

Rose glanced at her, and I saw a glow starting in her hand. I swiped a length of rebar and hurled it like a short javelin—

It caught Rose in the side of the head and knocked her off-kilter as a blast of red laser shot out of her hand and left a devastating trail behind it, a relic of the power Frankie had used so heavily in Edinburgh. She snapped her head back around at me as Eilish screamed and scrambled, running for cover behind a nearby house.

I seized another length of rebar, one about the length of my arm, then grabbed a second for my other hand. They were roughly uniform in length, straight pieces of steel that grooved roughly but fit just fine into the palms of my hands, like the eskrima sticks of my youth.

"What are you going to do with those?" she asked.

"Figured I'd go old school on you," I said, rising, my makeshift eskrima in a resting position, ready to use. "Maybe cram one of these up your flat ass and give it a twist, see if that's invulnerable. I'm guessing it's not, once you get past the—"

She came at me at warp speed, hyper powerful, and landed a hit that I barely—barely—managed to mitigate by turning aside at the last second. I still went flying, but I rolled out of it, pain screaming its way through my shoulder.

This was the problem with being a toddler fighting a heavyweight. One punch could end you. Something I knew from experience, because Rose had landed punches like that on me before, world-ending, life-stealing hits that could kill a normal person just from shock and trauma.

"Did you think it would be that easy?" she asked, coming at me again. This time I dropped, letting her skim overhead as she tapped me in the arm. It went numb all the way to the fingers and I nearly dropped my makeshift eskrima. She whirled around and came to a stop, hovering, lording it over me. "That you'd just—what? Find your confidence again and beat me through sheer pluck?" She laughed, howling like a nightmare, the sound echoing over the dead village. "I whipped you at your best, darling—what hope do you have at your worst?"

She shot at me like a hellbeast uncontained, bursting into flame as she did so. I was going to have to evade again, but it'd be more difficult each time to do so and avoid serious injury. She had a blazing look in her eye, even absent the fire, and I had a bad feeling she was going to do more than a glancing blow this time—

A chunk of concrete the size of a tire smashed into her, and Rose went spiraling off to the side. She crashed in the wreckage of a building and I caught a glimpse of Diana, darting back under cover, her work done for the moment. "Get out of sight, idiot! You're not going to win this by presenting your jaw and having her punch it until she's satisfied."

Points to the Goddess of the Hunt, who probably knew a thing or two about felling prey. I took advantage of the momentary distraction to dive behind a pile of rubble and started belly crawling around it at meta-speed, trying not to make too much noise as I circled.

"Oooh, that was a dirty trick," Rose said, and then grunted in pain. "But…I've always liked it dirty, my lass."

I started to say, "I think you mean 'your ass,' and I'm coming to help flatten that further in a minute," but I didn't because that would have been stupid and also given away my position. But mostly because it didn't quite hit the note of scorn I was looking for. So instead I kept crawling, pulling myself into a hole in a house's wall and into an abandoned bathroom.

"If you're not going to come out and face me…I guess I'll just have to up the stakes," Rose said, and suddenly the air was alive with…fire?

Aw, crap.

The roof above me lit off like tinder, a ball of flame landing on it, the one next door, the one past it—in the course of about ten seconds, she threw a ball of flame onto every single roof in the village. The one above me made an immediate impact, spreading across the timbers and catching the whole damned thing on fire in seconds.

There went my hiding place.

I crossed out of the bathroom, the ceiling writhing with flame above me, and crossed a living room to jump out an already-shattered window. I landed on the street, catching sight of Rose shooting overhead like a dog on the hunt. Bitch on the hunt? Whatever.

There was a pretty ominous feeling settled on my bones as I jumped back to my feet. I took off in the direction she'd gone, hoping that whoever she was chasing…Eilish or Diana…I'd get there soon enough to spare whichever of them it was from pretty certain death.

46.

Zack

They struck and struck at the vision of Rose that was presented to them. The winds howled above the village, screamed as though alive, clouds dancing in a miasma of light, and—

"Damn," Bjorn said, then jerked, screaming from the pain that Rose brought down on them all, not even laying a finger on them to do so. He was on a knee, his big shoulders heaving.

"Are we making any difference?" Eve was unsteady on her feet, the ground around them seeming to tilt. In the distance, beyond the swirling clouds, Rose's vision of the same village had gone hellish, the rooftops aflame beneath her and the lady herself zooming them toward some rabbiting prey moving beneath.

"Well, she hasn't smeared Sienna over the entire countryside yet," Bastian said, "so…yes?"

"It's coming at some cost," Harmon said, and here the President had a distinctly agonized look on his face. "I don't think…I've ever hurt this much in my life."

"Do any of you recall the days before when—no," Gavrikov said, staggering off the wall of a house, his face waxy pale, the way Zack recalled him in life. "It was only Wolfe and me, then. But…we could shoot pain into Sienna's mind, make her hurt if we wished. Nearly make her pass out,

279

through our own will."

"It'd be great if we could do that right now, then," Harmon said. "Maybe knock this psychotic Scot out, take a transfer to a less insane climate. The inside of Sienna's head is looking very promising right now."

"Just now, huh?" Zack asked, a little cynically. He could feel the pain arching over him, too, and it came in waves, whenever Rose turned her ire toward them.

"Boys and girl," Rose said, her own avatar within appearing before them once more. "I've had enough of your little rebellion here." The clouds were howling above. "I know you're mad at Mother, but—I don't bloody care. I've had enough of your shite for the day, and I'm ready to send you all to the dungeons."

"Yeah, the accommodations at Chez Sienna are sounding better all the time," Bastian said, and he lunged for her.

Bastian landed a fist against Rose's jaw, making little impact but for her to grit her teeth. Bjorn came in low after him and punched her in the gut hard enough to take her off her feet, but she remained planted like an oak.

"This is a battle of mind," Gavrikov said, calmly.

"I know that, you moron Russian," Harmon snapped at him.

"None of you has minds anymore," Rose said.

"No, we're inside yours," Gavrikov said, "but—we have *will*." He smiled. "And will…as you see from Sienna… triumphs."

And the Russian lit off, bursting into flame like himself of old, then shot at Rose like a rocket contrail.

She flinched away; she couldn't help it, seeing a demon of fire coming at her. Gavrikov slammed into her solidly, knocking her off her feet and landing atop her, still on fire. Rose let out a scream and Gavrikov went shooting up into the sky from her reprisal, but already Bjorn was howling, coming at her where she lay on the ground as Eve blasted away at her with light nets, webbing her to the ground—

"What can I do in all this?" Zack asked, the quiet whisper in the heart of the storm.

"Use your mind, fool!" Harmon shouted at him over the

chaos. "Use your imagination!"

Zack blinked. Imagination?

Oh, he could do that.

"MAKE WAY!" Zack shouted, a thousand missiles descending out of the sky, riding their imaginary rocket motors to the ground as Bjorn and Bastian leapt clear, and Eve zipped out of the way on glowing wings. They all thundered down on Rose, impacts blasting like a chain of nuclear bombs, leaving a mushroom cloud of fallout that was capped by Gavrikov doing exactly the same as he zipped back down to earth and blasted her solidly with a final explosion.

"That…was not that imaginative," Harmon said, staggering up to Zack.

"Well, it did something, at least," Zack said, watching the smoke.

The smoke blew away in an instant, and sitting, amidst charred, scarred ground, was Rose.

Unharmed.

"Did what?" Harmon shot back.

Zack looked up into the clouds, and saw…

"Huh," he said. "She's just…hovering there. Not looking at anything."

"Yes," Eve said, zipping by as she turned to aim herself toward Rose, "we're distracting her, you idiot—successfully. May I suggest we continue?"

Harmon stood there for just a second, an eyeblink, really. "The lady has a point."

"Yeah, let's go kick some flat ass," Zack said, and together they lurched back toward the fight.

47.

Sienna

Rose just halted in midair, hanging like her puppeteer decided to walk off for a pint and just leave her hanging. I couldn't pass up such a choice opportunity, of course, so I leapt into the air and smashed my rebar against the back of her neck.

She registered the force of the impact, but her invulnerable skin bent the metal as she lurched forward from the hit. She pinwheeled a half turn, then caught herself, and locked eyes with me, teeth bared, fury blazing within. "You think that's going to stop me?"

"I think it's a mosquito bite," I said, coming back to a landing and rolling out of it again. "But if I do about a million times, I'll even drain every ounce of your blood, Rose."

I heard her coming and threw myself sideways, smashing through the wall of a burning building. Without much time to react, I rolled back up again and threw myself out a window on the other side of the flaming house as Rose came wrecking-balling in behind me.

Rising to my feet in an alleyway between two burning houses, I scooted back slightly to obscure myself. Rose burst into a fit of coughing inside, and I realized her lungs probably weren't invulnerable either—not that such knowledge was going to do me worlds of good right now.

"Stop—stop it!" Rose shouted from within the house, and came crashing out through the wall a moment later, pawing at her own head as though trying to exorcise some demon within.

I could sympathize. I'd had those demons in my head before.

And would again, if this all went right. At the moment, that was still looking pretty dicey.

"We won't stop," I said, giving her a blow to the back of the head with the rebar again. I wasn't even sure if it was possible to break her bones with sheer blunt force, unless she was totally distracted, but...

Well...she didn't seem like the real world had her full attention.

I rained a series of blows down on her with my rebar eskrima, hammering her around the head and eyes. She shook it off, and started to throw a hand out at me, lashing wildly, and I threw myself back, rolling again.

Thank goodness I'd practiced those Aikido rolls a million times, even when I was fully powered, during the days of the agency. It was so much a part of my routine that I'd done them all the way up to coming to Scotland—albeit as more of a cardio exercise than serious anticipation of needing them to weather an attack.

Thanks, Mom. Old habits die hard.

Rose whipped a hand around again, and another of those walls of red, explosive light came blasting past, wrecking an already-on-fire house and cleaving it into collapse. It missed me by...uh...twenty feet or so, and I wondered if Rose was just completely out of her mind, distracted by the soul rebellion going on in her head, or if she'd seen Diana or Eilish hiding over there.

The answer came a moment later in the form of an actual car tire this time, heaved from just behind the collapsing building, as Diana blinked into sight for a second, frisbeeing the damned thing into the side of Rose's head. It bounced off, but she took the impact with punch drunk stupidity, wobbling as she shook off the hit.

When she came up again, she stared right at me. "You're

not making a dent, Sienna darling."

"I think I'm doing a little something," I said.

She shook her head. "You have no hope."

"I have lots of hope," I said. "Because now I know who you are, Rose." She shook her head, still trying to shake off the war going on inside her. "You're a coward." That darkened her eyes, and she locked on me. I sensed I only had a second to hit her again, so I gave it my best shot. "You're afraid of me, and you always have been. It's why you waited until I was on the run from the law, cut off from all my friends, and why you suckered me from the start, back in Edinburgh. Because you knew if you came at me head-on, when I was at my strongest, you'd get your flat ass handed to you."

"My…arse…is not…flat!" She screamed, and I had to wonder how off the charts demented she was that she latched on to that particular insult at this particular moment, with her village burning around her by her own hand and a bunch of pissed-off souls attacking her from within while me and my new friends were sniping at her from without.

"Well, it's not exactly a bubble, y'know—" I started to say, but had to cut it short when she zoomed at me in a scary burst of speed. I didn't quite evade her this time, and I knew it, seeing her zoom at me as time contracted around me. The air itself was alive with the energy of this fight, with the flames around us, and as I lunged to dive out of her path, I knew I wasn't going to make it in time. She was going to clip me, hard; I could feel it from the way the air was surging around her, disturbed by her passage and—

Wait.

No.

That wasn't her doing that—

The wind was alive and howling, sudden and furious, and Rose rocketed off-course like someone had blasted her with a jet engine. She couldn't turn quite quickly enough, and she crashed into the house burning behind me, shattering the walls and bringing the roof down on her.

My savior drifted down next to me, settling on his feet, his long hair whipping from the currents of air that he controlled. He shot me a look of thinly disguised relief, and then directed his attention toward the burning building where he'd just sent Rose with a solid effort, the sort of thing he'd never have been able to pull off before he'd gotten his powers boosted.

"New rules, Red," Reed said, calling out to Rose in the burning building, wherever she'd come to land. Seeing him was like someone had broken a dam of emotions around my heart, and I watched him as he stared with burning intensity toward the place where'd he sent my enemy—where he'd saved me from her. "You keep your damned flat ass away from my sister."

48.

Reed

I didn't get much of a chance to exchange words with Sienna, because right after I told Rose to keep her flat ass away, she came roaring back at us, and I was forced to shove Sienna one way—pointlessly, because she was already moving—while I went the other.

"What do you think is going to happen here?" Rose shouted, coming around, her clothing on fire at the sleeves, her hair even burning a couple embers. "Do you think you stand a ch—"

A boulder the size of a minibus drove her into the ground, which then seemed to swallow the Scottish girl up, churning against her like the tide.

Augustus dropped next to me, a look of intense concentration on his face. "Oh, I think we got a chance, crazy. Why are the redheads always crazy?"

"You better not be speaking from experience," Taneshia said, dropping down next to him.

"Nah, baby, you're the only one for me," Augustus said. "I got no time for crazy white girls."

"What the hell?" Sienna was rising to her feet. "Are you guys unpacking the clown car one at a time?"

"Well, we have to get unshrunk," I said, "and it didn't seem too wise to just unshrink the entire SR-71 in the middle of a battlefield. I mean, subtle it's not, y'know? Even Rose would notice that in her—what the hell is her state, anyway? Because she doesn't seem quite as focused and deadly as in the past."

"My souls are fighting her," Sienna said, and there was a trace of mischievous pride, like you'd see in a mother claiming credit for something bad one of her kids had done.

"Trying to get home to Momma, huh?" Jamal said as he appeared, almost out of thin air.

Sienna just smiled, ghostly. "That earthen thing isn't going to hold her for l—"

"It doesn't have to," came another voice from behind us. "Augustus!"

"I don't have to move it," Augustus said, concentrating on the boulder in the battlefield. "She's coming out right n—"

The boulder splintered and cracked, launching a few feet up in the air, and Rose was there, up to her waist in the hole, which was trying its best to drag her back into the earth.

Scott came riding in behind, the contents of some nearby creek or other body of water below his feet like a horse of water that he was riding like the Poseidon of legend. He jumped off it in a beautiful dismount, and the water horse came rushing down at Rose, hitting her full-bore and dragging her back into the hole. "Cap it!" Scott shouted, and Augustus did just that, bringing down the fragments of boulder and bricking her up within like a modern-day superpowered Montresor, leaving Rose to drown in Scott's makeshift well.

Byerly landed next to Sienna, and gave her the once-over. "You look…uh…"

"Half-dead?" she offered in return. She really did look… painfully thin. She was at least 90% there, but just enough off—just enough *Not Sienna* to make me worry.

But I didn't have time to worry about it *now*. There was more trouble on the horizon, and speaking of—I looked around quickly, finding what I was looking for just past one of the burning buildings. I pointed. "That mountain there. The one that looks like a boob."

"They all look like boobs, don't they?" Sienna's eyes were alight. "I've been saying this for months, they're like boob mountains."

"I don't think that looks like a boob," Scott said, following my finger, then looking back, surreptitiously, at Sienna—her chest, specifically. "It doesn't have any hang to it."

"Yeah, you wouldn't need any support for that," Augustus agreed. "It's like an expanded A cup at best—"

"This is the thing you discuss during the fight for our lives?" Eilish called over the flaming battlefield. She was still hiding, pretty wisely, I thought.

"Here she comes," Sienna said, turning all of our attention back to the center of the battle, where Augustus's cap on the well was cracking to pieces.

I angled my head slightly. "Olivia, Tracy—you are go. Knock it out of the park."

"Aye aye," Olivia said tightly. "Moving into position."

"Ready," Tracy said, his voice a little shaky. "Just give the word, boss." God, he sounded way overly eager.

"Who the hell are Olivia and Tracy?" Sienna asked. "How long have I been gone?"

The cap to Augustus's trap shattered and burst, and out came Rose, drenched and pissed off like nothing else, her skin on fire as the water evaporated off. "More dead people," Rose said, the crazy just leaking out. "That's who Olivia and Tracy are. More bloody dead p—"

Augustus corked her with another boulder to the face, perfectly timed, just as Scott reconstituted some of the water she'd evaporated and sent it right up her nose. Rose dangled in the air, caught between those two surprise attacks, drifting about a foot off the ground, in the middle of the village street.

"Duck and cover!" I shouted, grabbing for Sienna but finding her again already lunging behind the burning house next to us. I followed a second later; three months a prisoner/detainee, and my sister was still firing on all cylinders. The others were a half step behind us, and I peered out with the rest of them, around the corner.

Tracy was running up behind her, only a few feet away now, as Rose tried to shake off the combo attack that Augustus and Scott had just hit her with. She spat the water in an explosive burst, her own co-opted Poseidon powers allowing her to expel the distraction from her body. She shook her head, fighting against forces we couldn't see, and it gave Tracy the last second he needed to cover the distance between them—

The air around him was distorting as he charged her, the light bending past his body as he achieved some sort of breakaway speed beyond that which most metas could get to. He harnessed the power of momentum, building it on itself, and lowered his shoulder for the charge as he slammed into Rose's back—

She didn't break a single bone, but the impact was still a distinct WHOOMP! that echoed over the valley. Tracy's aim was perfect; Rose went tumbling ass over teakettle at Warp Nine, shooting past us like—well, like an SR-71 in perfect flight. She hurtled toward the end of the street—

Where Olivia waited, standing firmly planted, her thin, athletic frame in silhouette against all the fires. She took a couple steps to adjust her position—

Rose entered Olivia's personal space, her bubble, and now the air distorted around her. Rose reached Olivia at a rate of several hundred miles per hour, which was the same approximate speed she'd been launched from Olivia when we'd clashed back in Minnesota—

But Olivia's momentum powers had an amplifying effect, and when Rose reached Olivia's bubble...she accelerated.

Rose was caught for just a second in its depths, then she seemed to slingshot. Olivia stepped neatly out of the way and Rose was rocketed to a speed probably in the thousands of miles per hour; it was tough to judge with even a metahuman eye. In any case, she definitely broke some speed records as she flew toward the boob mountain, aimed by Olivia, and impacted on it so powerfully that the shockwave washed over the village a moment later, with a blast of dirt and fury to go along with it.

I coughed and hit the ground as it rushed past. "Do we have eyes on target?" I asked, listening to the static in my ear. "Did we get her?"

"Negative," J.J. answered. "I've got a drone deployed

overhead, and…she's not down. She's shaking it off. She's coming back for—jeez, she moves fast—"

Rose streaked into our midst, hovering overhead, her clothing ripped and in tatters, but there she stood, not even a drop of blood from an impact that would have killed the fricking dinosaurs. She blinked off the skull trauma that had rattled her head, looked at Sienna with a wide grin, and said, "Finally…I get what I want…"

Sienna's face was frozen, horrorstruck, as the dawning truth came down on her.

"…every one of your little friends," Rose said, eyes taking us in, each in turn. "And you, my darling…" and she looked at Sienna, spite burning in those glowing green eyes. "You get to watch every last one of them die in front of you…"

49.

Wolfe

"I might need more healing soon," Rose said, twisting around and kissing Wolfe full on the lips, while just outside she stared down this mad cavalry of Sienna's friends and family that had come to fight her, a bizarre army against this one woman.

So much strength, Wolfe thought. *Rose...will obliterate them all. Strength wins.*

"You will have it, should you need it," Wolfe said, something prickling at his guts.

"They will not break through my invulnerability," Mario said, half-faded, ghostly, his forehead broken into a deep sweat, even as he watched the scene before them play in the sky, like the movie theaters Sienna had taken Wolfe to in days past. "I will not fail you this time, my mistress."

"Other help is on the way," Rose said, watching the screen again. She'd just thrown down her threat against Sienna's little family. Wolfe knew, could taste the killer instinct at work.

The deaths would start soon...and Wolfe...Wolfe knew that the taste of blood was coming, and he tingled with the anticipation...

50.

Sienna

I plowed one of my rebar eskrima into Rose's jaw with bone-shattering force, knocking her mouth open. That done, I thrust the other into her mouth, ramming it into the back of her throat. "Open wide!" I said, cramming it back there. It hit something impossibly hard—I guess she had an iron gullet—and I buried it in almost to where I held it at the end, the sound of metal creaking and bending all the way.

Sensing her backlash, I flipped away, coming back to my feet with only one piece of rebar remaining. Rose staggered sideways, giant chunk of metal hanging about three inches out of her mouth, and then she commenced gagging.

"ALL RIGHT!" Guy Friday came leaping out of nowhere, suddenly back to full size, I assumed, and smashed into Rose with a punch that would have leveled a building. Rose flew sideways into a burning house and Friday was after her. "I'm going to beat you like a pinata for messing with my niece! UNCLE FRIDAY TO THE RESCUE!" And he disappeared into the burning building after her.

"Friday, no!" Reed shouted, then tossed a quick glance at the rest of us. "Scatter! Plan B!" And the crew damned sure did scatter, like cockroaches with the lights coming on (sorry, crew; best I could do) as Reed plunged into the remains of the burning building after Friday and Rose.

"Reed, don't chase after her!" I shouted, following him.

"She's got a cruel streak wider than my hips and she wants to kill all of you in front of me!" I was a hair slower because he was riding the wind, and I entered the building just as a strong surge of power hit it—

The burning house blew apart like someone had put a bomb inside it. I went flying, crashing into another burning house—in Rose's village, was there any other kind?—and managed to flip myself over to land, somewhat woozy, on my feet. My head was spinning from the impact, but I still had one rebar eskrima and most of my wits about me, so it was a net win.

The house that Reed had gone into, though—it was flattened. The roof had blown clear off, the fire was mostly out, the walls shattered and lying like someone had just knocked them over, breaking them like a gingerbread house in the process. I couldn't see the roof, and then it landed, bursting in a flaming pile on top of yet another burning house down the way.

And there, in the middle of the flattened slab, pieces of furniture smashed and shattered all around them, Friday was pounding the living snot out of Rose with both hands.

"—mess with my family—" He had her by the ruined shirt with one hand, obliterating her with punch after punch with the other. His knuckles were bleeding, and Rose's face was smeared with blood, though I doubted it was her own. Friday blasted her with one that knocked her into a flipping cartwheel into the next house, and that was when I noticed Reed, tugging at the back of Friday's shirt.

"PLAN B, FRIDAY!" Reed was shouting. Friday looked to be on the verge of tossing him off so that he could go after Rose again, but stopped mid-step, shrunk a couple feet, and then turned and ran.

Reed let him loose and then flew off in the other direction after making a hasty sign to me to get lost. At least, that was how I read it. It could have been "slap her" or "spank her," based on what he did. Probably get lost though, because the others made a little less sense.

Except for "spank her," because dammit, I was going to spank the hell out of Rose before this was over.

293

I followed my brother's lead in this case though, Rose's threat against my entire family still echoing in my mind, and made myself scarce as I listened to the sound of a very pissed off, dazed, unleashed succubus clawing her way out of a collapsed, burning building.

51.

Zack

"Admittedly, I probably haven't been in as many fights as you people have," Harmon said, his face racked with pain, "but even I know this…is not going so well for us."

"What was your first clue?" Eve Kappler asked, jolted as another spiking wave of pain ran through them all, almost making her dance as Zack watched, her face straining against it, her Germanic reserve holding—but only barely.

"I would say the agony," Bjorn said, his massive frame shaking, shoulders jolting. The hilltop around them seemed to be writhing, the ground itself almost alive, just another contributor to their searing anguish.

"I think she might be feeling it, too," Gavrikov called, shaking as they stood on the solid ground, heaving beneath them. "All we keep doing is pouring more pain on her—"

"And she's just taking it," Bastian said, staring at the figure hovering above them like—well, like a pissed-off goddess, scorned, furious, staring down at them with eyes literally aflame, as though Gavrikov had set fire to them. "Taking it—and dishing out more." The Quetzalcoatl grimaced as another wave thrashed through them.

"Anyone got…any ideas?" Zack said as his knees buckled beneath him. The clouds were howling, still, the residual remains of all those souls Rose had eaten whirling around in the strata of the sky above them, a formless, mindless mass.

Something pinged off Rose's head, outside of their little dream world, and they all watched on the vision in the sky as she reached out with a hand, catching something—

A dart. It had spanged off her invulnerable skin, the tip bent as it lay in her palm.

Rose's voice boomed out over the desolate, howling wastes in her mind, and outside it. "You think you can shoot me with suppressant?" Her eyes locked on a figure in the distance, grey hair blowing in the wind, and she rocketed toward him.

"Oh, shit, what's that guy's name?" Bastian asked. "That old sniper guy?"

"Phinneus Chalke," Zack said as Rose rocketed toward him. Chalke jumped, disappearing, gone by the time she reached him somehow. "What the—?"

Rose stared down at the empty ground below the sniper's perch, then howled. "I can feel you moving them around under that earth, Augustus, you wee bastard! When I find you, I'm going to take great pleasure in—"

A blue glow fell over Rose as a burst of superheated plasma hit her in the back, blinding Rose and, by extension, all of those in her head. "That was Veronika," Zack said. "Had to be."

"The sexpot, yes," Eve said. "I like her."

Rose moved closer to the ground, and a bolt of lightning struck her, was absorbed and channeled off a moment later, gone as swiftly as if it had never existed at all. "I'm wise to your tricks, you little mice," Rose shouted. Her voice thundered, everywhere, a loudspeaker all its own. "I know every move you can make—"

She was drifting past a tree when it caught her around the neck, dragging her forward and slamming her face into the bark. It thumped at her roughly and Rose fought back, something else pushing against her from behind, a sudden well of gravity shifting her, binding her from escape—

The tree limbs wailed on Rose, splinters of wood shattering all around her. Zack could hear the branches breaking as they toiled against her invulnerable flesh. Then a crackle of red energy flashed from behind and Rose straightened.

"That tickled," Rose shouted, ripping free of the tree and setting it aflame. "Kat, Gravity, and—I forget the name of that little darling who has a lightsaber power. What do you call her? Darth Insipid?"

"I call her friend." Sienna's voice in her ear prompted Rose to spin around just in time to catch an eskrima stick in the eye. "I call all of them that, though. By the by—losing an eye hurts, doesn't it?"

"Yes!" Bjorn shouted; the pain dropped for just a moment, the sky going red around them.

Rose looked up at her. Zack could see mostly clearly—Rose still had both eyes; one of them had just been shoved aside rather roughly to make way in the eye socket for the chunk of rebar. "I wouldn't know." She closed her eyelid and squeezed, and the rebar broke neatly in half, then the remaining chunk disgorged itself from her socket with another squeeze. "How are you going to feel when I kill those friends of yours? You still going to be quipping then? When I rip every last thing away from you?"

"Yeah," Sienna said, staring her down. "Unlike you, I was a fighter before I manifested, long before I unleashed my full powers. I grew up fighting, and I had to fight to find people who'd—well, love me."

"Nobody loves you, Sienna," Rose scoffed, sneering, but— Zack could feel the shift in her head, the clouds reddening further.

"Yeah, we totally traveled thousands of miles to kick your ass for the sport of it," Augustus's voice spoke from the dirt beneath her. Hands of earth reached out of the ground, seizing Rose and dragging her down. Scott appeared out of the sky, riding another wave of water as he flooded it toward her, washing it over her even as she lit aflame, trying to boil it off.

"That's the difference between you and me, Rose," Sienna said, punching her in the face, scooping up the rebar and bashing her with it, knocking the redhead back. "I never had to suck the mind out of anyone to get them to love me." Her eyes were burning, and she was hammering Rose again, bashing her in the face. "And no one—" she punched Rose in the mouth, rocking her head back, tilting the world around Zack and the others "—not one soul on this earth—" she struck again, and Rose stumbled, feet anchored by Augustus's rock-clad hands "—nor one that you stole, nor the ones you had factory installed—none of them love you, Rose. Nobody—loves—you—" And she pounded her with a flurry of blows, eyes burning as she struck each one, until—

Rose grabbed her by the bloody knuckles, kicking loose of Augustus's grasp. "Oh, but you're wrong about that, my dear. I have people who love me, now. Ones who will never let me down…right, Mario? Wolfe, darling?"

"Hit her now!" Harmon shouted, and everything in their little dream world lurched back into motion as Eve shot lights like machine bullets at the Rose hovering above them while Gavrikov, wreathed in flame, burst at her again, hitting her furiously. Bjorn roared and leapt into the fray, and Bastian—

Holy, shit, Bastian, Zack thought.

He roared and grew into a multistory dragon, and breathed blue flame that joined with Gavrikov's own to swirl around Rose.

On the screen to the outside world and here in her own, Rose screamed, twitched, and jerked, something beyond a sudden, furious wind that wrenched Sienna out of her grasp, tearing at the Scottish girl in question—

52.

Wolfe

The chaos was at high speed, frenzied and crazy, rumblings from within Rose as without. Wolfe was steady, Wolfe was watching, even as Rose's voice hit higher and higher levels of anger and despair.

"What are you doing!" she shouted, Mario's bare shadow quivering before her. "You idiot!"

"I...I am not doing anything...I...am keeping you saf—" His face was nearly blank, the sign of a soul almost faded to nothing, so little will remaining as to nearly not count.

"Why aren't any of her friends dead yet?" Rose spun on him, and Wolfe eyed her calmly. "How is this happening?"

"You want her to watch more than you want to win," Wolfe said.

Rose took that in. "I do. I want her to watch. I want her to—" The world seemed to rock around them, even here in Rose's little lounge, and she shot a daggered look at Mario, then grabbed at him. "Idiot! Do you feel that?"

"That's not...me!" Mario shook, ghostly, losing form. Fear was almost all that was left of him. He'd been a pitiful conquest, and Wolfe had watched her take him, digesting him, day by day. He'd heard that it was possible, dissolving a soul into yourself. Lethe had told him about it at one point.

Seeing it for himself, though...it didn't even involve stripping off the flesh, and yet somehow he found it...almost

299

repellent. A conquest, but not a worthy one.

"Stop failing me, Mario," Rose said, and Mario screamed. "Help me win this. Help me win this before I—"

And the world around them shook again, Wolfe maintaining his footing. "Remember your strength," he said, and Rose looked at him, just briefly, favoring him with a smile, before she turned her attention back to the war unfolding before them.

53.

Sienna

Reed's tornado ripped Rose away from me, and just in time, too. She was spazzing out, and it wasn't just the mean girl things I'd said about nobody loving her. I sensed a renewed onslaught from my souls, really giving her hell inside as Reed, Augustus and the others did their best to do the same from out here.

Rose was spasming, and I suspected there was a moment of vulnerability, but I needed to test it. So I grabbed a chunk of wood that was just sitting there next to where I'd landed, a fragment of one of these fallen houses, and took a running start.

I javelined it after a solid release, and it sailed for Rose. Reed must have seen it coming because he dissolved his tornado and it passed cleanly through, maybe with a little gust to aid it, and caught Rose—

Right in the gut, impaling her clean through.

Blood swelled at her midsection, soaking through her blouse, her jaw wagging as she stared mutely in horror at the wood pole sticking out of her belly.

"Angel, now!" Reed shouted, and a gun roared somewhere in the distance. Angel Gutierrez was a reflex type, like Diana and Phinneus, which meant her aim would be flawless—

The needle of suppressant bounced harmlessly off Rose's chest, and she looked up, scorn replacing the pain. She grabbed the wood stake I'd pushed through her, and ripped it free, leaving—well, a hole in her heart. Or another one, if you counted that big empty spot where her humanity should have been. "Wolfe, my darling…"

And before my very eyes, the wound I'd just caused this invulnerable girl…healed.

I almost gulped. A split second or so of vulnerability…

And Wolfe had just undone the damage I'd made.

"Sienna, we need to re-eval—" Reed said, and was cut off a second later as a chunk of rebar burst out of his chest on the right side. It popped through like an alien from those movies he used to love, and a sputter of blood dripped out of his lips a second later.

"No!" I shouted, and past him, I could see movement down the street. Mr. Blonde was waving at me in the distance, grin on his face, and more pieces of rebar lined up—

Something collided with me from the side, crashing into me and ending my distraction. "They're all going to suffer this fate sooner or later," Rose whispered in my ear as we smashed into another wall and brought down a flaming house around us.

She pinned me to the ground as the world burned above, below and on all sides of me.

Reed was down.

Because of me.

I looked into Rose's eyes, and saw hate burning back, like the fire that shrouded the ceiling above. I almost breathed in death, the black smoke hanging in the air, lit by the flames.

But instead…I looked Rose right in the eye…

And I begged.

"Please."

Rose just stared at me for a long second, then burst out laughing, throwing her head back and cackling. "You think I'll stop now? After I've got the better of you? After all this?" She looked back down at me, amusement lit among the dark shadows cast by the flame. "You're a bigger fool than I thought."

But I made my plea again, hoping it would fall on the right

ears.

Not hers.

"Wolfe…please."

Rose's face flashed with anger. "Too late, darling," she said, and something cold cut through it. "Wolfe is mine now. He does love me, you see…" And she put her hand to my face, delicate, a stroke of the cheek…

And left it there as it started to burn, burn against my skin, not the heat of the flames around us, but the power of her soul as it started to rip mine from my body.

54.

Wolfe

Norway
174 B.C.

Wolfe saw the child, Vivi, across the summery village. Voices were raised, other children were singing, playing, laughing. It was poison and bile to his ears, and he ignored it as best he could, trudging through on ground that had gone muddy from days of rain drenching the piney woodlands.

Now, though, the land was sun-drenched and full, light shining down upon them everywhere. Wolfe cast another look at the child, Vivi, who was still eyeing him, and took a breath.

This insult had gone on long enough.

He took a circuitous route, weaving around behind the little one, sneaking up through the underbrush behind a longhouse. Soundless, he was, making his approach. Odin didn't like violence in his village, but surely he wouldn't miss this little torment, this eye-burning freak if she went missing...

"Hello, Wolfe," Vivi said, without even turning, a little accent echoing in Wolfe's ears as he came up behind her.

Wolfe emerged from the brush, stirring a branch. It was the first noise he'd made since he'd entered the woods on the other side of the village. "Stop staring at the Wolfe."

Vivi turned, slowly, eyes intense. She said, "I can't."

Wolfe leaned in closer to the child, smelled the sweat of days without a bath, without going in the rain. "You won't be so smug when Wolfe rips your face off, little thing...little...doll."

Vivi just stared back, unblinking, blond hair hanging down in her eyes.

Wolfe gazed into those eyes. "What do you see? Your own future—without a face?" He growled.

Vivi did not stir, just stared. "No...I can't see my own future." A pause. "But I see yours."

Wolfe felt a tingle within, a little chill that made the hairs on his body stand on end. To this he said nothing.

"Your future is blood and death," Vivi said.

Wolfe smiled.

"And when the end of your days comes," Vivi said, head inclined, "you'll die for death in the land of the Scots...and you will go into it, willingly...

"...for love."

That cold tingle burst through Wolfe. "You lie," he whispered, staring into those eyes. "You lie. I won't—not for—for Lethe—for her, I won't—" He let out a roar, and came at the little waif. "You see that, do you?" He seized the child by the face. "How are you going to see anything else once I eat your eyes?" And ripped into the—

55.

Wolfe

Now

"Wolfe...please."

Sienna's voice was like the slow knife slicing through him. He'd felt the pain, the pangs, since he'd first heard her say that they were coming to this land, all the way back in London those months ago. He'd doubted, he'd feared...

And then he met Rose...and thought, perhaps, a reprieve was in order.

"Just listen to her beg," Rose said, crowing, delight just oozing out as she held her hand to Sienna's face. "So weak. Like prey." She breathed in Wolfe's ear, and the warmth spread through him—

As she always did. She knew how to make him tingle.

"Isn't it pathetic?" Rose asked, almost laughing. "She thought she was the most powerful person on the planet—and I showed her arse." She looked at Wolfe, triumph gleaming in her eyes. "I showed her."

"Yes," Wolfe agreed, feeling Rose's hand on him, touching him, that feeling—that ecstasy she brought spreading through him. "Your strength is unquestionably greater. You have gathered...so much unto yourself."

"I'm bloody unstoppable, darling," Rose said, eyes gleaming at him like a shining forest of green. "With your help—Wolfe, we're going slaughter the world."

He nodded, slowly. "Your power...makes it possible...in a way she never could have." And he leaned in to her embrace, felt the touch of her against him, that tingle—that warmth and feeling he never wanted to leave...

He whispered, "But I never loved *you*."

And he sank his teeth into her neck.

56.

Sienna

Rose recoiled from me just before her powers started to seriously drain me, letting out a scream that made it sound like someone had accidentally drizzled some wax in her bikini line that she'd just twisted loose. It was pain, it was emotion, it was fury—

And I didn't stick around to hear any more of it after she let loose of me, because I was out the window and down the street, figuring I'd be better off regrouping elsewhere than watching her shudder in a burning house that was about to come down around my ears.

"Whoa!" Someone almost collided with me as I turned a corner, then disappeared for a second, reappearing behind me. I spun, fist raised, then lowered it when I saw who it was.

"Greg," I said, slumping somewhat. My head was spinning; my entreaty to Wolfe appeared to have worked, for whatever that was worth. "Shouldn't you be circling in the plane? Very tiny circles?"

"Your telepath friend is minding it for me," Greg said, his thick body and short stature a strange mismatch, "and it's on autopilot."

"Zollers?" I frowned. "What's he doing up there?"

"Helping in his own way, he said. Coordinating viewpoints, data—then funneling people toward where their attacks will hit Rose in the blind side. Quicker than verbal communication."

So that was why we hadn't had a casualty yet, save for Reed and his wounding. *Thank you, Doc*, I said in my head.

Hurry up, Sienna, the answer came back, more strained than usual for Zollers. *I can't read her, but…she's getting more desperate by the minute, and she has strong mental defense too, but I'm working on it—and so is another friend of yours, from the inside.*

Harmon. I knew it.

She's powerful, Sienna, Zollers said. *And with that power…she can do a lot of damage if she gets desperate enough to pull out all the stops. She could make this town look like Glencoe, Minnesota.* That thought chilled me, since Glencoe was just a hole in the ground. Or worse.

On it, I said.

Greg looked around. "I, ah…" He looked around, taking in the chaos. "I've…somewhat missed this."

I looked at the burning buildings around us, and suddenly the dark skies were split with an artificial bolt of lightning crackling down from the heavens. Rose screamed in the distance, and I wondered who had done that to her. "You missed *this*?"

He shrugged. "I…being a better father to Eddie and a non-terrible husband to Morgan is rewarding, but—"

"Not a lot of adrenaline in that?" I asked. "I've got something for you that will get your juices flowing."

"Oh?" He quirked an eyebrow. "What's that?"

I explained.

He just stared at me once I was done. "Well…that will certainly be…exciting."

57.

Wolfe

She cast him out of the lounge, out of her little paradise, and it stung Wolfe a thousand times, a million times across his flesh. "Mario!" she screamed, howling into the void into which she had turned him out. It was nothing like that quiet box that Sienna had consigned him to when she was ireful, no…

This was…

It was…

A battle?

"Wolfe!" Zack's voice sounded, and in the midst of explosions and roars of a dragon and shouts from—was that Eve? And Bjorn? The blond-haired pretty-boy stood with something on his shoulder that looked like a tank. He handled it as though it were weightless, firing something bizarre into the distance, where the cacophony was breaking loose, a maelstrom of meta powers and explosions in so many colors as to look like a rainbow of fire and fury.

Wolfe hit the ground, and sprang back up, looking at the pretty-boy and his new artillery.

"Welcome to the party, pal," Zack said, doing a little appraising of his own.

"Sorry I'm late," Wolfe said, casting a quick eye to the fight down the way.

"You're just in time," Zack said, and here his voice

dropped. "We're getting our asses kicked."

Wolfe just stared at him for a long moment. "Well...let's stop doing that."

Zack grinned. "It's a better plan than we've been running with."

"Which was?"

He shrugged. "Kick this bitch's ass."

Wolfe nodded. "It's a good plan." And he ran off to help, throwing himself into the fight as though it would be the last of his life.

Because it seemed very much like the little Nordic child was right.

He was about to die, here in the land of the Scots...

...for love.

58.

Sienna

Zollers, I said, in my mind, once I had Greg all squared away, *how's Reed?*

Hurting, Zollers replied as I came around a corner. *He's down below. Kat's tending to him. Augustus is keeping them in the earth, but…Rose is almost certain to develop a counterattack since she knows it's happening. And soon, probably.*

Okay, I said, heat from one of the house fires rolling over me in a wave, sweat dripping down into my eyes. *I need a direct line into Rose's head.*

I need to talk to my souls.

Yeah, you didn't even need to say it. I could almost imagine Zollers's smile without seeing him, like a shadowy reminder in my head. *I don't know if I can get you in there. Her defenses—*

I know, I said. *But there's some of me in Rose, and some of Rose in here…*

You're such a dirty little girl, Sienna, Rose's voice spoke up, so opportunely timed.

Any chance you can just bridge us? I asked.

Maybe, Zollers said, but he didn't sound too sure. *I'm well bonded with your mind, but this Rose…she's trying to keep me out. If there is a part of your consciousness in her…it's possible. Let me tr—*

He didn't even get the word out before it was like I was jerked forward, like someone had snugged a rope around my waist and yanked me into a darker version of the village, one with a swirling red sky and—

Was that a bird's eye view through Rose's eyes? Playing on the clouds?

"That's dramatic," I said, and someone moved in front of me.

"Sienna," Zack said, spinning around. He looked ragged, but probably not as bad as I did. "How are you here?" His shoulders slumped, the light draining from his coffee-brown eyes. "She got you."

"She didn't get me," I said, waving him off as I took two steps toward him. "Zollers used the part of me that Rose absorbed to Trojan horse his way into her mind." I took a breath. "Zack…we have to get you guys out of here. I have a plan to deal with Rose, but…you need to get out first."

Zack was carrying…some kind of cannon on his shoulder the size of a minibus. He fired it and about a hundred rockets fell down on a howling maelstrom of a fight down below. "I like the sound of getting the hell out of here. How do we do it?"

"We need Harmon," I said, and started down the hill toward the fight. "Him plus Zollers working together, maybe they can—"

The trees whipped around us, and suddenly Gerry Harmon was standing there. His suit was torn and ragged, and his hair was more messed up than I could ever recall seeing it in life, even when he was a corpse. "I thought I felt you arrive."

"Here I am," I said. "Listen—can you download the others into my brain from Rose's? Like you did with Scott's memories back in Florida?"

Harmon opened his mouth, and I could see the emotions wrestling between them, warring with each other, and when he finally spoke…

Somehow, it sounded the death knell of so many hopes.

"No," he said, softly, simply. "She's too powerful, Sienna. We're fighting her as hard as we can…and it's the only thing keeping her from annihilating this entire town and all your people down there. This…" He looked almost ghostly grey, but tried to smile. "I think this is the end…for us." And he disappeared, and somehow I knew he'd leapt back into the action.

"What?" I asked the empty space where he'd stood, the pines rustling around us. "Zack, this is crazy. Talk some sense into—"

But Zack was gone, and in his place—

"Gavrikov," I said, as Aleksandr looked down at me, waxy pale, as I'd known him in life on the rare occasions when he'd dropped his flaming guard. "What are you—"

"We only have moments," Gavrikov said, smiling at me. He touched my arms. "Will you look after her for me?"

I opened my mouth to ask who, instinctively, but by the time the question formed...I knew the answer. "Klementina."

"Yes." His voice was soft, almost...sweet. Brotherly devotion. It made me think of Reed, taking a rebar through the chest for me.

"Of course I will," I said, and reached up to brush his face. He closed his eyes, and smiled. "I promised you peace." He opened them, surprised. "When I absorbed you...I promised you peace. I don't...guess I've lived up to that, have I?"

"Knowing that you will watch over her," Gavrikov said, his smile already disappearing, "will give me peace." And with that, he was gone, replaced by—

"Eve?" She was lit by shadow, and then the flame of a distant explosion.

"Would you keep an eye on Ariadne for me?" Eve asked, almost reluctant, like she thought I'd turn her down.

I gave her a slow nod. "I just checked on her in my dreams last night, in fact."

Eve smiled. "And?"

"She's well," I said, my voice suddenly very hoarse.

The vision around me broke for a second, and I could see the real village, torn by upheaval, the ground erupting. Greg's voice shouted, "I think it's coming soon!" and then I was back in the darkness, and Eve was gone, replaced by—

"Bastian." I looked at him, his skin dark, a hue to it almost like dragon flesh, and a distant smile perched on his lips.

"I'm sorry, Sienna," he said.

"For...what?" The darkness faded, the explosions and fighting dying down, just for a moment.

"For helping kill Zack," he said, and there was real remorse there, instantly undermined by his next words. "But…I'm also not sorry. Because you were without a doubt the finest warrior I ever worked with…so I'm sorry for what we did…but I'm not sorry at all for how you turned out." He looked at me, and his eyes glowed with pride. "Kick her ass."

And he was gone. Replaced by—

"Bjorn?" His hulking figure stood before me, bare-chested—naked, actually, but shadowed below the waist, thankfully.

"I hated you," Bjorn said, grinning. "But not as much as I hate this c—"

The world rocked around me again, and I was back in the burning village, Zollers whispering in my ear: *I can't hold this much longer. She's gone crazy, Sienna. She's seeking you; all her attention is on it, and she's going to catch you in just a few more s—*

Suddenly I was back in the woods, in the dark, and Gerry Harmon was standing there in front of me, his look not improved over how it had been moments before.

"You…don't want to escape?" I asked, staring right at him. "At least try?"

Harmon bowed his head, all his fancy moves and presidential acting gone. Here I saw a man without the face of his preparation, delivering something I'd…never seen from him before, not in the years I'd watched him on TV, and certainly not when he was living in my head for almost a year.

He was afraid.

"I don't think that's an option anymore," he said, more sedate than I'd ever seen him. "I—" He stopped, then just sat there for a minute in silence, and a slow, sad smile spread across his face. It didn't light his eyes, which was how I knew it was real. "You're going to be our only legacy left in the world. The sum of all my sacrifices up to now…and this last one, of course, the one I…never really wanted to give. So…believe that I am acting in your interests as well as mine when I say this…"

He looked me right in the eyes. "Sienna…do not go to Revelen. You are not ready for what waits for you there. Not now. Not ev—"

The world rocked around us again, and I broke into the real world once more, of fire and blood, and Rose screaming somewhere over it all.

Then I was back with Harmon again, in the darkness. "Why are you doing this, Harmon? This is crazy. You haven't tried to get ou—"

"I have tried," he said. "For months. The others could tell you. I've been looking, searching for an opportunity to get out." He kept his same, standoffish posture, there in his ragged suit. "I've sacrificed everything…everyone…that ever came close to me if the moment presented itself, all for my own ambitions…" He smiled, a ghostly one, still no mirth. "…to save the world—or so I told myself. And now…I find the only way I may end leaving my mark…actually saving the world…is by making sure that you're still in it. And strangely…I'm at peace with that idea."

He was gone a second later, only to be replaced by—

"Zack," I said, "Harmon just said—"

"I know," he said, and I'd forgotten how handsome his smile was. "We can all hear it, everything the others are saying over here. We're—tagging in and out of the fight, but it's…" He shook his head. "It's Rose's head. She's going to win." He took a hard breath. "I just wanted to tell you…I'm still in your corner." He smiled boyishly. "Do me a favor?"

"Anything," I said.

"I know you're going to get out from under this, all of it—all the shit you've been through in the last year," he said, and his smile evaporated; I could tell that whatever he wanted to say, he was taking it very seriously. "And when it's all done, Sienna, I want you to promise me—" He seized my hands with his own, cold and sweaty. "That you'll go out and have a life." His face crinkled. "I always wanted you to have a life, and—and if I know you're going, you're really going to try—then I will be okay marching into this."

"Oh, Zack," I said, feeling…choked up. "Yes. I—I promise. I will…try."

"That's all I can ask," he said, and he kissed me, just for a second…

316

...and then he was gone, and the world was cracking in half around me.

Rose floated overhead, her red hair glowing in the evil twilight hanging over the village, her pale skin almost as aglow as her hair.

And she smiled.

"Found you," she said. "At last."

59.

"How's your head?" I asked, completely casually, like I hadn't just been inside her brain.

She drifted down to me, and I could sense that reluctance that had owned her through our whole interaction, that desire to hold out, to keep putting the screws to me so she could watch me squirm in pain. It was the ultimate human instinct, and it hit me there, at the last, why Rose had done this to me all along, held back.

I was the closest thing she had in the world to a friend at this point.

She really didn't have anyone that loved her.

"Not as bad as yours is going to be," she said with a smirk, and suddenly I was hit with that dragging sensation, back to the dark, back to—

"Wolfe," I said, and he lingered there in the murk, farther than the others had…almost out of reach.

He stood with his back to me, hulking, this brute of a creature that had scared me worse than I'd ever been scared in my entire life. Next to him, Rose was a piker, just some random idiot off the street with godlike powers and a grudge to burn.

It was against Wolfe that I'd really learned to test my strength and find out what I was made of.

And here…in the darkness with him, I felt, maybe for the first time, a little more of a human sense to him, something that had probably been buried under thousands of years of dust and pain.

"Sienna…" he said, acknowledging me at last, even though I knew he'd had to "tag out" to come here and speak to me. "I…" He didn't finish.

"I know, Wolfe," I said, and somehow, I thought I did know what he was going to say—some variant of, "I'm sorry for helping your psychohosebeast stalker heal from wounds that should have killed her flat, dumb, ginger ass." Instead I just said, "I know."

"You're like her," Wolfe said, still unwilling to face me. I knew for the first time who he meant—Lethe. "A hunter. It's in your blood." He rasped every word, and turned his head a little to look at me out of the corner of his eye. "I should have known. I could taste it the first time I—"

"Gross," I said. "Crossing a line there. Back it up."

"Sorry," Wolfe said. And he meant it. "I served her…and her father before her…I've served Death all my life, in many forms…just as I served you."

"I'm just glad that 'To Serve Sienna' didn't turn out to be a cookbook."

He stirred with faint amusement. "You were stronger, Sienna." He looked me right in the eye. "Stronger than you ever knew. Strong enough to take everything the world threw at you—and it threw a lot. An endless succession of these…threats. This is another of those. You have a plan?"

I nodded.

He looked right back at me, dark eyes in shadows. "You should get to it, then."

I stared into the darkness, at Wolfe, and I said…

"I can't." Something was tearing at me on the inside. "Without the others—"

And then he was gone, replaced by:

"You know it always comes down to this," Harmon said, smooth voice eliding over the explosions in the woods. "A meta like Rose…"

"…is only vulnerable for an instant," Aleksandr Gavrikov said, appearing where Harmon had been a second earlier. "And…"

"…you must take your shot," Eve Kappler said, with the

ghost of a smile as she took up for them, "when…"

"…you get the chance," Bjorn said. "You…"

"…have to kill her, Sienna," Zack said, stern resolve all painted across his handsome face.

"You can't expect me to do this to you—to all of you," I said, and my voice was choked, hoarse. "You can't make me—"

"We've never been able to make you do anything," Eve said. "This is your choice."

"This is the mission, Sienna," Bastian said, calm, cool, military resolve exuded with every word.

"Rose won't stop with you," Harmon said. "Her anger, her vengeance…killing you won't fill that empty spot inside her. All of that…it's going to spill over to the rest of this country…and the rest of the world. Ask your friend Zollers, when he gets a peek inside…it'll happen.

"I see now that we weren't that different," Harmon said, and his old smile was back, lacking the usual smugness. It was tight, sad. "I wanted to save the world by perfecting it. You just wanted to save the people in it, so they could live their lives. Well…now's your chance. Again." He looked me in the eye, and there was real warmth there. "You've saved the world—and people—so much. Always laying your life on the line…"

"It's our turn now…" Zack said, strong and clear.

"…to repay the favor…" Gavrikov said.

"Now it's our turn…" Eve said.

"…to save you," Wolfe said.

"But…" I could barely speak, my throat was closing up.

"This is the end for you, Sienna darling." Rose's voice crackled like thunder as the world broke around me and I was back in the burning village, less than a second after I'd left last time. She was hovering over me, about to strike—

"Congratulations," Bjorn said, and he, too, was smiling, though it was dark, an ill-humored look.

I just stared at him. "What?"

"You changed us," Gavrikov said.

"I think I speak for everyone when I say—I was never the noble, self-sacrificing type, Sienna," Harmon said, still pale, the strain of battle I couldn't see showing on his face. "This will sound strange, but...it's been a pleasure getting to know your mind...in a way I never knew anyone else's before." And he faded away, and somehow I knew...it was for the last time.

"You know what you have to do," Wolfe said, and suddenly the darkness was stripped away, and—

I was face to face with Rose, only twenty feet away, and she was there, ready to strike, face aglow with fury, and I knew—

This time...she wasn't going to let me walk away.

Do it, Zack's voice intruded on my thoughts. *Do it, NOW!*

I hesitated, my stomach dropping as I let my hand fall to my side.

Become...like her. Take up...your legacy. Wolfe's growl filled my head, maybe for the last time...

I pulled the pistol that Mac had given me, raising the Walther PPK so the sights aligned perfectly with Rose's forehead.

She laughed at me. "You've lost your ever-loving mind, Sienna darling."

"No...you took it," I whispered.

"And I'm about to take the rest," she said, and started to move—

Become...her, Wolfe whispered, voice rising to a frenzy, pushing me to action. *Do it. Become—*

"Death," I whispered.

And I pulled the trigger.

60.

The roar of the gun made him smile in a way that sound never had. It had been a fool's weapon. A coward's weapon, for as long as they'd existed, at least in his eyes.

But now…

Now…

Now it was the hammer of the righteous, come to deliver him to his promised destiny.

"Been nice knowing you guys," Zack said quietly, as they all watched it come together.

Death.

He felt the surge of pride as it hit—

61.

Sienna

Rose didn't know what hit her.

The Walther jumped in my hand, lipping fire out in the dark, a bullet blasting free of the chamber at 1,000 feet per second. It was a little bullet, 9 by 9.5 millimeters, a tiny little thing...

That got much smaller in flight, as Greg Vansen, riding on the tip, used his powers to take it down to the molecular level.

It passed through Rose's invulnerable skin at a size too small for her to even feel it, but as soon as it was through the skin, and the bone—

It got big again.

Greg appeared out the back side of her head, shrinking through just as he'd entered it, at the subatomic level, then resuming his normal size and tumbling back to the earth. He landed like he was stepping off a curb, but Rose...

Rose just hung there for a second, wobbling, as that hollow-point .380—now over an inch in diameter, if Greg had followed my instructions—bounced around in Rose's invincible skull, unable to escape.

She dropped a second later, blood running out of her nose, eyes glassy and staring at the sky above.

Rose Steward was dead.

"Long live the queen of mean," I said, mostly to myself, as

I clutched my Walther, the smoke still wafting off the barrel.

Somewhere in the distance, I could hear the rush of water. Scott, probably trying to put out the fires.

The earth was no longer shaking. It opened, sprouting like a flower, across the street, and my friends started to emerge.

"That…was an impressively thought-out strategy," Greg said, keeping his distance as he commended me. "Also…I wouldn't care to do that ever again. Can we consider our debt—?"

"We're square, Greg," I said. "Thank you."

"Sienna?" Reed's voice reached me where I stood, planted in place, in the same spot where I'd fired at Rose. He struggled his way over to me, still clutching his shoulder stiffly, Kat a few steps behind him. "Are you…?"

I blinked at him.

My brother had come to save me.

My friends—my family—had come to save me.

"I'm fine, Reed," I lied, putting on the brave face, smiling, impossibly tightly, even though I wanted, so badly, to do anything but. "I'm…just fine…"

62.

Reed

The fires took some time to put out, and the chaos took a while to subside. We did a head count, and made sure we had as many coming out of the fight as we'd had going in. In this...we were pleasantly surprised.

And in one case...unpleasantly so.

"I just called him Mr. Blonde," Sienna said, staring down the street at the man whom Eilish—her new Irish friend, and apparently Breandan's old girlfriend—had dancing a little jig in the middle of the street, completely under her control. "No idea what his real name is."

I frowned. "He looks nothing like Michael Madsen."

"Cease your geekery," Sienna tossed back at me. A trace of regret fell over her features, and she added, "You know what? Don't cease it. Keep it up." She bumped into my shoulder, lightly. "I've missed it." She was...almost normal.

But that gap between her as she was...and what she was now?

I had a feeling she was putting on the bravest face in the history of brave faces.

"Should we...turn him loose?" I asked, looking at the blonde man. "You know—now that Rose is dead? And since we're leaving?"

She shrugged, and waved Eilish over. It took a few seconds, but she came, her little puppet following like he was

325

on a string. "What's up?" she asked, in some bizarre combination of an Irish and a London accent. It was subtle, but I'd worked in Europe enough to know that she'd clearly had some fade in from living in the big city for too long.

"Turn him loose," Sienna said, nodding at Mr. Blonde. "We want to see what he has to say now that Rose is dead. He probably just wants to go back to being a normal person or something—"

"Okay," Eilish said, and then shrugged. "Done. He's—"

"I will kill you," Mr. Blonde said, head turning right toward Sienna.

"Hold it right there," Eilish said as he started toward her. "No hurting her." And he damned sure stopped.

But he still had the most hateful look on his face. "Not today then. Maybe not tomorrow." His eyes blazed as he looked at Sienna. "But you killed my mistress. And someday, when you least expect it, I will come for you. And I will make you pay."

Sienna just sort of looked at him, almost inscrutable, then said, "Awww. So one person did love her, I guess."

"I will come for you when your back is turned," Mr. Blonde went on, building up a head of steam in his threats. "Put me in prison for a year, a thousand years—I will turn all my thoughts toward getting out. And when I taste free air again, know that my mind will be fixed not on food, or fun or frivolities—"

"Getting laid is probably right out too, eh?" Eilish asked.

"—and I will kill you," he said, with burning eyes. "I will kill y—"

The wood beam landed right through his head, pushed by a gust of wind that I'd used to bring it aloft and now, bring it down in the center of his skull at about a hundred miles an hour. It swept straight through, crushing in via the top of his head and burying itself neatly in the middle of him, perfectly invisible where it rested somewhere in his chest and innards.

I looked at him calmly, but I was a storm inside. "Nope," I said, as his body toppled over. "You won't."

63.

Sienna

After Reed's quite impressive display of protecting me—a sure sign that I wasn't the only one who'd changed after this little adventure—we gathered, a few of us, to see off one of our number who was staying behind.

"Thank you, Diana," I said, and meant it wholeheartedly. "I couldn't have asked for a better guide—and I wouldn't have made it without you."

"If you see my brother again…" Diana said, kind of glazing over the nice things I'd said to her, "punch him in the face and tell him it was from me." She looked at Reed, and stepped toward him like she was going to kiss him, but he dodged, and she grinned. "I can smell her on you." Without bothering to explain what that meant, she turned on her heel and stalked off, presumably back to the Audi, which—we'd checked—was surprisingly whole and all right.

"I kinda want to go with her," Eilish said, lingering. "Just until tomorrow, you know. She's going back to Mac's, right?" She sighed. "I liked Mac."

"Of course you did," I said as we watched Diana turn a corner and disappear from sight. "He's Manannán Mac Lir."

Eilish blinked a few times. "Manannán—Mac—oh!" She spun on me. "Why did no one tell me this? Me, in the house of Manannán Mac Lir! I'm Irish, for crying out loud! I should have been consulted! Informed!" She squinted, as if in thought. "And why is an Irish god living in Scotland?"

Turning my back on those questions, I looked at Reed. He was still clutching his shoulder, but he had regained his coloration. "Are you ready to go home?"

I smiled, but it was painfully forced. "Yes," I said, even though I knew that when I got on that plane, we weren't going home, not really. We were going back to the US, sure, but…that wasn't home.

But it'd have to be close enough.

For now.

64.

There was a party in the house/travel chamber that Greg had secured beneath his seat on the SR-71, and soon enough we were streaking through the sky in high style, albeit shrunken to the size of dust mites. I tried to ignore the worrisome parts of that as I circulated among my friends and the people who had come to rescue me.

It would have felt wrong to just ignore them, to shut myself away, to disappear into one of the upstairs bedrooms without at least making an effort to make the rounds, to look every single one of them in the eye and thank them for coming.

With some of them...it was easier than others.

"Please don't upend my entire life again," Jamie Barton said, and she really was pleading. "My daughter—I haven't seen her in months. I was dating this guy from the bank, and it was going really well until I completely disappeared for months—"

"I'm so sorry, Jamie," I said, staring at her across a small end table in the living room, a Scotch in my hand. Greg had a fully stocked bar, complete with full-sized booze bottles. Best airline ever. The table rattled, just slightly, with the motion of the plane, and I looked down at the legs of the table. He'd even bolted them in.

"There's the girl of the hour," Augustus said, making his way over. We'd talked like...twelve times thus far since the end of the fight, but that Augustus...what a social butterfly.

"Hey, Taneshia," I said to her for the sixth time tonight. She smiled tightly, and had an iron grip on Augustus's arm. She steered him away at the last second, and I wondered if he'd had a few too many.

Yeah, probably, I thought as I took a sip of Scotch. But after a fight like that…who didn't want a little liquid stress relief?

"Please," Jamie said one last time, rising. Her eyes communicated the message again, and I made the biggest mea culpa face I could. I couldn't blame her; if somehow something she did had turned my life to utter crap and sent my family into hiding for months? I'd have been pissed, too.

Of course, my life was already kind of wrecked that way, but hey…beggars can't be choosers. Or something. It was good Scotch.

I felt a strong hand on my shoulder, and looked up to find Veronika there, not nearly so sneeringly smug as usual. She looked…pretty closely guarded, actually, like she was surveying me, looking for weakness. "How are you?" she asked. No leer.

"I'm wonderful, thanks to you all." It was my practiced answer. And total bullshit.

"Hm," she said, making a little sound. "I know you've got other people to talk to, but…" She leaned in. "If you ever do need to talk…" And she looked me dead in the eyes, and I knew—

She knew I was lying.

"You call me," she said, serious as I'd ever seen her. "Anytime." And she got up and left, nothing more to say.

Dr. Zollers caught my eye from across the room, and nodded once. I couldn't tell for sure what he was thinking, but…he knew what I was thinking, so I read it as…

You can leave now.

And I did. Gathered up my Scotch and headed for the stairs. I passed by J.J. and Abby, asleep on the couch, her head in his lap, and I felt a little pang of…

Something.

"You still owe me," Cassidy Ellis said, passing me as she came down the stairs. That was all she said, nothing else, and her skinny ass just disappeared out of sight toward the dining room.

"I'll get right on that," I said, raising my glass to the archway where she'd vanished. "Tomorrow." And I strolled up the stairs, alone.

It was relatively quiet up here, the muffled sounds of the party below especially quieted. I wondered if Greg had introduced some kind of insulation to the plane, something between the walls that would take out all the noise. I put my ear up to one of the doors that was closed and heard—

Nothing. Not a sound.

With a sigh of relief, I moved down the hall and found an open door, and snuck through it.

The room was nothing too fancy—a bed, a dresser, a little half bath, and a tiny closet up against the far wall. What more did you need, really?

Nothing. I didn't need anything else.

All I needed was the closet.

I locked the door and walked across the room, draining the last of my Scotch before I reached it. I deposited the empty glass on the dresser and left it there, figuring I'd pick it up in a few hours.

Because right now...

I just needed to be...

Alone.

"I just took a shot of chloridamide," I lied to myself. "That's why I can't hear them in my head." It was all the worse for the fact that it had been months since I'd heard any of them.

Until today.

Until the last time, today.

And now...I'd never hear any of their voices again.

I stepped into the empty closet and slid the door shut behind me. The light faded, leaving me in darkness.

It was a little slice of home, my own little makeshift box, flying high in the sky, shrunken to the size of an insect.

Here...now...alone...truly alone...

I let the brave face fall away.

Here, in the privacy of my own little box...I could finally

admit the truth to myself.

She'd taken...*everything* from me. Or so it felt.

And in the silence of the darkness, I cried, with no one to hear me...

And mourned the loss of my souls, and wondered what was left of Sienna Nealon without them.

Epilogue

Bredoccia, Revelen

He was a man in a castle, and had been known by many names.

One of them—one of the best known—was Vlad.

There were others. Ones he preferred. None that carried quite the fear, the…cachet…of the allusion to the famous "vampire" of legend.

But it was silly, for he…was not a vampire. He had never drunk so much as an ounce of blood, he did not fear the sun—despite his complexion as evidence to the contrary. Garlic and crucifixes bothered him not at all.

He sat in his office, an aging edifice of stone and turrets, and contemplated the news he'd just been given.

Rose Steward had been killed by Sienna Nealon.

He'd met the redhead. Gotten the full measure of her, enough to feel comfortable supplying her with endless amounts of the serum. It was a simple enough matter, and cheap. And it had bought her cooperation, after a fashion. He doubted it would have stuck, once she had achieved her aims, but…it seemed a minimal investment for a possible return.

Spinning in his chair, he looked out on the window on the darkened land below. Revelen had been a backwater of Eastern Europe for centuries. A peasant people, first oppressed by kings, then by the Soviet Union, now oppressed by their poor lot. Not a natural resource to call their own, they were left with nothing but open land…

And a flexible willingness to listen to a ruler who had quietly removed the boot of the Soviets from their necks, and kept any others from landing upon them.

Rose Steward was dead, and with her…his minimal investment in her success, in her burning feud against Sienna Nealon.

The man smiled, distantly pleased. *It would always have come to this,* he told himself. An inevitable meeting.

She was tired. Weary. Probably near broken after the fight it would have taken to bring down Rose. He could wait—just a little longer—before effecting his plans for her.

And soon enough…Sienna Nealon wouldn't be a problem anymore…at all.

Sienna Nealon Will Return in

APEX

Out of the Box
Book 18

Coming February 1, 2018!

Author's Note

Thanks for reading! If you want to know immediately when future books become available, take sixty seconds and sign up for my NEW RELEASE EMAIL ALERTS by visiting my website. I don't sell your information and I only send out emails when I have a new book out. The reason you should sign up for this is because I don't always set release dates, and even if you're following me on Facebook (robertJcrane (Author)) or Twitter (@robertJcrane), it's easy to miss my book announcements because...well, because social media is an imprecise thing.

Come join the discussion on my website:
http://www.robertjcrane.com!

Cheers,
Robert J. Crane

ACKNOWLEDGMENTS

Editorial/Literary Janitorial duties performed by Nick Bowman and Jeffrey Bryan. Final proofing was once more handled by the illustrious Jo Evans. Any errors you see in the text, however, are the result of me rejecting changes.

The cover was once more designed with exceeding skill by Karri Klawiter of Artbykarri.com.

The formatting was provided by nickbowman-editing.com.

Thanks to John Clifford for both being a first reader and also letting Sienna once again beclown him on the page.

Also, thanks to Jennifer Ellison (J Ells) for reading ahead (and epically fast) to let me know my instincts were on target with this one.

Once more, thanks to my parents, my in-laws, my kids and my wife, for helping me keep things together.

Other Works by Robert J. Crane

World of Sanctuary
Epic Fantasy

Defender: The Sanctuary Series, Volume One
Avenger: The Sanctuary Series, Volume Two
Champion: The Sanctuary Series, Volume Three
Crusader: The Sanctuary Series, Volume Four
Sanctuary Tales, Volume One - A Short Story Collection
Thy Father's Shadow: The Sanctuary Series, Volume 4.5
Master: The Sanctuary Series, Volume Five
Fated in Darkness: The Sanctuary Series, Volume 5.5
Warlord: The Sanctuary Series, Volume Six
Heretic: The Sanctuary Series, Volume Seven
Legend: The Sanctuary Series, Volume Eight
Ghosts of Sanctuary: The Sanctuary Series, Volume Nine*
(Coming 2018, at earliest.)

A Haven in Ash: Ashes of Luukessia, Volume One* *(with Michael Winstone—Coming Late 2017!)*
A Respite From Storms: Ashes of Luukessia, Volume Two* *(with Michael Winstone—Coming 2018!)*

The Girl in the Box
and
Out of the Box
Contemporary Urban Fantasy

Alone: The Girl in the Box, Book 1
Untouched: The Girl in the Box, Book 2
Soulless: The Girl in the Box, Book 3
Family: The Girl in the Box, Book 4
Omega: The Girl in the Box, Book 5

Broken: The Girl in the Box, Book 6
Enemies: The Girl in the Box, Book 7
Legacy: The Girl in the Box, Book 8
Destiny: The Girl in the Box, Book 9
Power: The Girl in the Box, Book 10

Limitless: Out of the Box, Book 1
In the Wind: Out of the Box, Book 2
Ruthless: Out of the Box, Book 3
Grounded: Out of the Box, Book 4
Tormented: Out of the Box, Book 5
Vengeful: Out of the Box, Book 6
Sea Change: Out of the Box, Book 7
Painkiller: Out of the Box, Book 8
Masks: Out of the Box, Book 9
Prisoners: Out of the Box, Book 10
Unyielding: Out of the Box, Book 11
Hollow: Out of the Box, Book 12
Toxicity: Out of the Box, Book 13
Small Things: Out of the Box, Book 14
Hunters: Out of the Box, Book 15
Badder: Out of the Box, Book 16
Apex: Out of the Box, Book 18* *(Coming February 1, 2018!)*
Time: Out of the Box, Book 19* *(Coming May 2018!)*
Driven: Out of the Box, Book 20* *(Coming July 2018!)*

Southern Watch
Contemporary Urban Fantasy

Called: Southern Watch, Book 1
Depths: Southern Watch, Book 2
Corrupted: Southern Watch, Book 3
Unearthed: Southern Watch, Book 4
Legion: Southern Watch, Book 5
Starling: Southern Watch, Book 6
Forsaken: South Watch, Book 7* *(Come Late 2018—Tentatively)*

The Shattered Dome Series
(with Nicholas J. Ambrose)
Sci-Fi

Voiceless: The Shattered Dome, Book 1
Unspeakable: The Shattered Dome, Book 2* *(Coming 2018!)*

The Mira Brand Adventures
Contemporary Urban Fantasy

The World Beneath: The Mira Brand Adventures, Book 1
The Tide of Ages: The Mira Brand Adventures, Book 2
The City of Lies: The Mira Brand Adventures, Book 3
The King of the Skies: The Mira Brand Adventures, Book 4*
(Coming Late 2017/Early 2018!)

Liars and Vampires
(with Lauren Harper)
Contemporary Urban Fantasy

No One Will Believe You: Liars and Vampires, Book 1*
(Coming Early 2018!)
Someone Should Save Her: Liars and Vampires, Book 2*
(Coming Early 2018!)
You Can't Go Home Again: Liars and Vampires, Book 3*
(Coming Early 2018!)

* Forthcoming, Subject to Change

CPSIA information can be obtained
at www.ICGtesting.com
Printed in the USA
LVOW10s1626130218
566429LV00011B/623/P